PRINCESS NINJAS

silver dragon

Writer
Dave Franchini

Artwork
Eduardo Garcia

Colors
Robby Bevard
Maxflan Araujo

Letters
Fabio Amelia
Maurizio Clausi
(Arancia Studios)

Editor
Christina Barbieri

Cover Artwork
Manuel Preitano

Production & Design
Christopher Cote
Ashley Vanacore

Managing Editor
Jennifer Bermel

Publisher
Joe Brusha

Silver dragon
SILVERDRAGONBOOKS.COM

Joe Brusha • President & Chief Creative Officer
Ralph Tedesco • VP Film & Television
Christopher Cote • Art Director
Dave Franchini • Editor
Christina Barbieri • Assistant Editor
Kellie Supplee • Assistant Editor
Ashley Vanacore • Graphic Designer
Lauren Klasik • Director of Sales & Marketing
Jennifer Bermel • Business Development & Licensing Manage
Jason Condeelis • Direct Sales Representative
Rebecca Pons • Marketing & VIP Coordinator
Eden Pio • Social Media Manager
Stu Kropnick • Operations Manager

Princess Ninjas Trade Paperback, May, 2019. First Printing. Published by Silver Dragon Books, 433 Caredean Drive, Ste. C, Horshar Pennsylvania 19044.

ISBN: 978-1942275909

PRINCESS NINJAS

Story One
Princess Ninjas 04

Story Two
Dark Magic Forest 50

Story Three
Unfriendly Faces 96

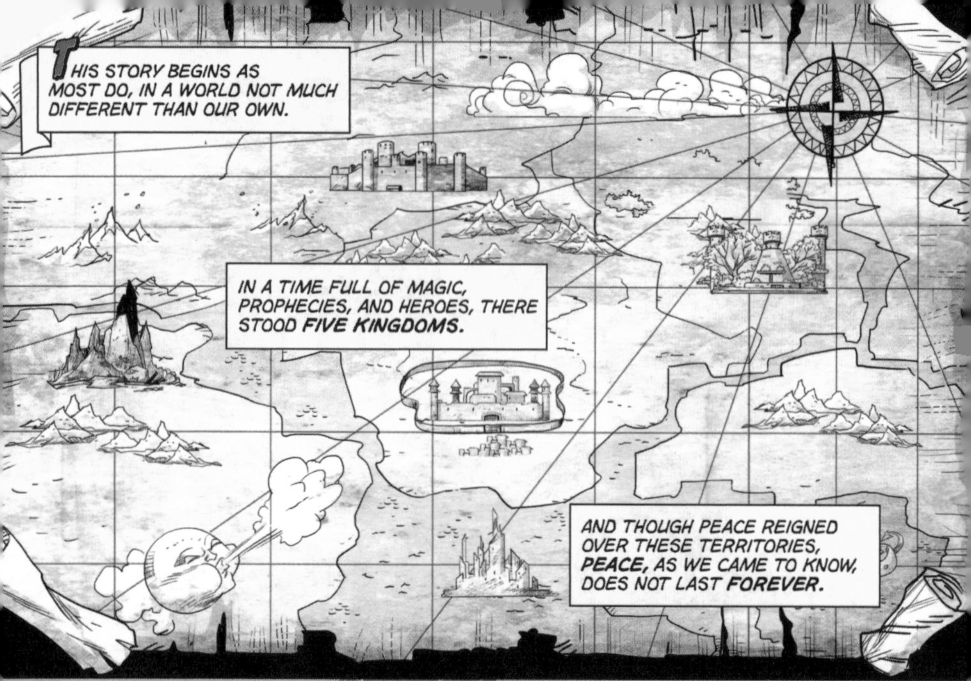
THIS STORY BEGINS AS MOST DO, IN A WORLD NOT MUCH DIFFERENT THAN OUR OWN.
IN A TIME FULL OF MAGIC, PROPHECIES, AND HEROES, THERE STOOD FIVE KINGDOMS.
AND THOUGH PEACE REIGNED OVER THESE TERRITORIES, PEACE, AS WE CAME TO KNOW, DOES NOT LAST FOREVER.

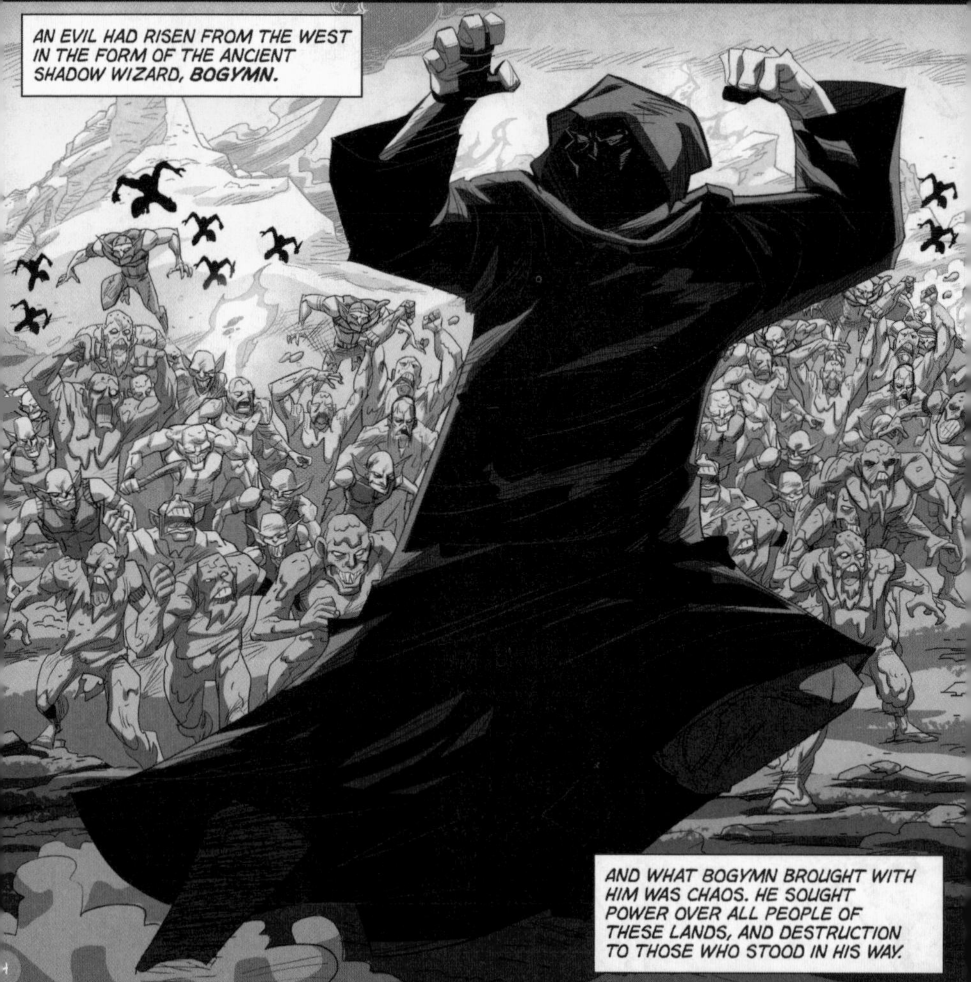
AN EVIL HAD RISEN FROM THE WEST IN THE FORM OF THE ANCIENT SHADOW WIZARD, BOGYMN.
AND WHAT BOGYMN BROUGHT WITH HIM WAS CHAOS. HE SOUGHT POWER OVER ALL PEOPLE OF THESE LANDS, AND DESTRUCTION TO THOSE WHO STOOD IN HIS WAY.

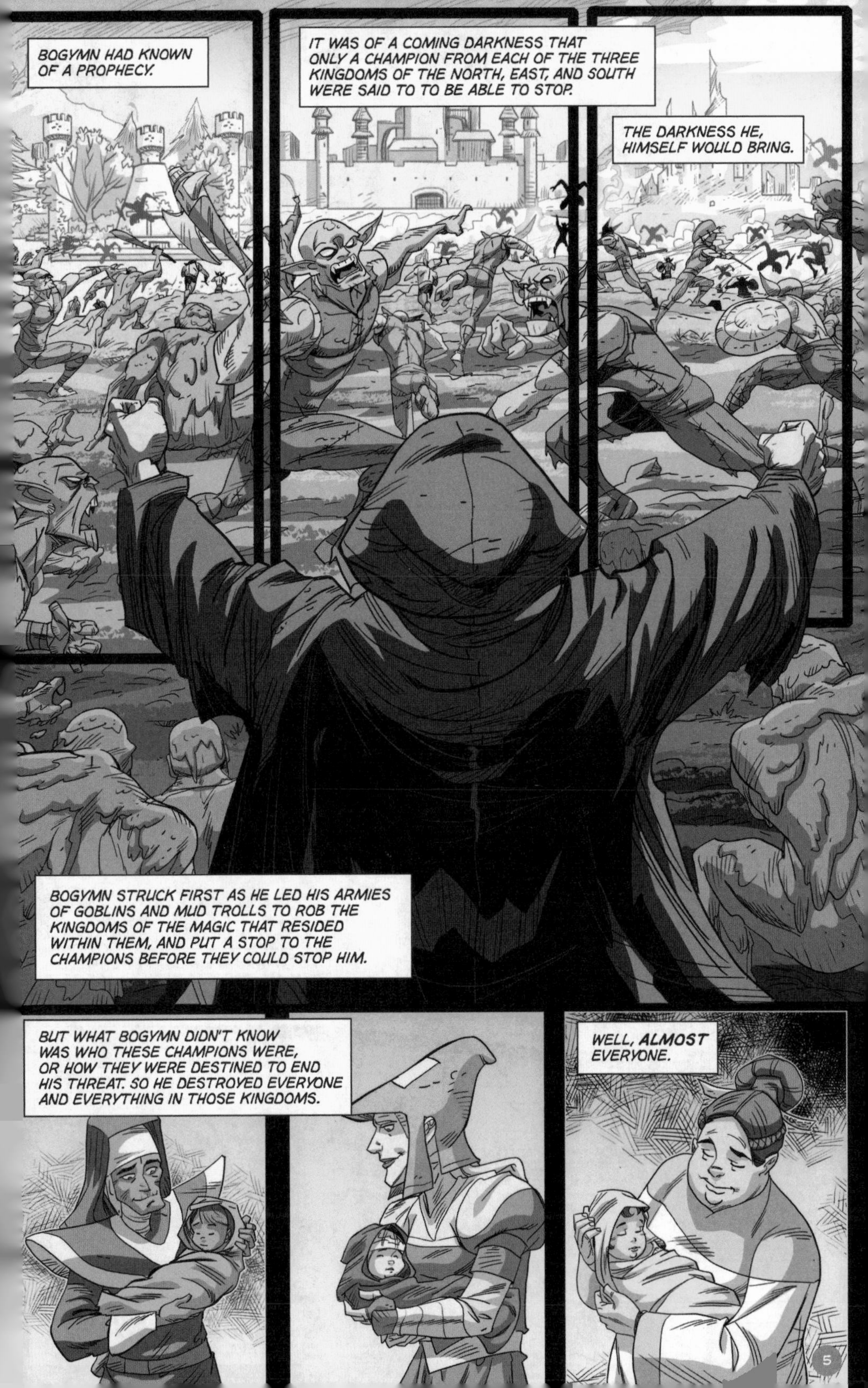
BOGYMN HAD KNOWN OF A PROPHECY.
IT WAS OF A COMING DARKNESS THAT ONLY A CHAMPION FROM EACH OF THE THREE KINGDOMS OF THE NORTH, EAST, AND SOUTH WERE SAID TO TO BE ABLE TO STOP.
THE DARKNESS HE, HIMSELF WOULD BRING.
BOGYMN STRUCK FIRST AS HE LED HIS ARMIES OF GOBLINS AND MUD TROLLS TO ROB THE KINGDOMS OF THE MAGIC THAT RESIDED WITHIN THEM, AND PUT A STOP TO THE CHAMPIONS BEFORE THEY COULD STOP HIM.
BUT WHAT BOGYMN DIDN'T KNOW WAS WHO THESE CHAMPIONS WERE, OR HOW THEY WERE DESTINED TO END HIS THREAT. SO HE DESTROYED EVERYONE AND EVERYTHING IN THOSE KINGDOMS.
WELL, **ALMOST** EVERYONE.

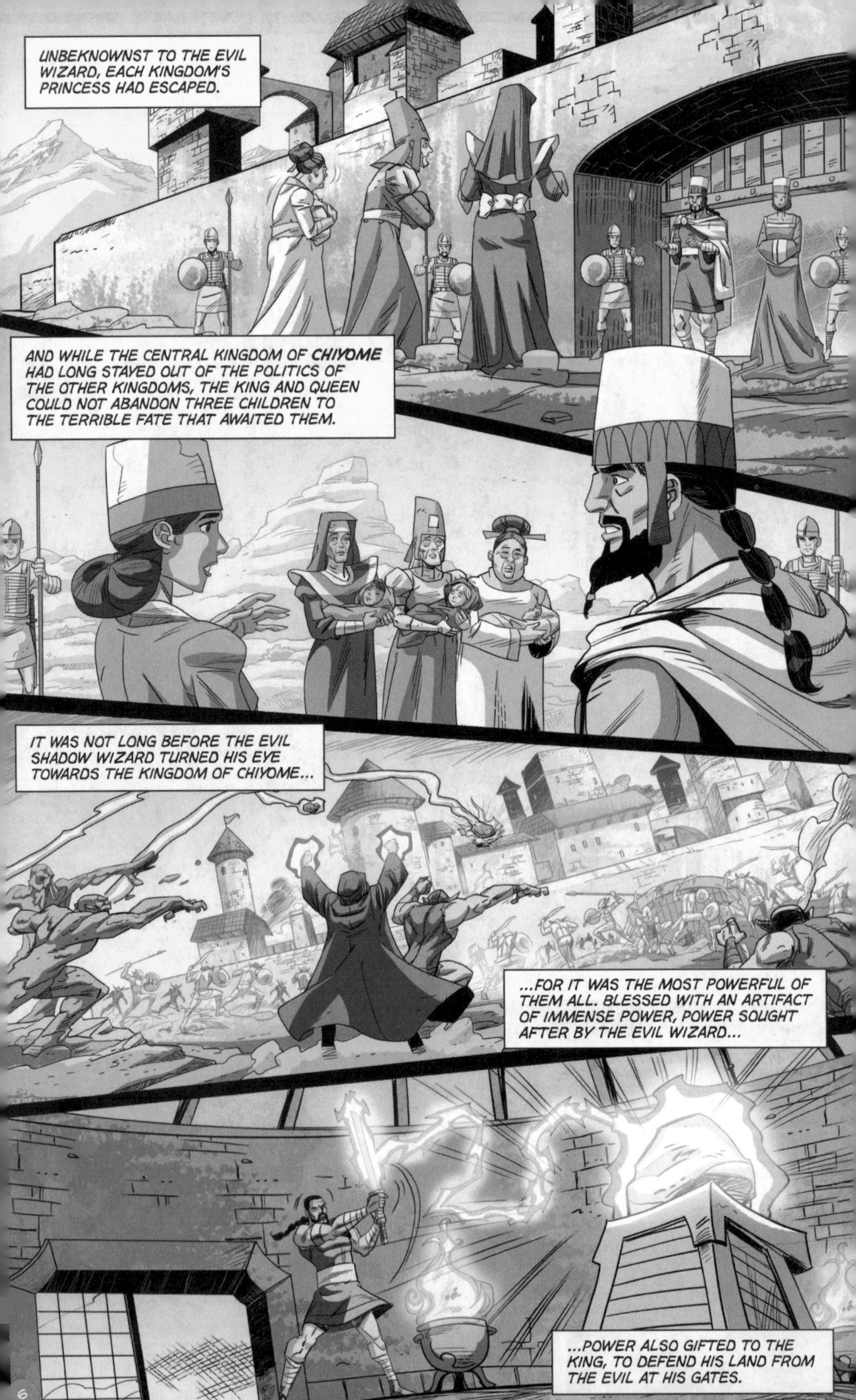
UNBEKNOWNST TO THE EVIL WIZARD, EACH KINGDOM'S PRINCESS HAD ESCAPED.
AND WHILE THE CENTRAL KINGDOM OF **CHIYOME** HAD LONG STAYED OUT OF THE POLITICS OF THE OTHER KINGDOMS, THE KING AND QUEEN COULD NOT ABANDON THREE CHILDREN TO THE TERRIBLE FATE THAT AWAITED THEM.
IT WAS NOT LONG BEFORE THE EVIL SHADOW WIZARD TURNED HIS EYE TOWARDS THE KINGDOM OF CHIYOME...
...FOR IT WAS THE MOST POWERFUL OF THEM ALL. BLESSED WITH AN ARTIFACT OF IMMENSE POWER, POWER SOUGHT AFTER BY THE EVIL WIZARD...
...POWER ALSO GIFTED TO THE KING, TO DEFEND HIS LAND FROM THE EVIL AT HIS GATES.

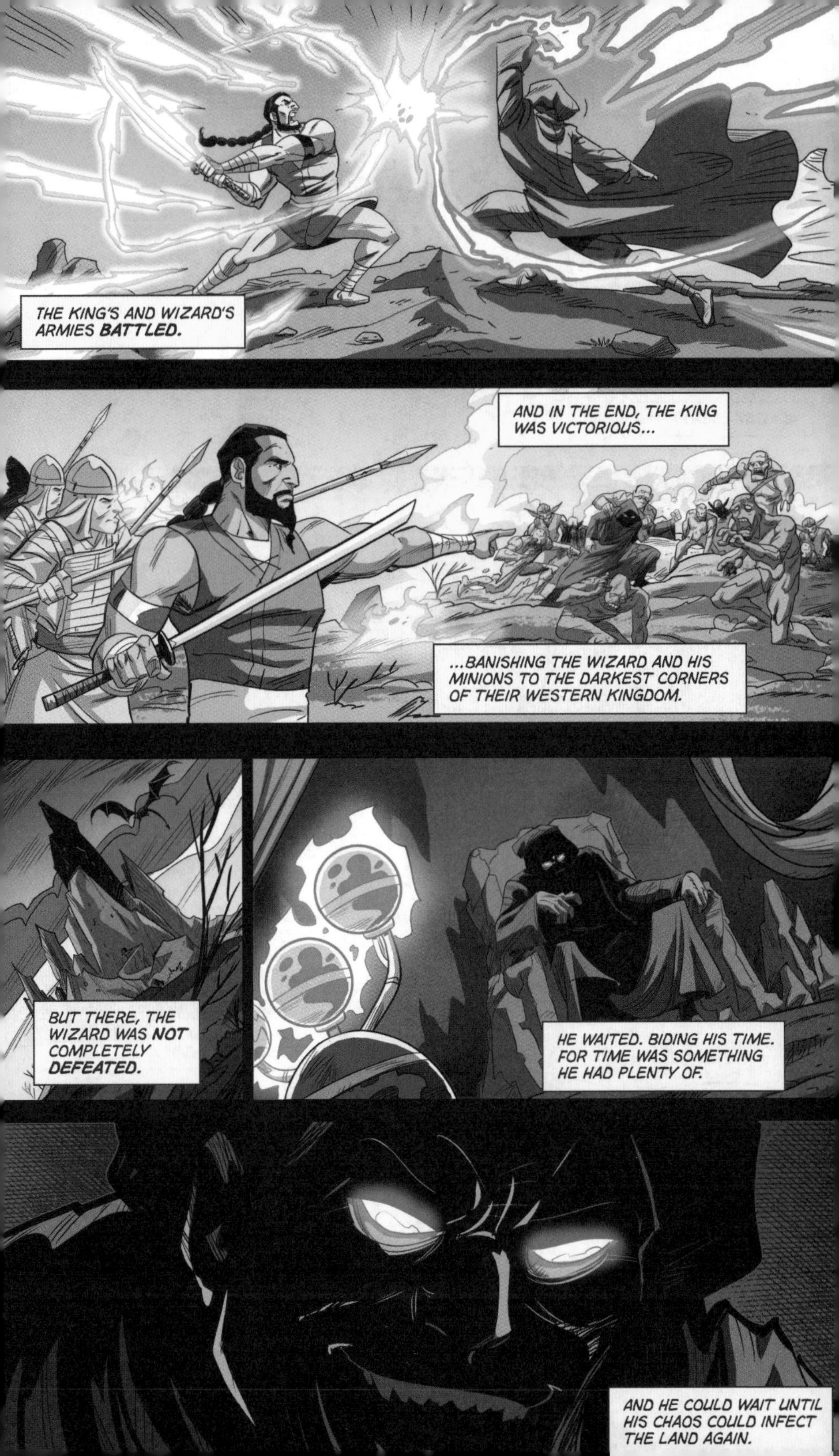
THE KING'S AND WIZARD'S ARMIES BATTLED.
AND IN THE END, THE KING WAS VICTORIOUS...
...BANISHING THE WIZARD AND HIS MINIONS TO THE DARKEST CORNERS OF THEIR WESTERN KINGDOM.
BUT THERE, THE WIZARD WAS NOT COMPLETELY DEFEATED.
HE WAITED. BIDING HIS TIME. FOR TIME WAS SOMETHING HE HAD PLENTY OF.
AND HE COULD WAIT UNTIL HIS CHAOS COULD INFECT THE LAND AGAIN.

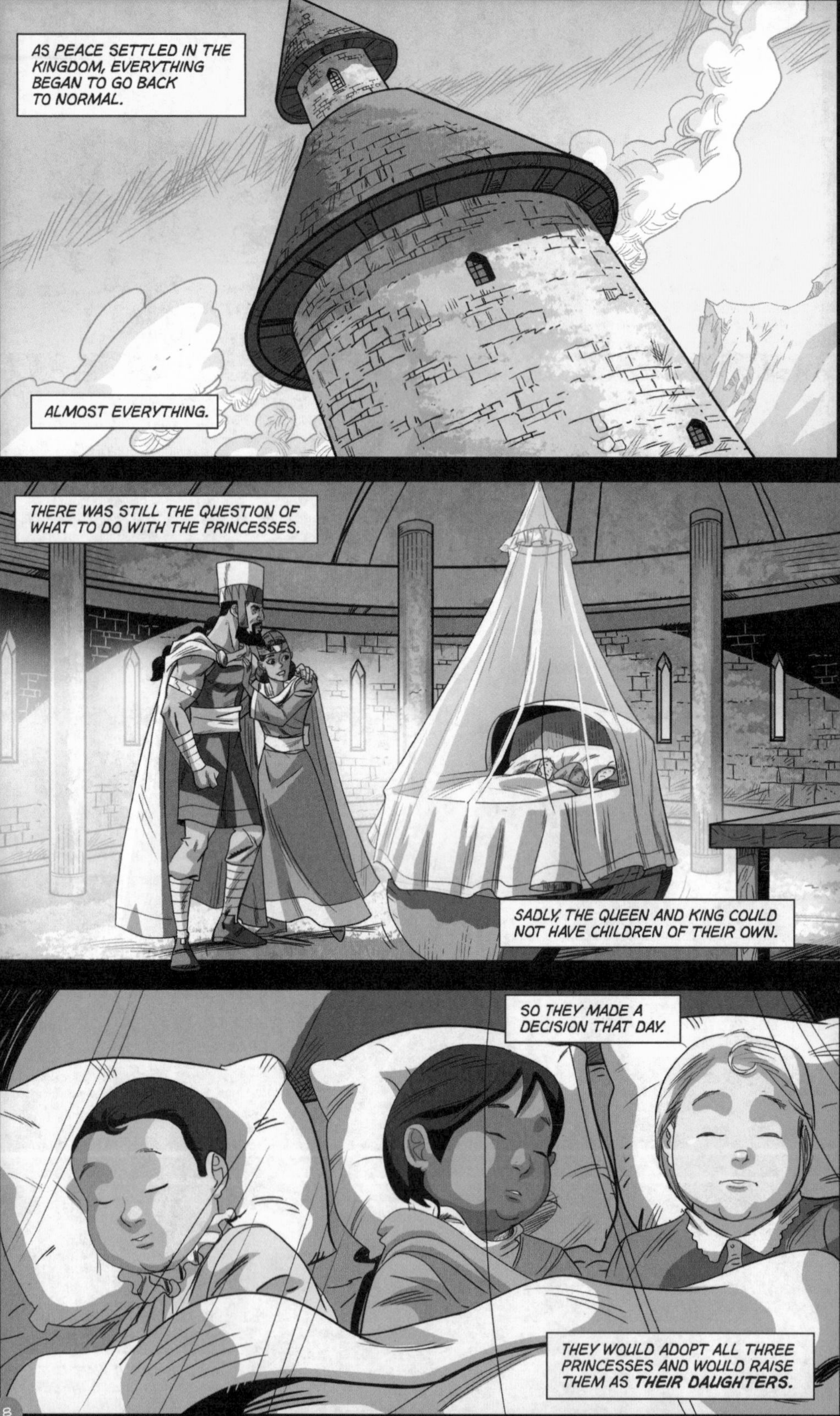
AS PEACE SETTLED IN THE KINGDOM, EVERYTHING BEGAN TO GO BACK TO NORMAL.
ALMOST EVERYTHING.
THERE WAS STILL THE QUESTION OF WHAT TO DO WITH THE PRINCESSES.
SADLY, THE QUEEN AND KING COULD NOT HAVE CHILDREN OF THEIR OWN.
SO THEY MADE A DECISION THAT DAY.
THEY WOULD ADOPT ALL THREE PRINCESSES AND WOULD RAISE THEM AS **THEIR DAUGHTERS.**

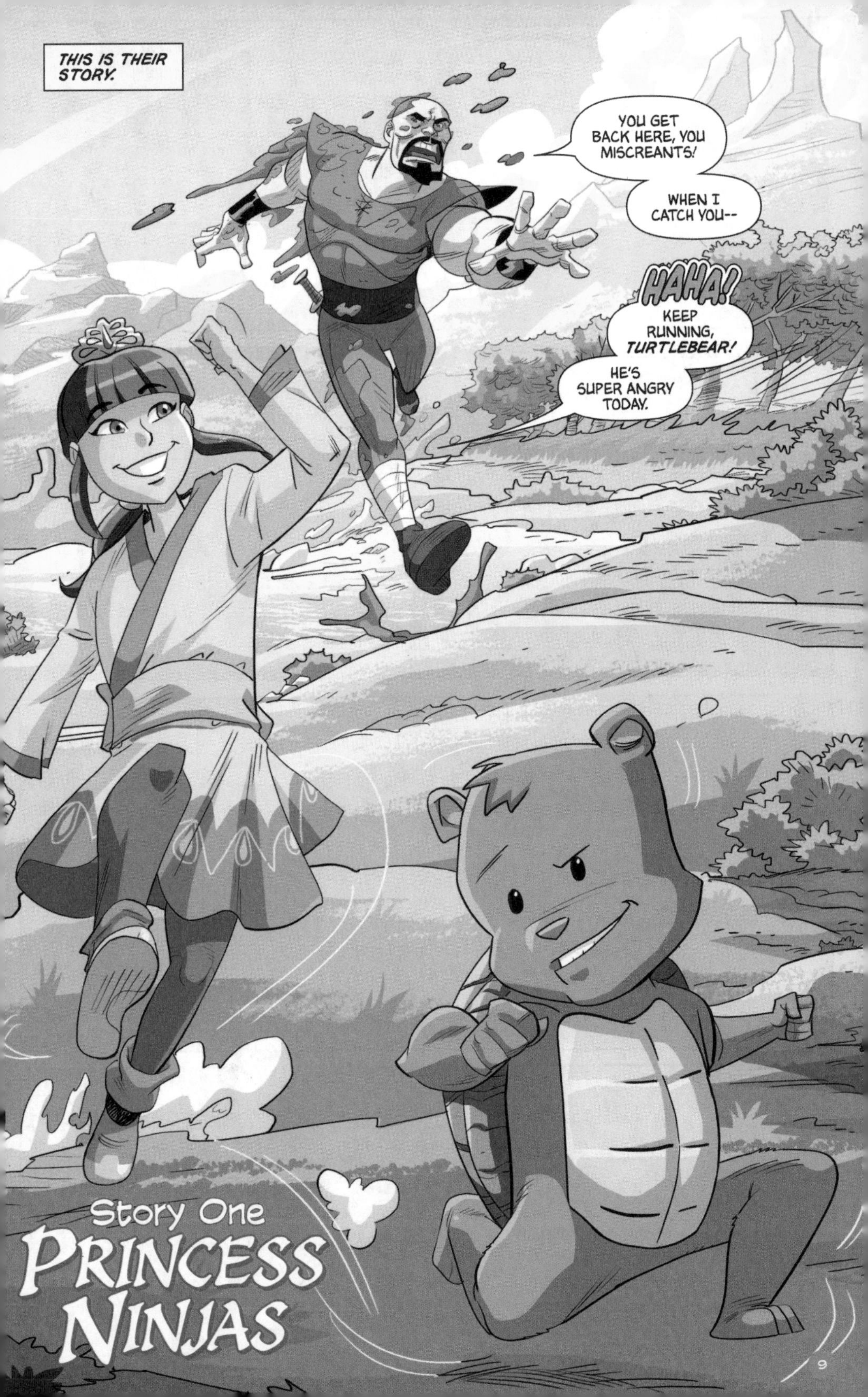
THIS IS THEIR STORY.
YOU GET BACK HERE, YOU MISCREANTS!
WHEN I CATCH YOU--
HAHA!
KEEP RUNNING, *TURTLEBEAR!*
HE'S SUPER ANGRY TODAY.
Story One
PRINCESS NINJAS

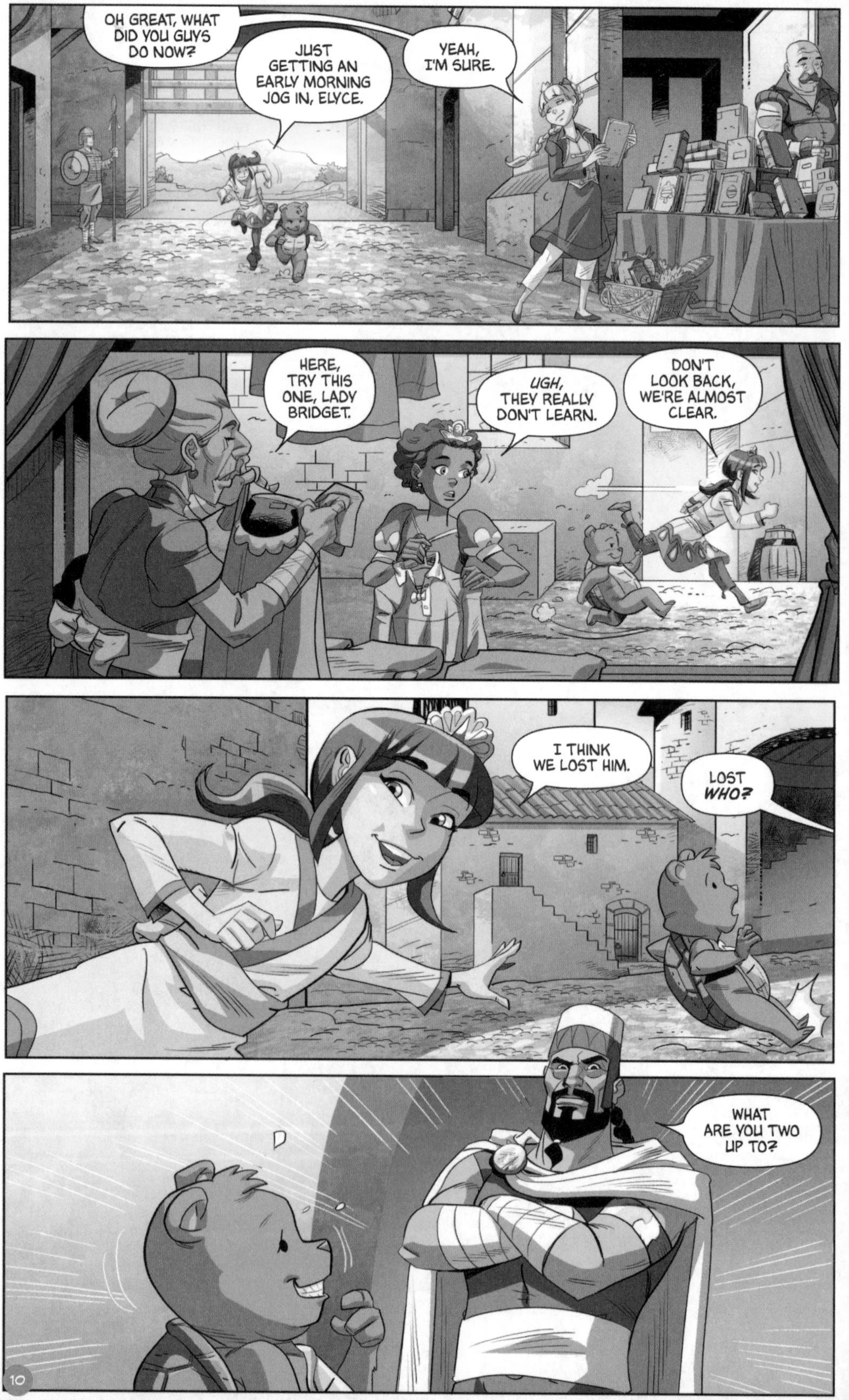
OH GREAT, WHAT DID YOU GUYS DO NOW?
JUST GETTING AN EARLY MORNING JOG IN, ELYCE.
YEAH, I'M SURE.
HERE, TRY THIS ONE, LADY BRIDGET.
UGH, THEY REALLY DON'T LEARN.
DON'T LOOK BACK, WE'RE ALMOST CLEAR.
I THINK WE LOST HIM.
LOST ***WHO?***
WHAT ARE YOU TWO UP TO?

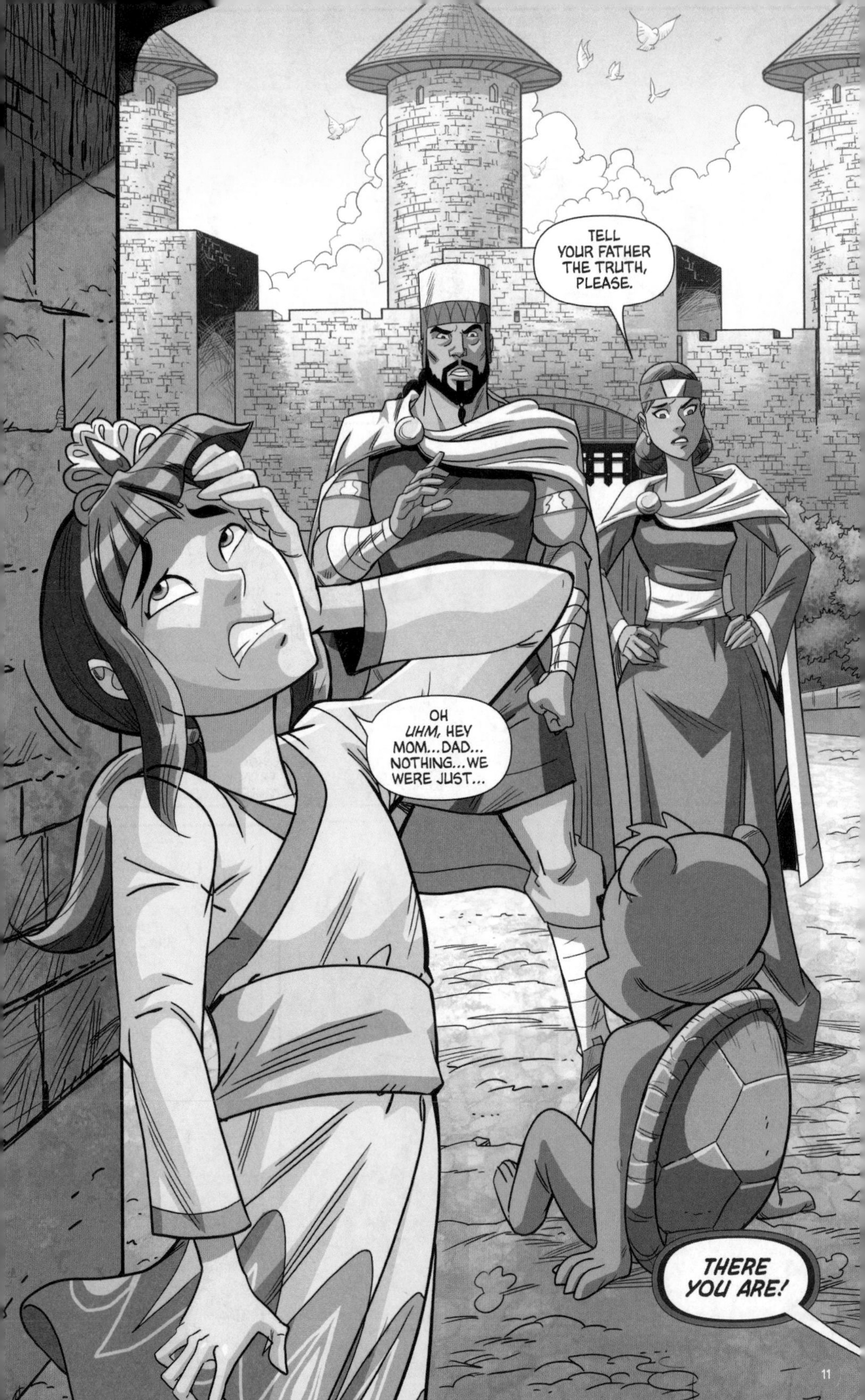
TELL YOUR FATHER THE TRUTH, PLEASE.
OH *UHM*, HEY MOM...DAD... NOTHING...WE WERE JUST...
THERE YOU ARE!

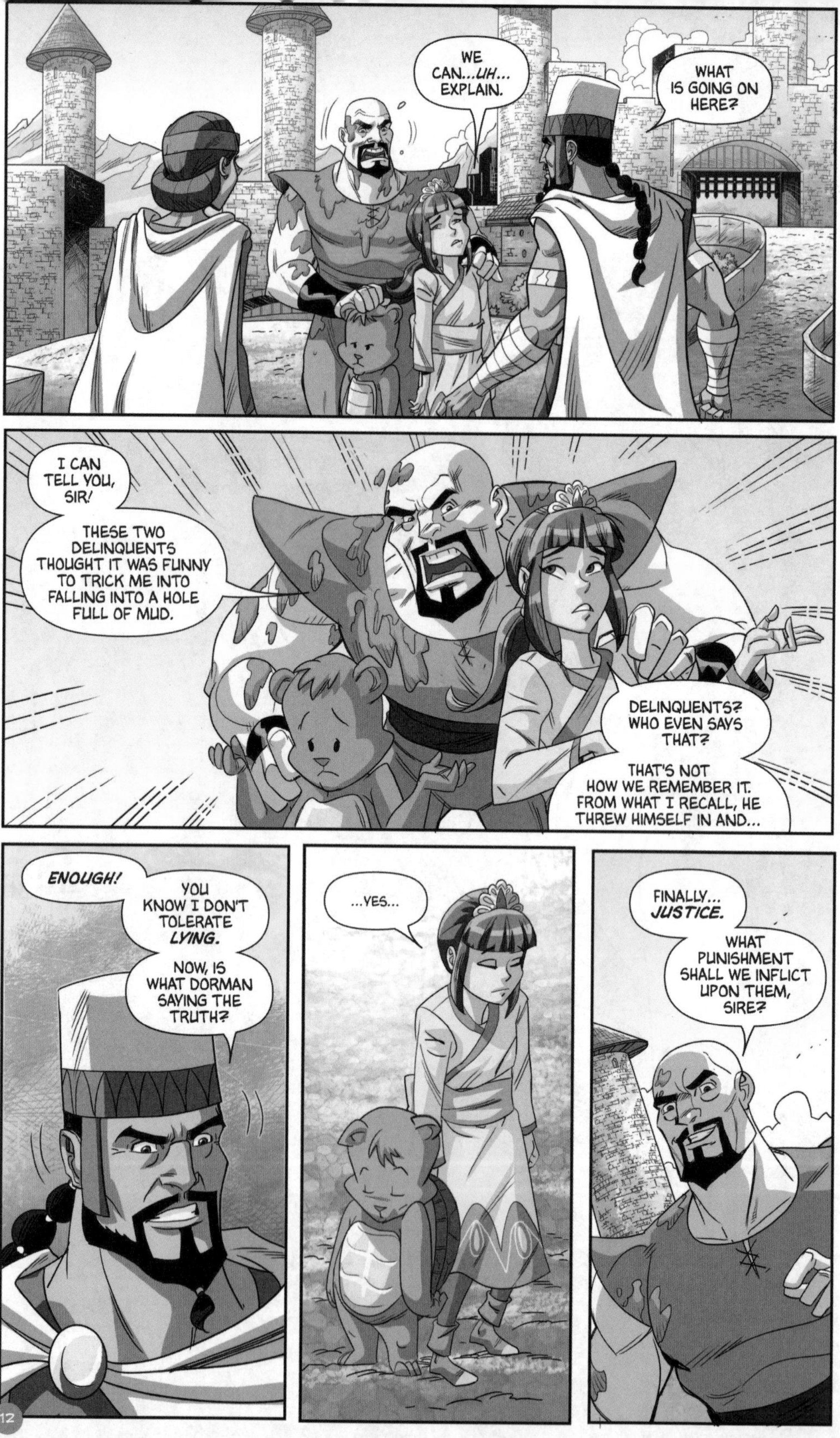
WE CAN...UH... EXPLAIN.
WHAT IS GOING ON HERE?
I CAN TELL YOU, SIR!
THESE TWO DELINQUENTS THOUGHT IT WAS FUNNY TO TRICK ME INTO FALLING INTO A HOLE FULL OF MUD.
DELINQUENTS? WHO EVEN SAYS THAT?
THAT'S NOT HOW WE REMEMBER IT. FROM WHAT I RECALL, HE THREW HIMSELF IN AND...
ENOUGH!
YOU KNOW I DON'T TOLERATE LYING.
NOW, IS WHAT DORMAN SAYING THE TRUTH?
...YES...
FINALLY... JUSTICE.
WHAT PUNISHMENT SHALL WE INFLICT UPON THEM, SIRE?

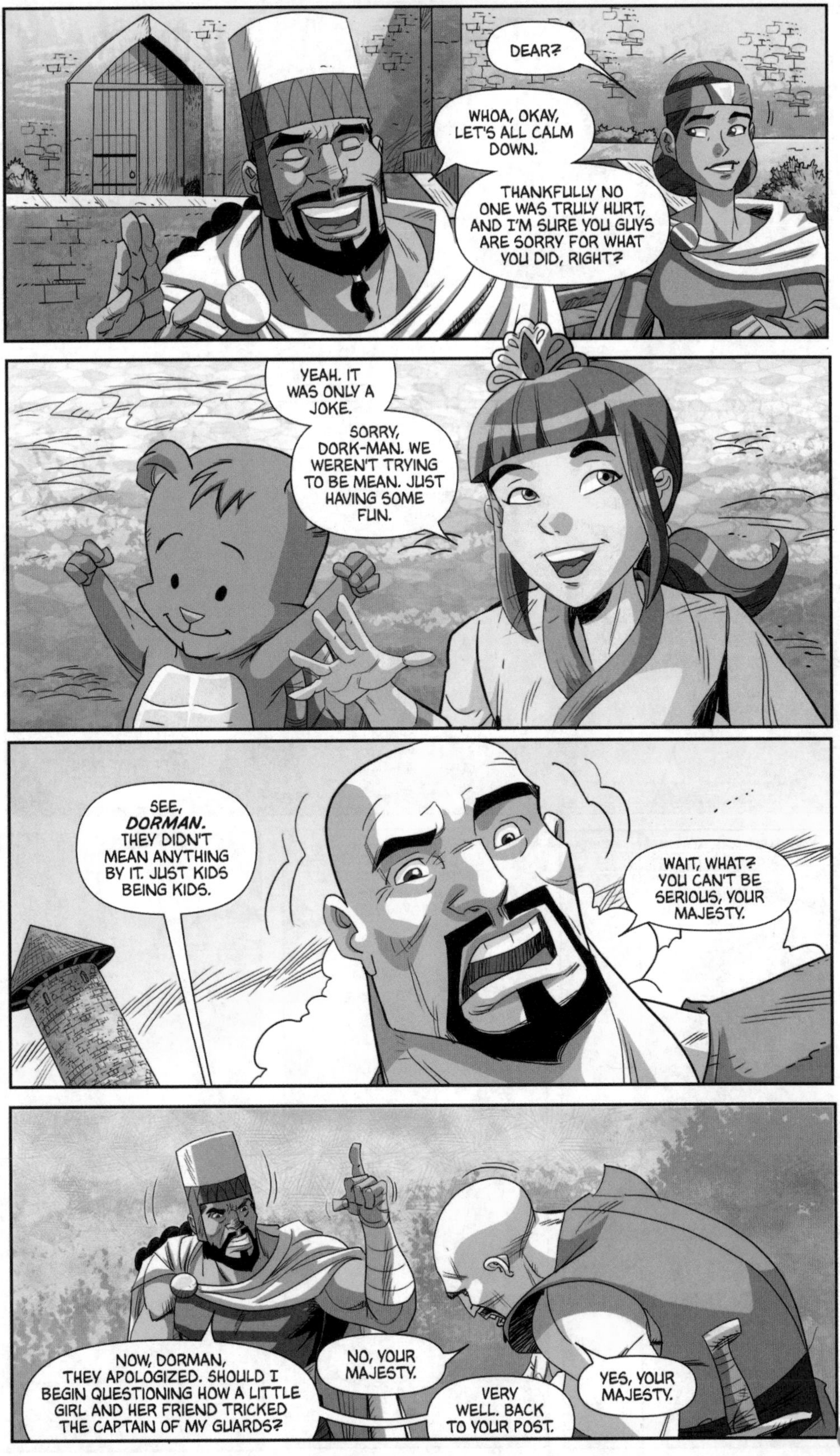
DEAR?
WHOA, OKAY, LET'S ALL CALM DOWN.
THANKFULLY NO ONE WAS TRULY HURT, AND I'M SURE YOU GUYS ARE SORRY FOR WHAT YOU DID, RIGHT?
YEAH. IT WAS ONLY A JOKE.
SORRY, DORK-MAN. WE WEREN'T TRYING TO BE MEAN. JUST HAVING SOME FUN.
SEE, **DORMAN.** THEY DIDN'T MEAN ANYTHING BY IT. JUST KIDS BEING KIDS.
WAIT, WHAT? YOU CAN'T BE SERIOUS, YOUR MAJESTY.
NOW, DORMAN, THEY APOLOGIZED. SHOULD I BEGIN QUESTIONING HOW A LITTLE GIRL AND HER FRIEND TRICKED THE CAPTAIN OF MY GUARDS?
NO, YOUR MAJESTY.
VERY WELL. BACK TO YOUR POST.
YES, YOUR MAJESTY.

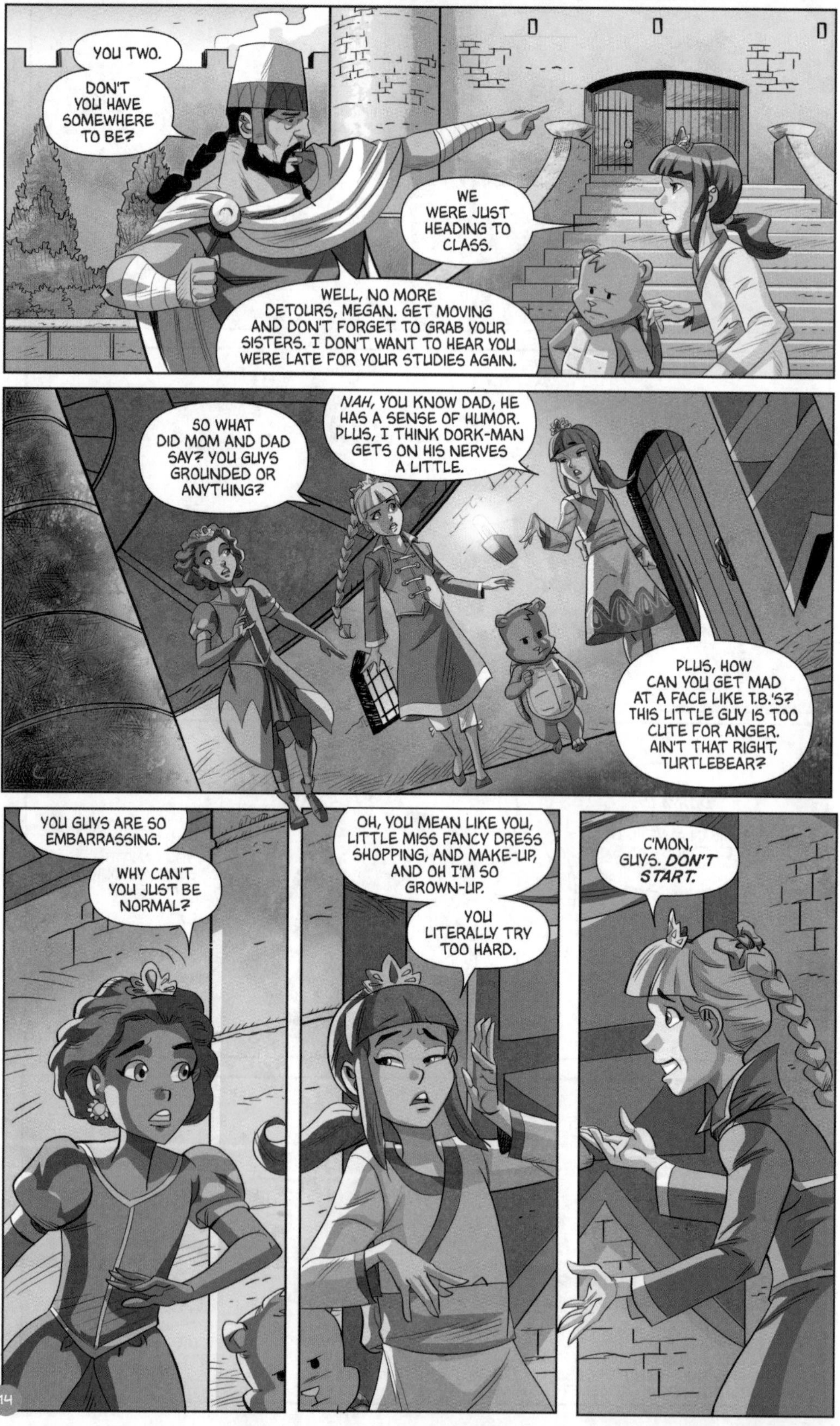
YOU TWO.
DON'T YOU HAVE SOMEWHERE TO BE?
WE WERE JUST HEADING TO CLASS.
WELL, NO MORE DETOURS, MEGAN. GET MOVING AND DON'T FORGET TO GRAB YOUR SISTERS. I DON'T WANT TO HEAR YOU WERE LATE FOR YOUR STUDIES AGAIN.
SO WHAT DID MOM AND DAD SAY? YOU GUYS GROUNDED OR ANYTHING?
NAH, YOU KNOW DAD, HE HAS A SENSE OF HUMOR. PLUS, I THINK DORK-MAN GETS ON HIS NERVES A LITTLE.
PLUS, HOW CAN YOU GET MAD AT A FACE LIKE T.B.'S? THIS LITTLE GUY IS TOO CUTE FOR ANGER. AIN'T THAT RIGHT, TURTLEBEAR?
YOU GUYS ARE SO EMBARRASSING.
WHY CAN'T YOU JUST BE NORMAL?
OH, YOU MEAN LIKE YOU, LITTLE MISS FANCY DRESS SHOPPING, AND MAKE-UP, AND OH I'M SO GROWN-UP.
YOU LITERALLY TRY TOO HARD.
C'MON, GUYS. ***DON'T START.***

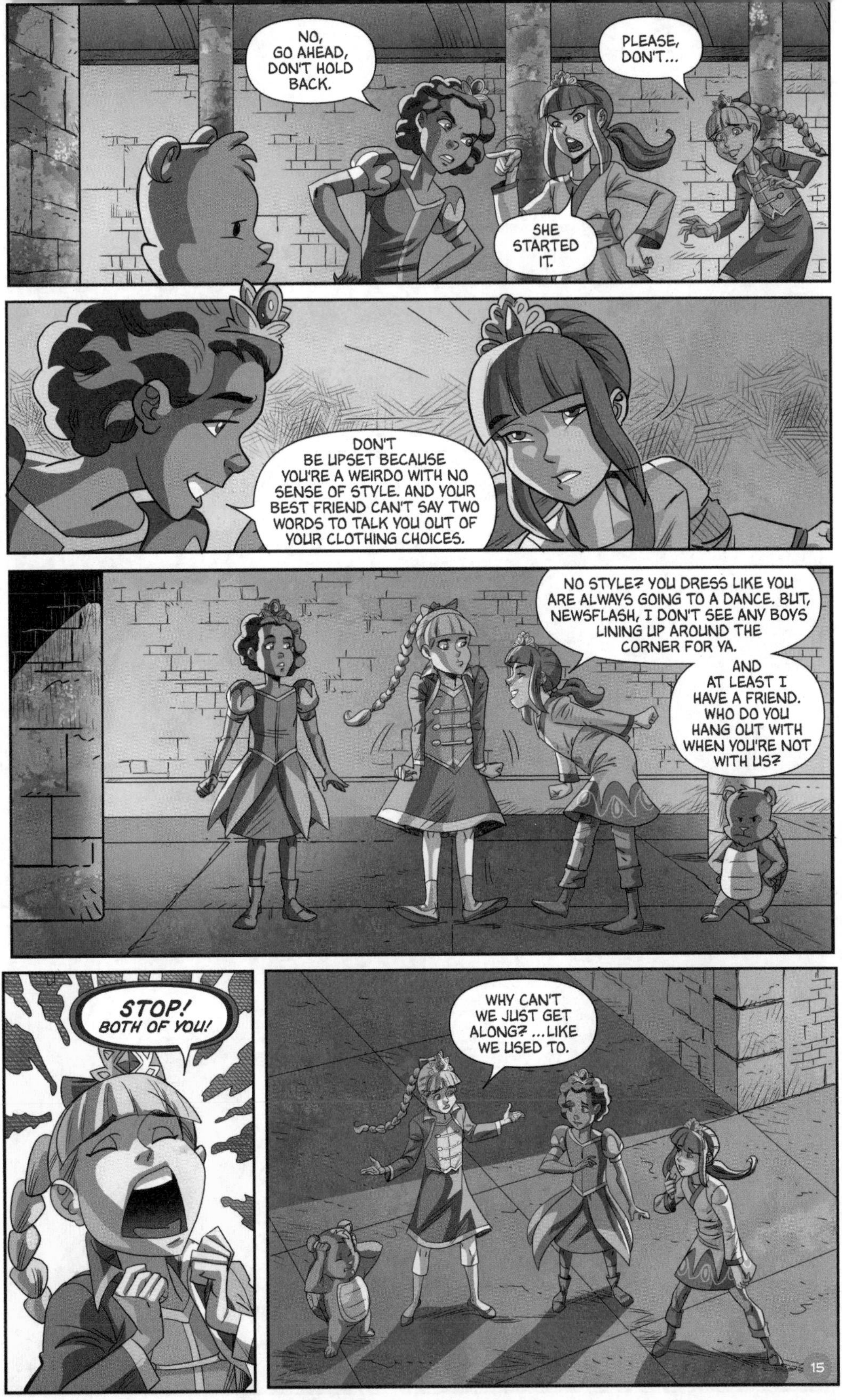
NO, GO AHEAD, DON'T HOLD BACK.
PLEASE, DON'T...
SHE STARTED IT.
DON'T BE UPSET BECAUSE YOU'RE A WEIRDO WITH NO SENSE OF STYLE. AND YOUR BEST FRIEND CAN'T SAY TWO WORDS TO TALK YOU OUT OF YOUR CLOTHING CHOICES.
NO STYLE? YOU DRESS LIKE YOU ARE ALWAYS GOING TO A DANCE. BUT, NEWSFLASH, I DON'T SEE ANY BOYS LINING UP AROUND THE CORNER FOR YA.
AND AT LEAST I HAVE A FRIEND. WHO DO YOU HANG OUT WITH WHEN YOU'RE NOT WITH US?
STOP! BOTH OF YOU!
WHY CAN'T WE JUST GET ALONG? ...LIKE WE USED TO.

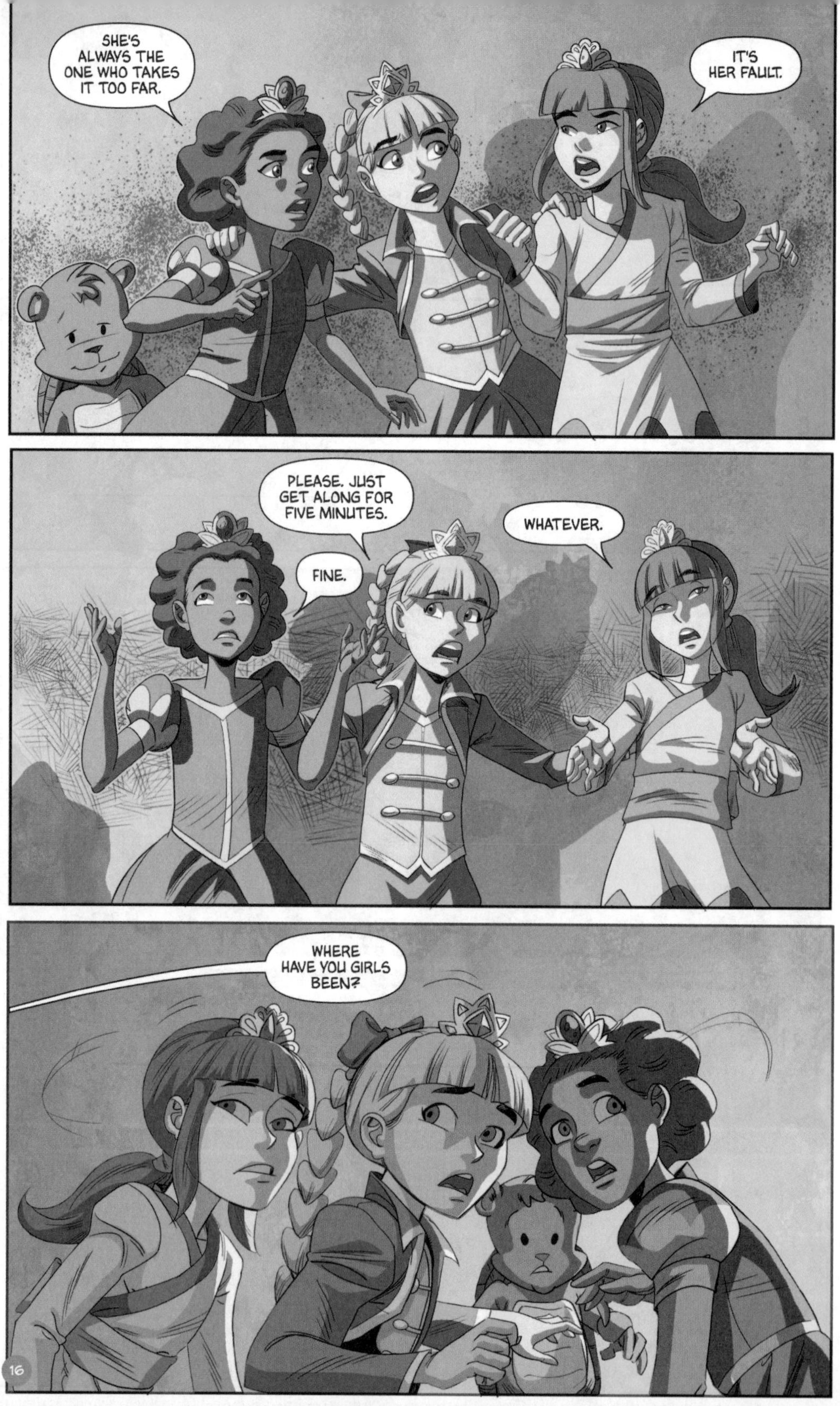
SHE'S ALWAYS THE ONE WHO TAKES IT TOO FAR.
IT'S HER FAULT.
PLEASE. JUST GET ALONG FOR FIVE MINUTES.
FINE.
WHATEVER.
WHERE HAVE YOU GIRLS BEEN?

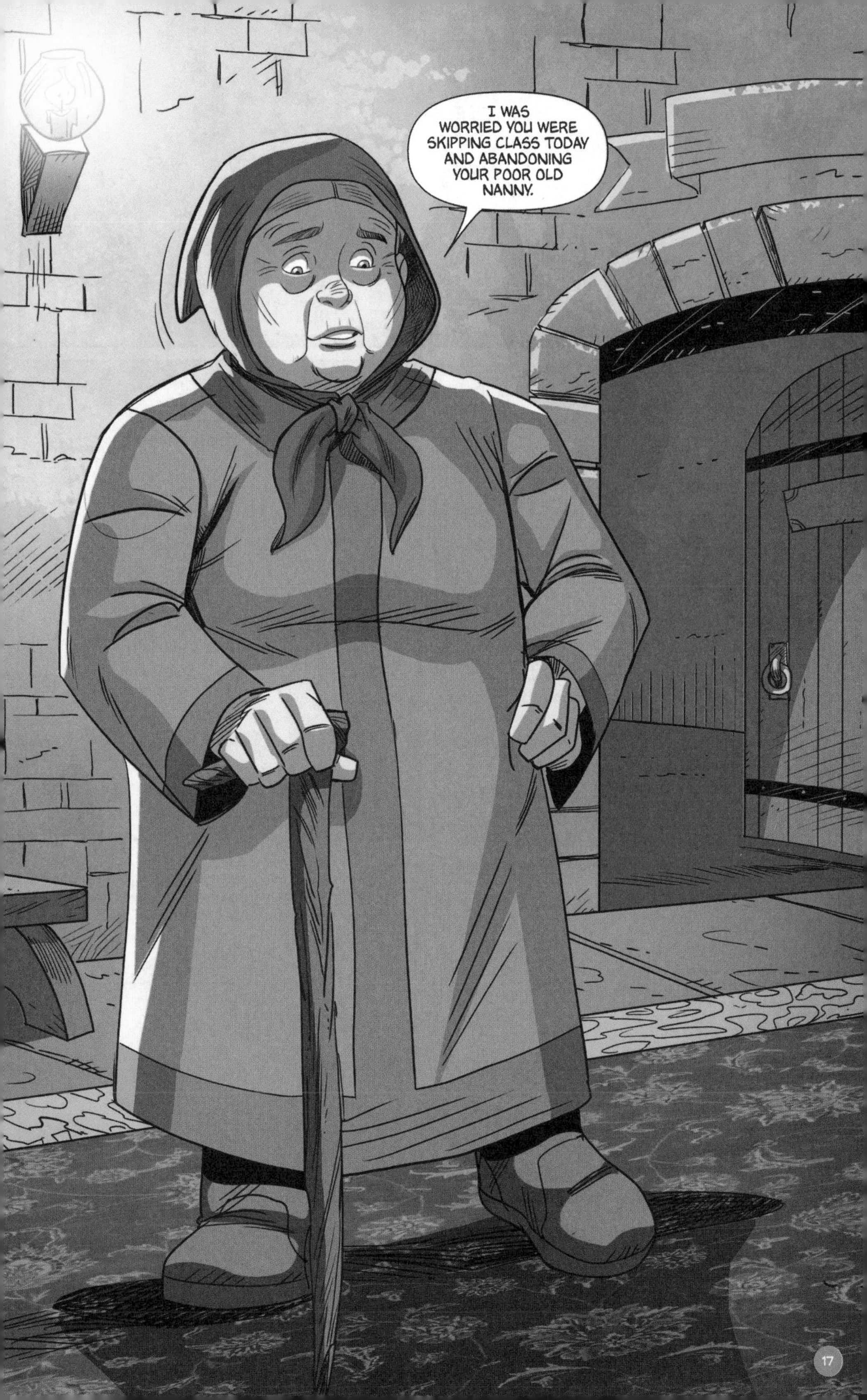
I WAS WORRIED YOU WERE SKIPPING CLASS TODAY AND ABANDONING YOUR POOR OLD NANNY.

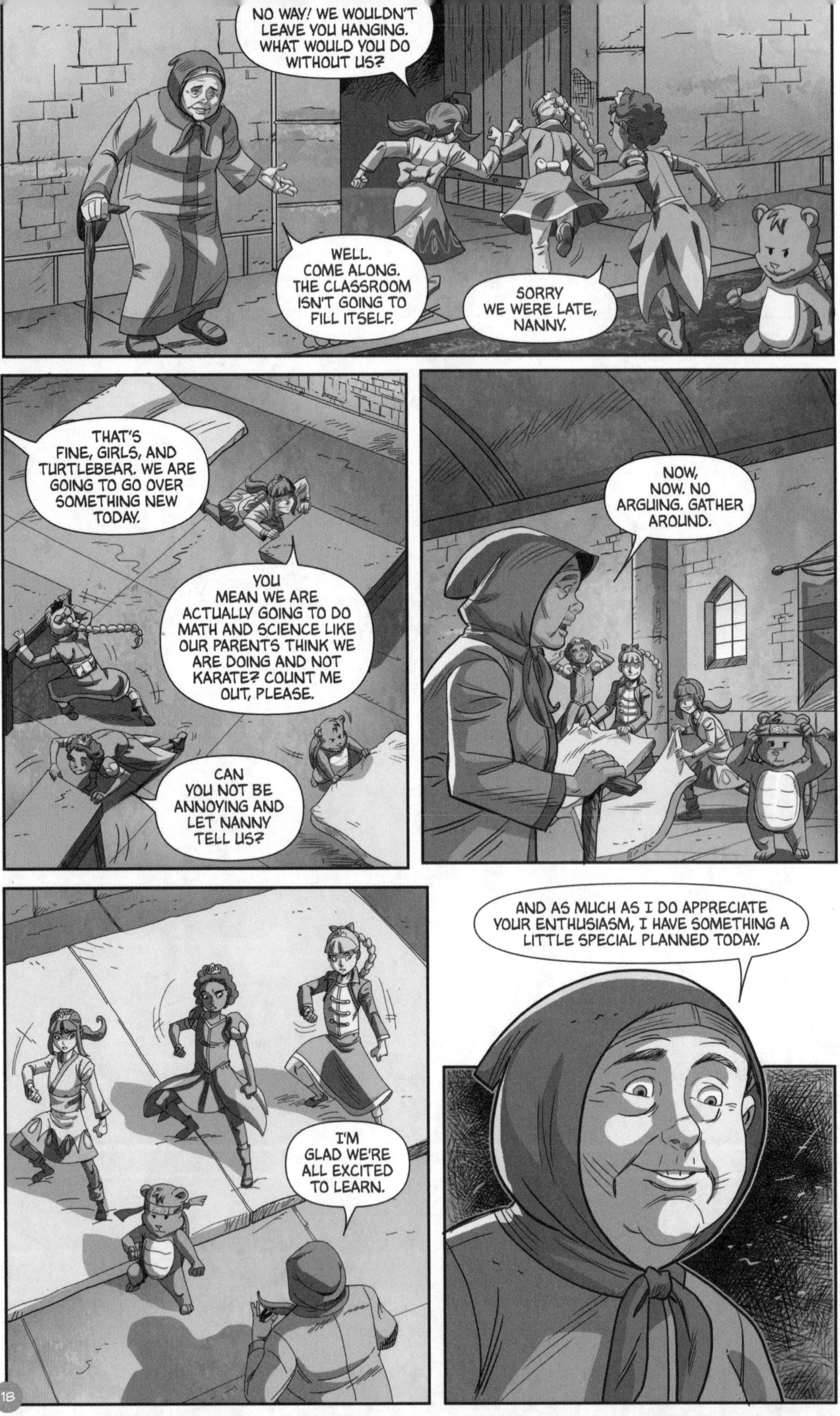
NO WAY! WE WOULDN'T LEAVE YOU HANGING. WHAT WOULD YOU DO WITHOUT US?
WELL. COME ALONG. THE CLASSROOM ISN'T GOING TO FILL ITSELF.
SORRY WE WERE LATE, NANNY.
THAT'S FINE, GIRLS, AND TURTLEBEAR. WE ARE GOING TO GO OVER SOMETHING NEW TODAY.
YOU MEAN WE ARE ACTUALLY GOING TO DO MATH AND SCIENCE LIKE OUR PARENTS THINK WE ARE DOING AND NOT KARATE? COUNT ME OUT, PLEASE.
CAN YOU NOT BE ANNOYING AND LET NANNY TELL US?
NOW, NOW. NO ARGUING. GATHER AROUND.
I'M GLAD WE'RE ALL EXCITED TO LEARN.
AND AS MUCH AS I DO APPRECIATE YOUR ENTHUSIASM, I HAVE SOMETHING A LITTLE SPECIAL PLANNED TODAY.

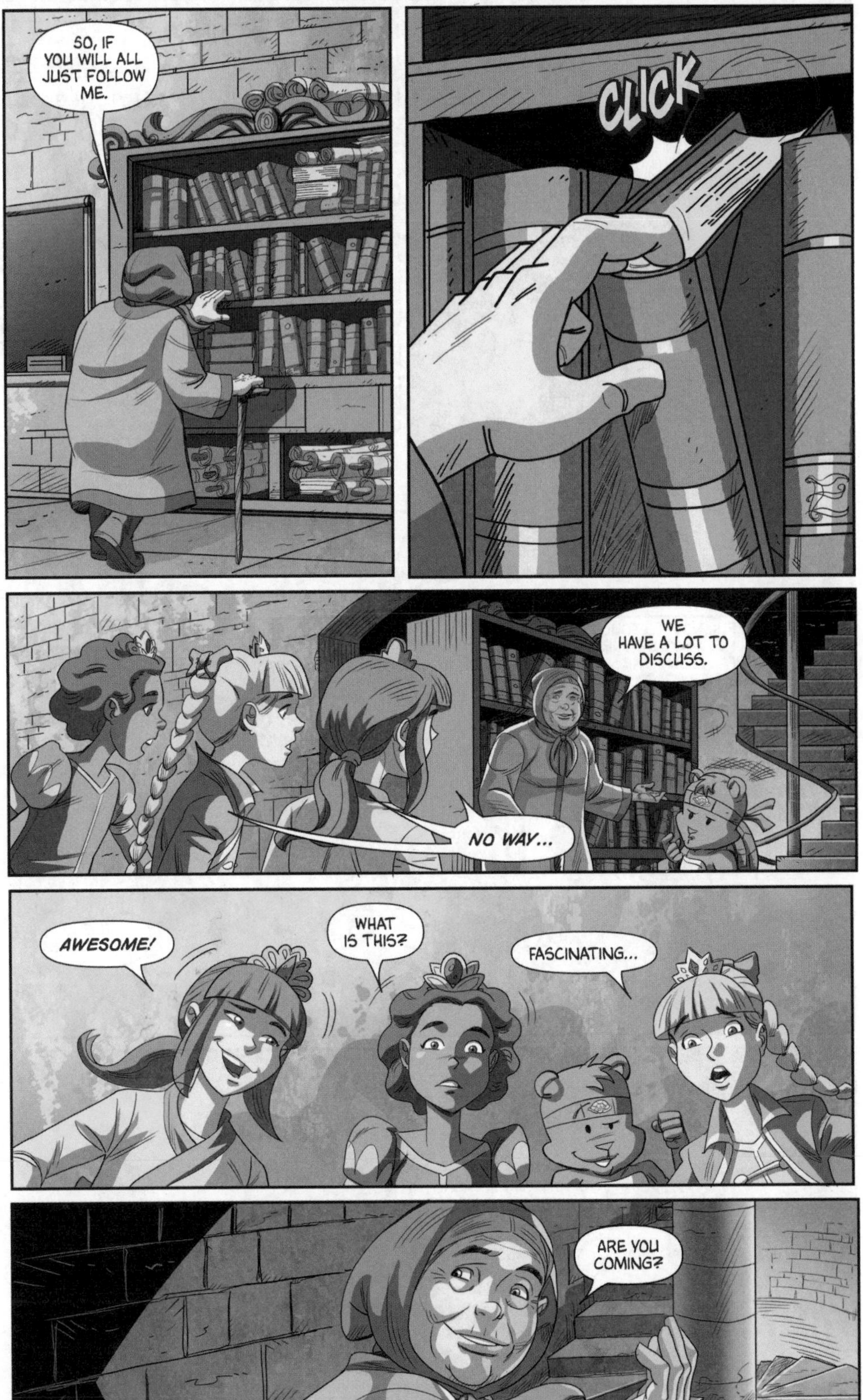
SO, IF YOU WILL ALL JUST FOLLOW ME.
CLICK
WE HAVE A LOT TO DISCUSS.
NO WAY...
AWESOME!
WHAT IS THIS?
FASCINATING...
ARE YOU COMING?

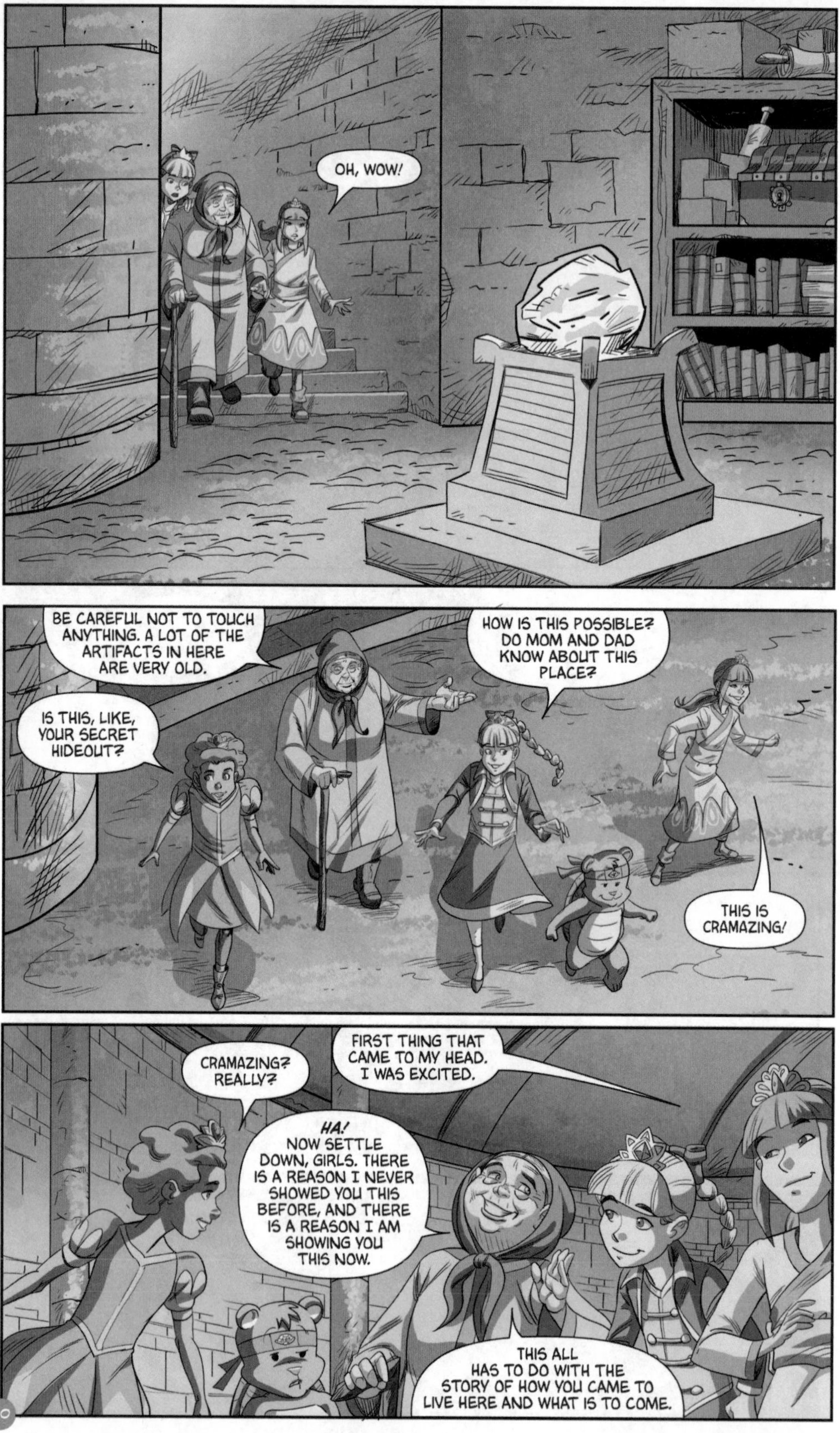

OH, WOW!
BE CAREFUL NOT TO TOUCH ANYTHING. A LOT OF THE ARTIFACTS IN HERE ARE VERY OLD.
IS THIS, LIKE, YOUR SECRET HIDEOUT?
HOW IS THIS POSSIBLE? DO MOM AND DAD KNOW ABOUT THIS PLACE?
...
THIS IS CRAMAZING!
CRAMAZING? REALLY?
FIRST THING THAT CAME TO MY HEAD. I WAS EXCITED.
HA! NOW SETTLE DOWN, GIRLS. THERE IS A REASON I NEVER SHOWED YOU THIS BEFORE, AND THERE IS A REASON I AM SHOWING YOU THIS NOW.
THIS ALL HAS TO DO WITH THE STORY OF HOW YOU CAME TO LIVE HERE AND WHAT IS TO COME.

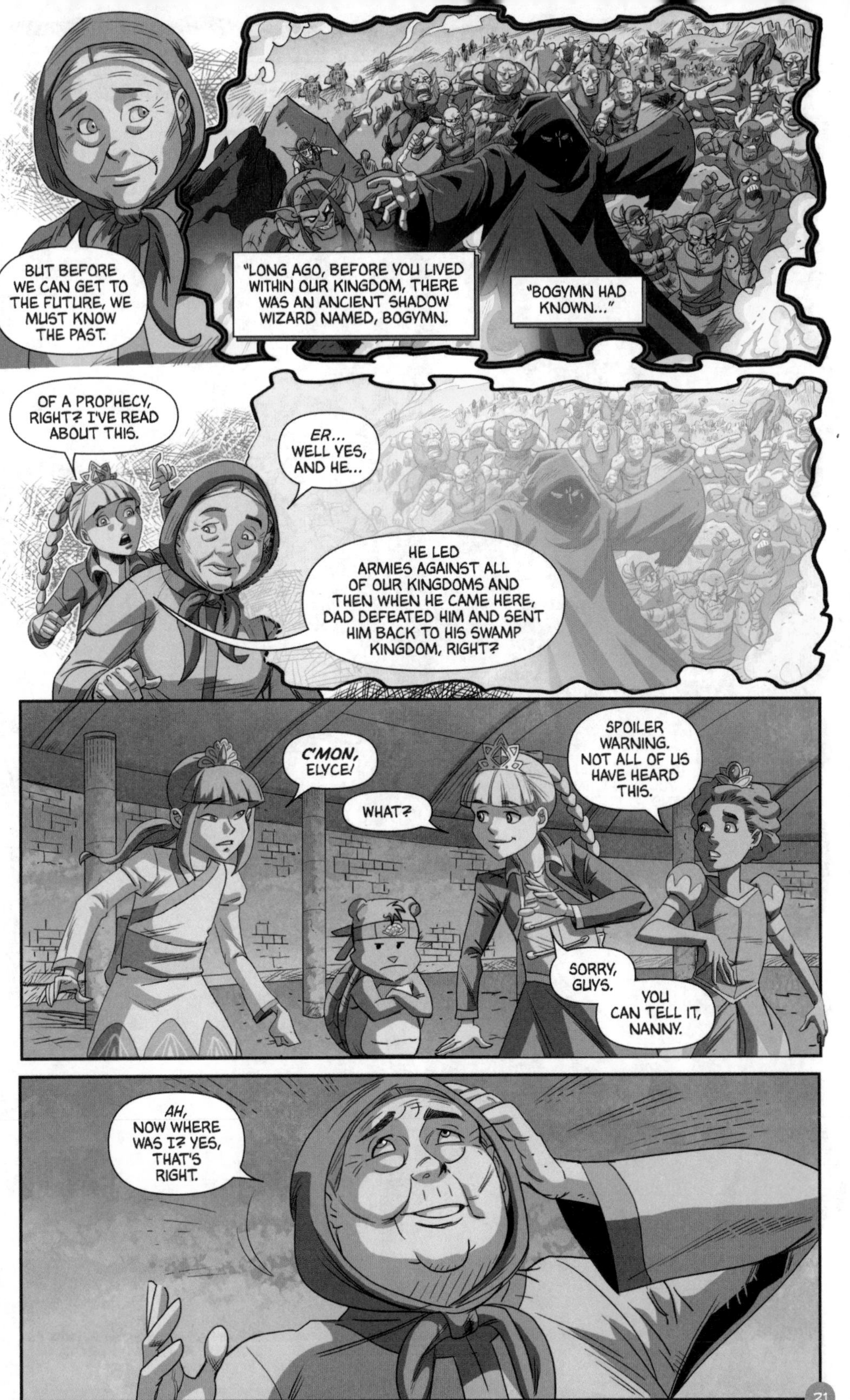
BUT BEFORE WE CAN GET TO THE FUTURE, WE MUST KNOW THE PAST.
"LONG AGO, BEFORE YOU LIVED WITHIN OUR KINGDOM, THERE WAS AN ANCIENT SHADOW WIZARD NAMED, BOGYMN.
"BOGYMN HAD KNOWN..."
OF A PROPHECY, RIGHT? I'VE READ ABOUT THIS.
ER... WELL YES, AND HE...
HE LED ARMIES AGAINST ALL OF OUR KINGDOMS AND THEN WHEN HE CAME HERE, DAD DEFEATED HIM AND SENT HIM BACK TO HIS SWAMP KINGDOM, RIGHT?
C'MON, ELYCE!
WHAT?
SPOILER WARNING. NOT ALL OF US HAVE HEARD THIS.
SORRY, GUYS.
YOU CAN TELL IT, NANNY.
AH, NOW WHERE WAS I? YES, THAT'S RIGHT.

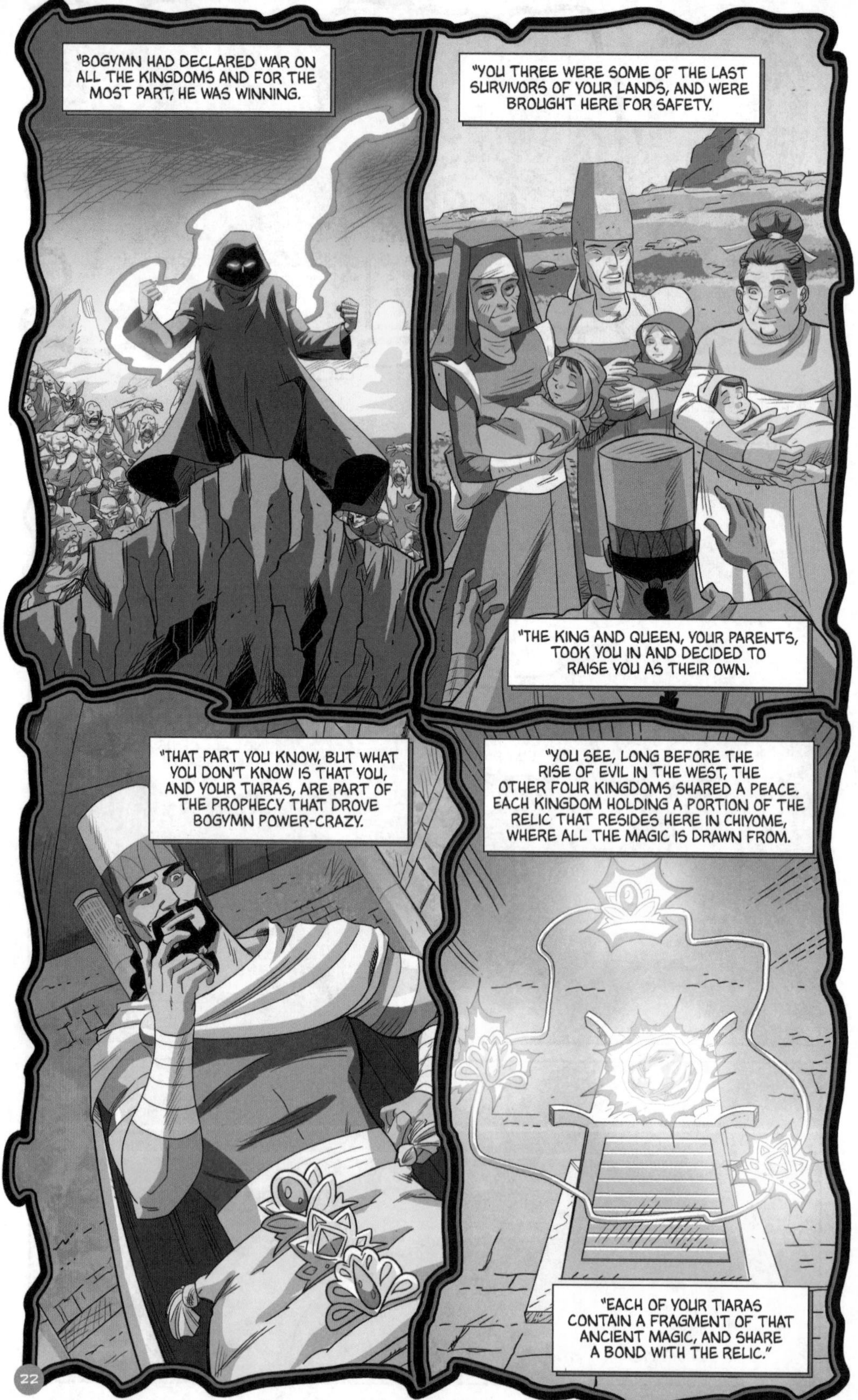
"BOGYMN HAD DECLARED WAR ON ALL THE KINGDOMS AND FOR THE MOST PART, HE WAS WINNING.
"YOU THREE WERE SOME OF THE LAST SURVIVORS OF YOUR LANDS, AND WERE BROUGHT HERE FOR SAFETY.
"THE KING AND QUEEN, YOUR PARENTS, TOOK YOU IN AND DECIDED TO RAISE YOU AS THEIR OWN.
"THAT PART YOU KNOW, BUT WHAT YOU DON'T KNOW IS THAT YOU, AND YOUR TIARAS, ARE PART OF THE PROPHECY THAT DROVE BOGYMN POWER-CRAZY.
"YOU SEE, LONG BEFORE THE RISE OF EVIL IN THE WEST, THE OTHER FOUR KINGDOMS SHARED A PEACE. EACH KINGDOM HOLDING A PORTION OF THE RELIC THAT RESIDES HERE IN CHIYOME, WHERE ALL THE MAGIC IS DRAWN FROM.
"EACH OF YOUR TIARAS CONTAIN A FRAGMENT OF THAT ANCIENT MAGIC, AND SHARE A BOND WITH THE RELIC."

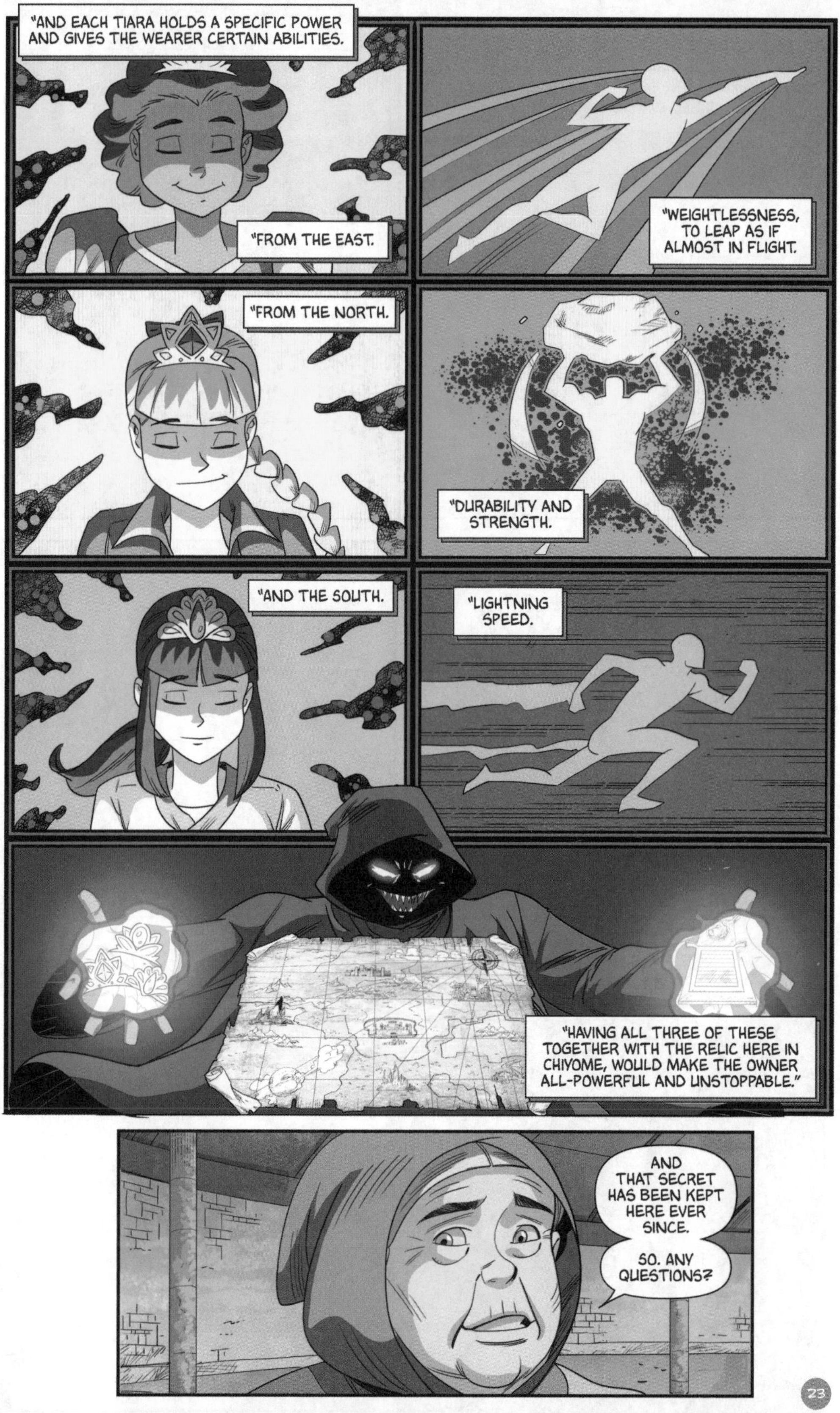

"AND EACH TIARA HOLDS A SPECIFIC POWER AND GIVES THE WEARER CERTAIN ABILITIES.
"FROM THE EAST.
"WEIGHTLESSNESS, TO LEAP AS IF ALMOST IN FLIGHT.
"FROM THE NORTH.
"DURABILITY AND STRENGTH.
"AND THE SOUTH.
"LIGHTNING SPEED.
"HAVING ALL THREE OF THESE TOGETHER WITH THE RELIC HERE IN CHIYOME, WOULD MAKE THE OWNER ALL-POWERFUL AND UNSTOPPABLE."
AND THAT SECRET HAS BEEN KEPT HERE EVER SINCE.
SO. ANY QUESTIONS?

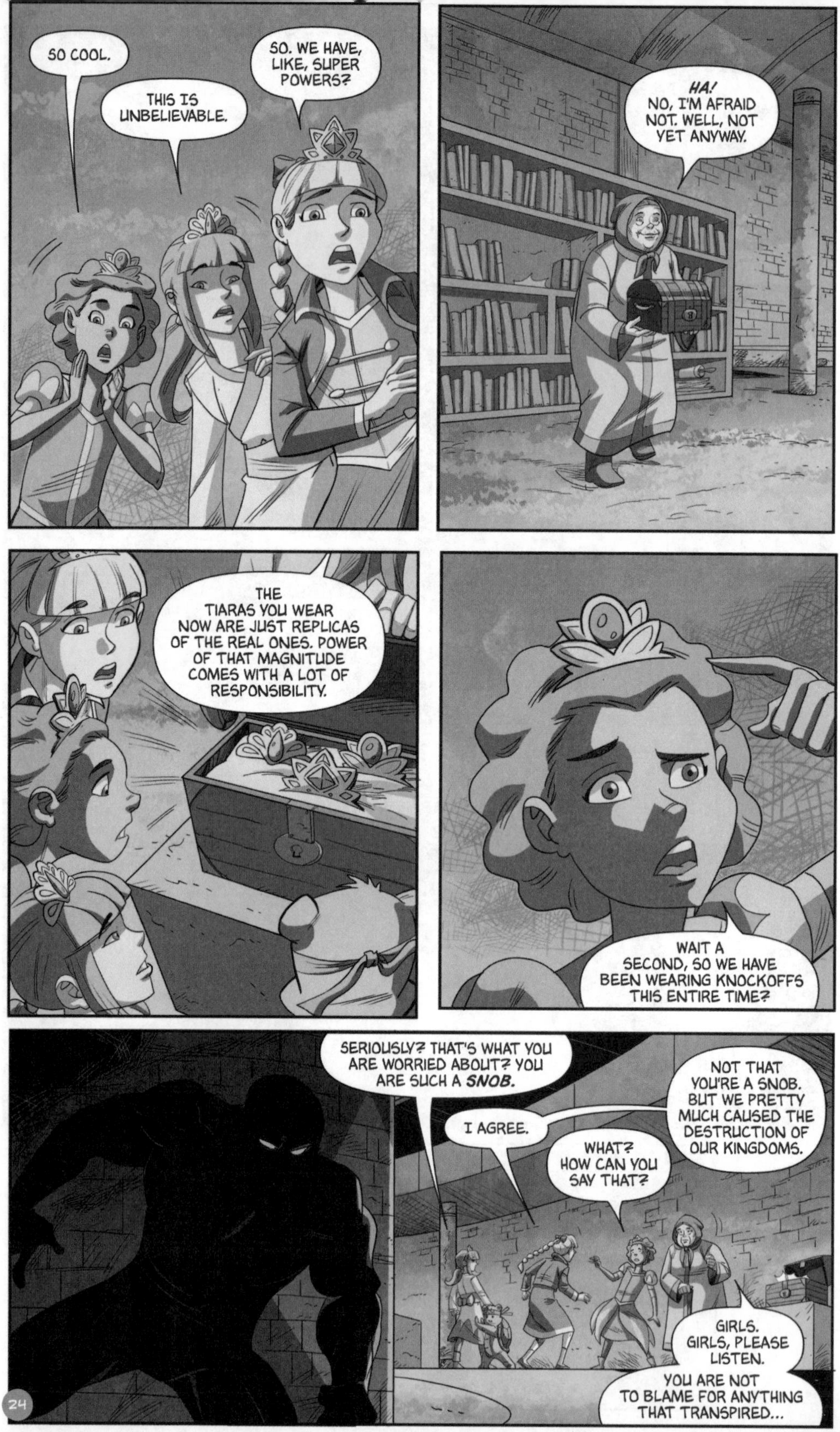
SO COOL.
THIS IS UNBELIEVABLE.
SO. WE HAVE, LIKE, SUPER POWERS?
HA! NO, I'M AFRAID NOT. WELL, NOT YET ANYWAY.
THE TIARAS YOU WEAR NOW ARE JUST REPLICAS OF THE REAL ONES. POWER OF THAT MAGNITUDE COMES WITH A LOT OF RESPONSIBILITY.
WAIT A SECOND, SO WE HAVE BEEN WEARING KNOCKOFFS THIS ENTIRE TIME?
SERIOUSLY? THAT'S WHAT YOU ARE WORRIED ABOUT? YOU ARE SUCH A SNOB.
I AGREE.
NOT THAT YOU'RE A SNOB. BUT WE PRETTY MUCH CAUSED THE DESTRUCTION OF OUR KINGDOMS.
WHAT? HOW CAN YOU SAY THAT?
GIRLS. GIRLS, PLEASE LISTEN.
YOU ARE NOT TO BLAME FOR ANYTHING THAT TRANSPIRED...

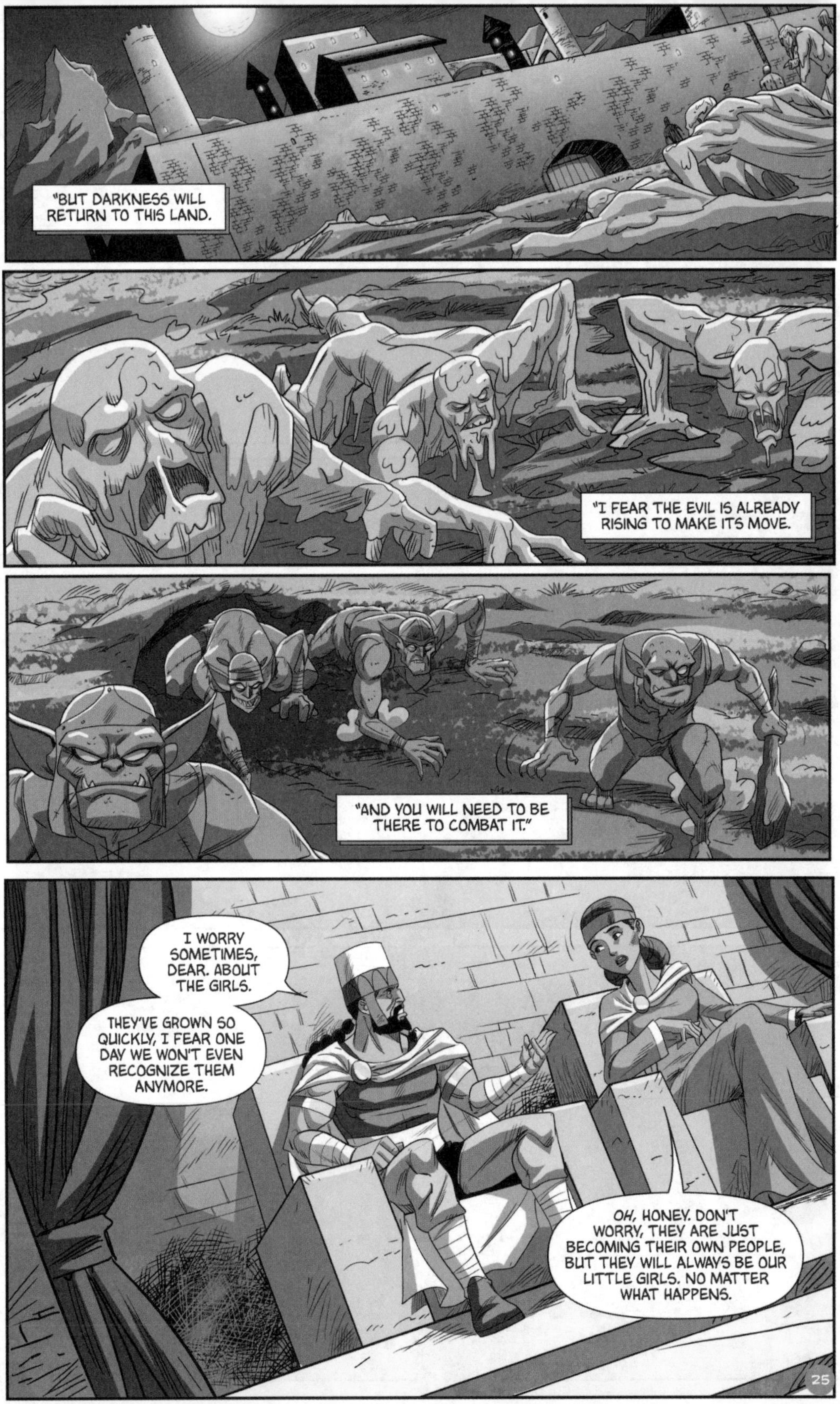
"BUT DARKNESS WILL RETURN TO THIS LAND.
"I FEAR THE EVIL IS ALREADY RISING TO MAKE ITS MOVE.
"AND YOU WILL NEED TO BE THERE TO COMBAT IT."
I WORRY SOMETIMES, DEAR. ABOUT THE GIRLS.
THEY'VE GROWN SO QUICKLY, I FEAR ONE DAY WE WON'T EVEN RECOGNIZE THEM ANYMORE.
OH, HONEY. DON'T WORRY, THEY ARE JUST BECOMING THEIR OWN PEOPLE, BUT THEY WILL ALWAYS BE OUR LITTLE GIRLS. NO MATTER WHAT HAPPENS.

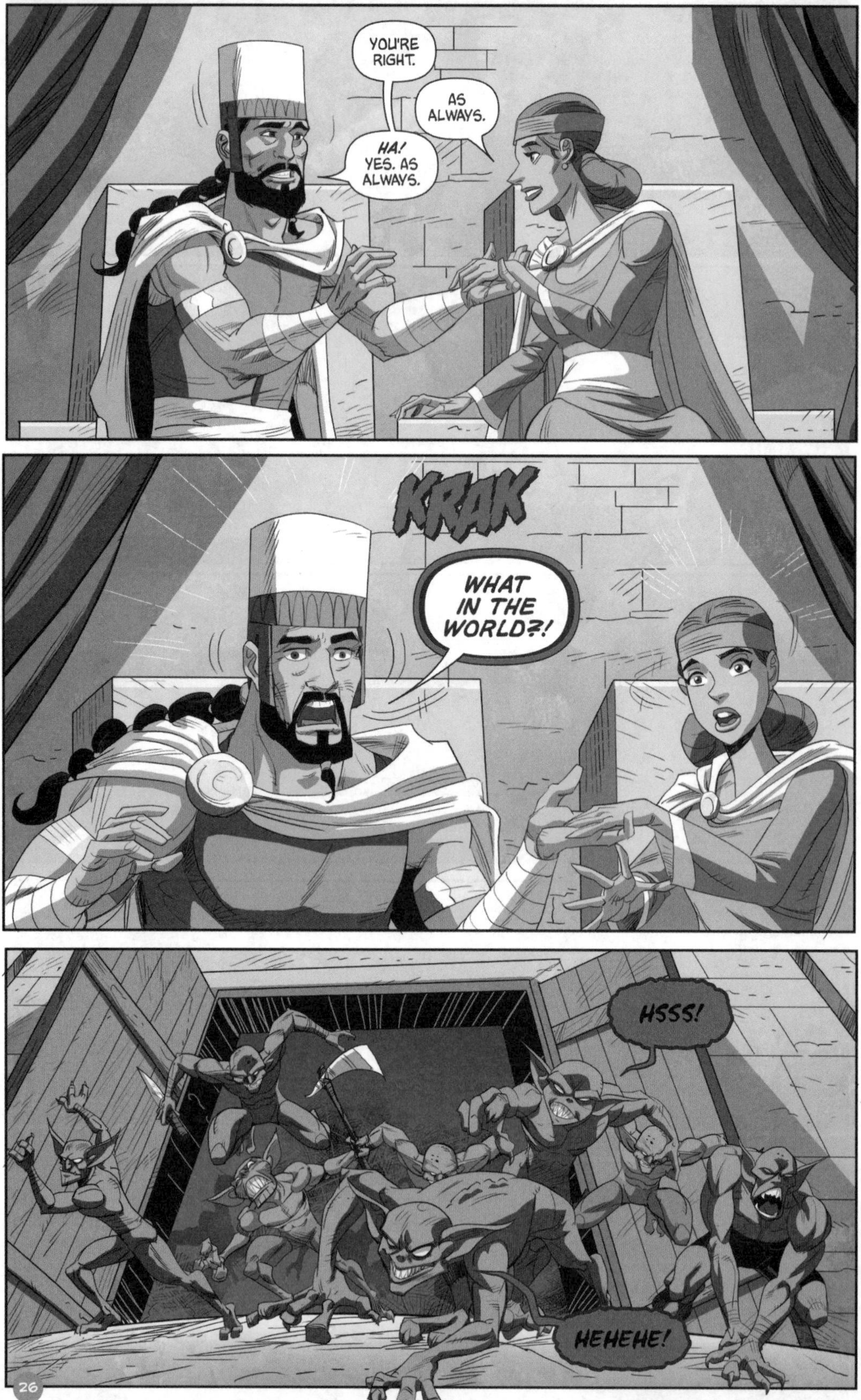
YOU'RE RIGHT.
AS ALWAYS.
HA! YES. AS ALWAYS.
KRAK
WHAT IN THE WORLD?!
HSSS!
HEHEHE!

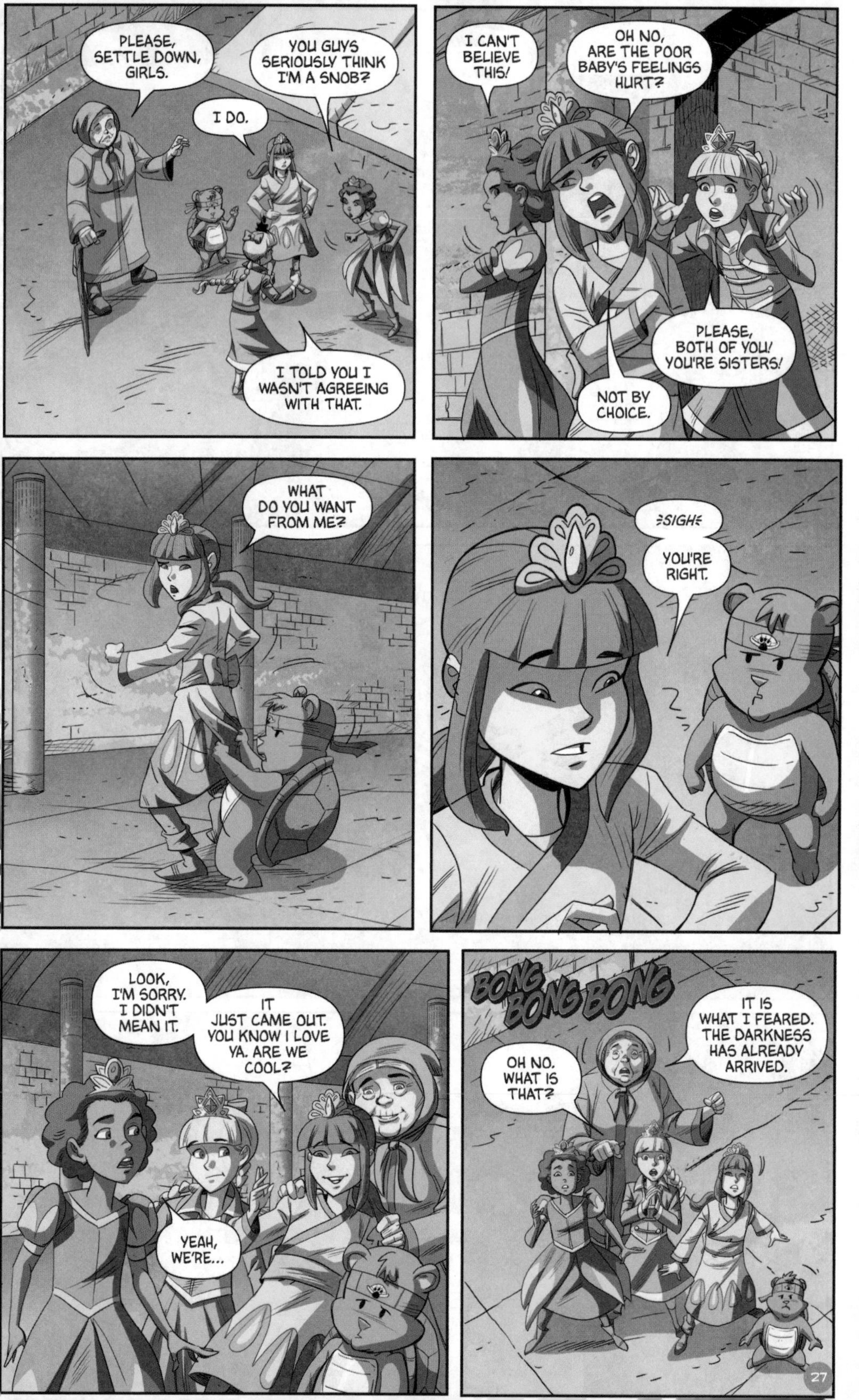
PLEASE, SETTLE DOWN, GIRLS.
YOU GUYS SERIOUSLY THINK I'M A SNOB?
I DO.
I TOLD YOU I WASN'T AGREEING WITH THAT.
I CAN'T BELIEVE THIS!
OH NO, ARE THE POOR BABY'S FEELINGS HURT?
PLEASE, BOTH OF YOU! YOU'RE SISTERS!
NOT BY CHOICE.
WHAT DO YOU WANT FROM ME?
SIGH
YOU'RE RIGHT.
LOOK, I'M SORRY. I DIDN'T MEAN IT.
IT JUST CAME OUT. YOU KNOW I LOVE YA. ARE WE COOL?
YEAH, WE'RE...
BONG BONG BONG
IT IS WHAT I FEARED. THE DARKNESS HAS ALREADY ARRIVED.
OH NO. WHAT IS THAT?
27

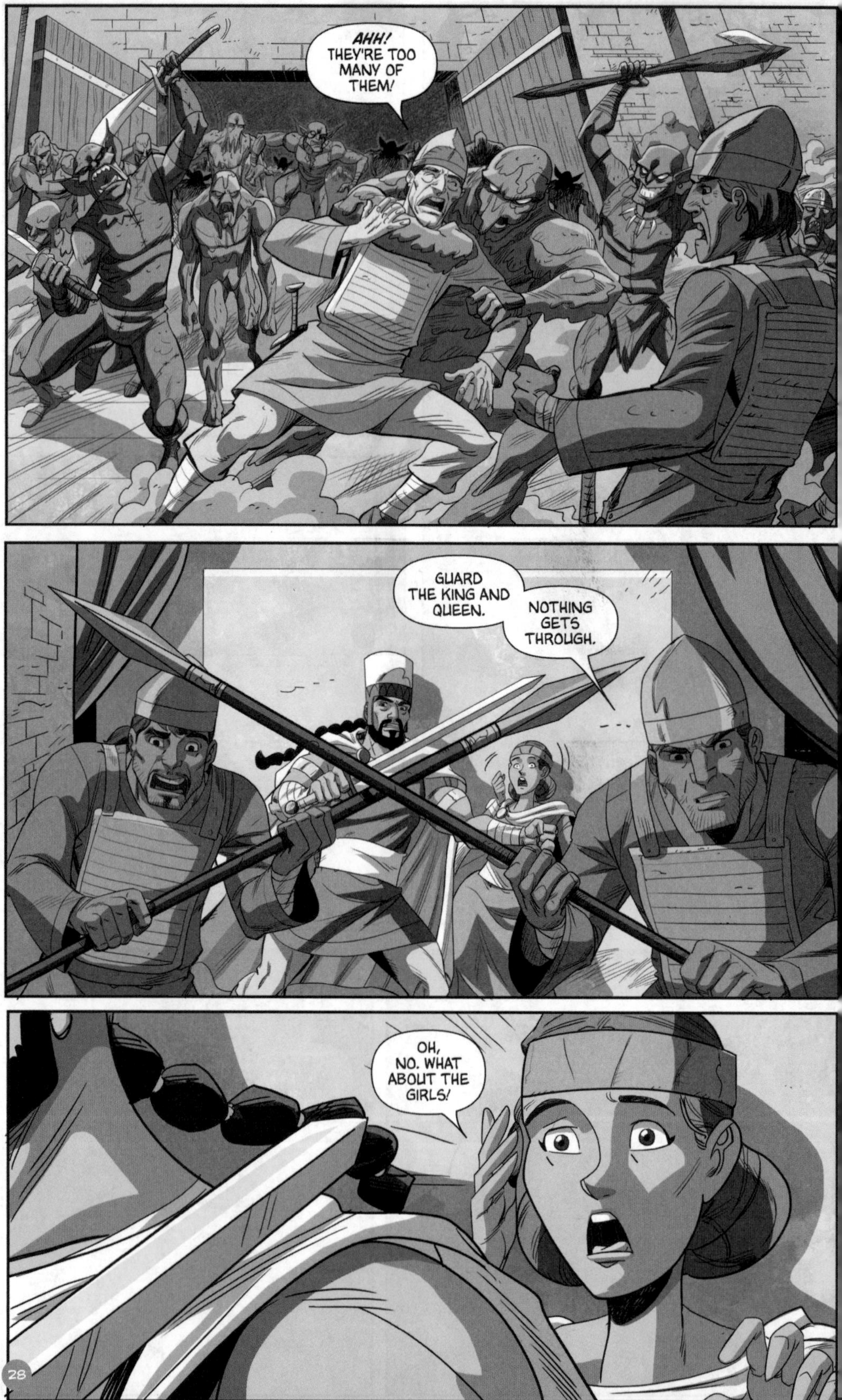
AHH! THEY'RE TOO MANY OF THEM!
GUARD THE KING AND QUEEN.
NOTHING GETS THROUGH.
OH, NO. WHAT ABOUT THE GIRLS!

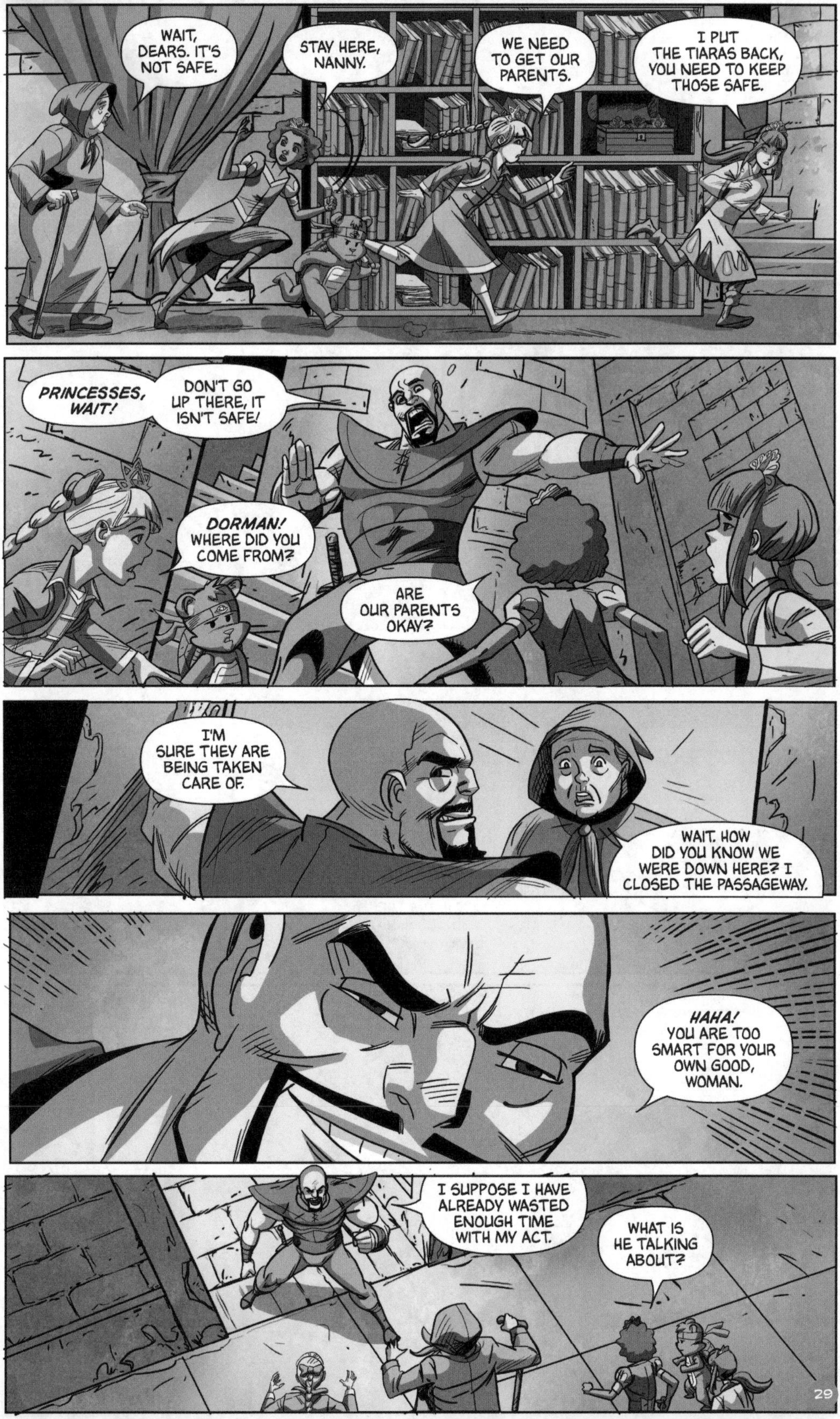
WAIT, DEARS. IT'S NOT SAFE.
STAY HERE, NANNY.
WE NEED TO GET OUR PARENTS.
I PUT THE TIARAS BACK, YOU NEED TO KEEP THOSE SAFE.
PRINCESSES, WAIT!
DON'T GO UP THERE, IT ISN'T SAFE!
DORMAN! WHERE DID YOU COME FROM?
ARE OUR PARENTS OKAY?
I'M SURE THEY ARE BEING TAKEN CARE OF.
WAIT. HOW DID YOU KNOW WE WERE DOWN HERE? I CLOSED THE PASSAGEWAY.
HAHA! YOU ARE TOO SMART FOR YOUR OWN GOOD, WOMAN.
I SUPPOSE I HAVE ALREADY WASTED ENOUGH TIME WITH MY ACT.
WHAT IS HE TALKING ABOUT?

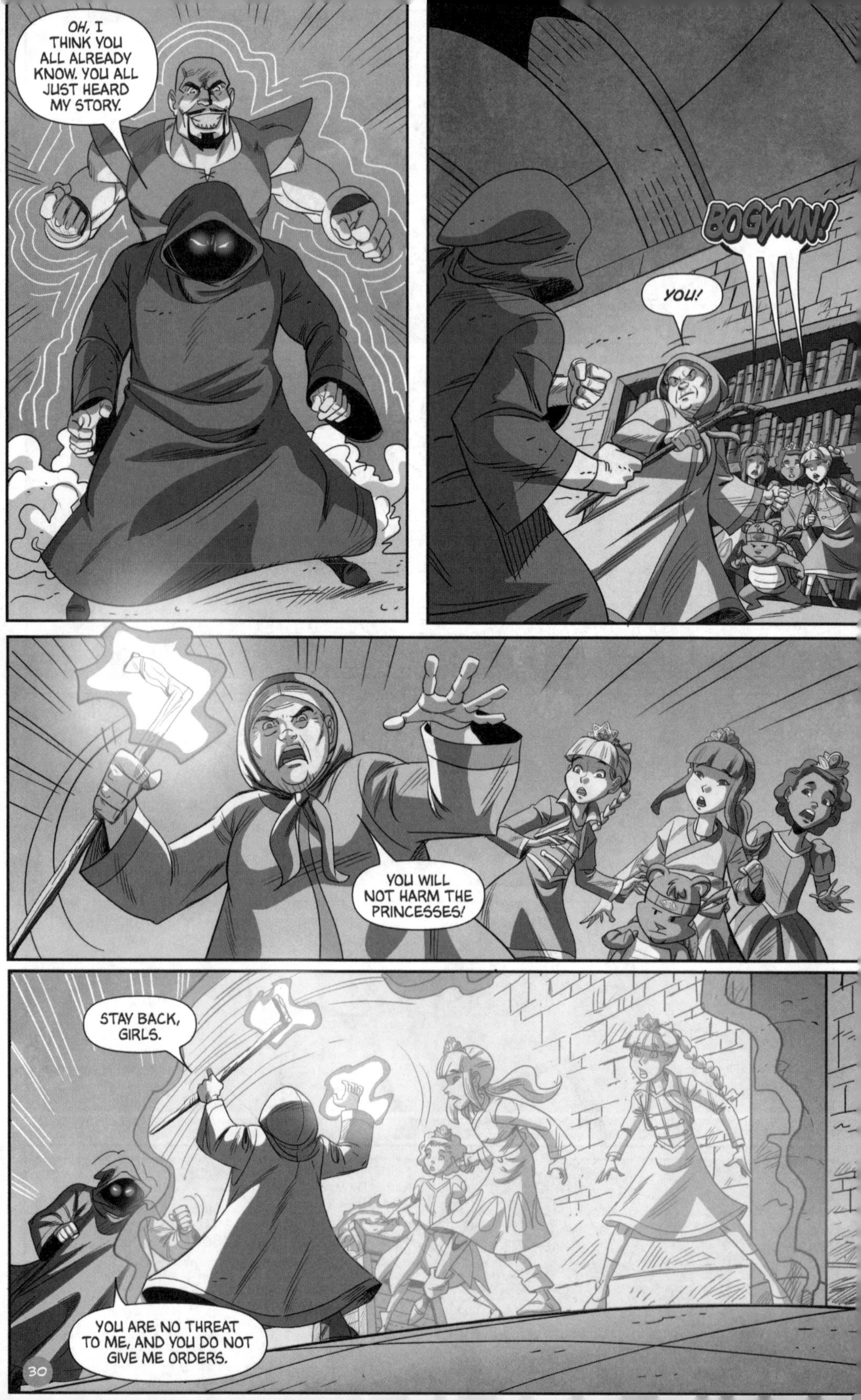

OH, I THINK YOU ALL ALREADY KNOW. YOU ALL JUST HEARD MY STORY.
BOGYMN!
YOU!
YOU WILL NOT HARM THE PRINCESSES!
STAY BACK, GIRLS.
YOU ARE NO THREAT TO ME, AND YOU DO NOT GIVE ME ORDERS.

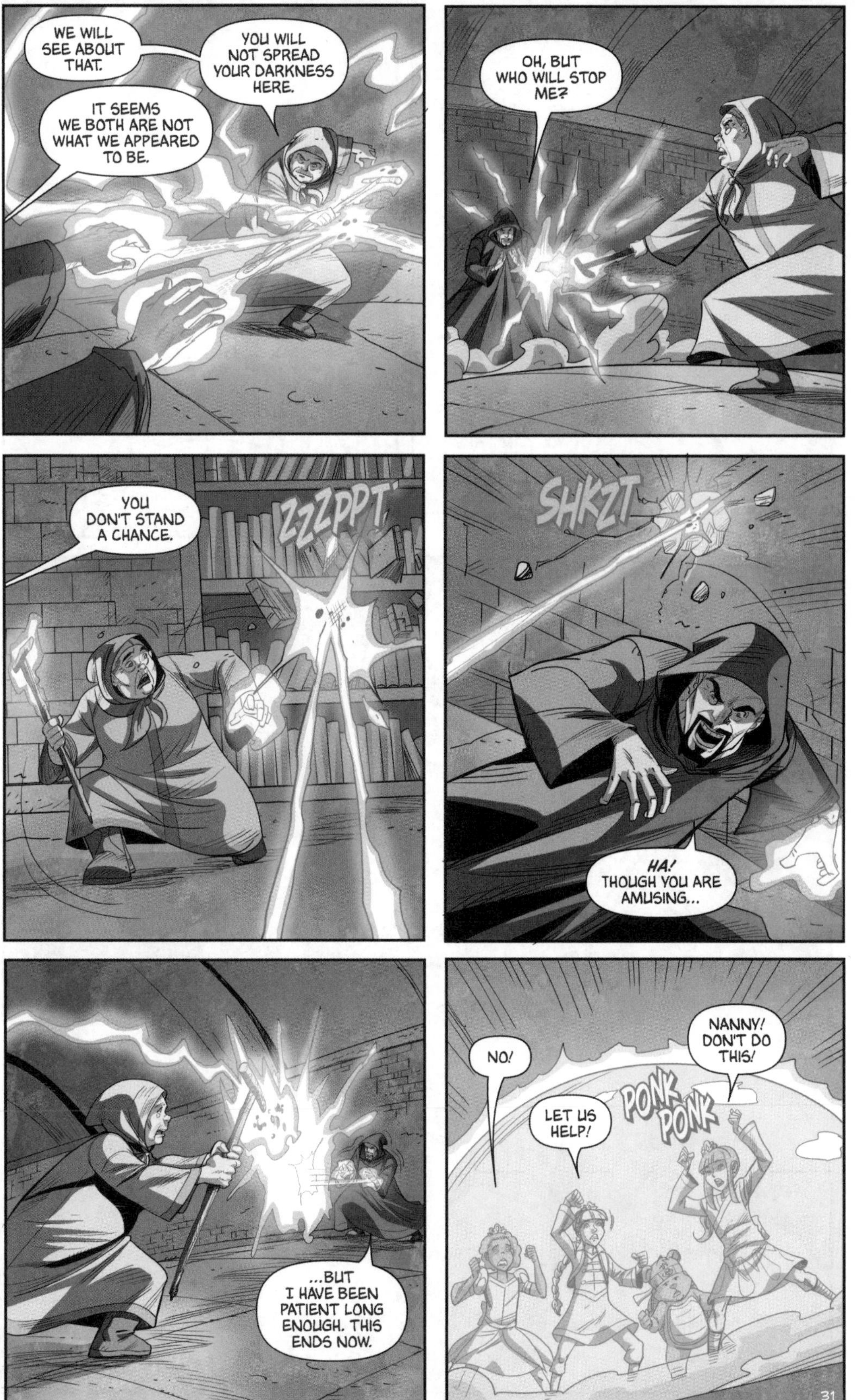
WE WILL SEE ABOUT THAT.
YOU WILL NOT SPREAD YOUR DARKNESS HERE.
IT SEEMS WE BOTH ARE NOT WHAT WE APPEARED TO BE.
OH, BUT WHO WILL STOP ME?
YOU DON'T STAND A CHANCE.
ZZZPPT
SHKZT
HA! THOUGH YOU ARE AMUSING...
...BUT I HAVE BEEN PATIENT LONG ENOUGH. THIS ENDS NOW.
NO!
LET US HELP!
PONK
PONK
NANNY! DON'T DO THIS!

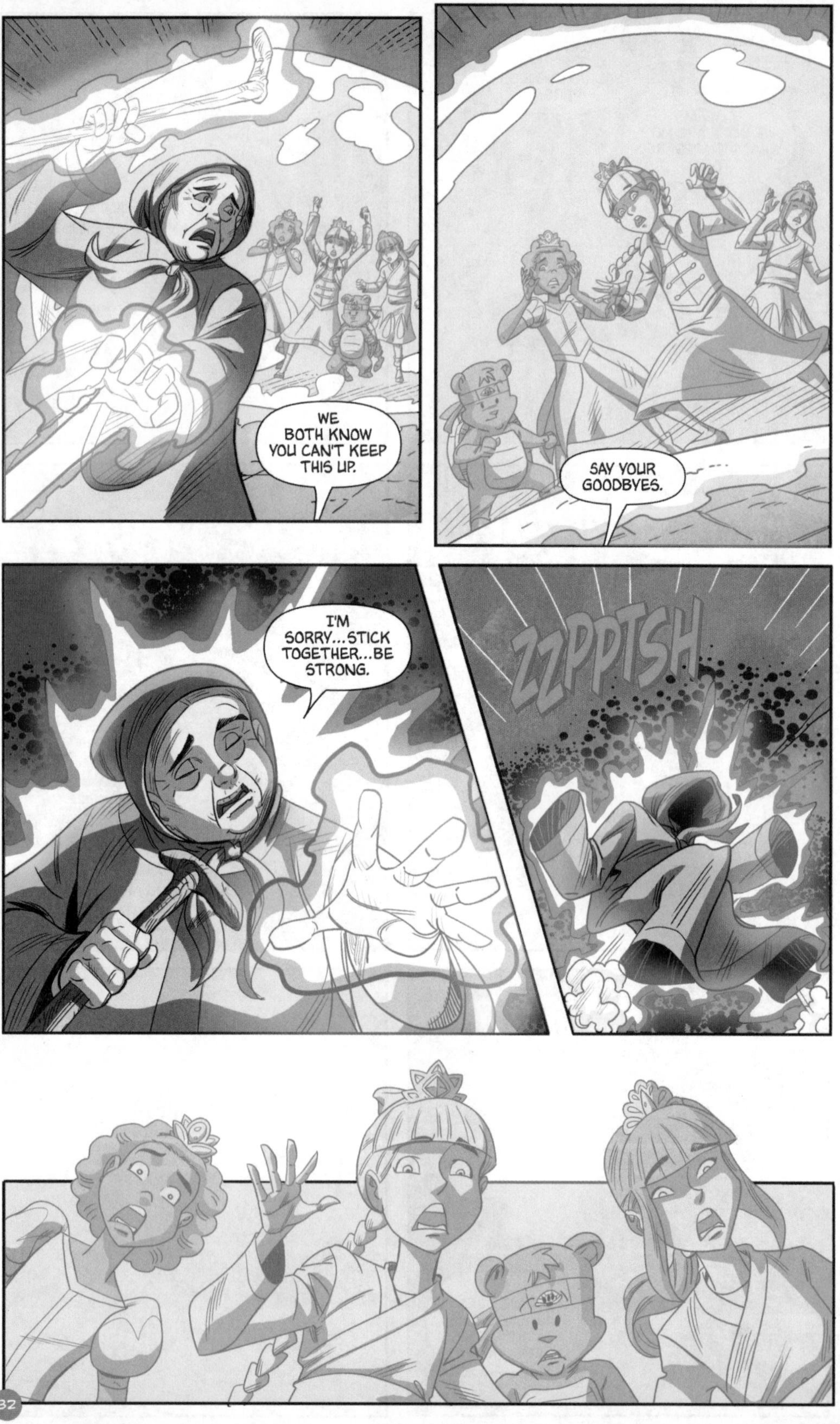
WE BOTH KNOW YOU CAN'T KEEP THIS UP.
SAY YOUR GOODBYES.
I'M SORRY...STICK TOGETHER...BE STRONG.
ZZPPPTSH

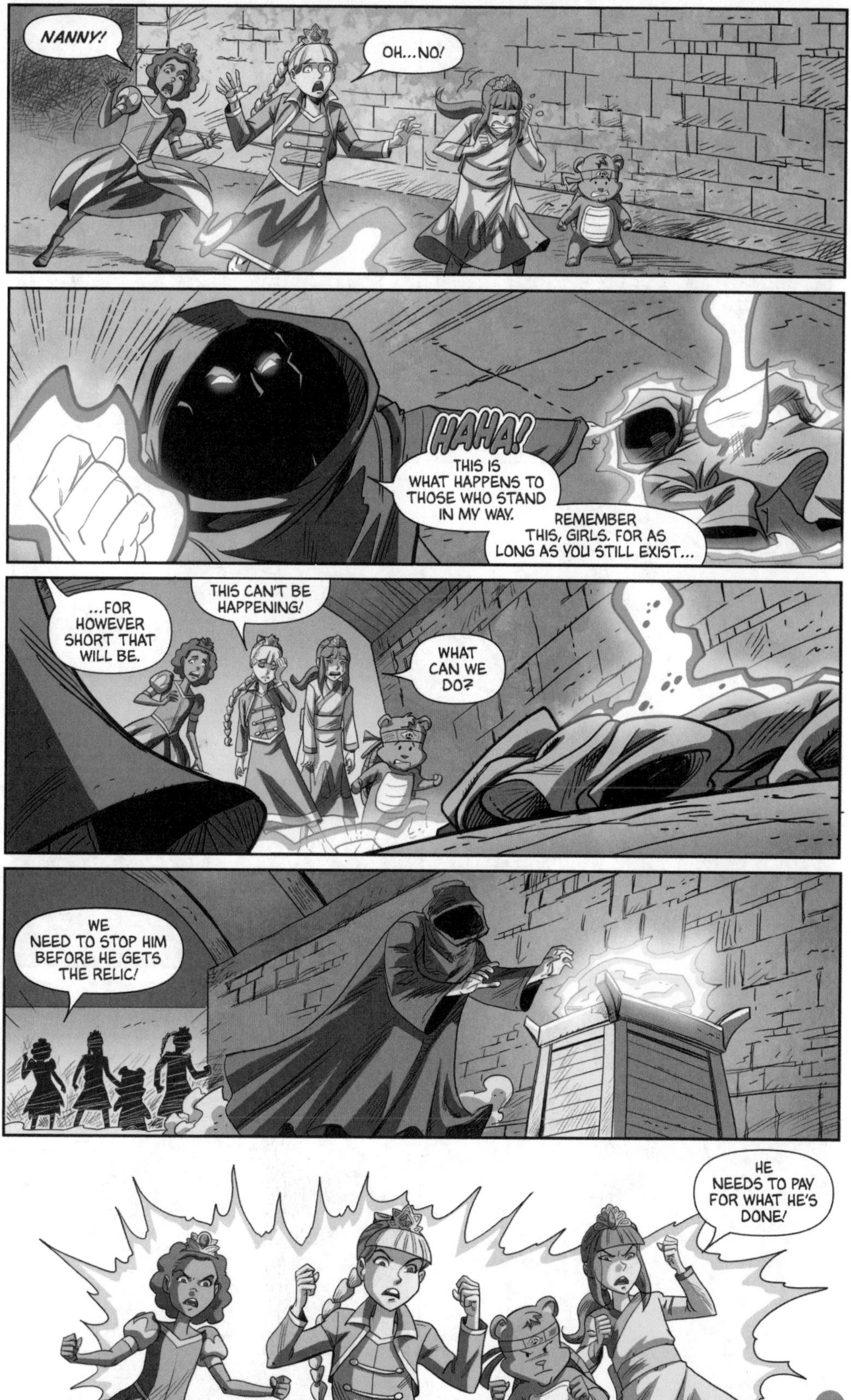
NANNY!
OH...NO!
HAHA!
THIS IS WHAT HAPPENS TO THOSE WHO STAND IN MY WAY.
REMEMBER THIS, GIRLS. FOR AS LONG AS YOU STILL EXIST...
...FOR HOWEVER SHORT THAT WILL BE.
THIS CAN'T BE HAPPENING!
WHAT CAN WE DO?
WE NEED TO STOP HIM BEFORE HE GETS THE RELIC!
HE NEEDS TO PAY FOR WHAT HE'S DONE!

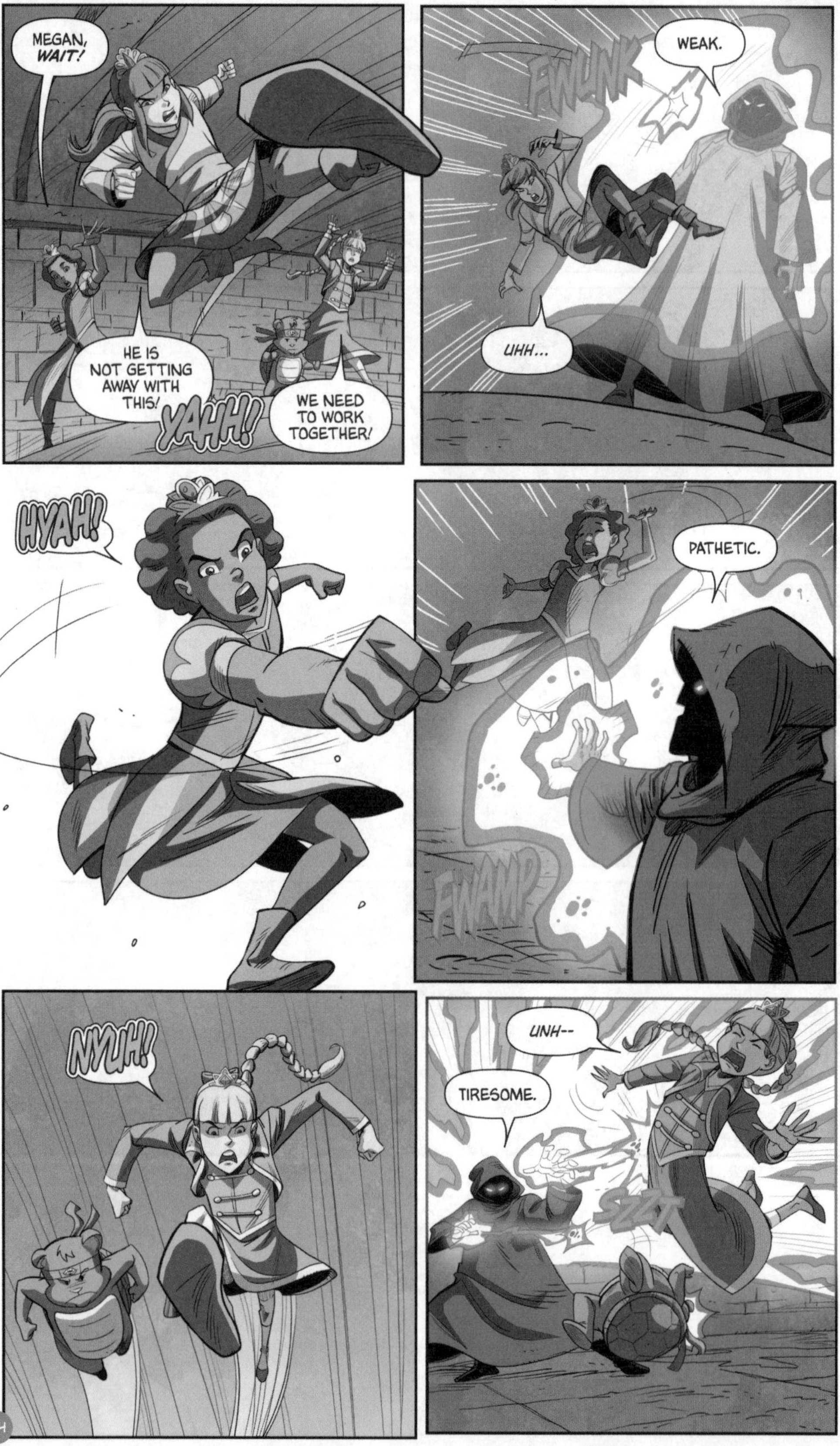

MEGAN, WAIT!
HE IS NOT GETTING AWAY WITH THIS!
YAHH!
WE NEED TO WORK TOGETHER!
FWUNK
WEAK.
UHH...
HYAH!
PATHETIC.
FWAMP
NYUH!
UNH--
TIRESOME.
SZZT

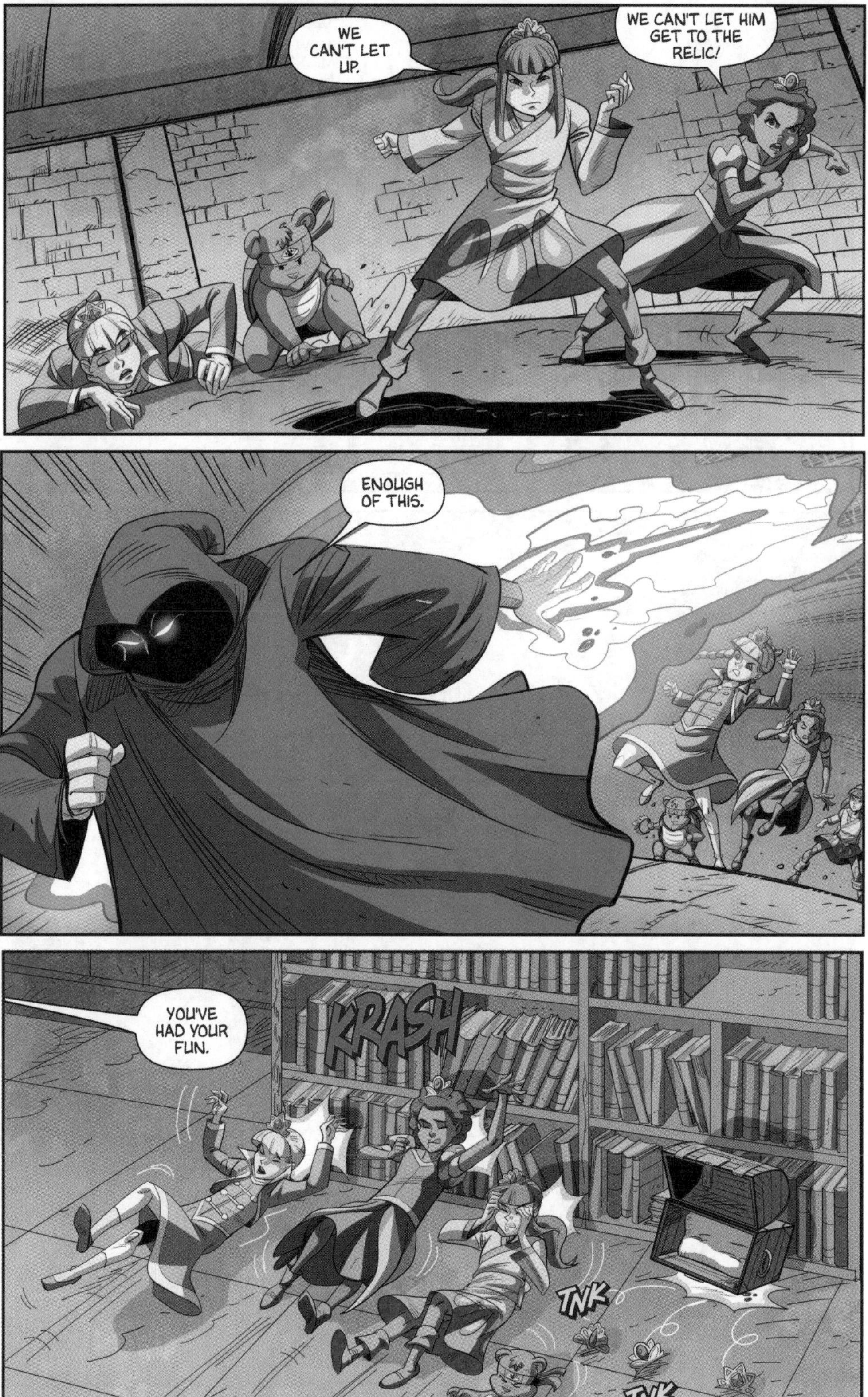
WE CAN'T LET UP.
WE CAN'T LET HIM GET TO THE RELIC!
ENOUGH OF THIS.
YOU'VE HAD YOUR FUN.
KRASH
TNK
TNK
TNK

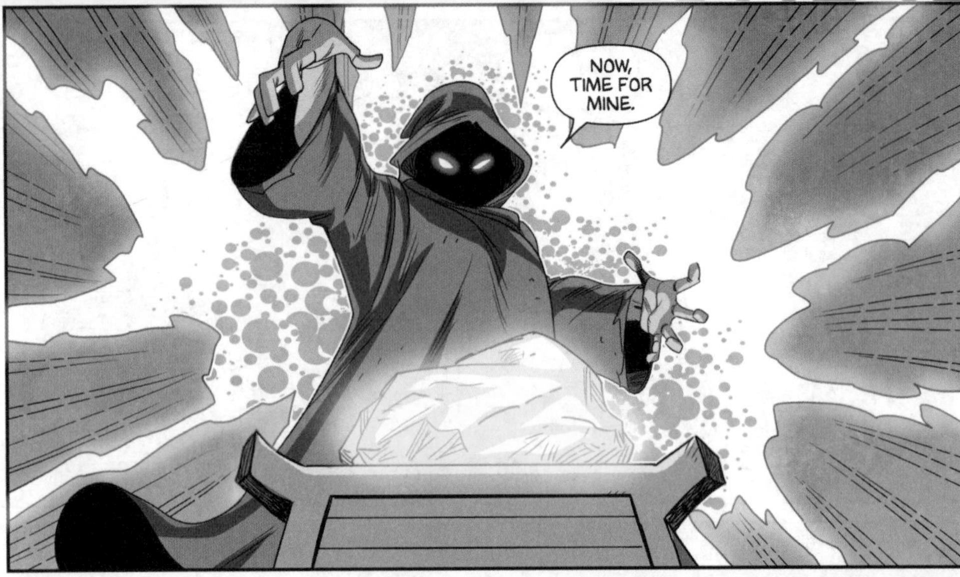
NOW, TIME FOR MINE.

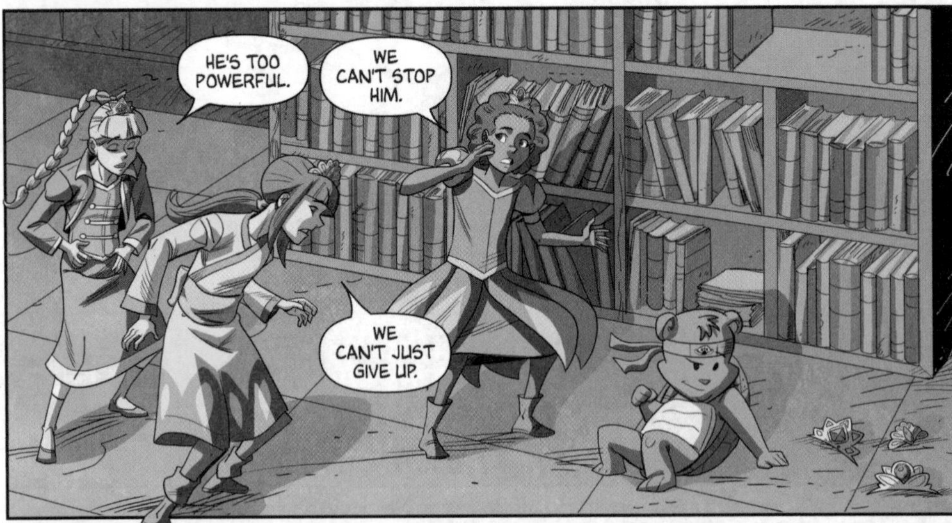
HE'S TOO POWERFUL.
WE CAN'T STOP HIM.
WE CAN'T JUST GIVE UP.

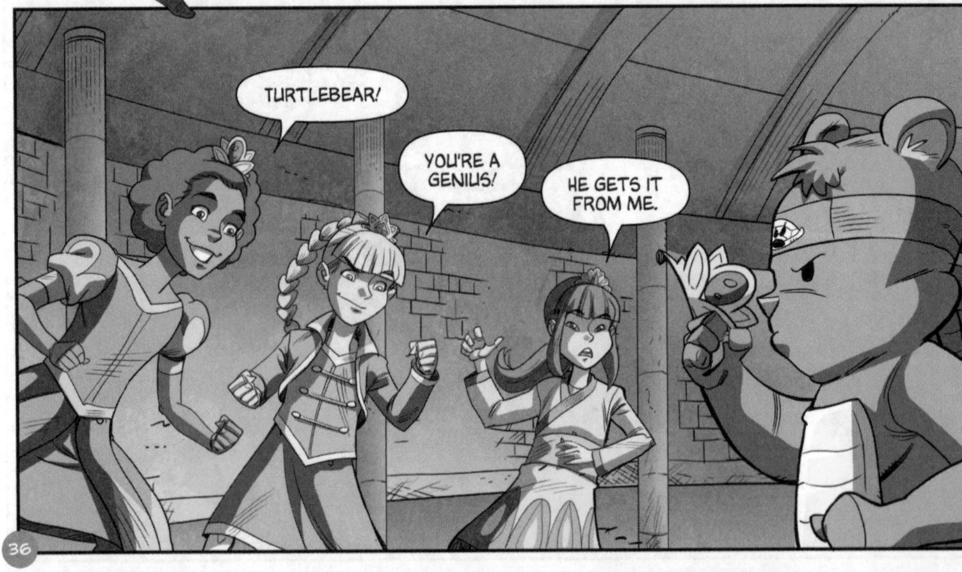
TURTLEBEAR!
YOU'RE A GENIUS!
HE GETS IT FROM ME.

HOW DO YOU THINK THEY WORK?

LET'S PUT THEM ON AND FIND OUT.

HERE GOES NOTHING.

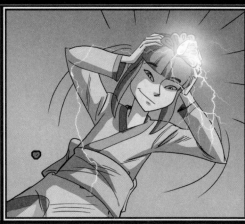

FINALLY. AFTER ALL THESE YEARS OF PLANNING AND WAITING.

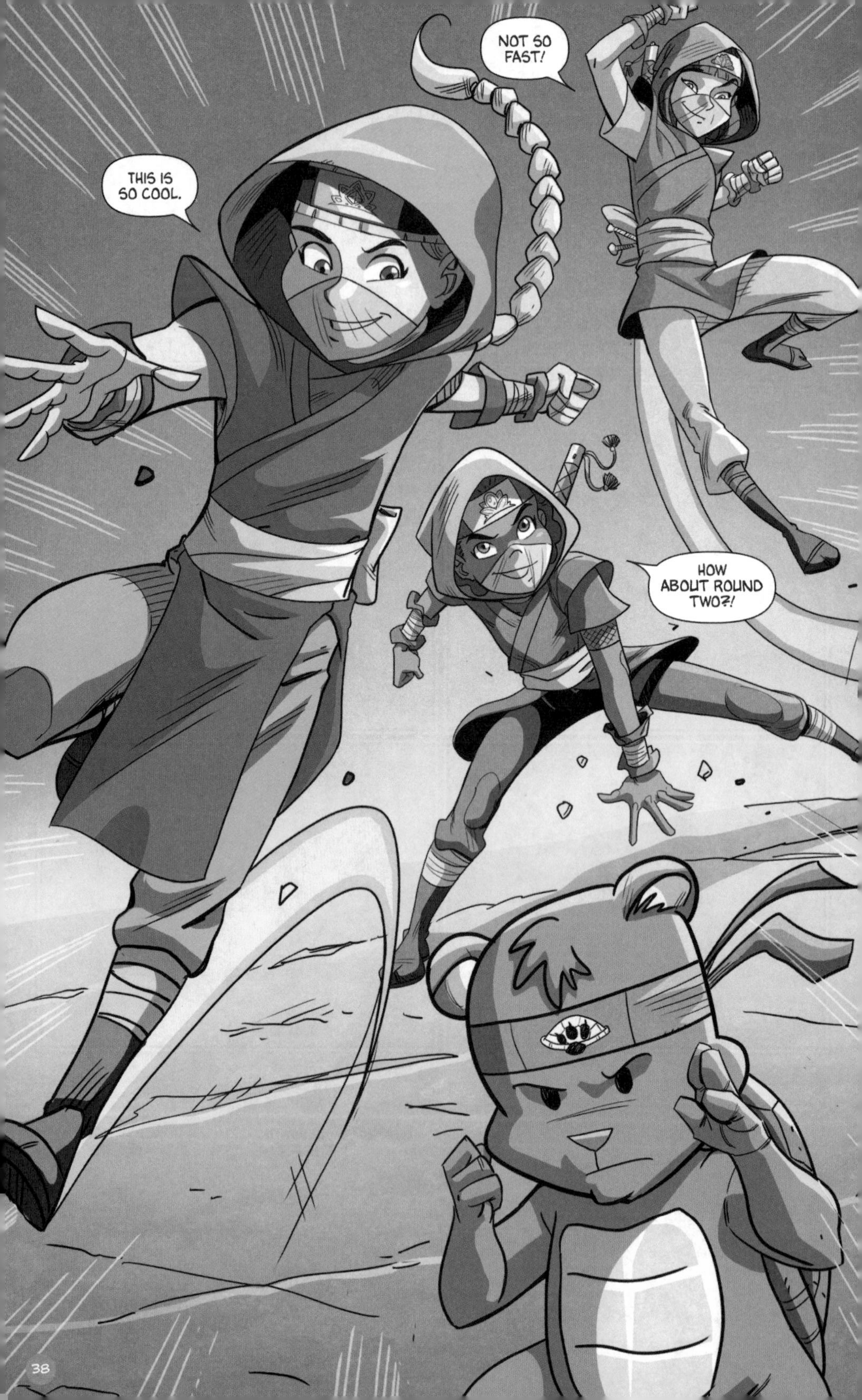
NOT SO FAST!
THIS IS SO COOL.
HOW ABOUT ROUND TWO?!

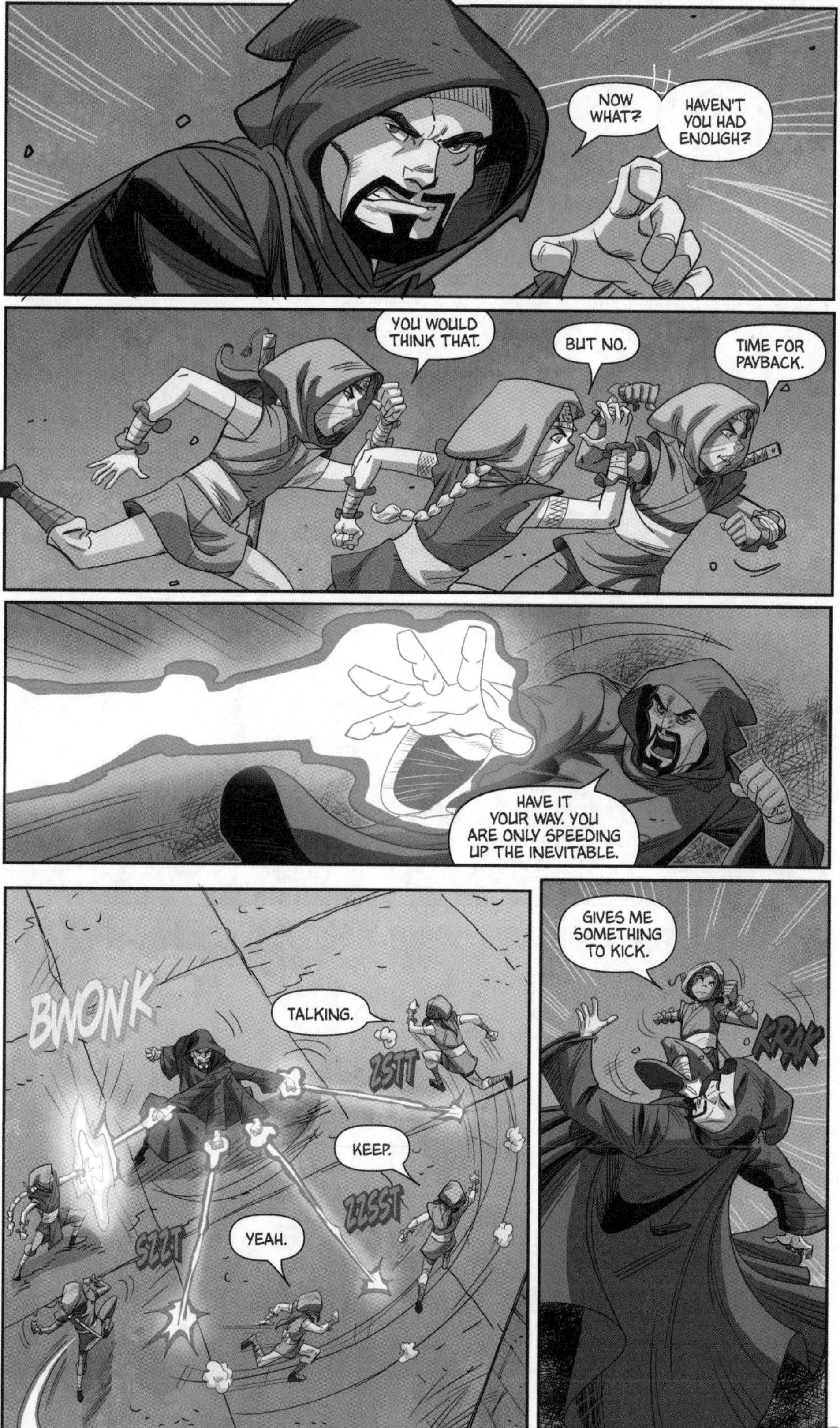
NOW WHAT?
HAVEN'T YOU HAD ENOUGH?
YOU WOULD THINK THAT.
BUT NO.
TIME FOR PAYBACK.
HAVE IT YOUR WAY. YOU ARE ONLY SPEEDING UP THE INEVITABLE.
BWONK
TALKING.
ZSTT
KEEP.
ZZSST
SZZT
YEAH.
GIVES ME SOMETHING TO KICK.
KRAK

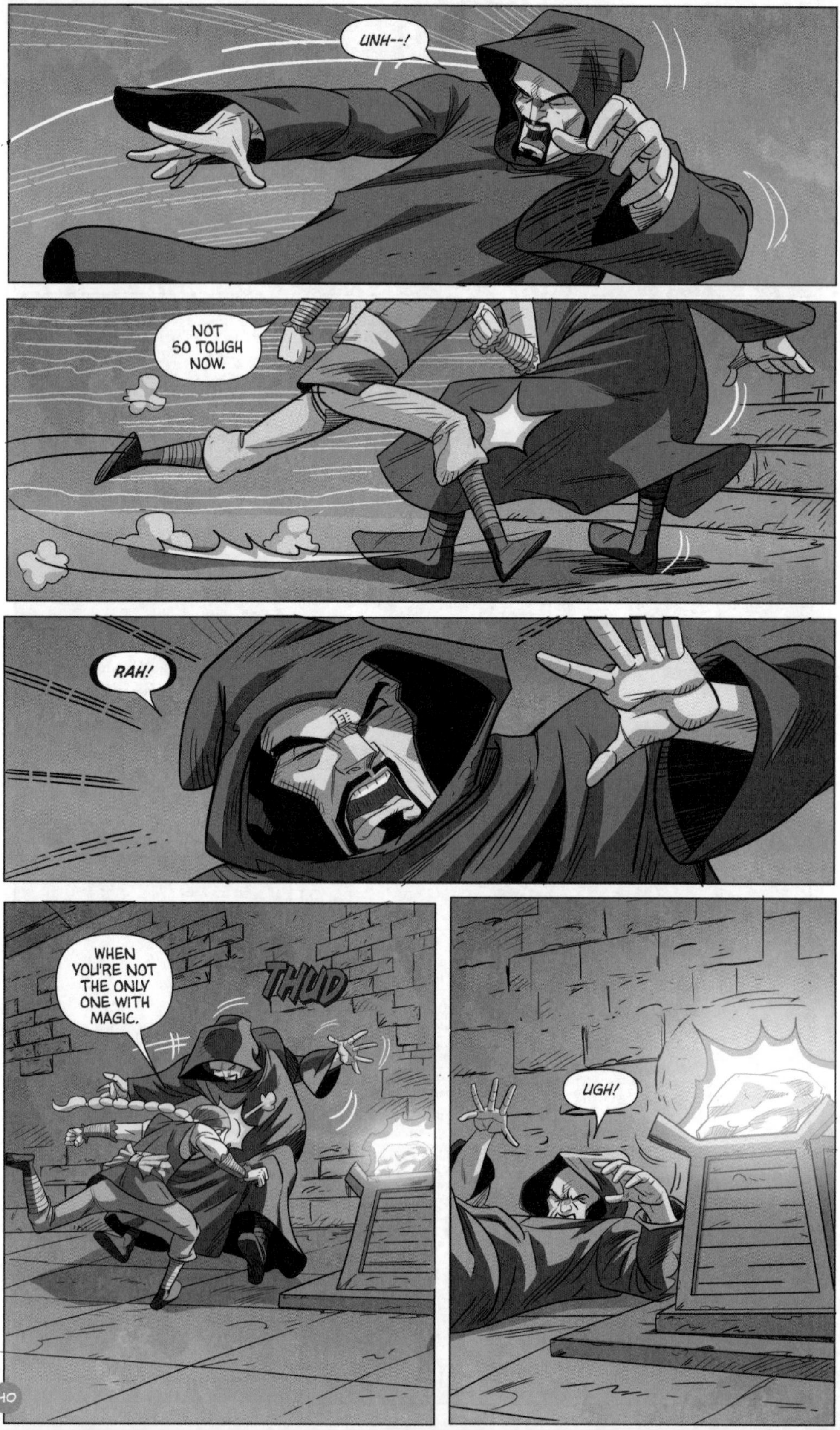
UNH--!
NOT SO TOUGH NOW.
RAH!
WHEN YOU'RE NOT THE ONLY ONE WITH MAGIC.
THUD
UGH!

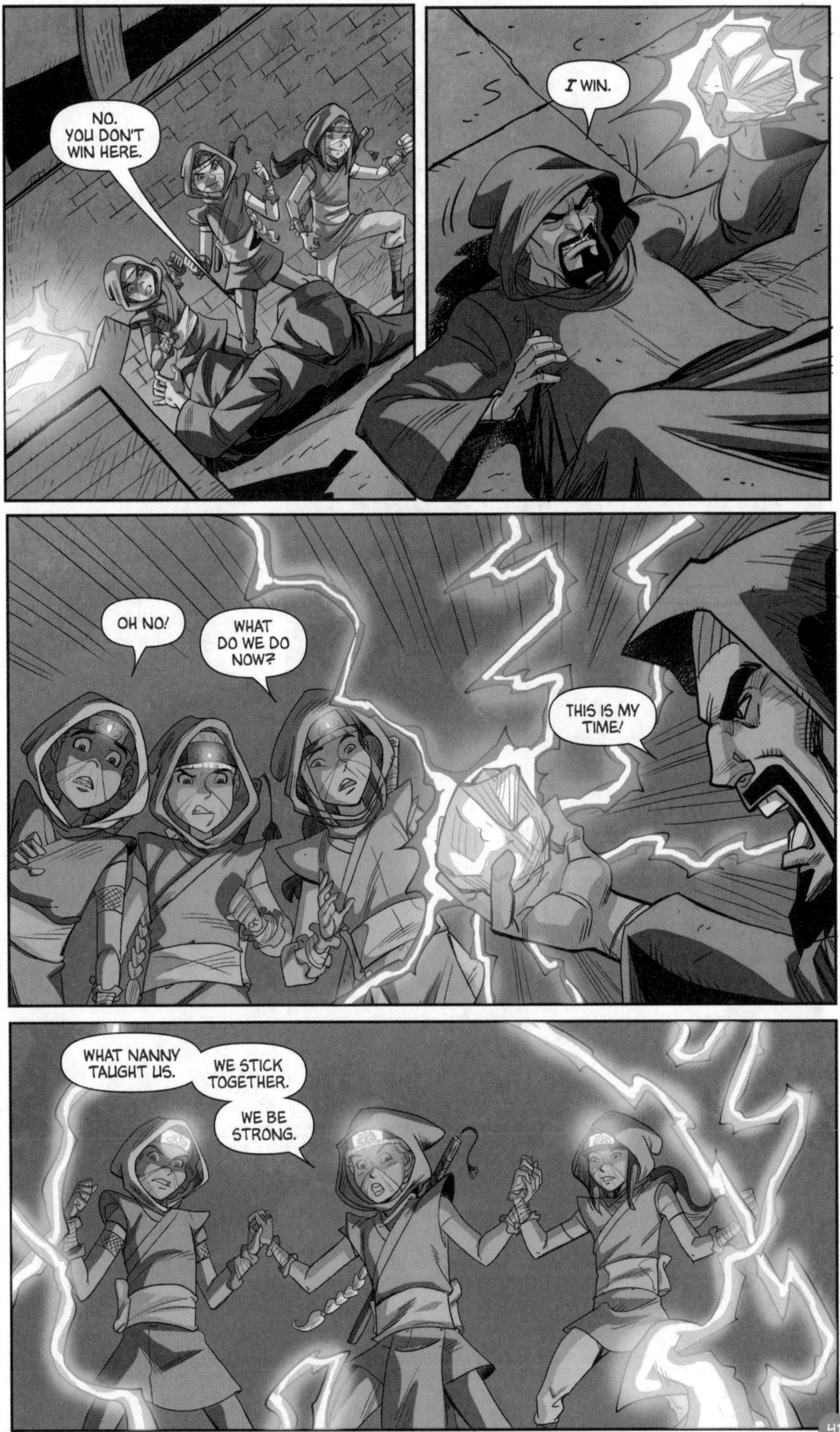
NO. YOU DON'T WIN HERE.
I WIN.
OH NO!
WHAT DO WE DO NOW?
THIS IS MY TIME!
WHAT NANNY TAUGHT US.
WE STICK TOGETHER.
WE BE STRONG.

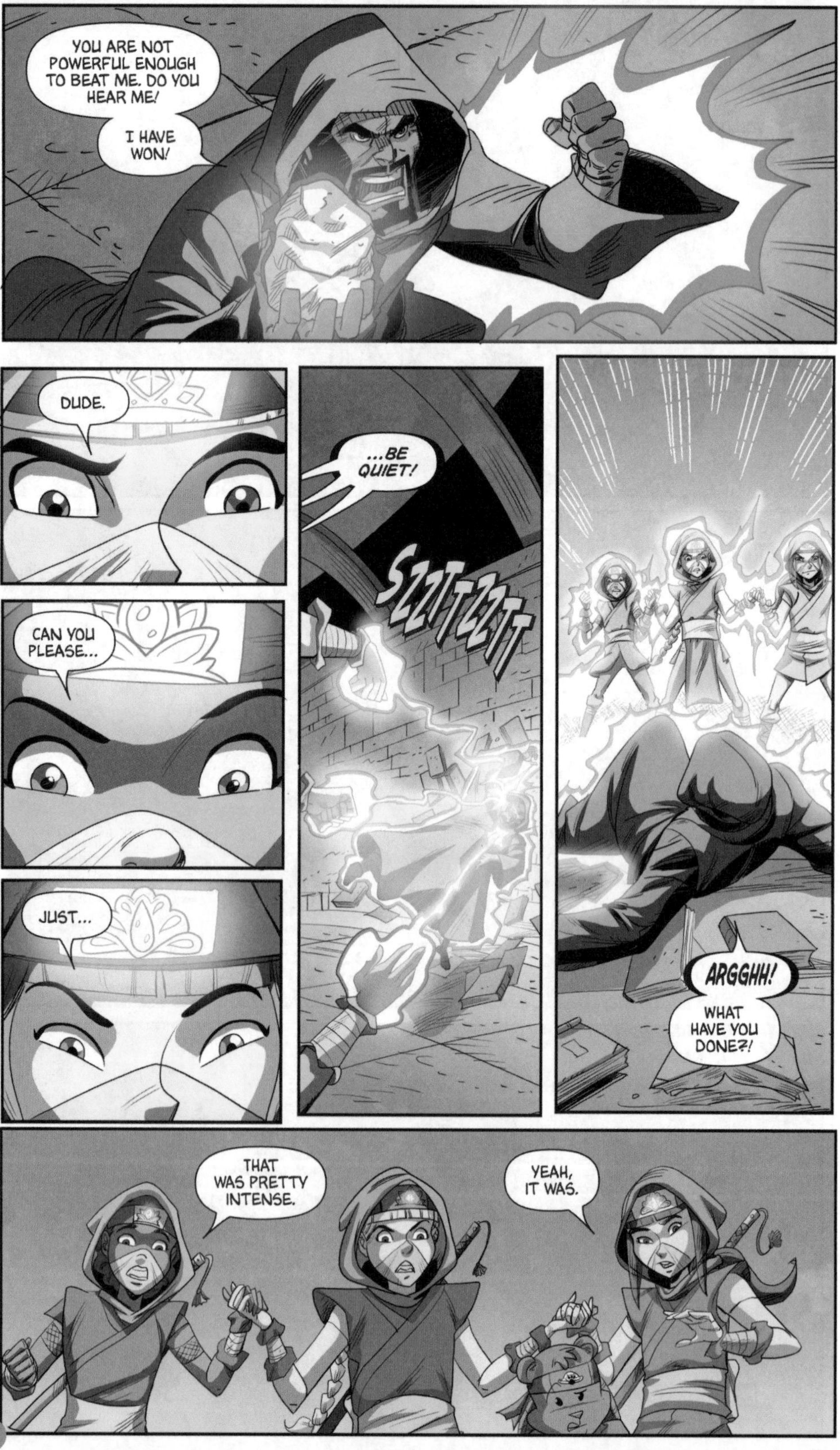
YOU ARE NOT POWERFUL ENOUGH TO BEAT ME. DO YOU HEAR ME!
I HAVE WON!
DUDE.
CAN YOU PLEASE...
JUST...
...BE QUIET!
SZZTTZZTT
ARGGHH!
WHAT HAVE YOU DONE?!
THAT WAS PRETTY INTENSE.
YEAH, IT WAS.

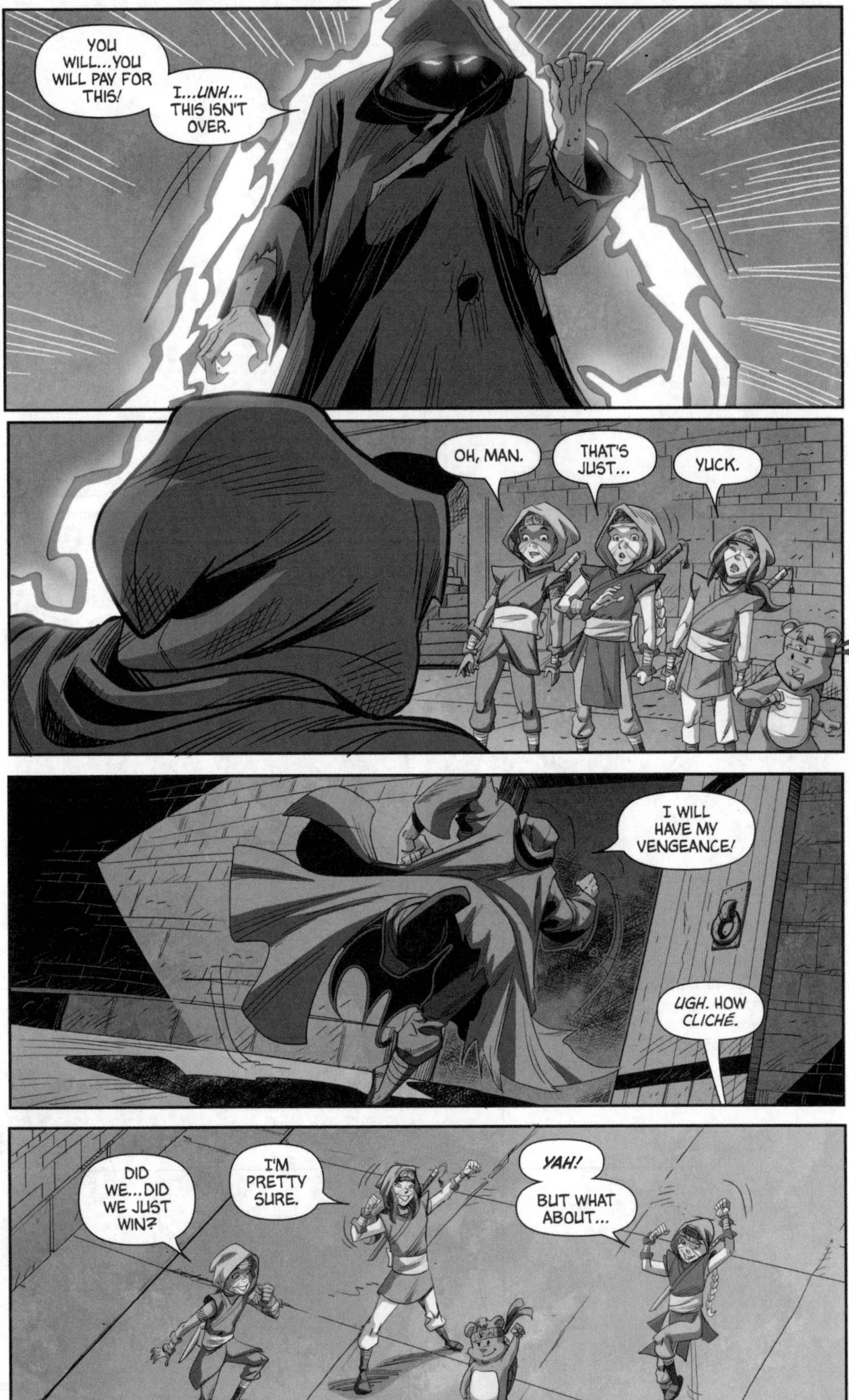
YOU WILL...YOU WILL PAY FOR THIS!
I...UNH... THIS ISN'T OVER.
OH, MAN.
THAT'S JUST...
YUCK.
I WILL HAVE MY VENGEANCE!
UGH. HOW CLICHÉ.
DID WE...DID WE JUST WIN?
I'M PRETTY SURE.
YAH!
BUT WHAT ABOUT...

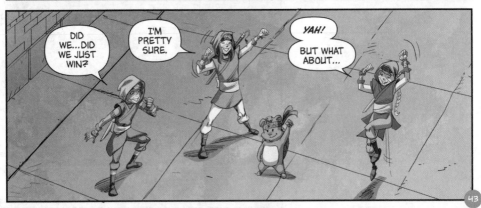

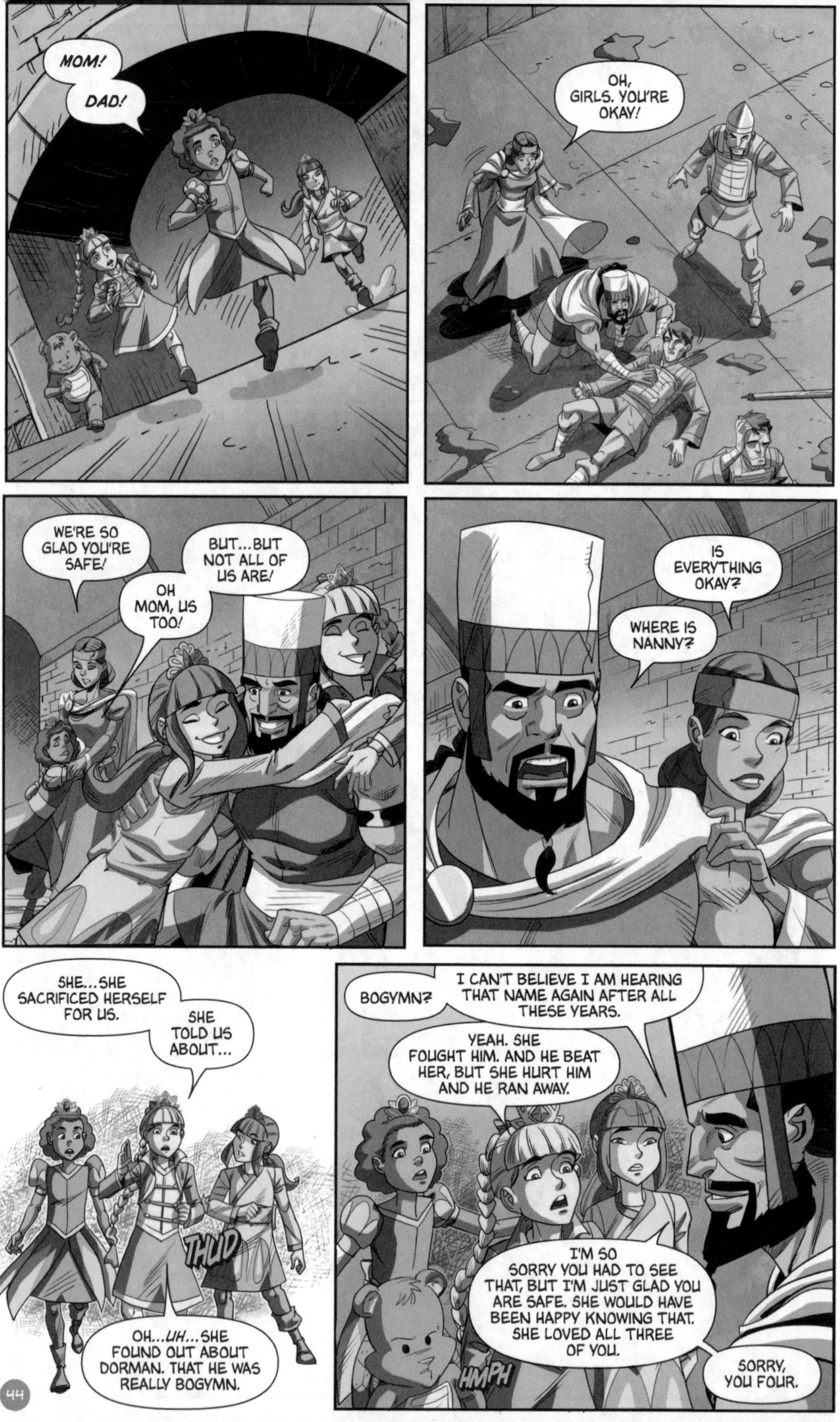
MOM!
DAD!
OH, GIRLS. YOU'RE OKAY!
WE'RE SO GLAD YOU'RE SAFE!
OH MOM, US TOO!
BUT...BUT NOT ALL OF US ARE!
IS EVERYTHING OKAY?
WHERE IS NANNY?
SHE...SHE SACRIFICED HERSELF FOR US.
SHE TOLD US ABOUT...
THUD
OH...UH...SHE FOUND OUT ABOUT DORMAN. THAT HE WAS REALLY BOGYMN.
BOGYMN?
I CAN'T BELIEVE I AM HEARING THAT NAME AGAIN AFTER ALL THESE YEARS.
YEAH. SHE FOUGHT HIM. AND HE BEAT HER, BUT SHE HURT HIM AND HE RAN AWAY.
I'M SO SORRY YOU HAD TO SEE THAT, BUT I'M JUST GLAD YOU ARE SAFE. SHE WOULD HAVE BEEN HAPPY KNOWING THAT. SHE LOVED ALL THREE OF YOU.
HMPH
SORRY, YOU FOUR.

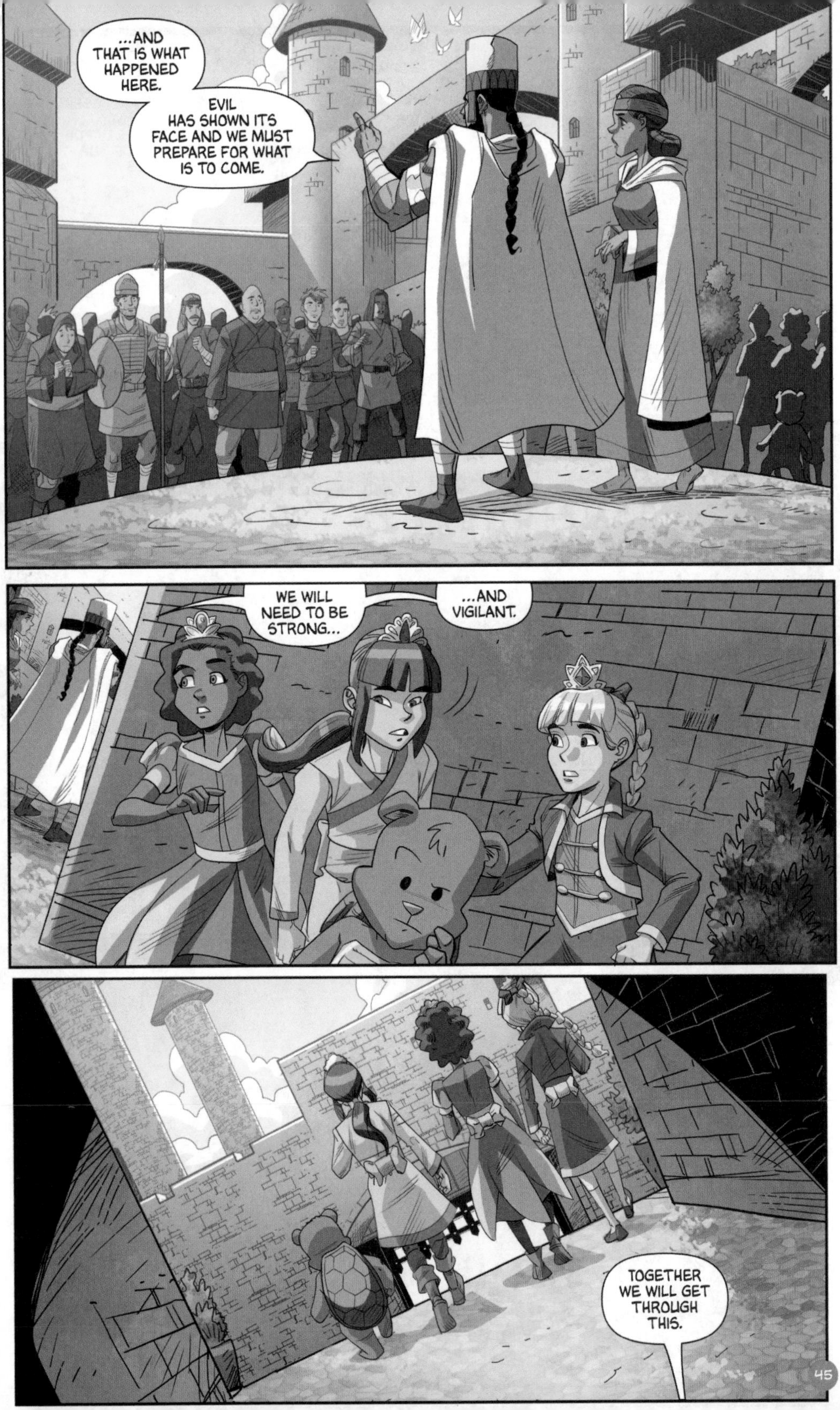
...AND THAT IS WHAT HAPPENED HERE.
EVIL HAS SHOWN ITS FACE AND WE MUST PREPARE FOR WHAT IS TO COME.
WE WILL NEED TO BE STRONG...
...AND VIGILANT.
TOGETHER WE WILL GET THROUGH THIS.

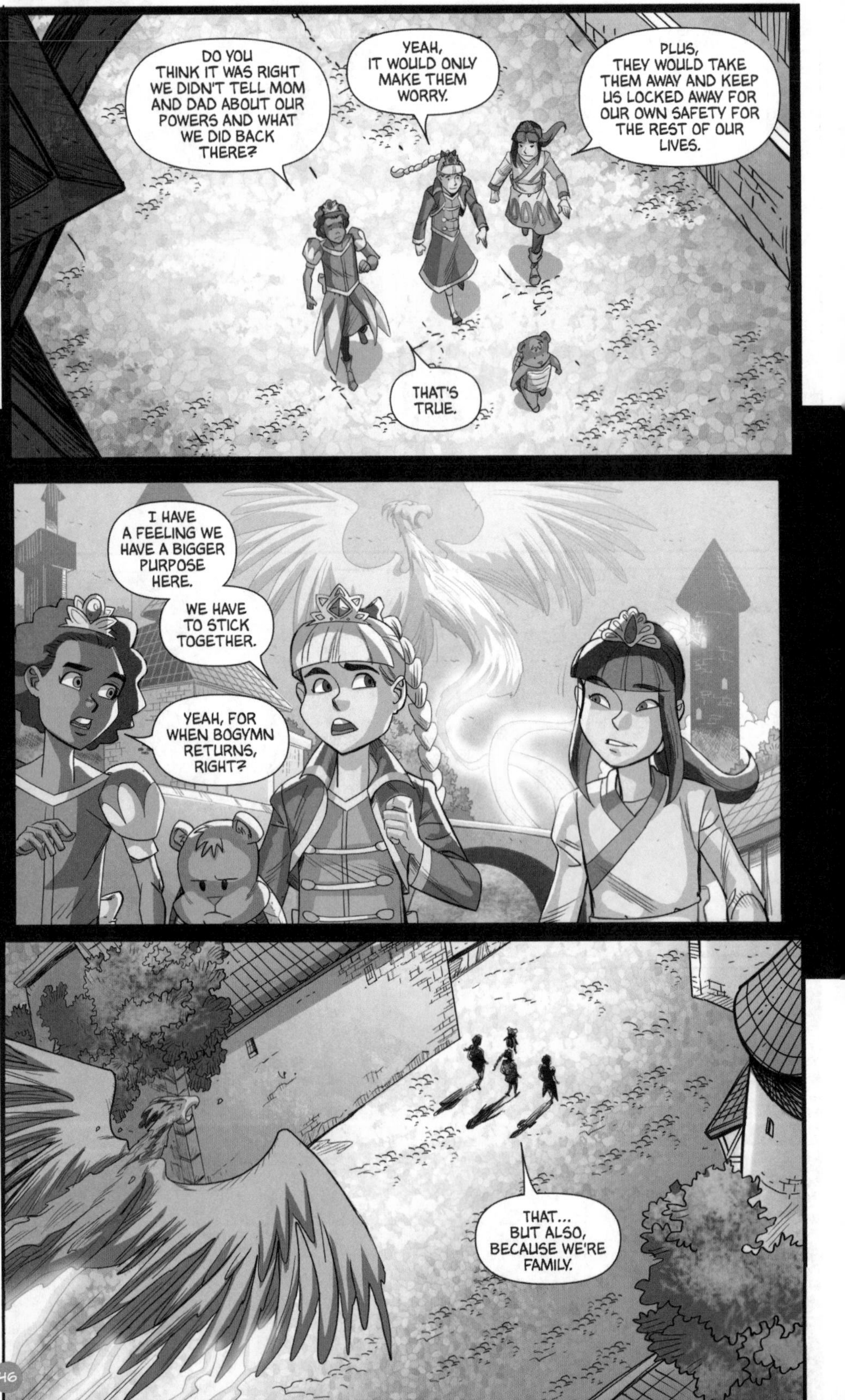
DO YOU THINK IT WAS RIGHT WE DIDN'T TELL MOM AND DAD ABOUT OUR POWERS AND WHAT WE DID BACK THERE?
YEAH, IT WOULD ONLY MAKE THEM WORRY.
PLUS, THEY WOULD TAKE THEM AWAY AND KEEP US LOCKED AWAY FOR OUR OWN SAFETY FOR THE REST OF OUR LIVES.
THAT'S TRUE.
I HAVE A FEELING WE HAVE A BIGGER PURPOSE HERE.
WE HAVE TO STICK TOGETHER.
YEAH, FOR WHEN BOGYMN RETURNS, RIGHT?
THAT... BUT ALSO, BECAUSE WE'RE FAMILY.

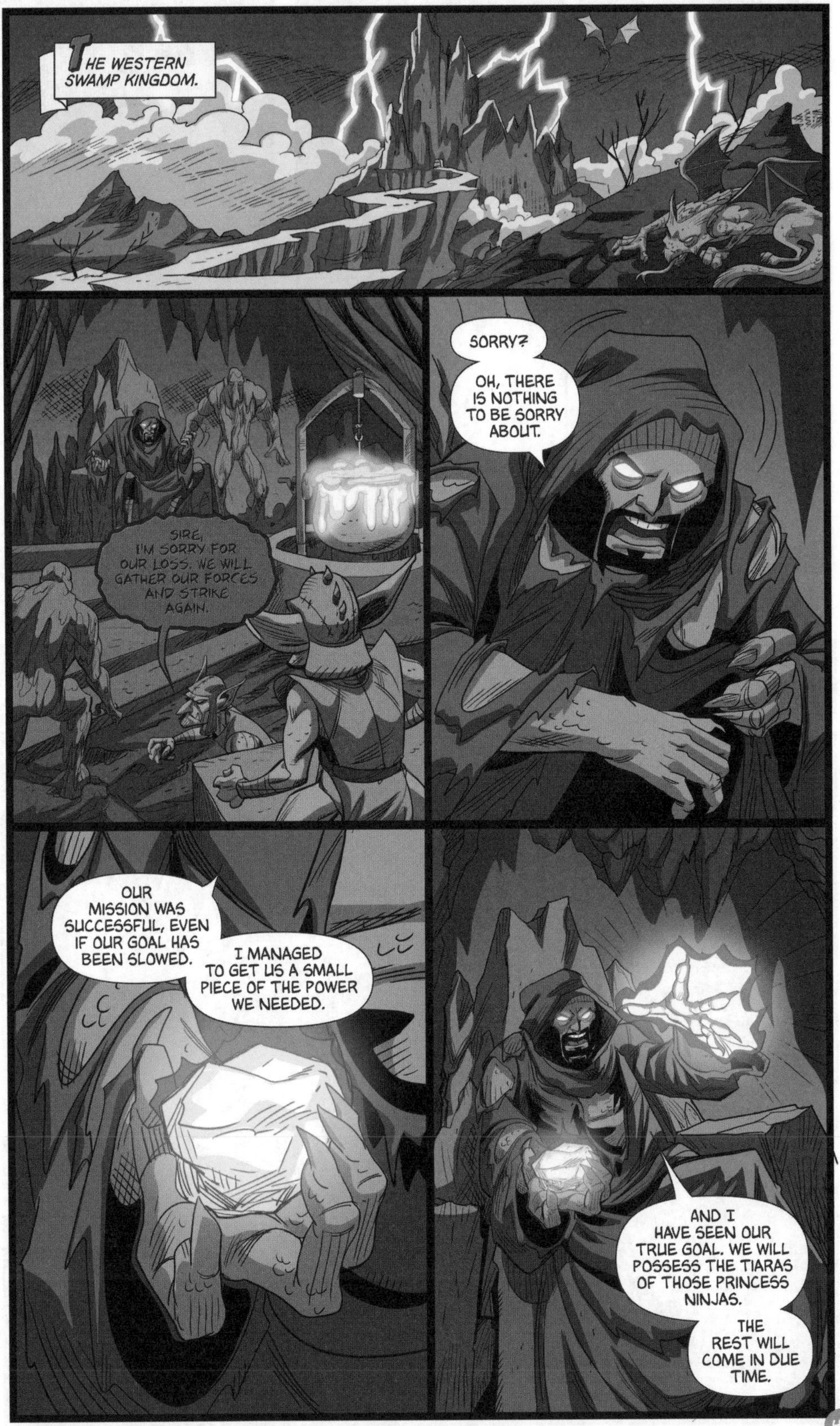
THE WESTERN SWAMP KINGDOM.
SIRE, I'M SORRY FOR OUR LOSS. WE WILL GATHER OUR FORCES AND STRIKE AGAIN.
SORRY?
OH, THERE IS NOTHING TO BE SORRY ABOUT.
OUR MISSION WAS SUCCESSFUL, EVEN IF OUR GOAL HAS BEEN SLOWED.
I MANAGED TO GET US A SMALL PIECE OF THE POWER WE NEEDED.
AND I HAVE SEEN OUR TRUE GOAL. WE WILL POSSESS THE TIARAS OF THOSE PRINCESS NINJAS.
THE REST WILL COME IN DUE TIME.

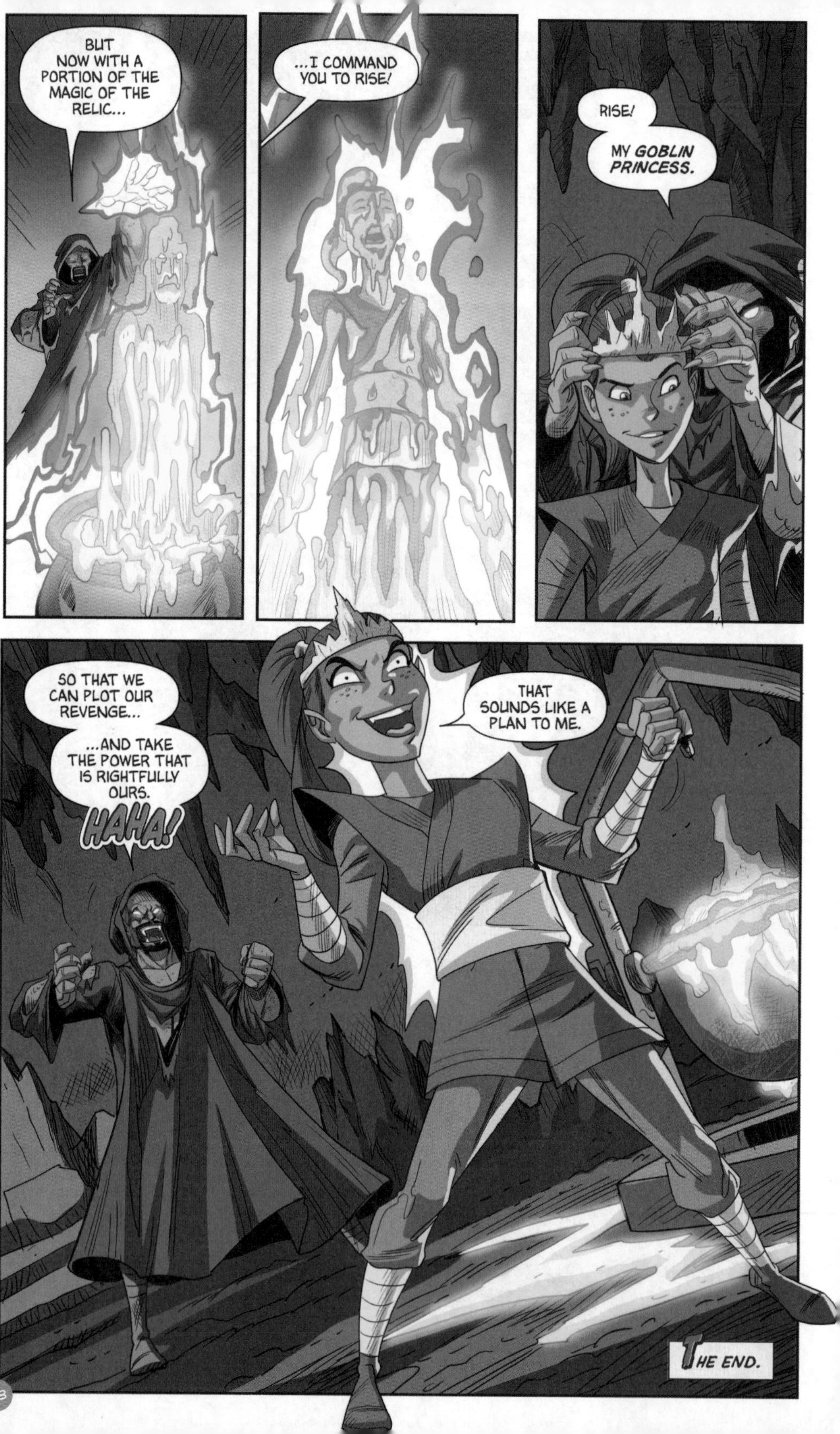
BUT NOW WITH A PORTION OF THE MAGIC OF THE RELIC...
...I COMMAND YOU TO RISE!
RISE!
MY GOBLIN PRINCESS.
SO THAT WE CAN PLOT OUR REVENGE...
...AND TAKE THE POWER THAT IS RIGHTFULLY OURS.
HAHA!
THAT SOUNDS LIKE A PLAN TO ME.
THE END.

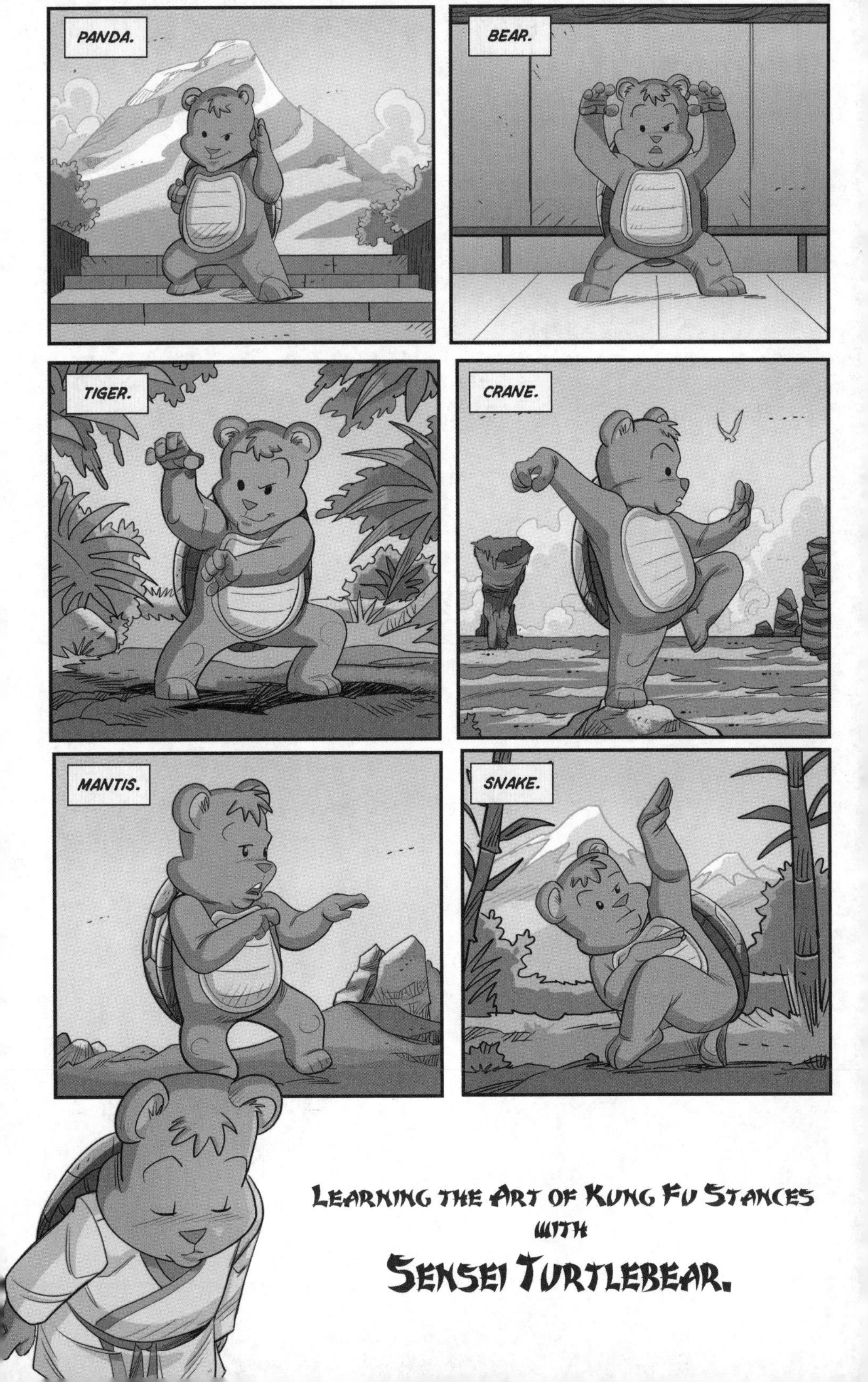
PANDA.
BEAR.
TIGER.
CRANE.
MANTIS.
SNAKE.
LEARNING THE ART OF KUNG FU STANCES
WITH
SENSEI TURTLEBEAR.

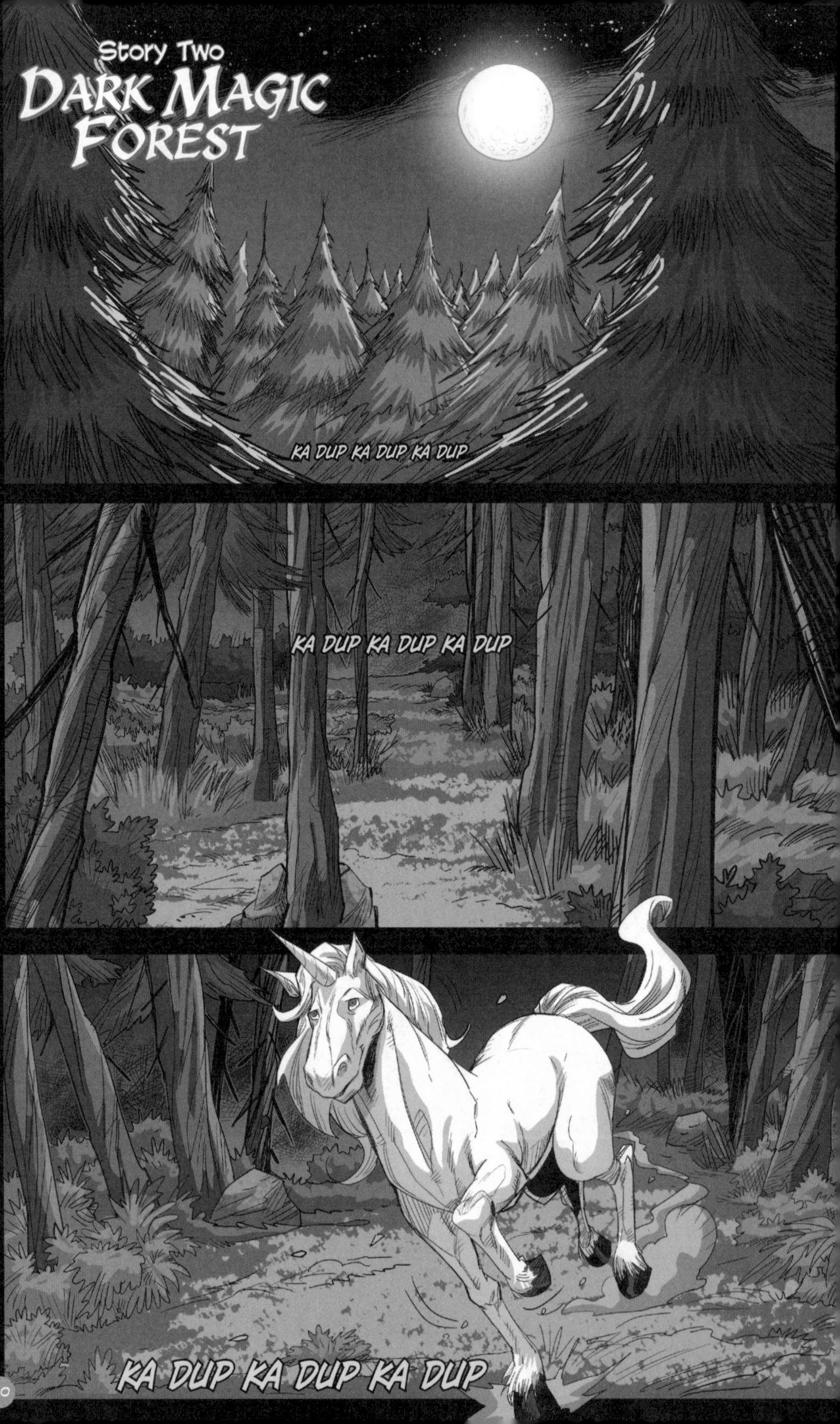
Story Two
DARK MAGIC FOREST
KA DUP KA DUP KA DUP
KA DUP KA DUP KA DUP
KA DUP KA DUP KA DUP

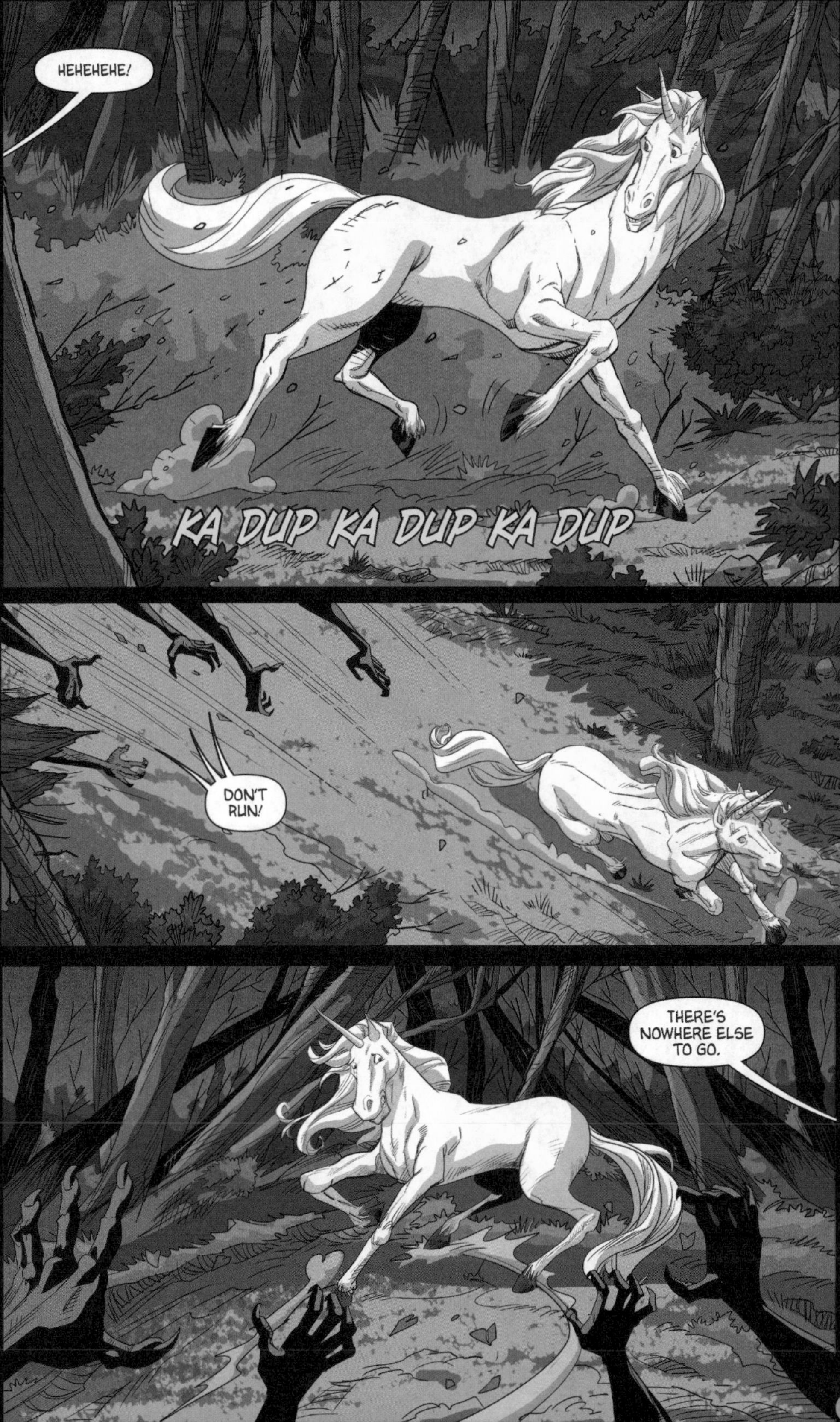
HEHEHEHE!
KA DUP KA DUP KA DUP
DON'T RUN!
THERE'S NOWHERE ELSE TO GO.

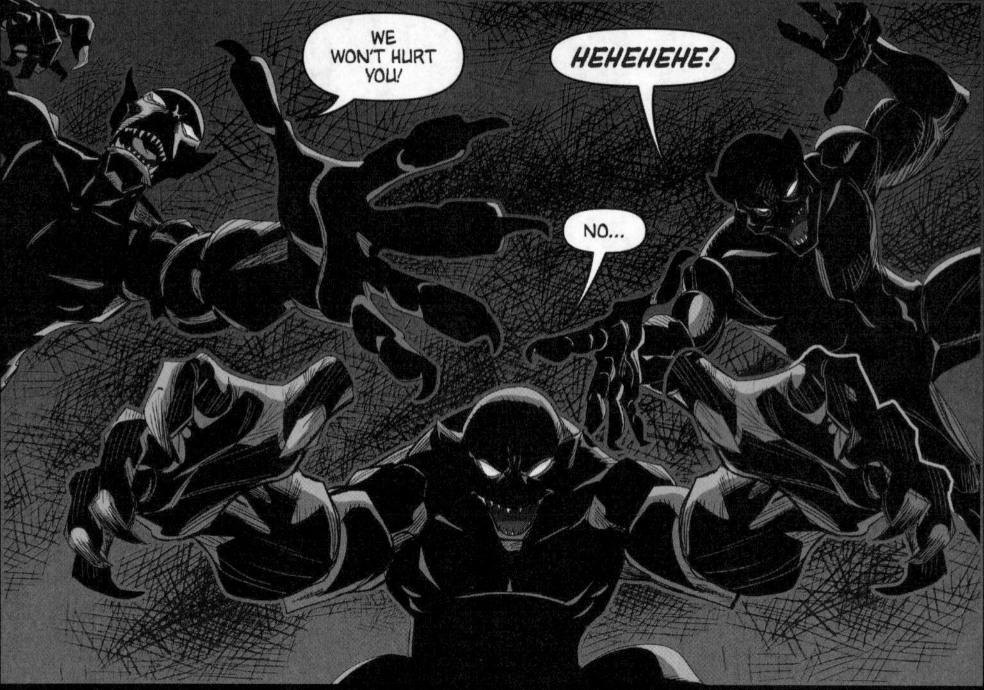
WE WON'T HURT YOU!
HEHEHEHE!
NO...

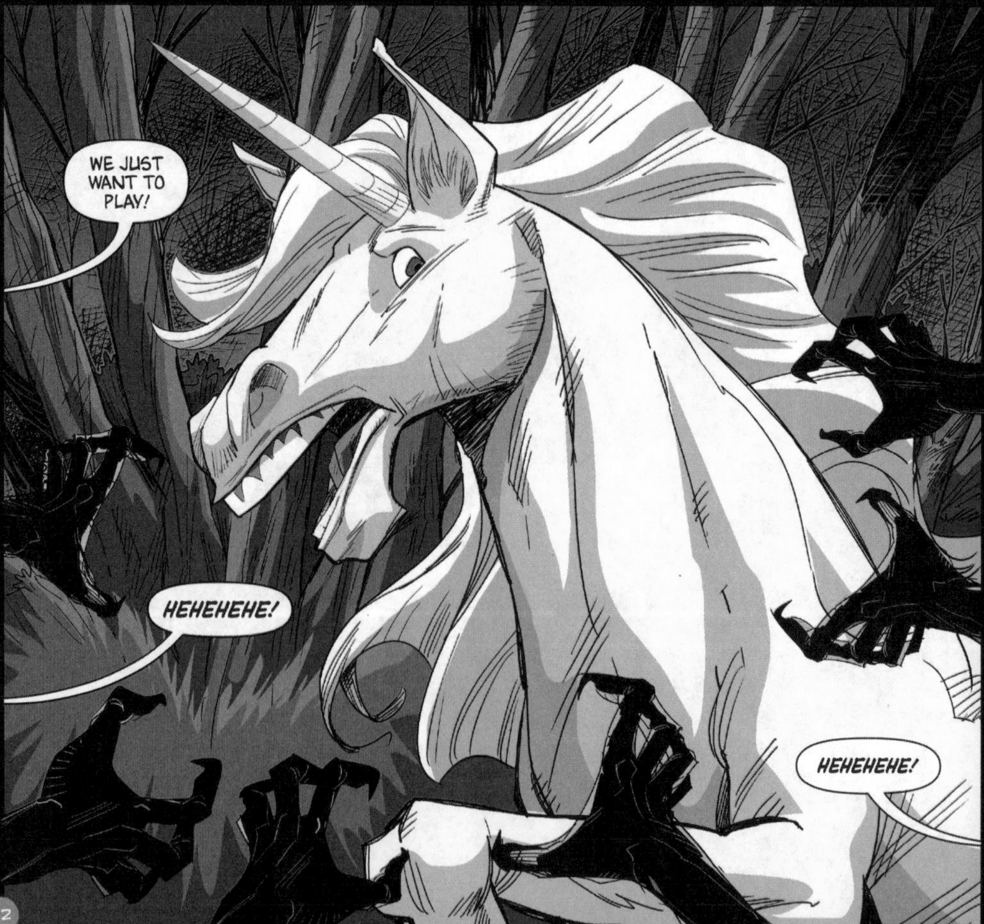
WE JUST WANT TO PLAY!
HEHEHEHE!
HEHEHEHE!

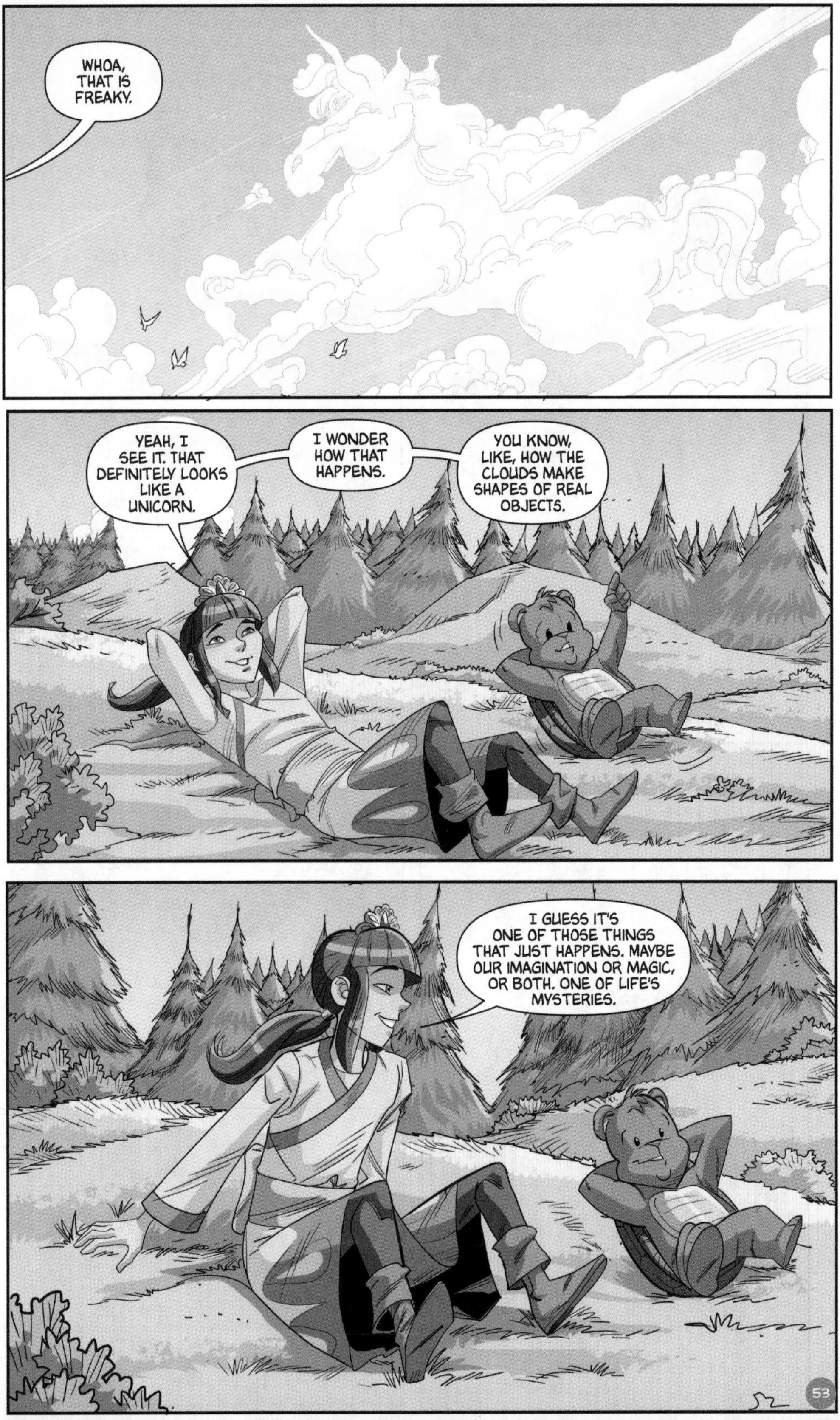
WHOA, THAT IS FREAKY.
YEAH, I SEE IT. THAT DEFINITELY LOOKS LIKE A UNICORN.
I WONDER HOW THAT HAPPENS.
YOU KNOW, LIKE, HOW THE CLOUDS MAKE SHAPES OF REAL OBJECTS.
I GUESS IT'S ONE OF THOSE THINGS THAT JUST HAPPENS. MAYBE OUR IMAGINATION OR MAGIC, OR BOTH. ONE OF LIFE'S MYSTERIES.

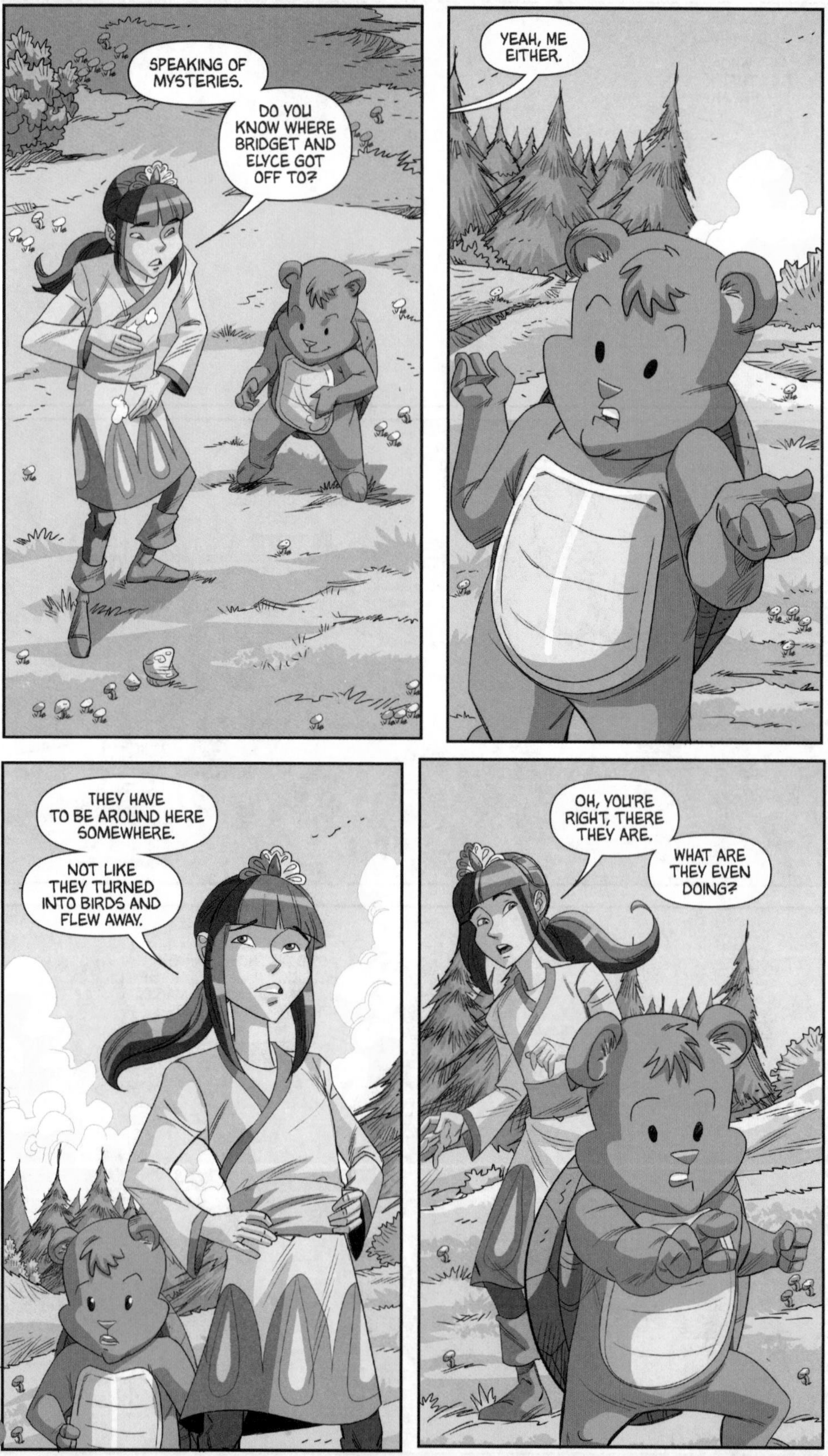
SPEAKING OF MYSTERIES.
DO YOU KNOW WHERE BRIDGET AND ELYCE GOT OFF TO?
YEAH, ME EITHER.
THEY HAVE TO BE AROUND HERE SOMEWHERE.
NOT LIKE THEY TURNED INTO BIRDS AND FLEW AWAY.
OH, YOU'RE RIGHT, THERE THEY ARE.
WHAT ARE THEY EVEN DOING?

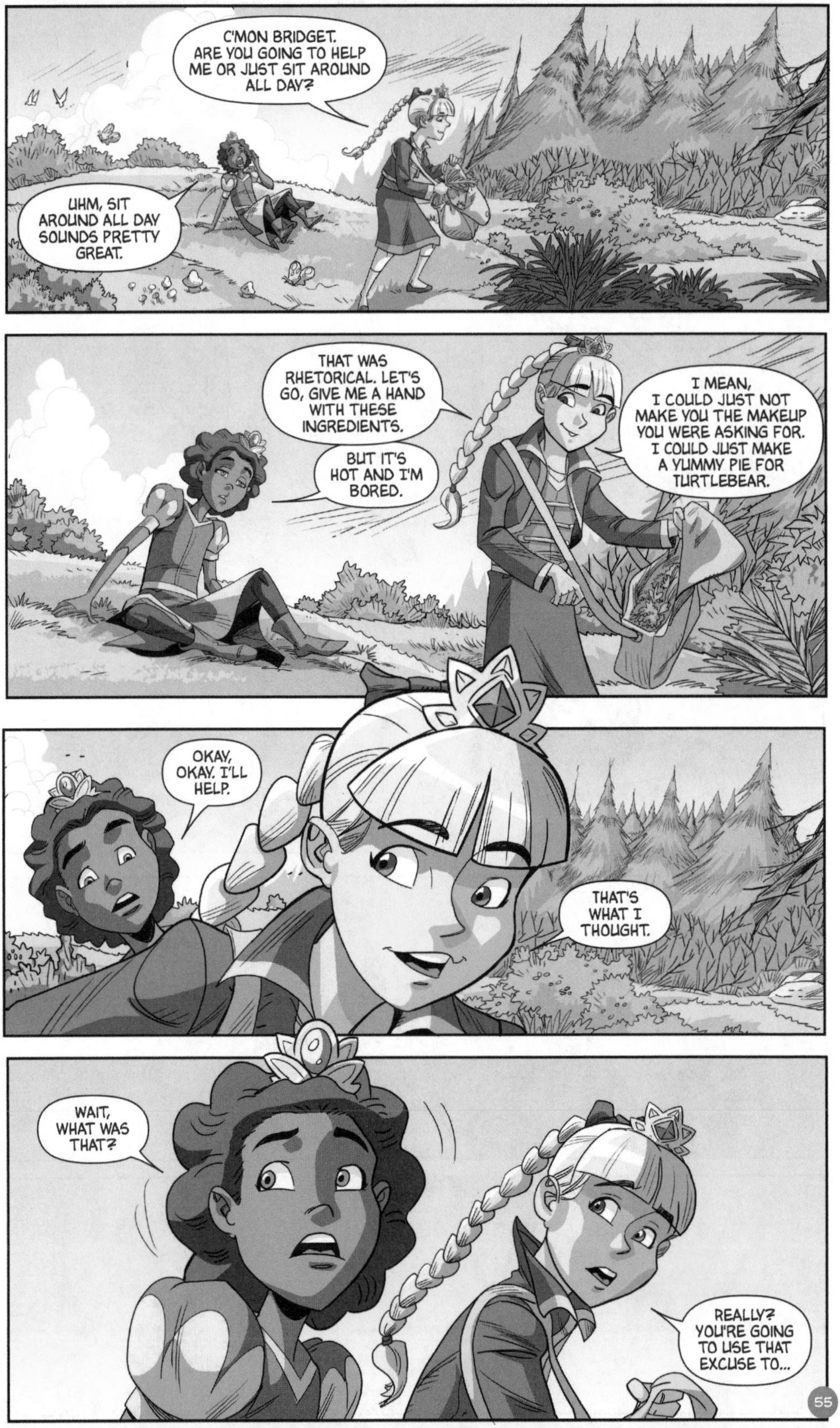
C'MON BRIDGET. ARE YOU GOING TO HELP ME OR JUST SIT AROUND ALL DAY?
UHM, SIT AROUND ALL DAY SOUNDS PRETTY GREAT.
THAT WAS RHETORICAL. LET'S GO, GIVE ME A HAND WITH THESE INGREDIENTS.
BUT IT'S HOT AND I'M BORED.
I MEAN, I COULD JUST NOT MAKE YOU THE MAKEUP YOU WERE ASKING FOR. I COULD JUST MAKE A YUMMY PIE FOR TURTLEBEAR.
OKAY, OKAY. I'LL HELP.
THAT'S WHAT I THOUGHT.
WAIT, WHAT WAS THAT?
REALLY? YOU'RE GOING TO USE THAT EXCUSE TO...

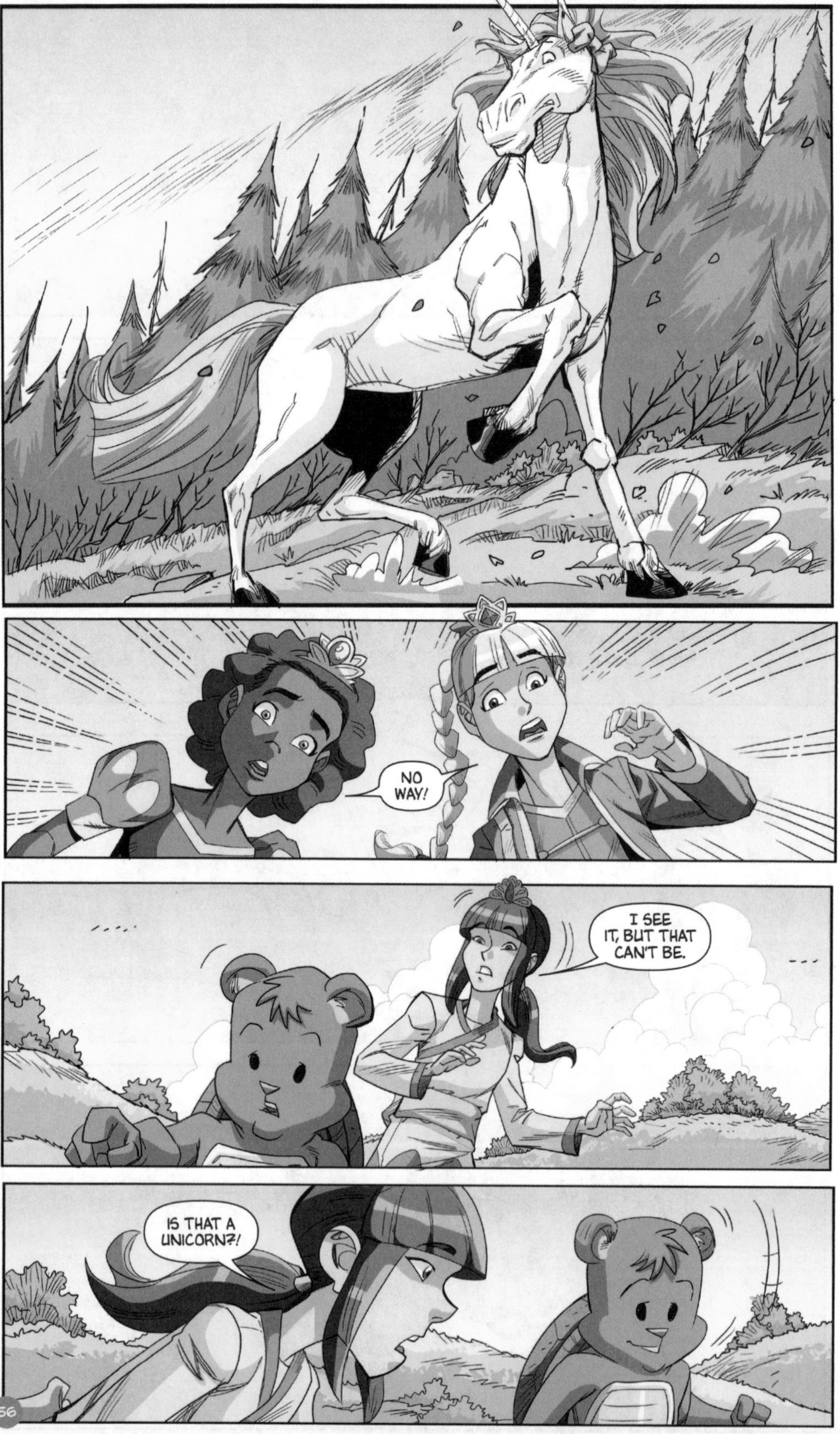
NO WAY!
I SEE IT, BUT THAT CAN'T BE.
IS THAT A UNICORN?!

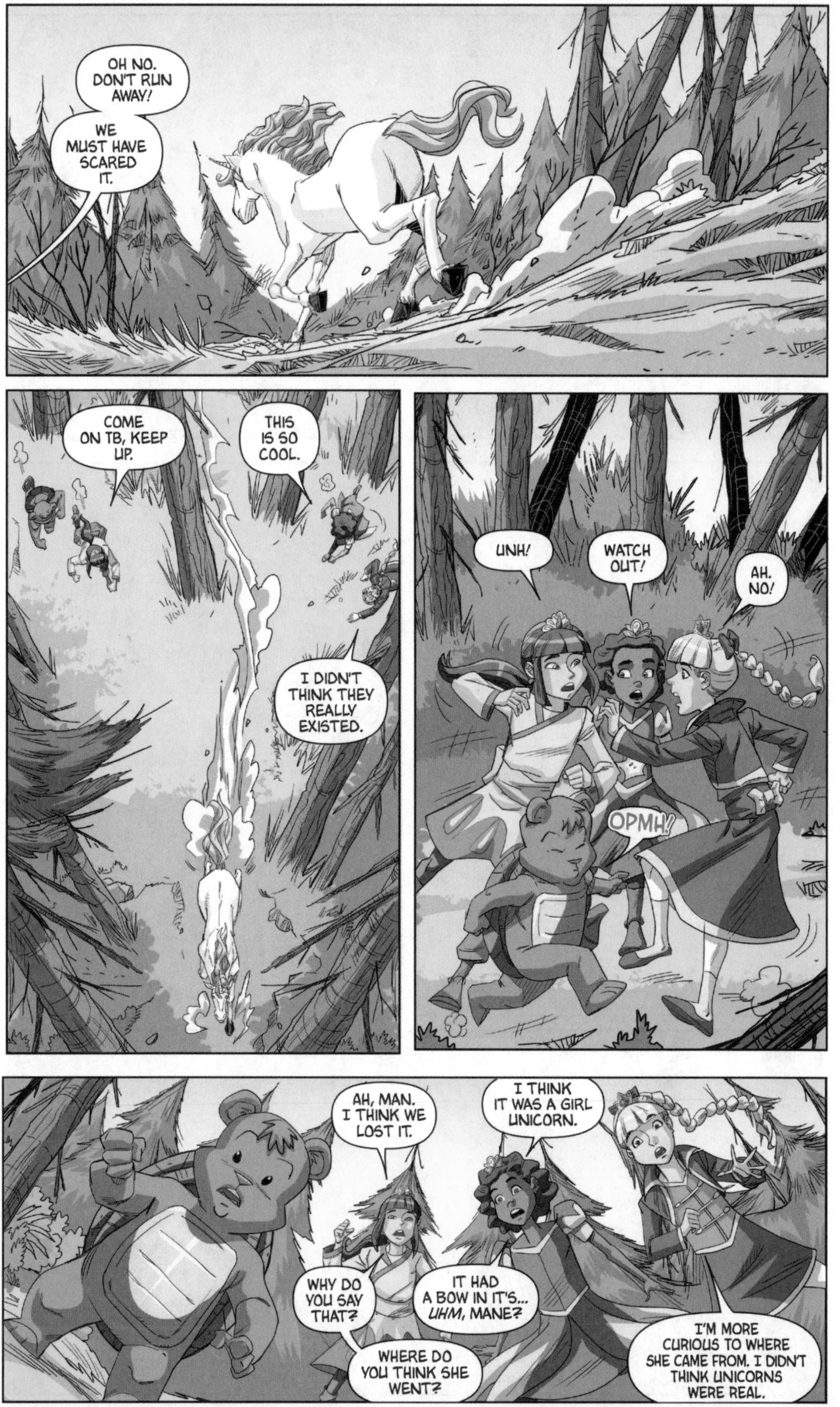
OH NO. DON'T RUN AWAY!
WE MUST HAVE SCARED IT.
COME ON TB, KEEP UP.
THIS IS SO COOL.
I DIDN'T THINK THEY REALLY EXISTED.
UNH!
WATCH OUT!
AH. NO!
OPMH!
AH, MAN. I THINK WE LOST IT.
I THINK IT WAS A GIRL UNICORN.
WHY DO YOU SAY THAT?
IT HAD A BOW IN IT'S... UHM, MANE?
WHERE DO YOU THINK SHE WENT?
I'M MORE CURIOUS TO WHERE SHE CAME FROM. I DIDN'T THINK UNICORNS WERE REAL.

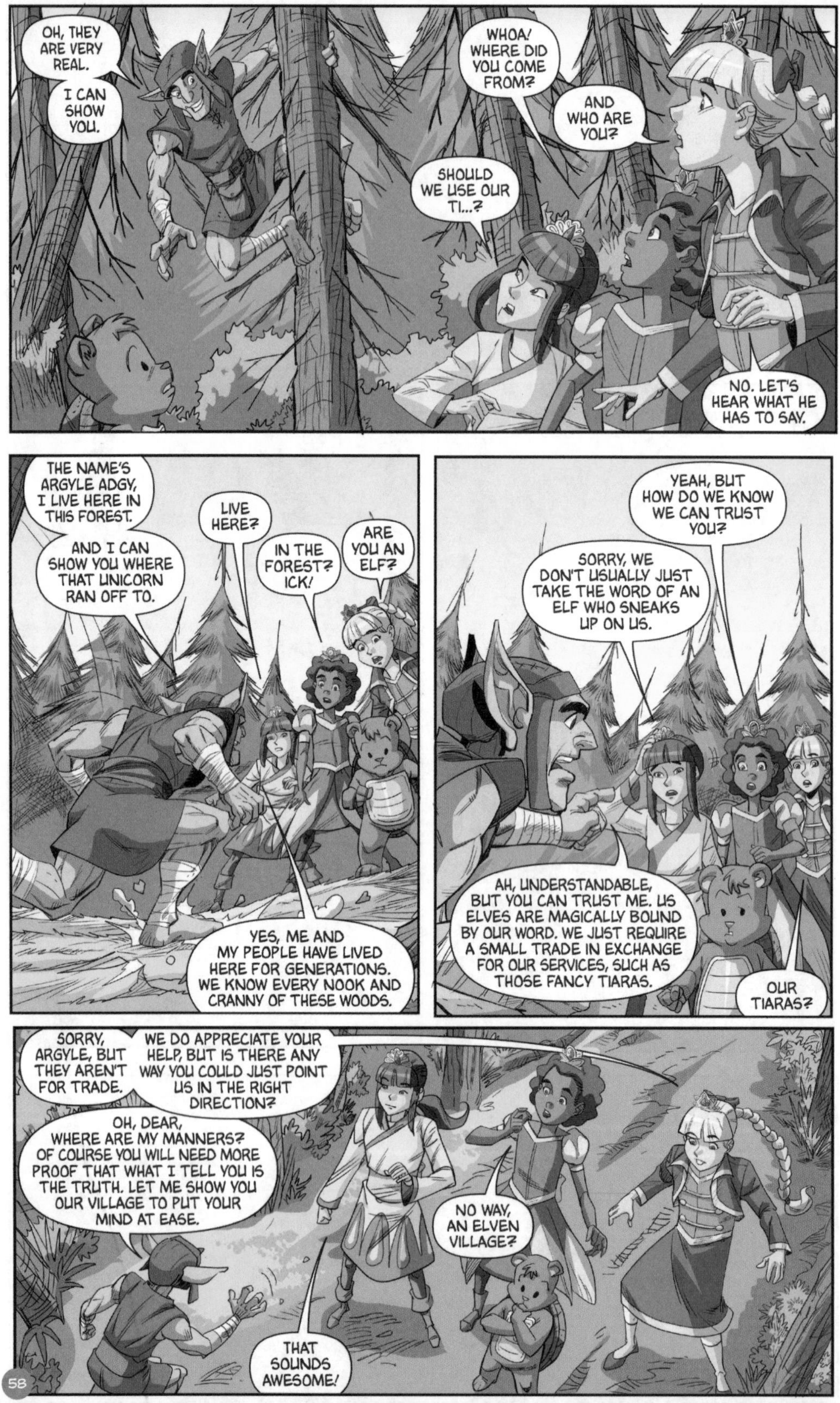
OH, THEY ARE VERY REAL.
I CAN SHOW YOU.
WHOA! WHERE DID YOU COME FROM?
AND WHO ARE YOU?
SHOULD WE USE OUR TI...?
NO. LET'S HEAR WHAT HE HAS TO SAY.
THE NAME'S ARGYLE ADGY, I LIVE HERE IN THIS FOREST.
AND I CAN SHOW YOU WHERE THAT UNICORN RAN OFF TO.
LIVE HERE?
IN THE FOREST? ICK!
ARE YOU AN ELF?
YES, ME AND MY PEOPLE HAVE LIVED HERE FOR GENERATIONS. WE KNOW EVERY NOOK AND CRANNY OF THESE WOODS.
YEAH, BUT HOW DO WE KNOW WE CAN TRUST YOU?
SORRY, WE DON'T USUALLY JUST TAKE THE WORD OF AN ELF WHO SNEAKS UP ON US.
AH, UNDERSTANDABLE, BUT YOU CAN TRUST ME. US ELVES ARE MAGICALLY BOUND BY OUR WORD. WE JUST REQUIRE A SMALL TRADE IN EXCHANGE FOR OUR SERVICES, SUCH AS THOSE FANCY TIARAS.
OUR TIARAS?
SORRY, ARGYLE, BUT THEY AREN'T FOR TRADE.
WE DO APPRECIATE YOUR HELP, BUT IS THERE ANY WAY YOU COULD JUST POINT US IN THE RIGHT DIRECTION?
OH, DEAR, WHERE ARE MY MANNERS? OF COURSE YOU WILL NEED MORE PROOF THAT WHAT I TELL YOU IS THE TRUTH. LET ME SHOW YOU OUR VILLAGE TO PUT YOUR MIND AT EASE.
NO WAY, AN ELVEN VILLAGE?
THAT SOUNDS AWESOME!

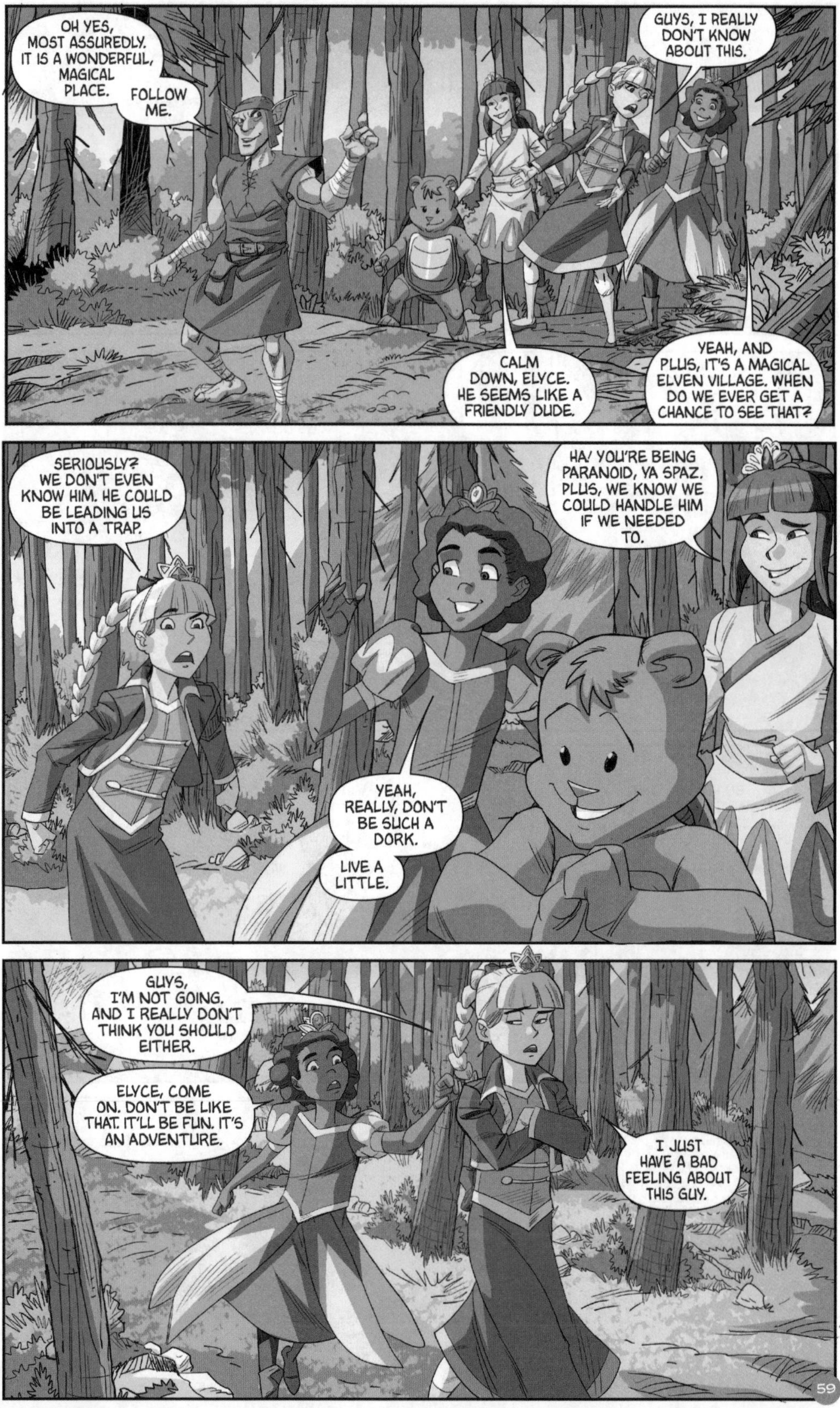
OH YES, MOST ASSUREDLY. IT IS A WONDERFUL, MAGICAL PLACE.
FOLLOW ME.
GUYS, I REALLY DON'T KNOW ABOUT THIS.
CALM DOWN, ELYCE. HE SEEMS LIKE A FRIENDLY DUDE.
YEAH, AND PLUS, IT'S A MAGICAL ELVEN VILLAGE. WHEN DO WE EVER GET A CHANCE TO SEE THAT?
SERIOUSLY? WE DON'T EVEN KNOW HIM. HE COULD BE LEADING US INTO A TRAP.
HA! YOU'RE BEING PARANOID, YA SPAZ. PLUS, WE KNOW WE COULD HANDLE HIM IF WE NEEDED TO.
YEAH, REALLY, DON'T BE SUCH A DORK.
LIVE A LITTLE.
GUYS, I'M NOT GOING. AND I REALLY DON'T THINK YOU SHOULD EITHER.
ELYCE, COME ON. DON'T BE LIKE THAT. IT'LL BE FUN. IT'S AN ADVENTURE.
I JUST HAVE A BAD FEELING ABOUT THIS GUY.

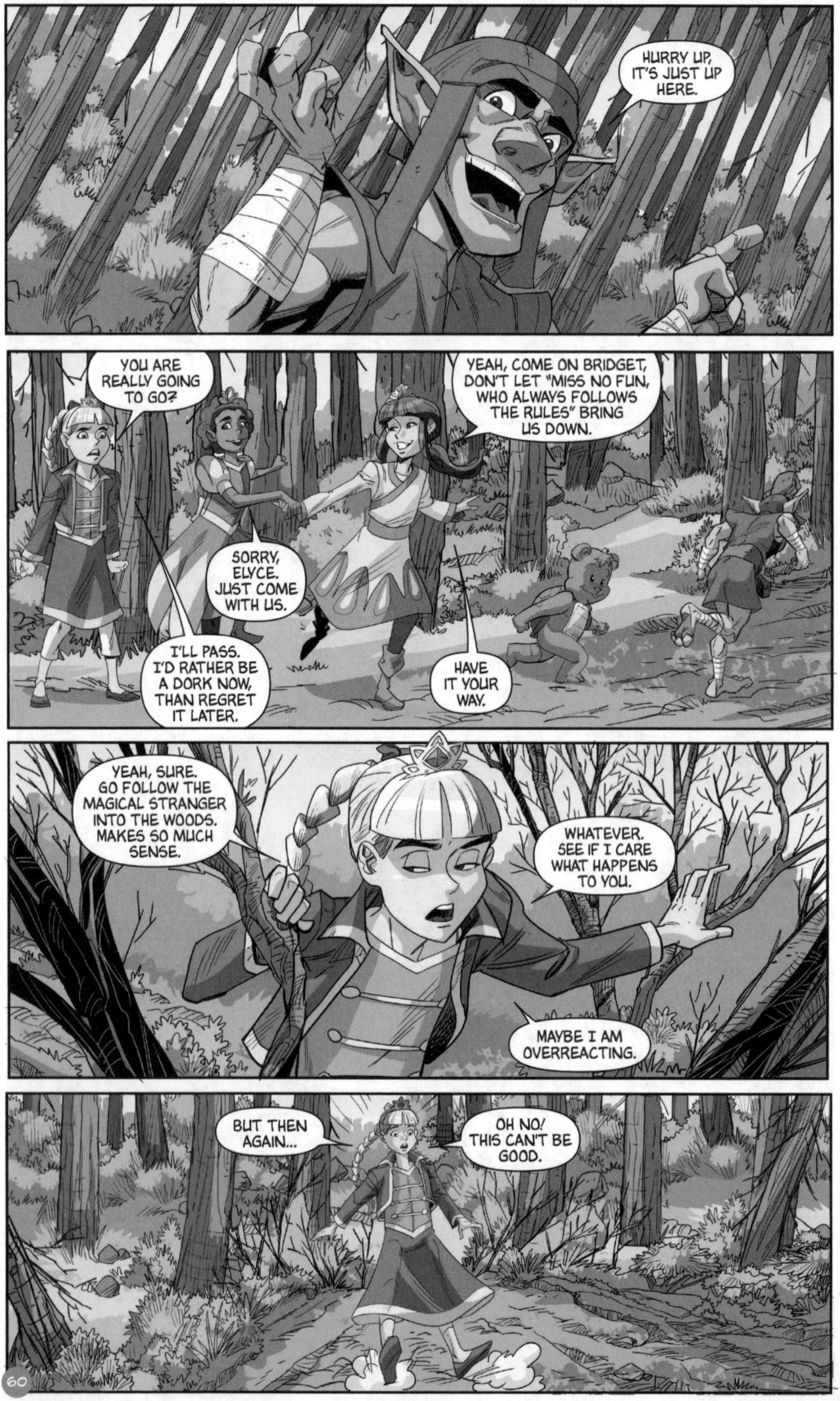
HURRY UP, IT'S JUST UP HERE.
YOU ARE REALLY GOING TO GO?
YEAH, COME ON BRIDGET, DON'T LET "MISS NO FUN, WHO ALWAYS FOLLOWS THE RULES" BRING US DOWN.
SORRY, ELYCE. JUST COME WITH US.
I'LL PASS. I'D RATHER BE A DORK NOW, THAN REGRET IT LATER.
HAVE IT YOUR WAY.
YEAH, SURE. GO FOLLOW THE MAGICAL STRANGER INTO THE WOODS. MAKES SO MUCH SENSE.
WHATEVER. SEE IF I CARE WHAT HAPPENS TO YOU.
MAYBE I AM OVERREACTING.
BUT THEN AGAIN...
OH NO! THIS CAN'T BE GOOD.

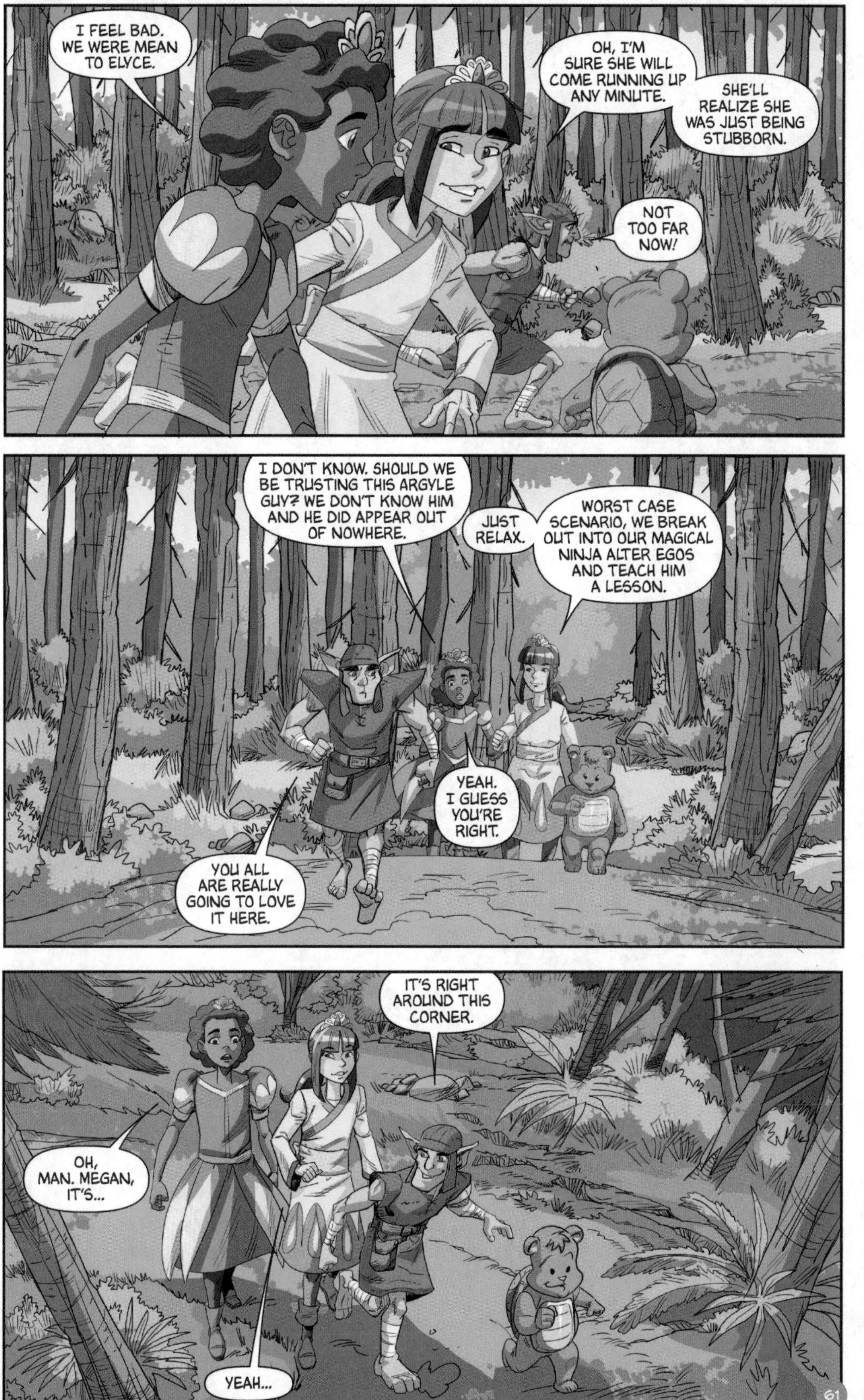
I FEEL BAD. WE WERE MEAN TO ELYCE.
OH, I'M SURE SHE WILL COME RUNNING UP ANY MINUTE.
SHE'LL REALIZE SHE WAS JUST BEING STUBBORN.
NOT TOO FAR NOW!
I DON'T KNOW. SHOULD WE BE TRUSTING THIS ARGYLE GUY? WE DON'T KNOW HIM AND HE DID APPEAR OUT OF NOWHERE.
JUST RELAX.
WORST CASE SCENARIO, WE BREAK OUT INTO OUR MAGICAL NINJA ALTER EGOS AND TEACH HIM A LESSON.
YEAH. I GUESS YOU'RE RIGHT.
YOU ALL ARE REALLY GOING TO LOVE IT HERE.
IT'S RIGHT AROUND THIS CORNER.
OH, MAN. MEGAN, IT'S...
YEAH...

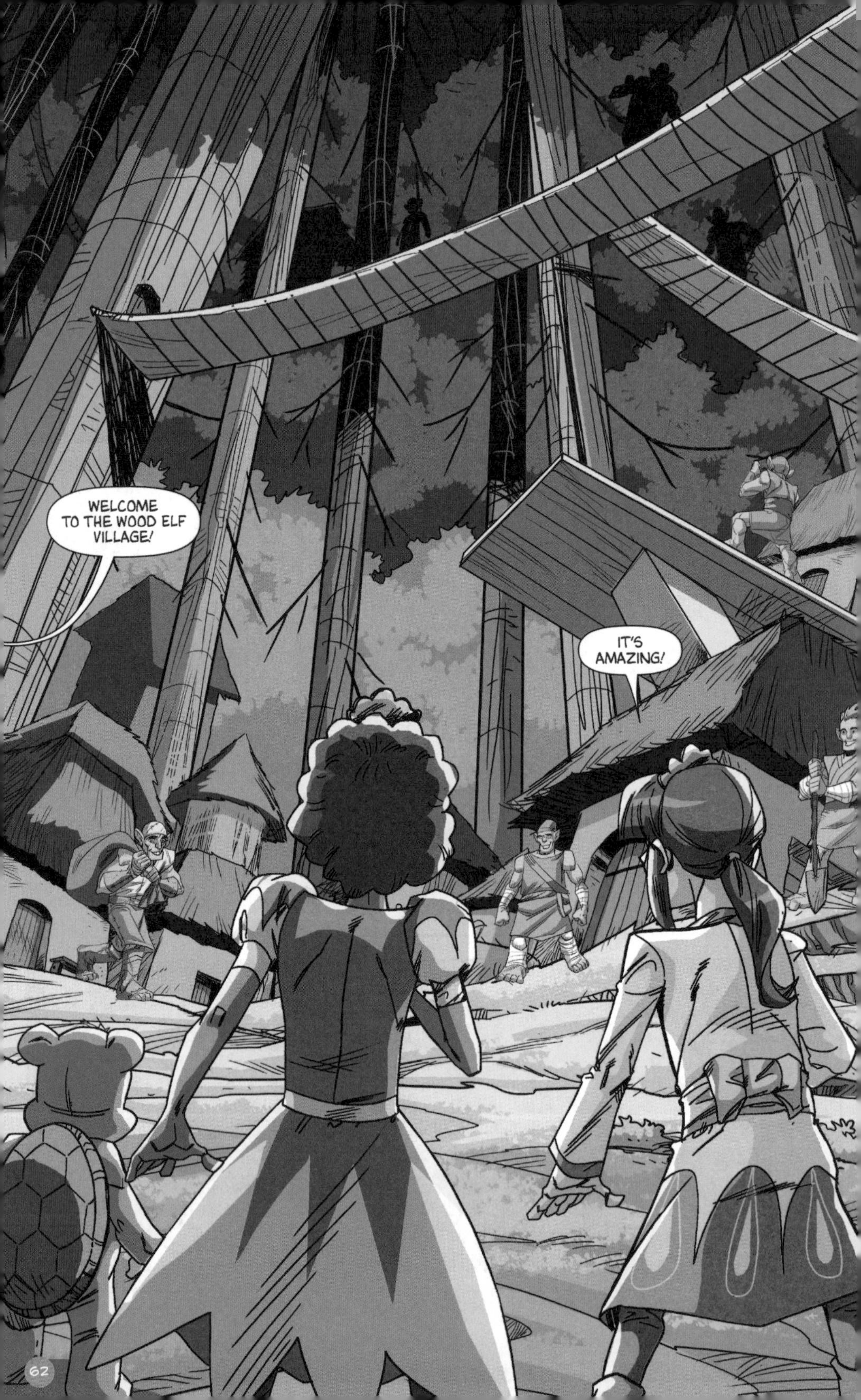
WELCOME TO THE WOOD ELF VILLAGE!
IT'S AMAZING!

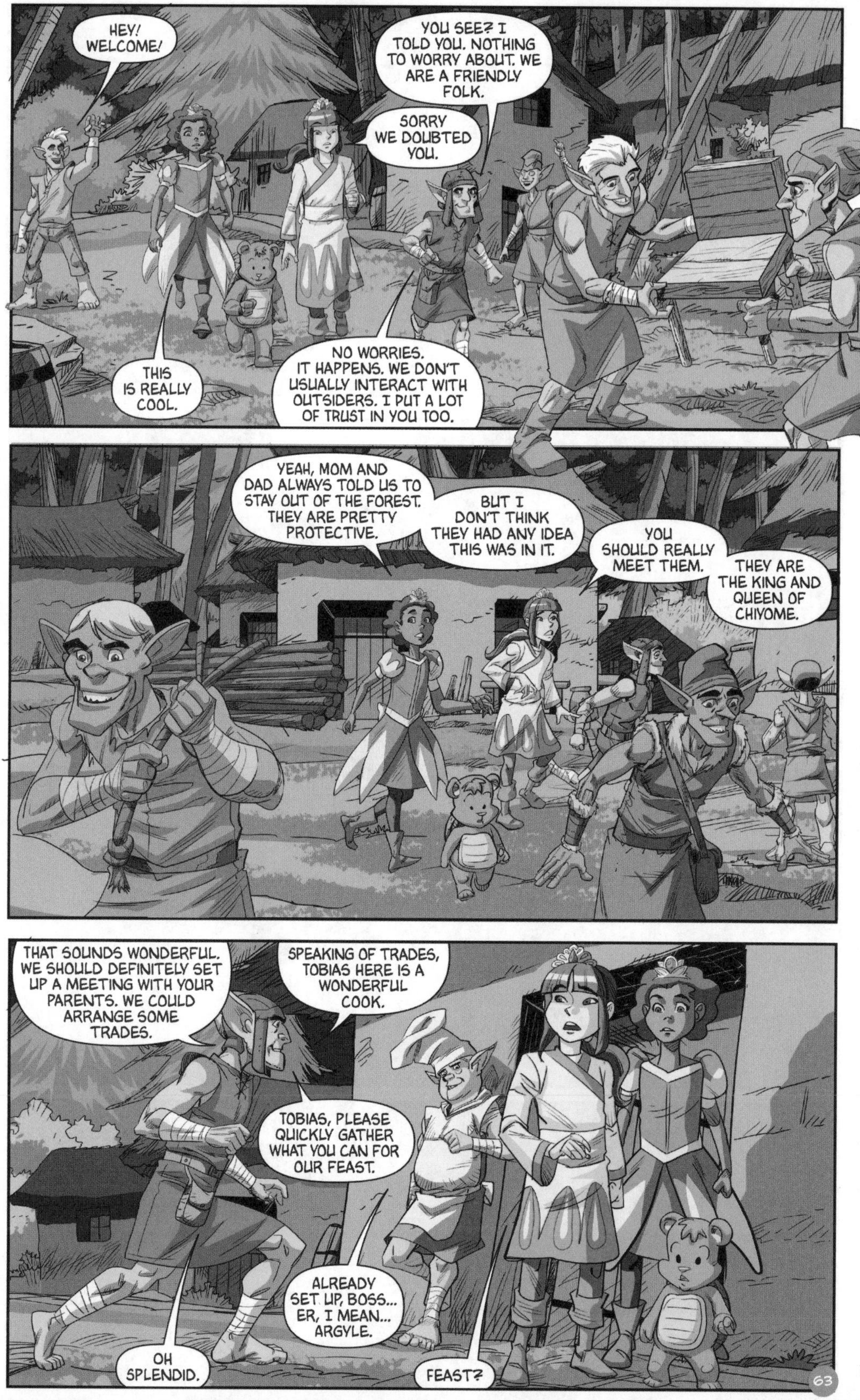
HEY! WELCOME!
YOU SEE? I TOLD YOU. NOTHING TO WORRY ABOUT. WE ARE A FRIENDLY FOLK.
SORRY WE DOUBTED YOU.
THIS IS REALLY COOL.
NO WORRIES. IT HAPPENS. WE DON'T USUALLY INTERACT WITH OUTSIDERS. I PUT A LOT OF TRUST IN YOU TOO.
YEAH, MOM AND DAD ALWAYS TOLD US TO STAY OUT OF THE FOREST. THEY ARE PRETTY PROTECTIVE.
BUT I DON'T THINK THEY HAD ANY IDEA THIS WAS IN IT.
YOU SHOULD REALLY MEET THEM.
THEY ARE THE KING AND QUEEN OF CHIYOME.
THAT SOUNDS WONDERFUL. WE SHOULD DEFINITELY SET UP A MEETING WITH YOUR PARENTS. WE COULD ARRANGE SOME TRADES.
SPEAKING OF TRADES, TOBIAS HERE IS A WONDERFUL COOK.
TOBIAS, PLEASE QUICKLY GATHER WHAT YOU CAN FOR OUR FEAST.
ALREADY SET UP, BOSS... ER, I MEAN... ARGYLE.
OH SPLENDID.
FEAST?

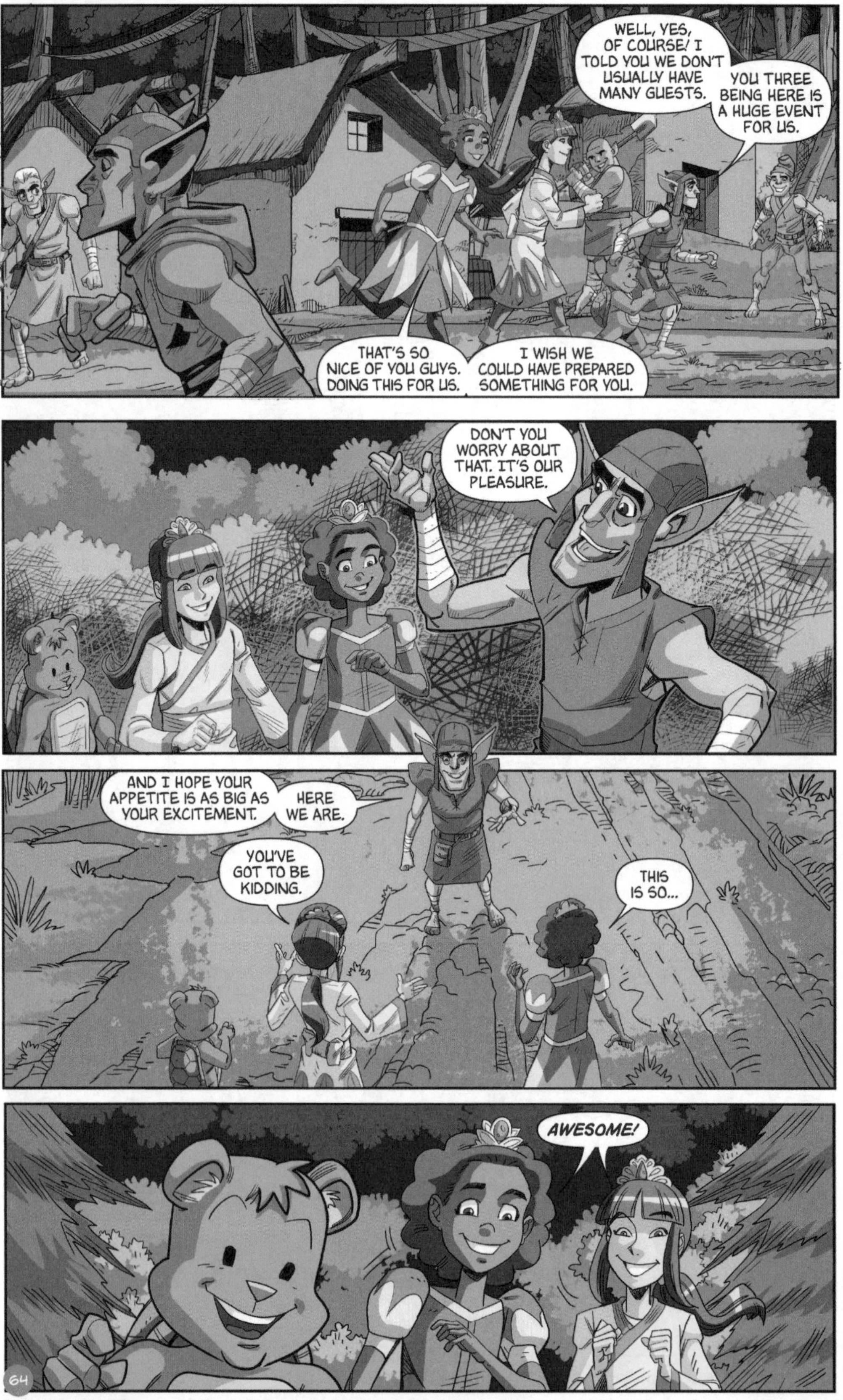
WELL, YES, OF COURSE! I TOLD YOU WE DON'T USUALLY HAVE MANY GUESTS.
YOU THREE BEING HERE IS A HUGE EVENT FOR US.
THAT'S SO NICE OF YOU GUYS. DOING THIS FOR US.
I WISH WE COULD HAVE PREPARED SOMETHING FOR YOU.
DON'T YOU WORRY ABOUT THAT. IT'S OUR PLEASURE.
AND I HOPE YOUR APPETITE IS AS BIG AS YOUR EXCITEMENT.
HERE WE ARE.
YOU'VE GOT TO BE KIDDING.
THIS IS SO...
AWESOME!

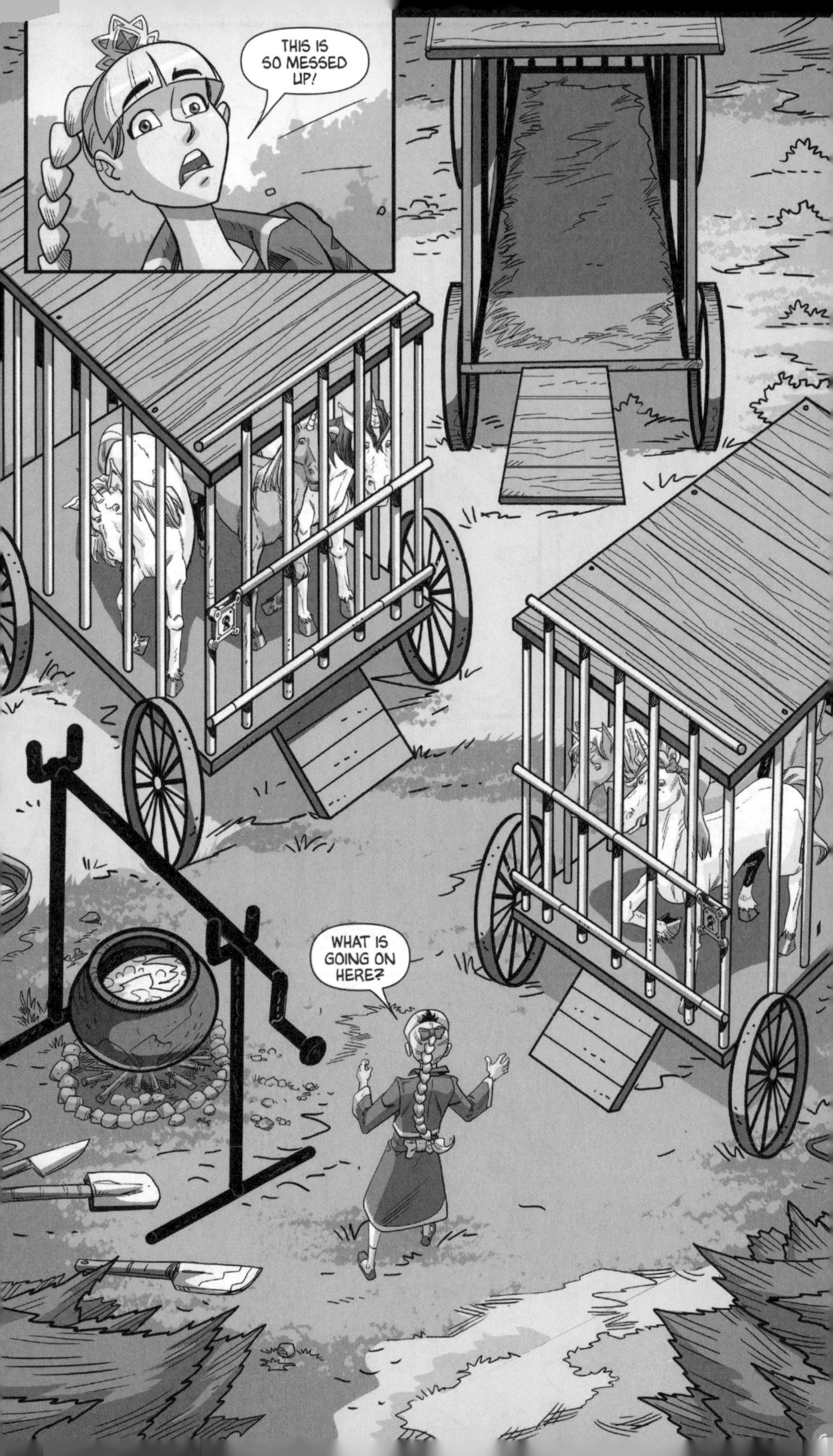
THIS IS SO MESSED UP!
WHAT IS GOING ON HERE?

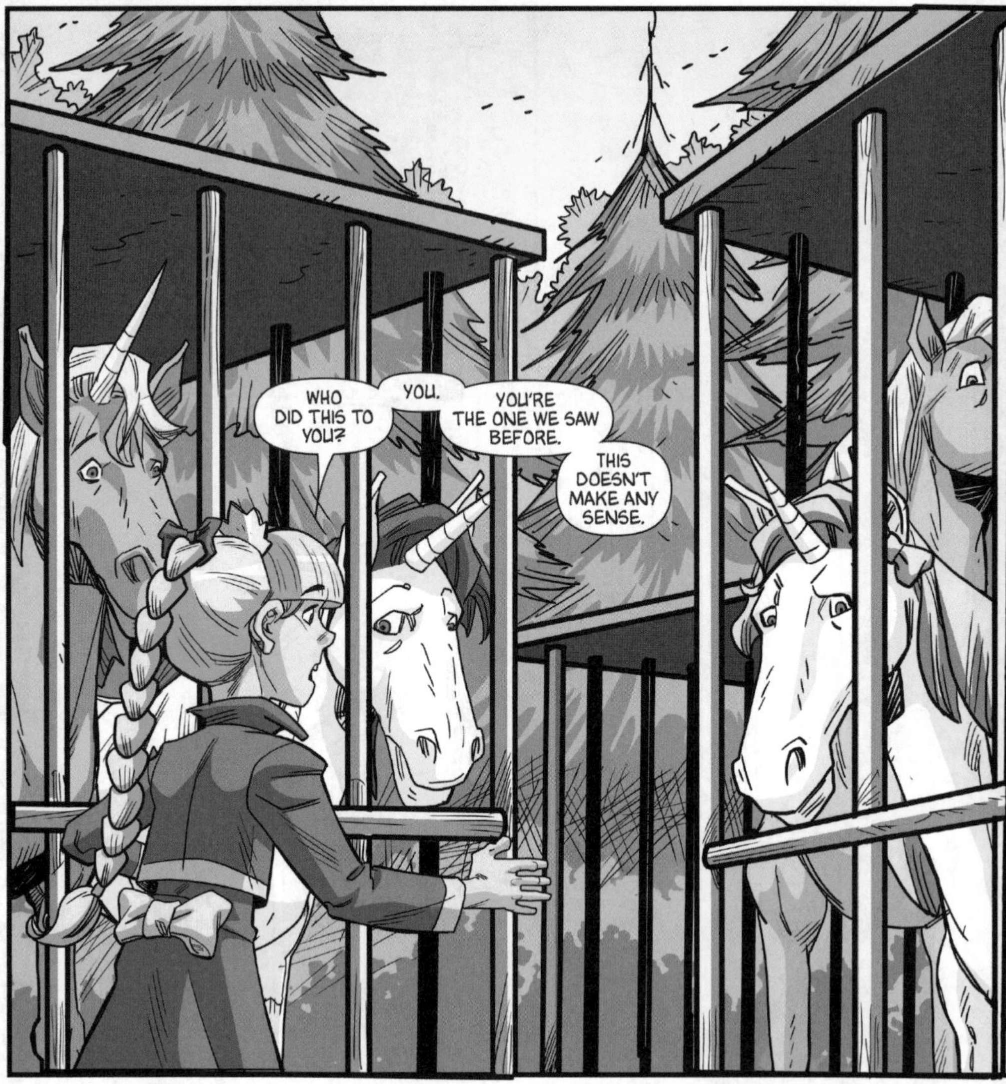
WHO DID THIS TO YOU?
YOU.
YOU'RE THE ONE WE SAW BEFORE.
THIS DOESN'T MAKE ANY SENSE.

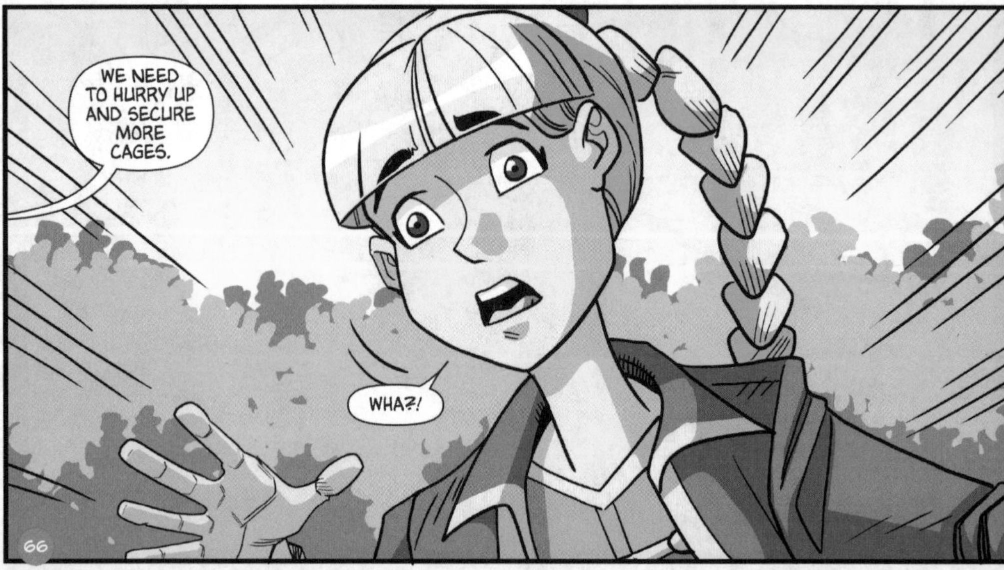
WE NEED TO HURRY UP AND SECURE MORE CAGES.
WHA?!

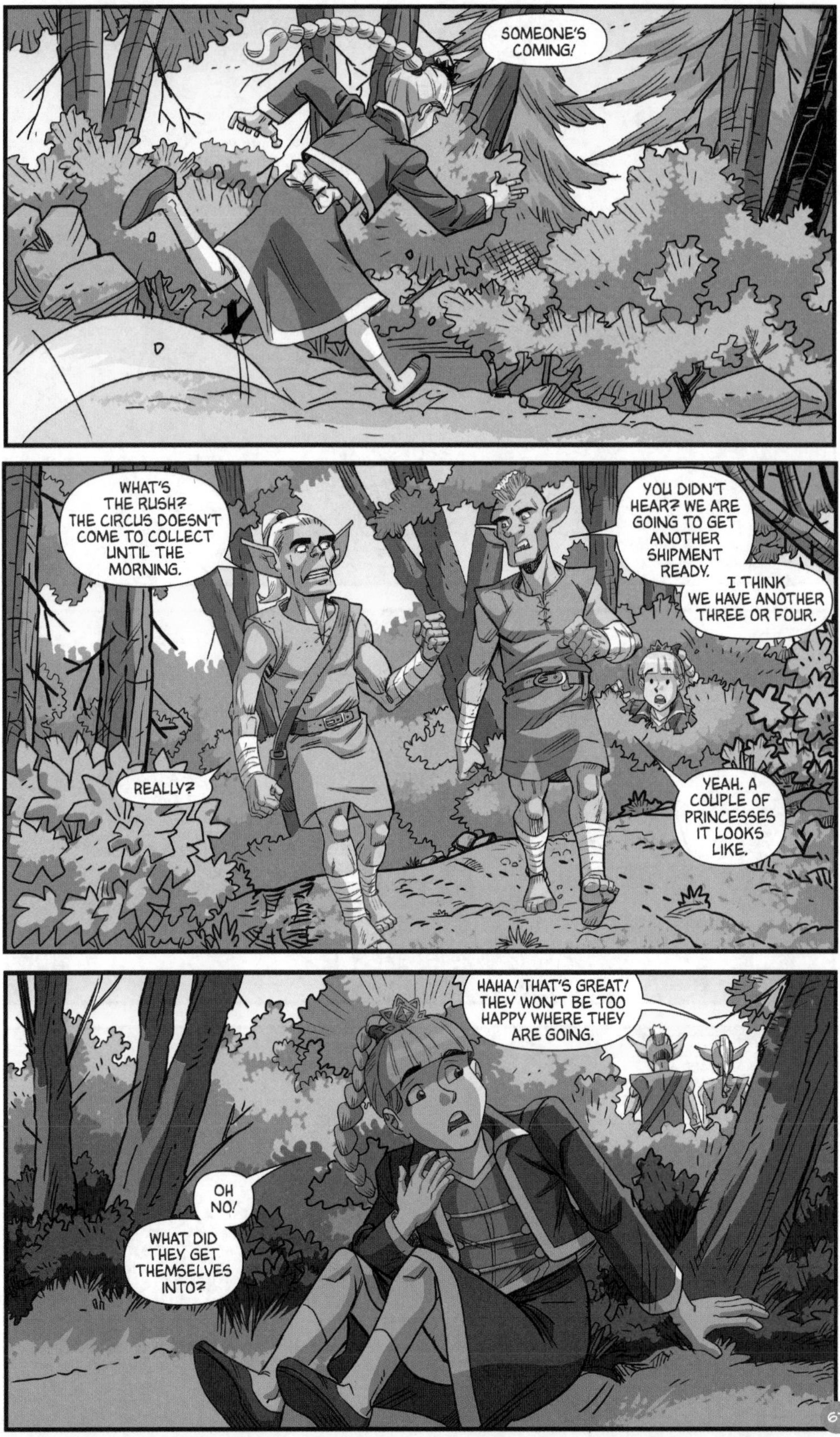
SOMEONE'S COMING!
WHAT'S THE RUSH? THE CIRCUS DOESN'T COME TO COLLECT UNTIL THE MORNING.
YOU DIDN'T HEAR? WE ARE GOING TO GET ANOTHER SHIPMENT READY.
I THINK WE HAVE ANOTHER THREE OR FOUR.
REALLY?
YEAH. A COUPLE OF PRINCESSES IT LOOKS LIKE.
HAHA! THAT'S GREAT! THEY WON'T BE TOO HAPPY WHERE THEY ARE GOING.
OH NO!
WHAT DID THEY GET THEMSELVES INTO?

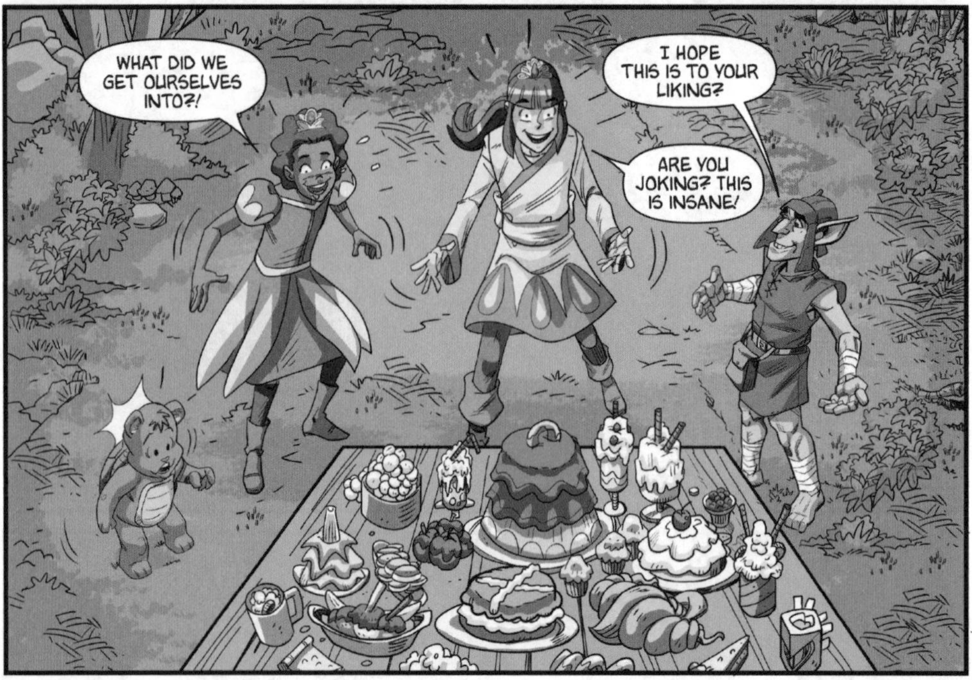
WHAT DID WE GET OURSELVES INTO?!
I HOPE THIS IS TO YOUR LIKING?
ARE YOU JOKING? THIS IS INSANE!

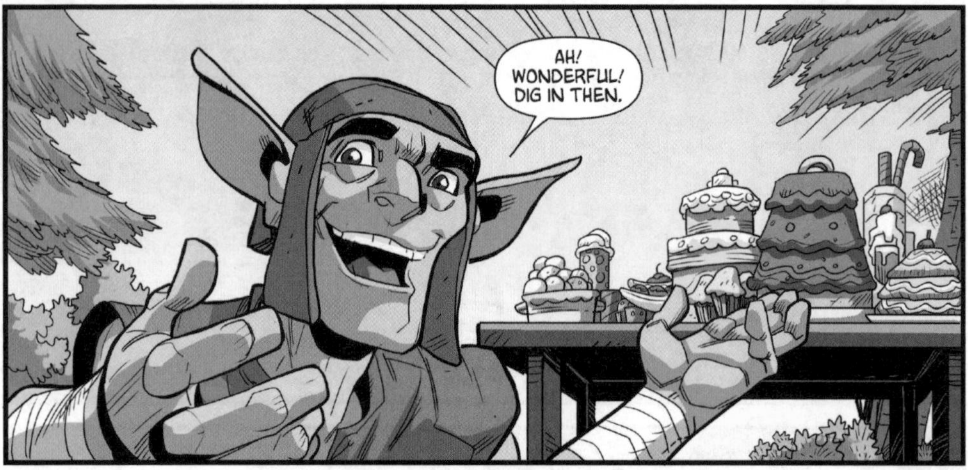
AH! WONDERFUL! DIG IN THEN.

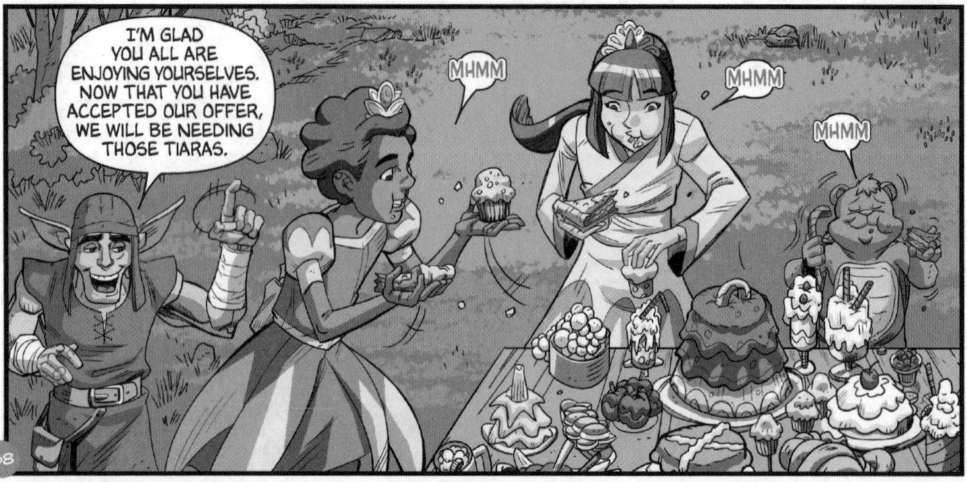
I'M GLAD YOU ALL ARE ENJOYING YOURSELVES. NOW THAT YOU HAVE ACCEPTED OUR OFFER, WE WILL BE NEEDING THOSE TIARAS.
MHMM
MHMM
MHMM

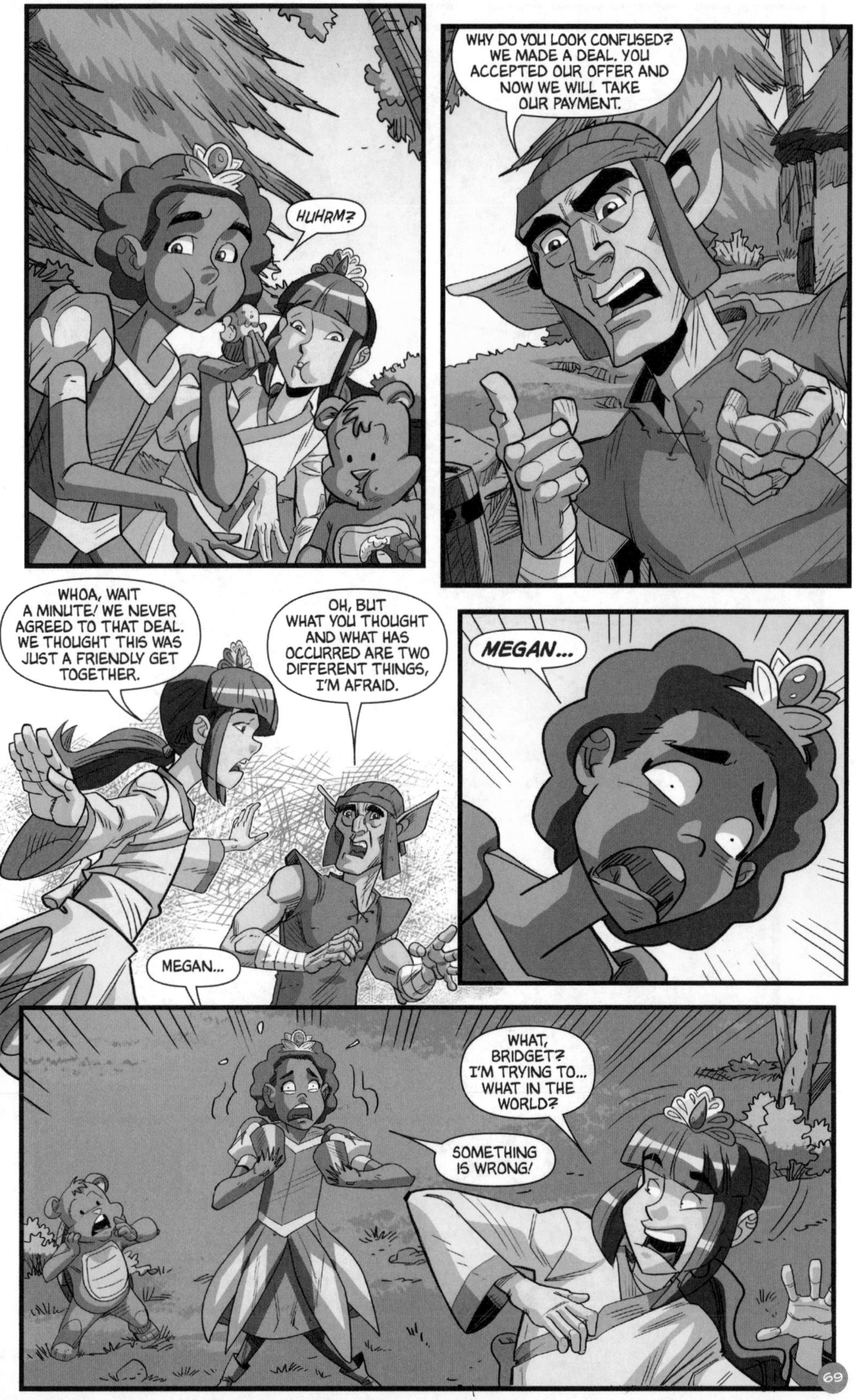
HUHRM?
WHY DO YOU LOOK CONFUSED? WE MADE A DEAL. YOU ACCEPTED OUR OFFER AND NOW WE WILL TAKE OUR PAYMENT.
WHOA, WAIT A MINUTE! WE NEVER AGREED TO THAT DEAL. WE THOUGHT THIS WAS JUST A FRIENDLY GET TOGETHER.
OH, BUT WHAT YOU THOUGHT AND WHAT HAS OCCURRED ARE TWO DIFFERENT THINGS, I'M AFRAID.
MEGAN...
MEGAN...
WHAT, BRIDGET? I'M TRYING TO... WHAT IN THE WORLD?
SOMETHING IS WRONG!

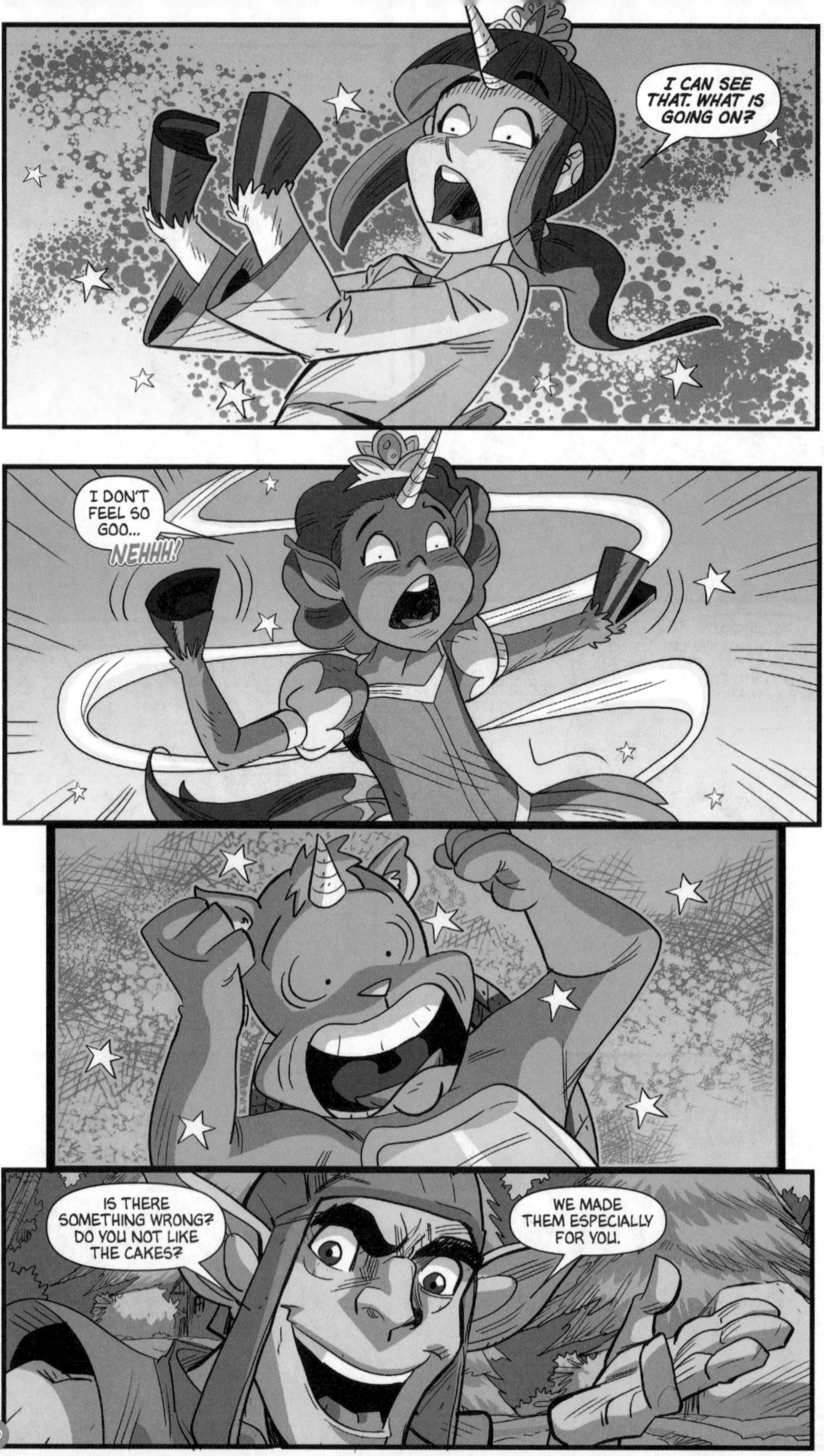
I CAN SEE THAT. WHAT IS GOING ON?
I DON'T FEEL SO GOO... NEHHH!
IS THERE SOMETHING WRONG? DO YOU NOT LIKE THE CAKES?
WE MADE THEM ESPECIALLY FOR YOU.

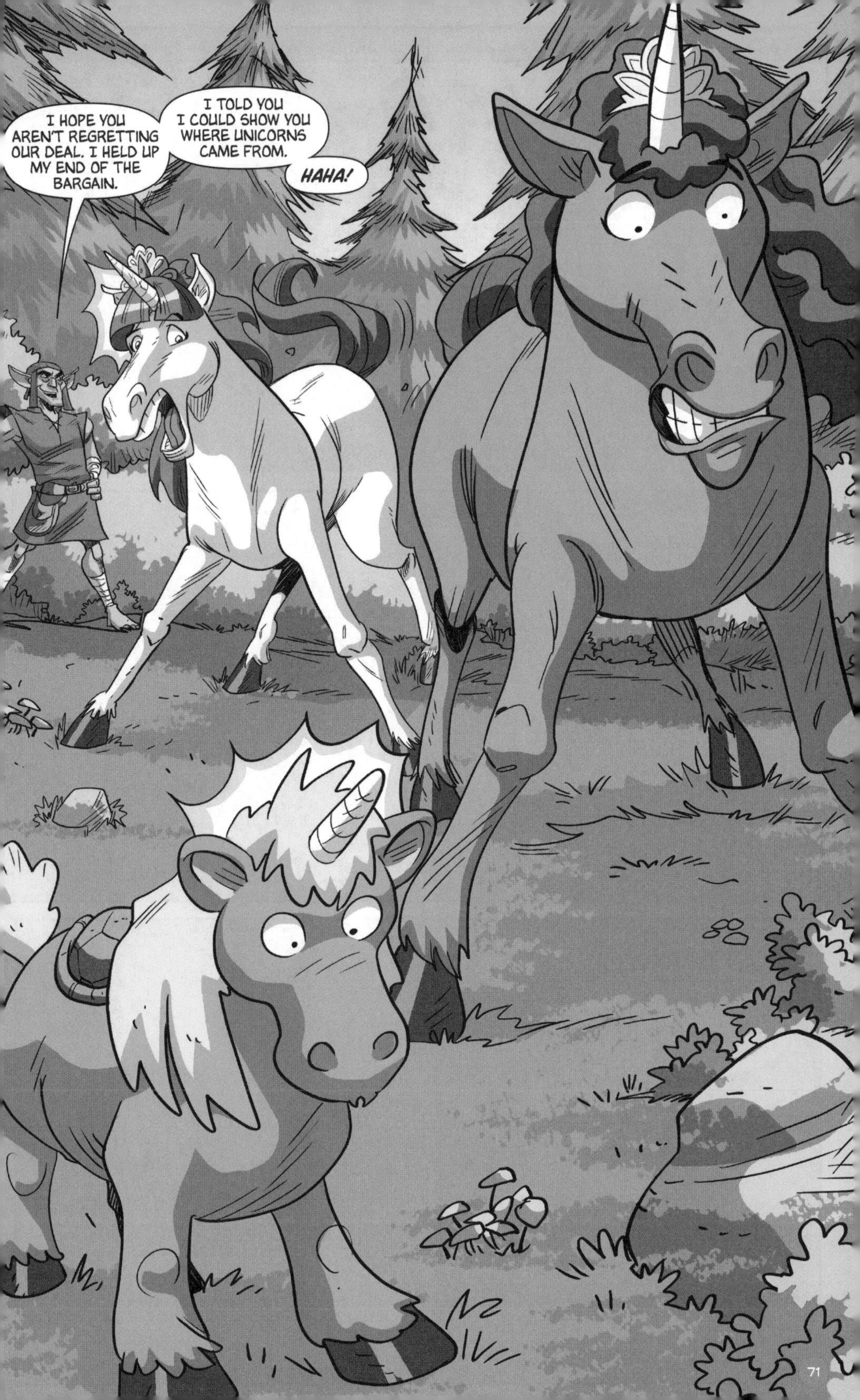
I HOPE YOU AREN'T REGRETTING OUR DEAL. I HELD UP MY END OF THE BARGAIN.
I TOLD YOU I COULD SHOW YOU WHERE UNICORNS CAME FROM.
HAHA!

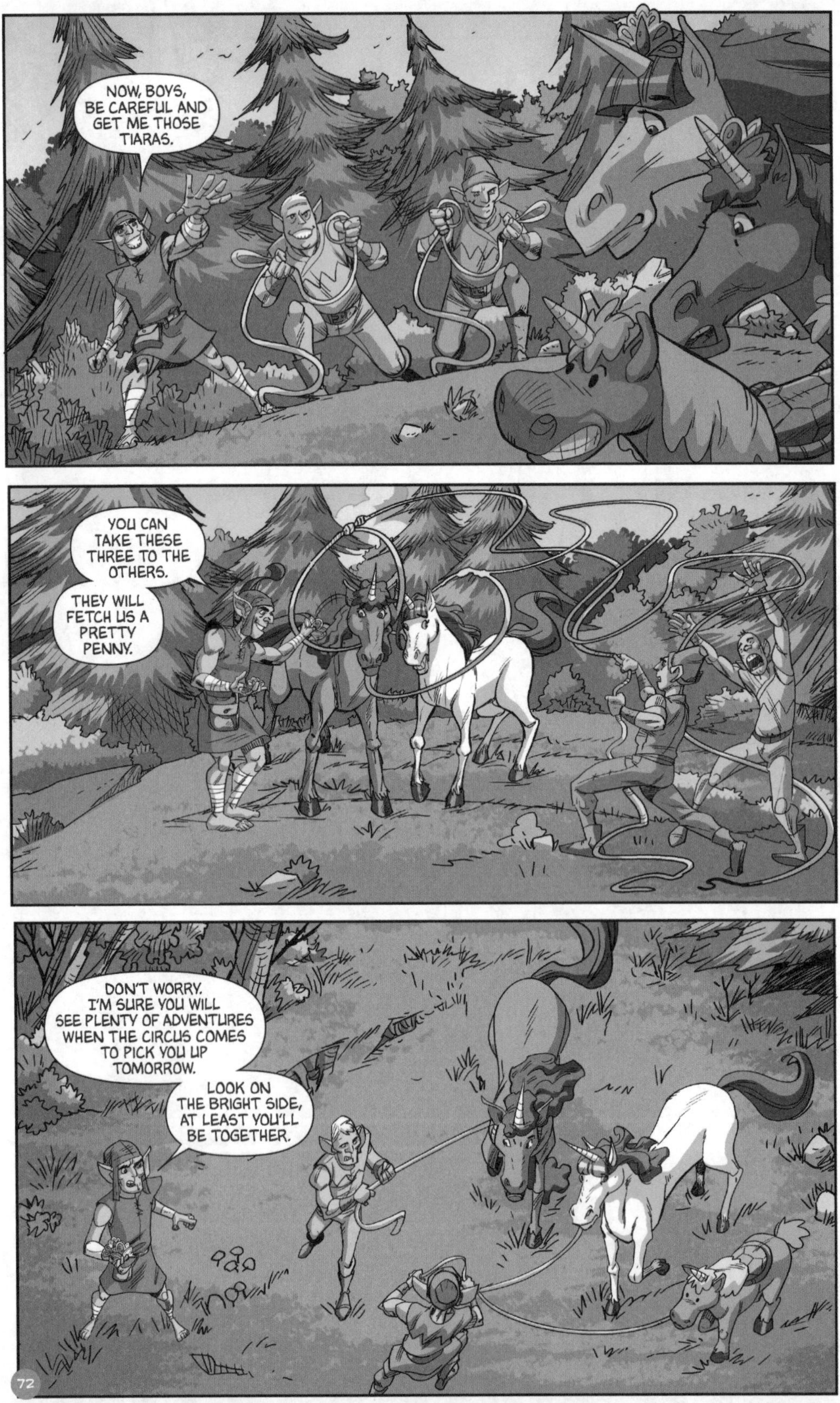
NOW, BOYS, BE CAREFUL AND GET ME THOSE TIARAS.
YOU CAN TAKE THESE THREE TO THE OTHERS.
THEY WILL FETCH US A PRETTY PENNY.
DON'T WORRY. I'M SURE YOU WILL SEE PLENTY OF ADVENTURES WHEN THE CIRCUS COMES TO PICK YOU UP TOMORROW.
LOOK ON THE BRIGHT SIDE, AT LEAST YOU'LL BE TOGETHER.

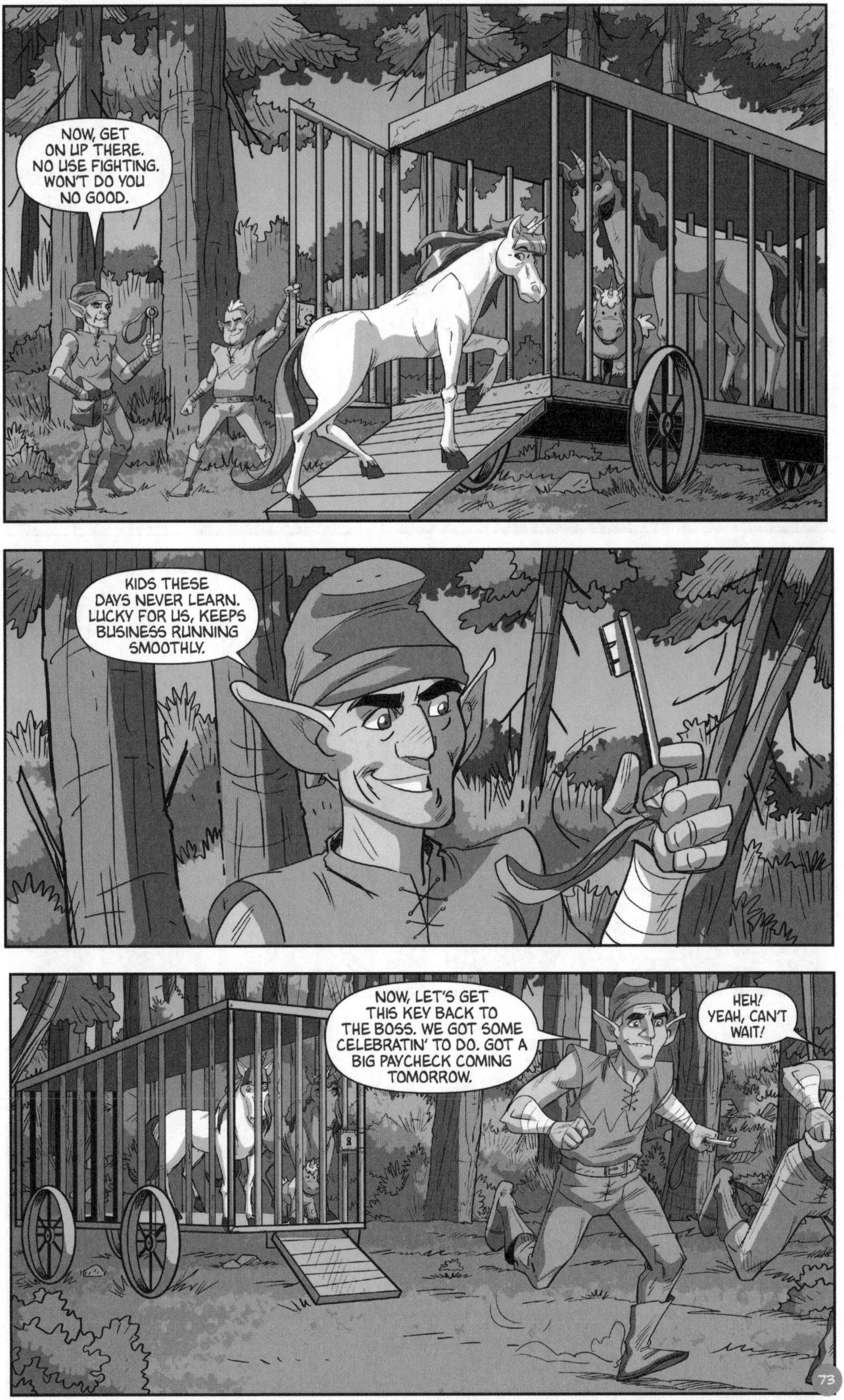
NOW, GET ON UP THERE. NO USE FIGHTING. WON'T DO YOU NO GOOD.
KIDS THESE DAYS NEVER LEARN. LUCKY FOR US, KEEPS BUSINESS RUNNING SMOOTHLY.
NOW, LET'S GET THIS KEY BACK TO THE BOSS. WE GOT SOME CELEBRATIN' TO DO. GOT A BIG PAYCHECK COMING TOMORROW.
HEH! YEAH, CAN'T WAIT!

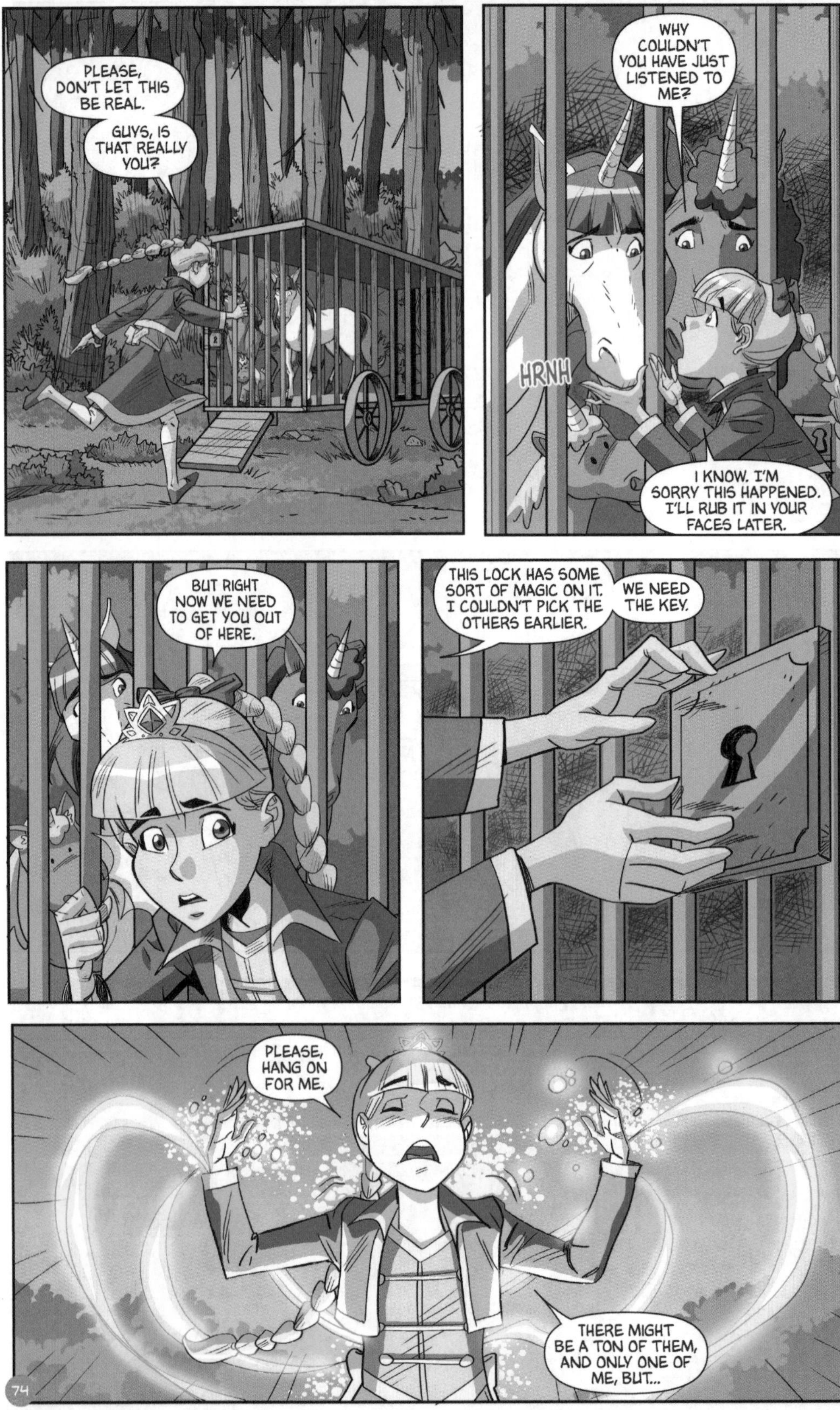
PLEASE, DON'T LET THIS BE REAL.
GUYS, IS THAT REALLY YOU?
WHY COULDN'T YOU HAVE JUST LISTENED TO ME?
HRNH
I KNOW. I'M SORRY THIS HAPPENED. I'LL RUB IT IN YOUR FACES LATER.
BUT RIGHT NOW WE NEED TO GET YOU OUT OF HERE.
THIS LOCK HAS SOME SORT OF MAGIC ON IT. I COULDN'T PICK THE OTHERS EARLIER.
WE NEED THE KEY.
PLEASE, HANG ON FOR ME.
THERE MIGHT BE A TON OF THEM, AND ONLY ONE OF ME, BUT...

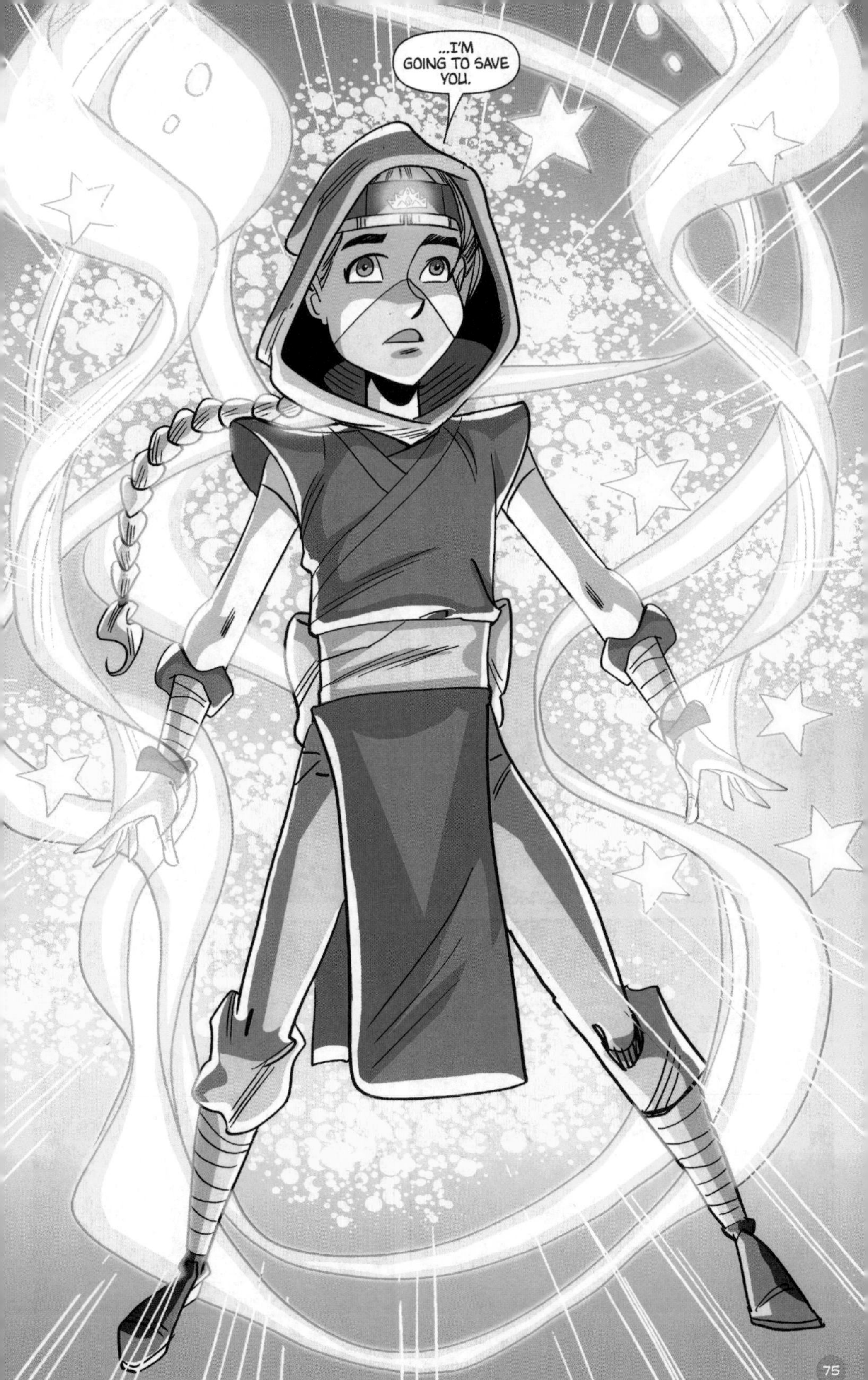
...I'M GOING TO SAVE YOU.

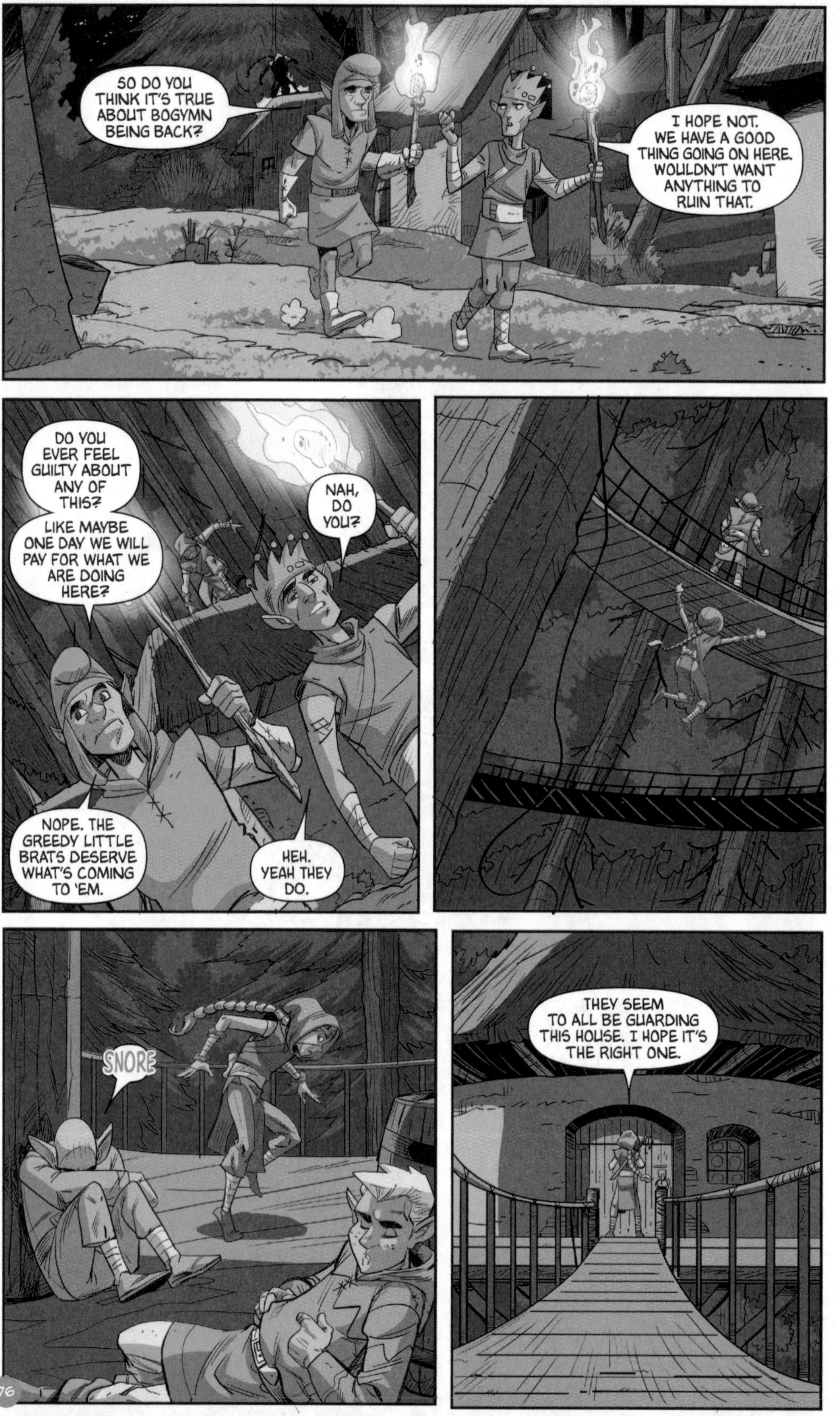
SO DO YOU THINK IT'S TRUE ABOUT BOGYMN BEING BACK?
I HOPE NOT. WE HAVE A GOOD THING GOING ON HERE. WOULDN'T WANT ANYTHING TO RUIN THAT.
DO YOU EVER FEEL GUILTY ABOUT ANY OF THIS?
LIKE MAYBE ONE DAY WE WILL PAY FOR WHAT WE ARE DOING HERE?
NAH, DO YOU?
NOPE. THE GREEDY LITTLE BRATS DESERVE WHAT'S COMING TO 'EM.
HEH. YEAH THEY DO.
SNORE
THEY SEEM TO ALL BE GUARDING THIS HOUSE. I HOPE IT'S THE RIGHT ONE.

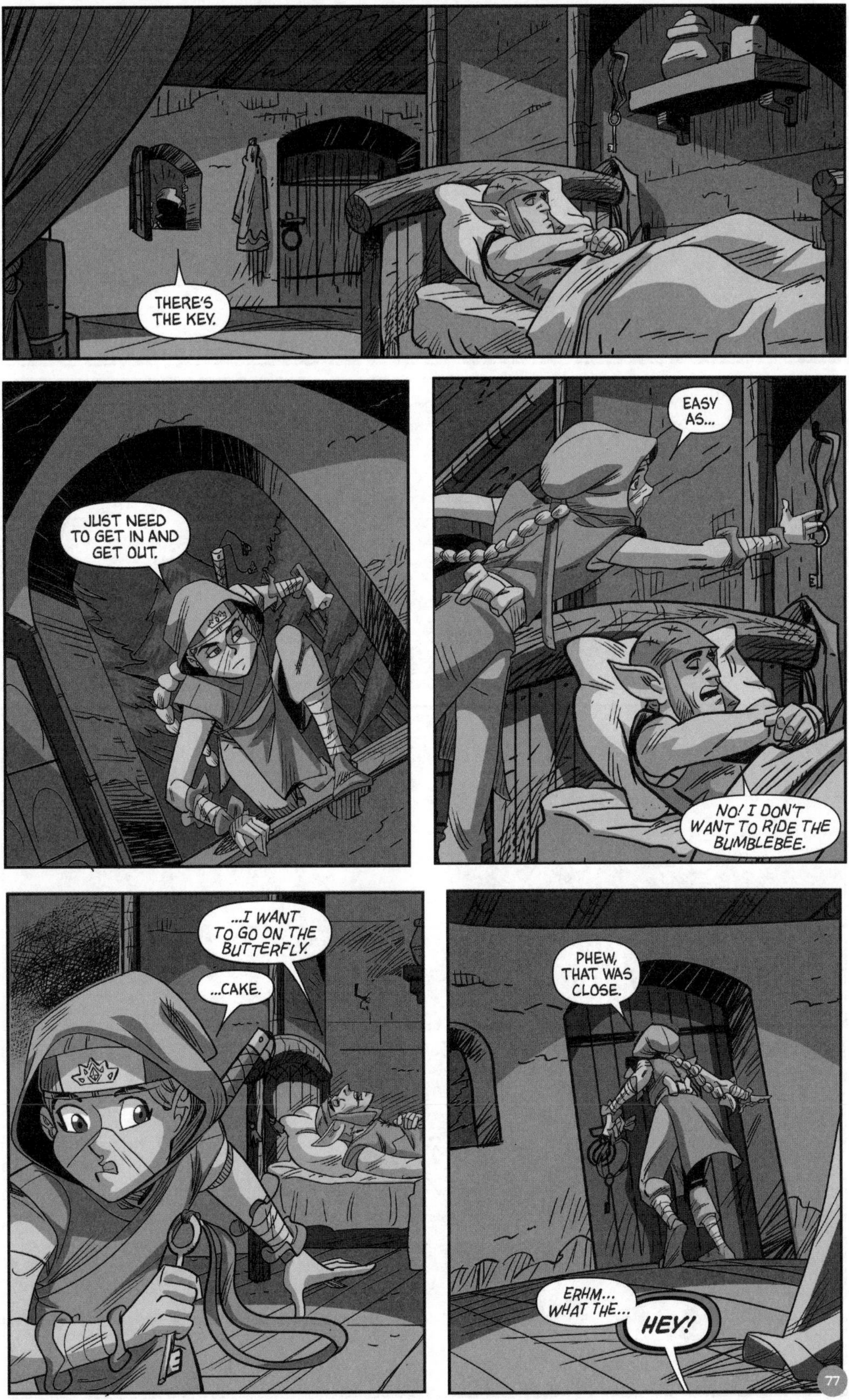
THERE'S THE KEY.
JUST NEED TO GET IN AND GET OUT.
EASY AS...
NO! I DON'T WANT TO RIDE THE BUMBLEBEE.
...I WANT TO GO ON THE BUTTERFLY.
...CAKE.
PHEW, THAT WAS CLOSE.
ERHM... WHAT THE...
HEY!

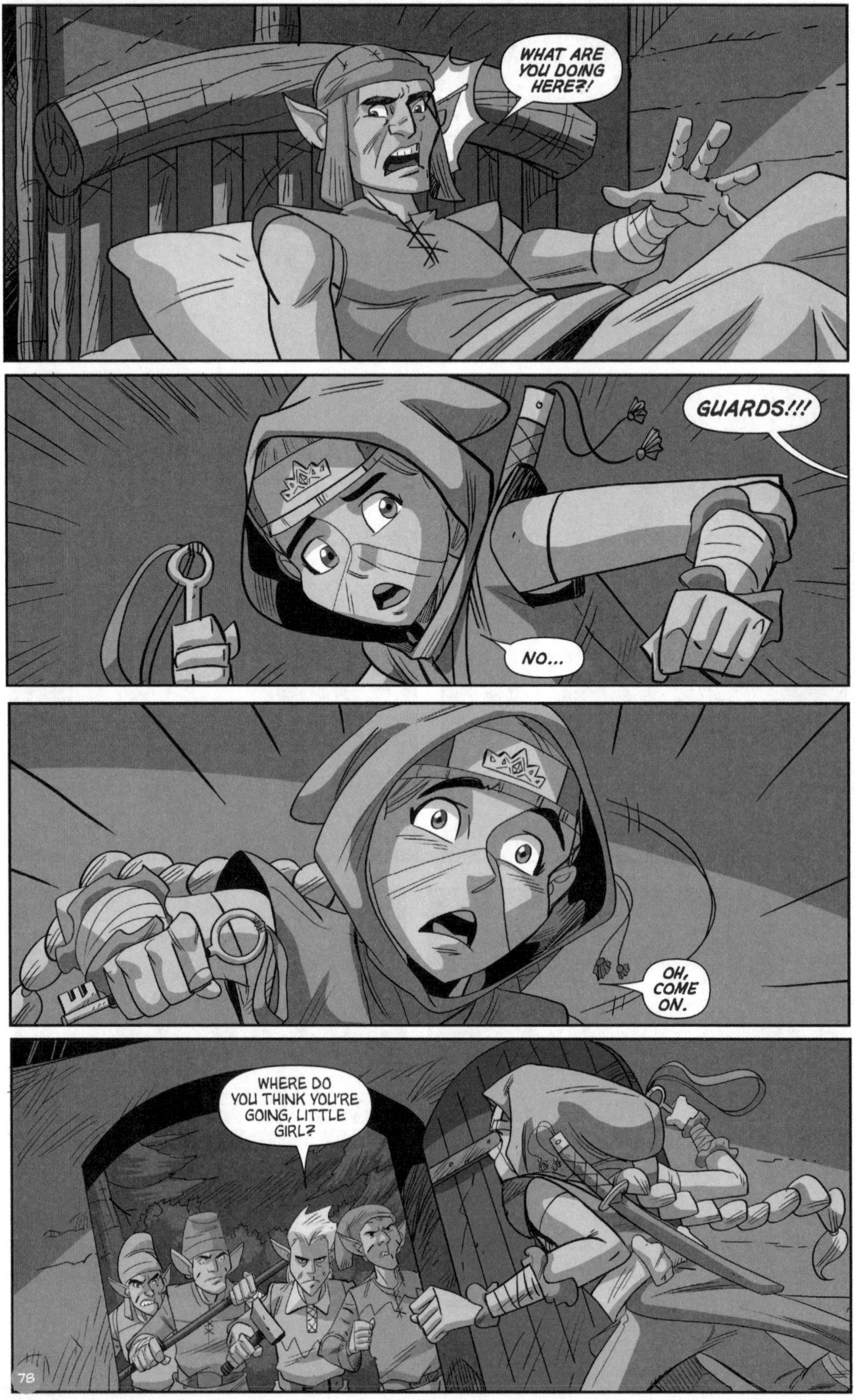
WHAT ARE YOU DOING HERE?!
GUARDS!!!
NO...
OH, COME ON.
WHERE DO YOU THINK YOU'RE GOING, LITTLE GIRL?

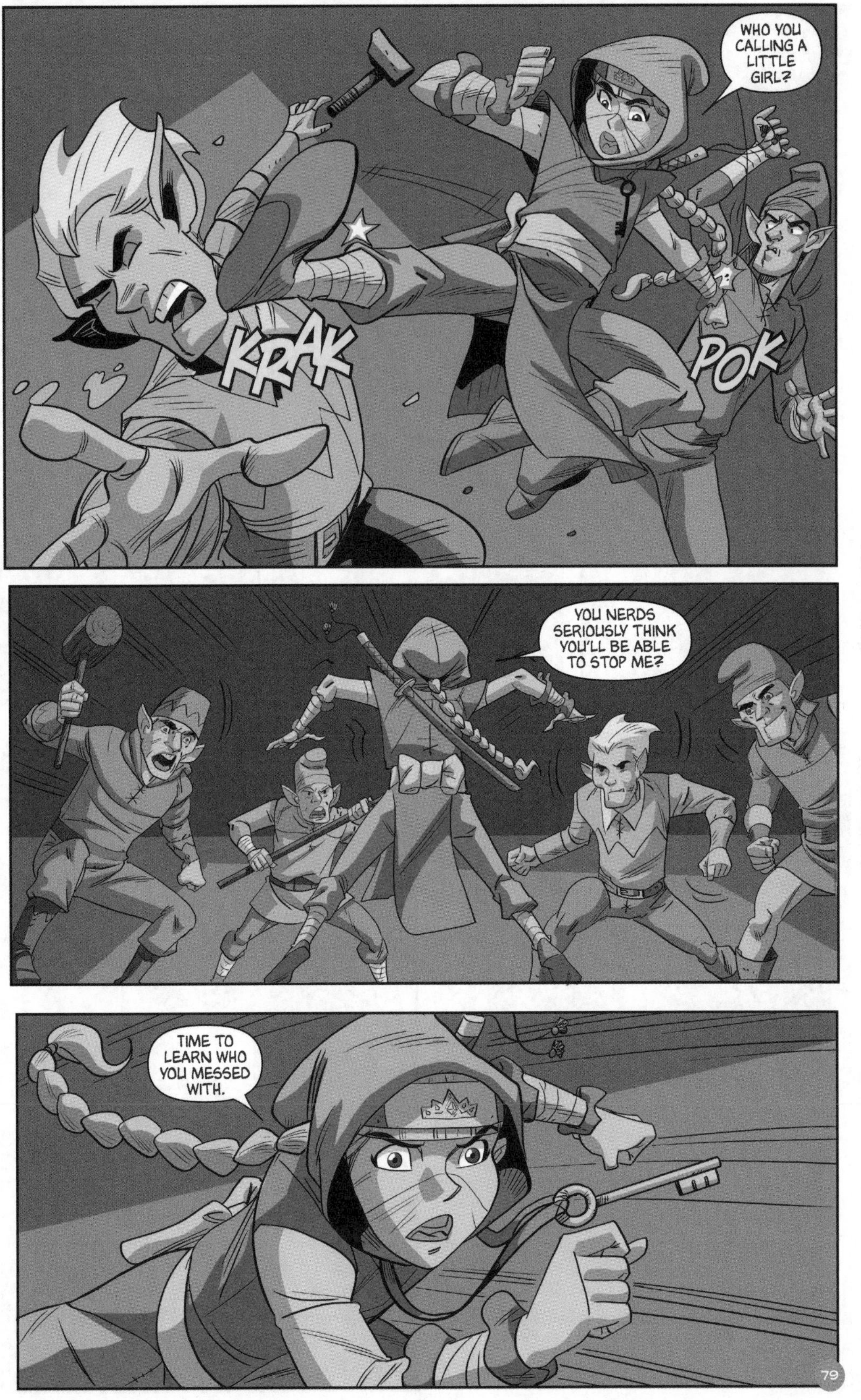
WHO YOU CALLING A LITTLE GIRL?
KRAK
POK
YOU NERDS SERIOUSLY THINK YOU'LL BE ABLE TO STOP ME?
TIME TO LEARN WHO YOU MESSED WITH.

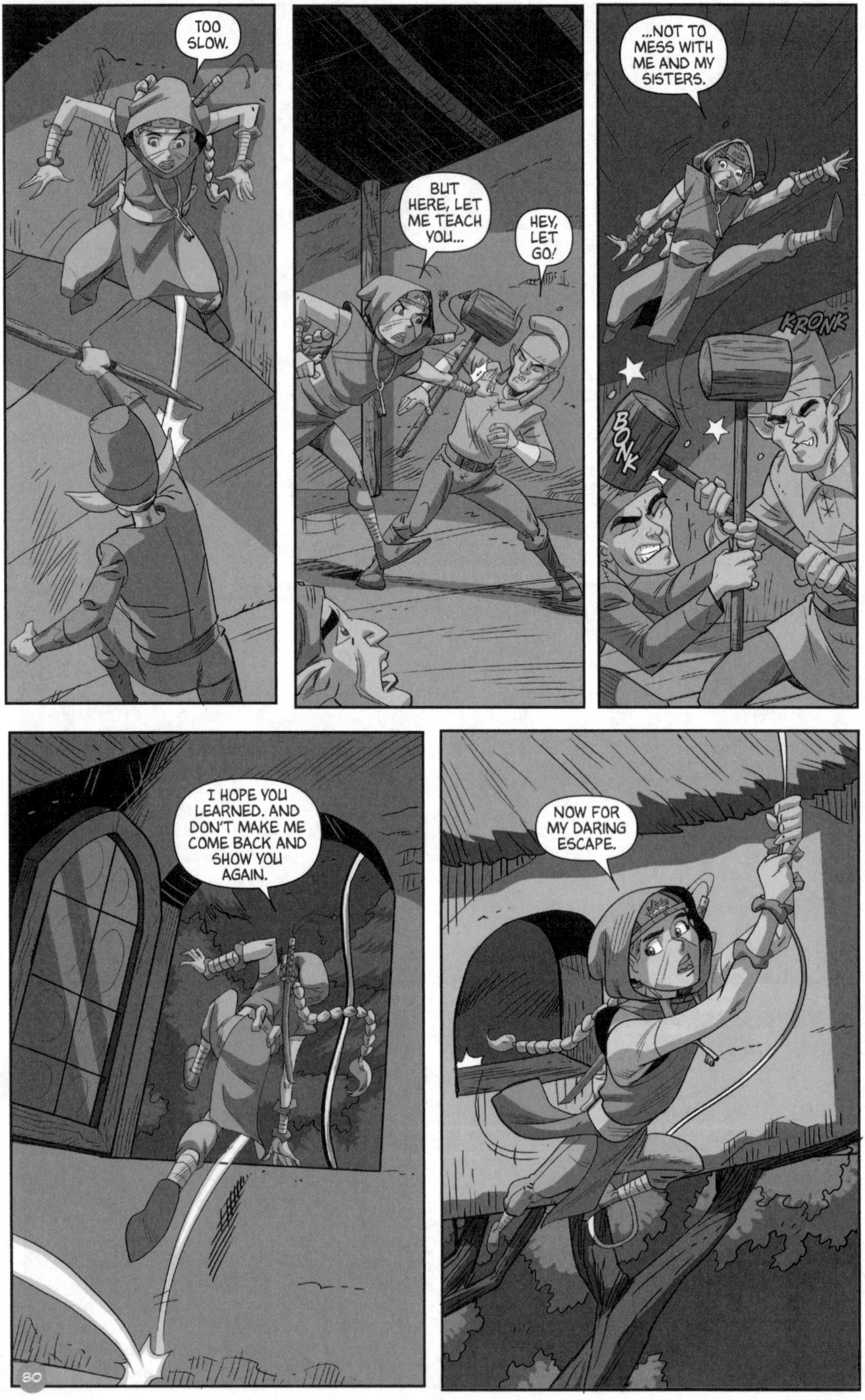
TOO SLOW.
BUT HERE, LET ME TEACH YOU...
HEY, LET GO!
...NOT TO MESS WITH ME AND MY SISTERS.
KRONK
BONK
I HOPE YOU LEARNED. AND DON'T MAKE ME COME BACK AND SHOW YOU AGAIN.
NOW FOR MY DARING ESCAPE.

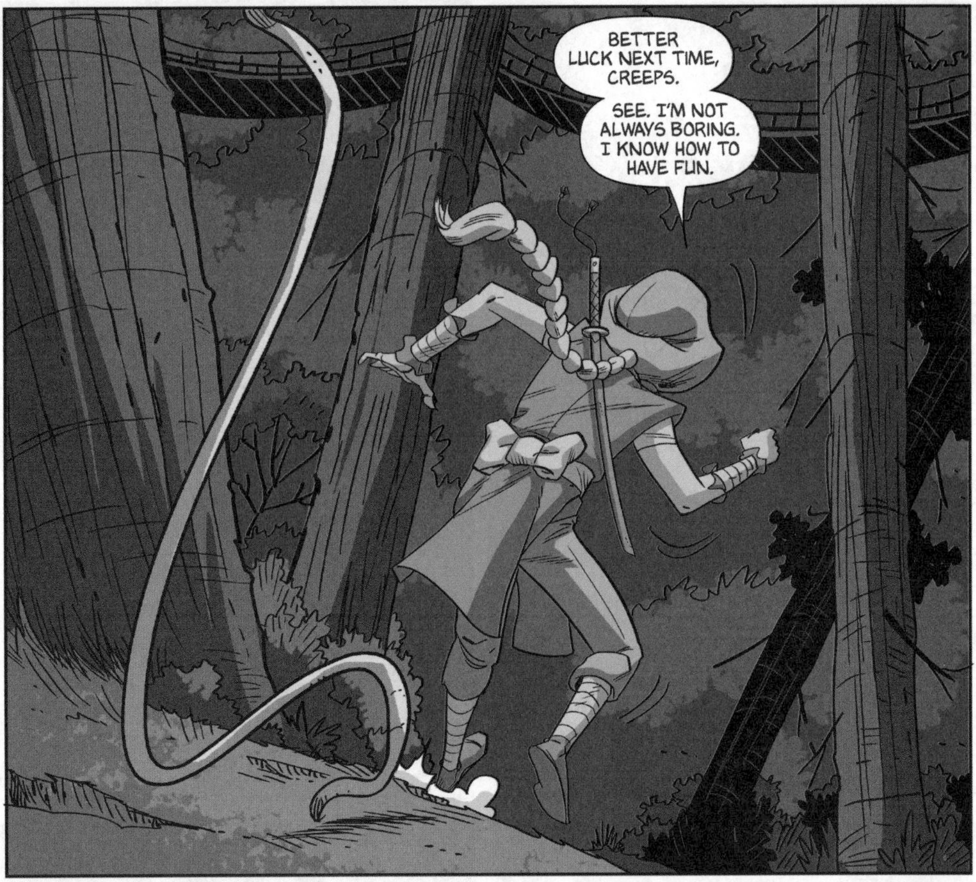
BETTER LUCK NEXT TIME, CREEPS.
SEE. I'M NOT ALWAYS BORING. I KNOW HOW TO HAVE FUN.

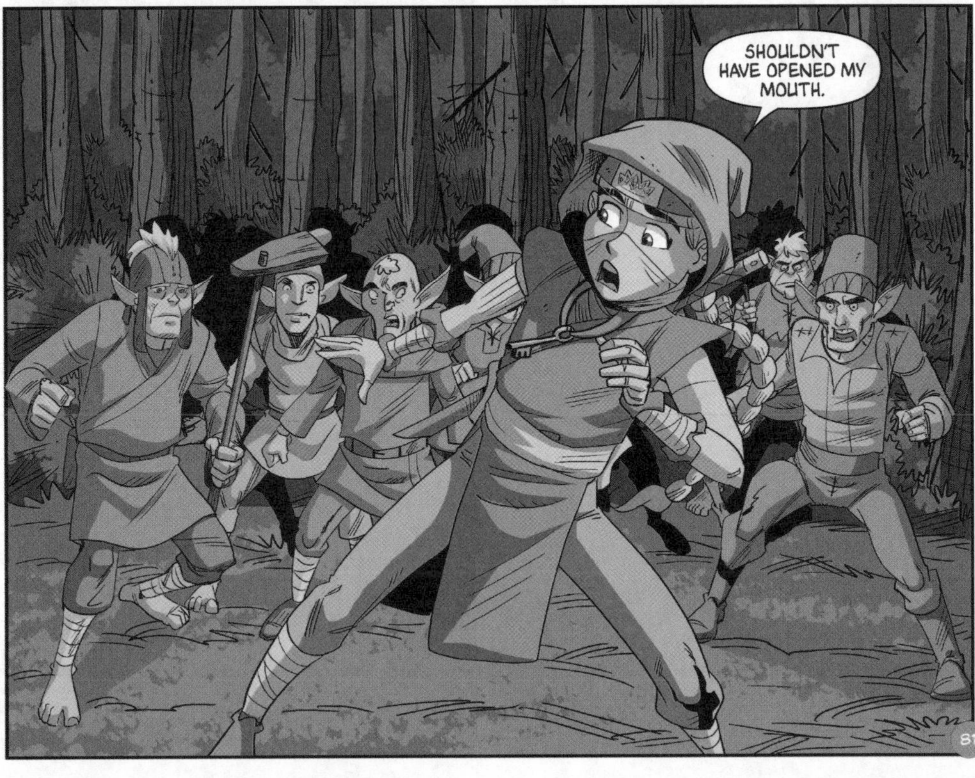
SHOULDN'T HAVE OPENED MY MOUTH.

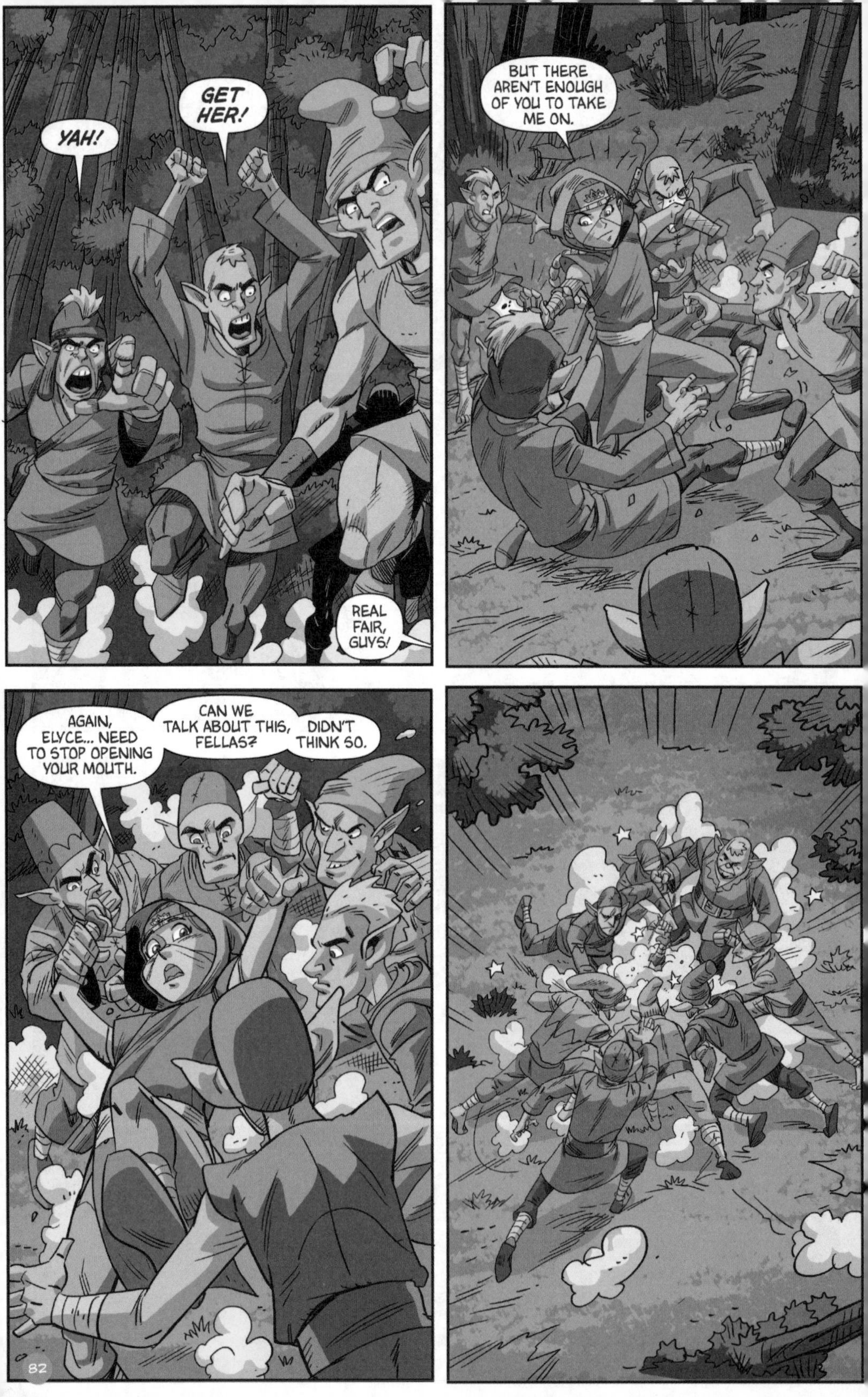
YAH!
GET HER!
REAL FAIR, GUYS!
BUT THERE AREN'T ENOUGH OF YOU TO TAKE ME ON.
AGAIN, ELYCE... NEED TO STOP OPENING YOUR MOUTH.
CAN WE TALK ABOUT THIS, FELLAS?
DIDN'T THINK SO.

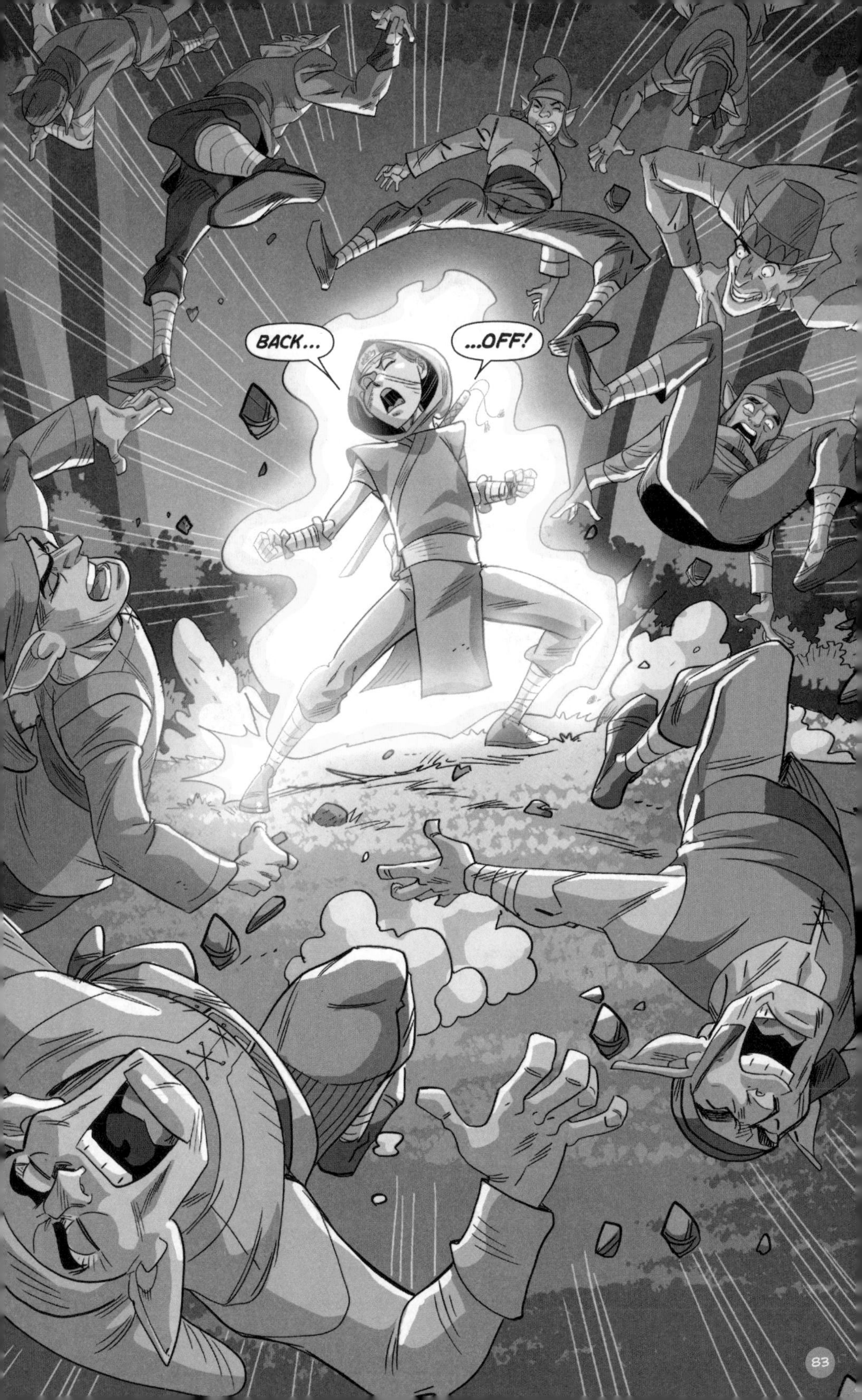
BACK...
...OFF!

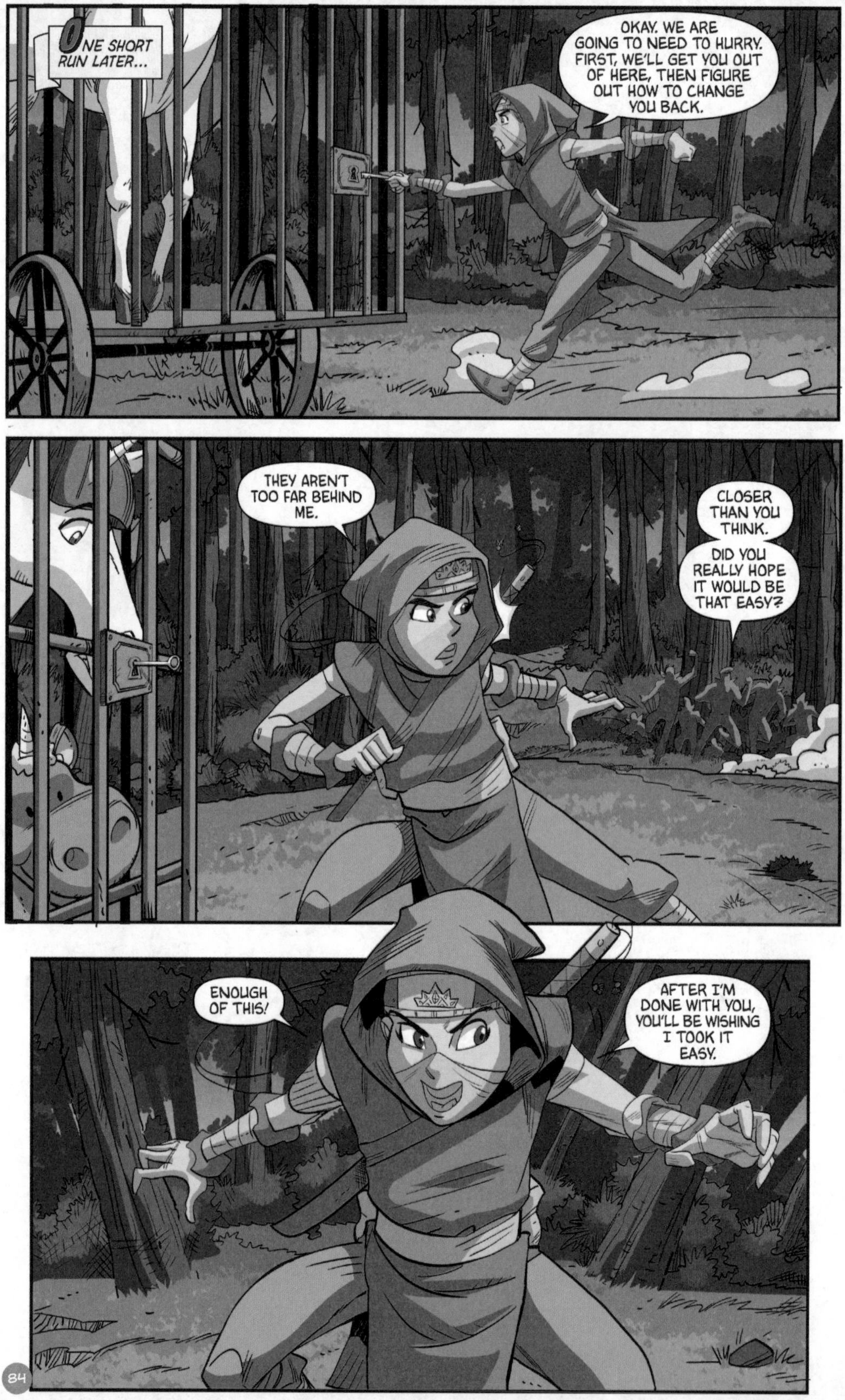
ONE SHORT RUN LATER...
OKAY. WE ARE GOING TO NEED TO HURRY. FIRST, WE'LL GET YOU OUT OF HERE, THEN FIGURE OUT HOW TO CHANGE YOU BACK.
THEY AREN'T TOO FAR BEHIND ME.
CLOSER THAN YOU THINK.
DID YOU REALLY HOPE IT WOULD BE THAT EASY?
ENOUGH OF THIS!
AFTER I'M DONE WITH YOU, YOU'LL BE WISHING I TOOK IT EASY.

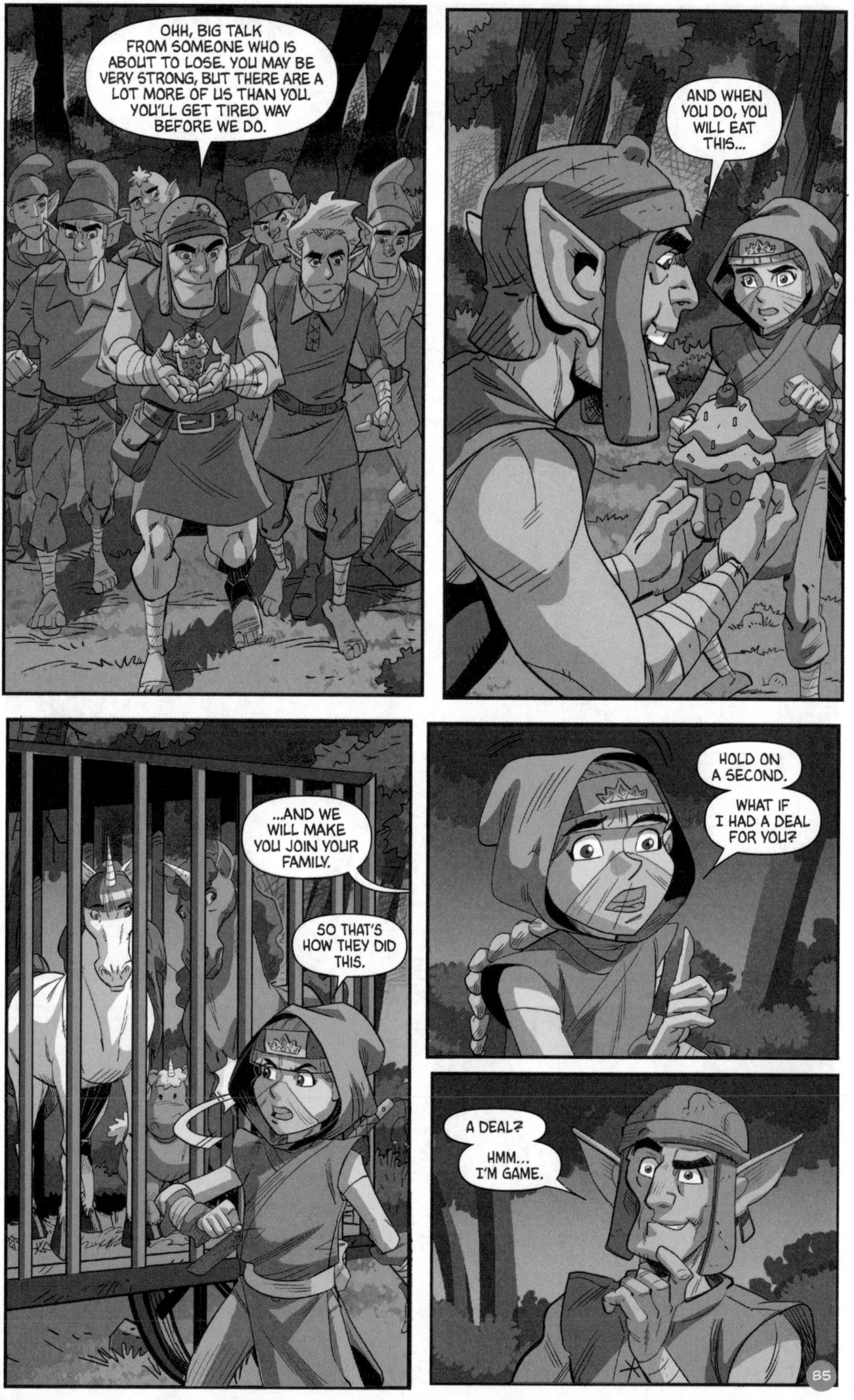
OHH, BIG TALK FROM SOMEONE WHO IS ABOUT TO LOSE. YOU MAY BE VERY STRONG, BUT THERE ARE A LOT MORE OF US THAN YOU. YOU'LL GET TIRED WAY BEFORE WE DO.
AND WHEN YOU DO, YOU WILL EAT THIS...
...AND WE WILL MAKE YOU JOIN YOUR FAMILY.
SO THAT'S HOW THEY DID THIS.
HOLD ON A SECOND.
WHAT IF I HAD A DEAL FOR YOU?
A DEAL?
HMM... I'M GAME.

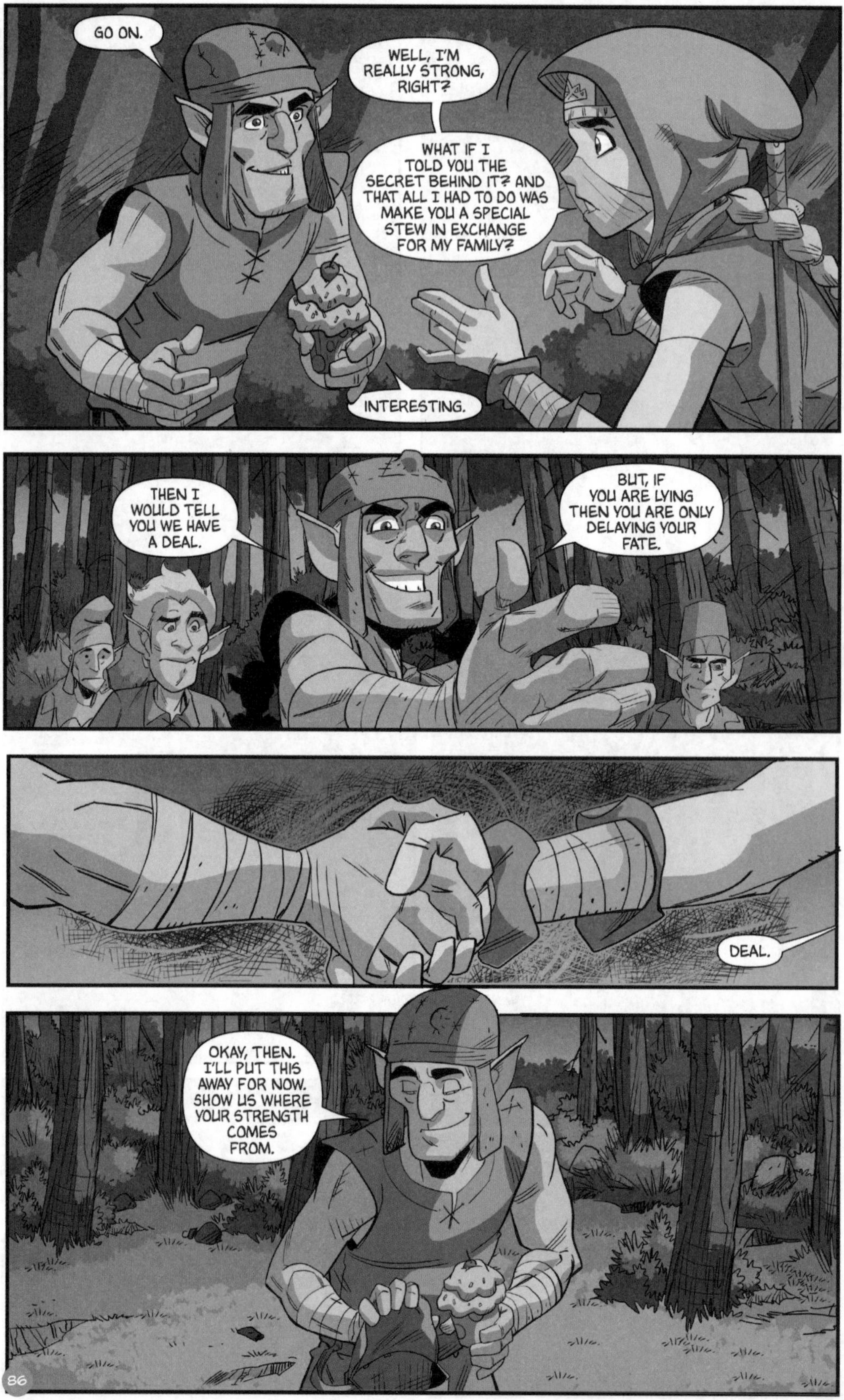
GO ON.
WELL, I'M REALLY STRONG, RIGHT?
WHAT IF I TOLD YOU THE SECRET BEHIND IT? AND THAT ALL I HAD TO DO WAS MAKE YOU A SPECIAL STEW IN EXCHANGE FOR MY FAMILY?
INTERESTING.
THEN I WOULD TELL YOU WE HAVE A DEAL.
BUT, IF YOU ARE LYING THEN YOU ARE ONLY DELAYING YOUR FATE.
DEAL.
OKAY, THEN. I'LL PUT THIS AWAY FOR NOW. SHOW US WHERE YOUR STRENGTH COMES FROM.

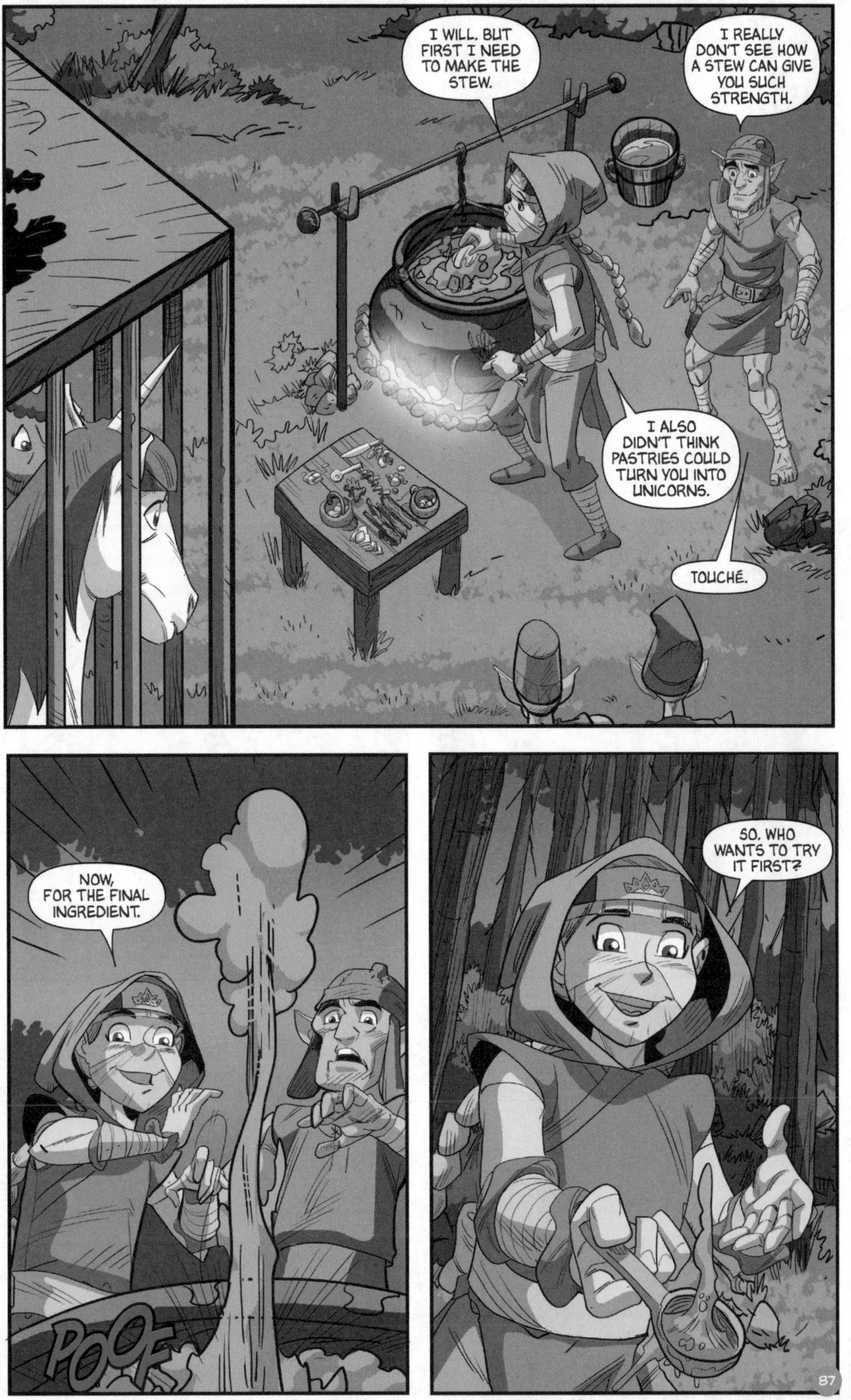
I WILL. BUT FIRST I NEED TO MAKE THE STEW.
I REALLY DON'T SEE HOW A STEW CAN GIVE YOU SUCH STRENGTH.
I ALSO DIDN'T THINK PASTRIES COULD TURN YOU INTO UNICORNS.
TOUCHÉ.
NOW, FOR THE FINAL INGREDIENT.
POOF
SO. WHO WANTS TO TRY IT FIRST?

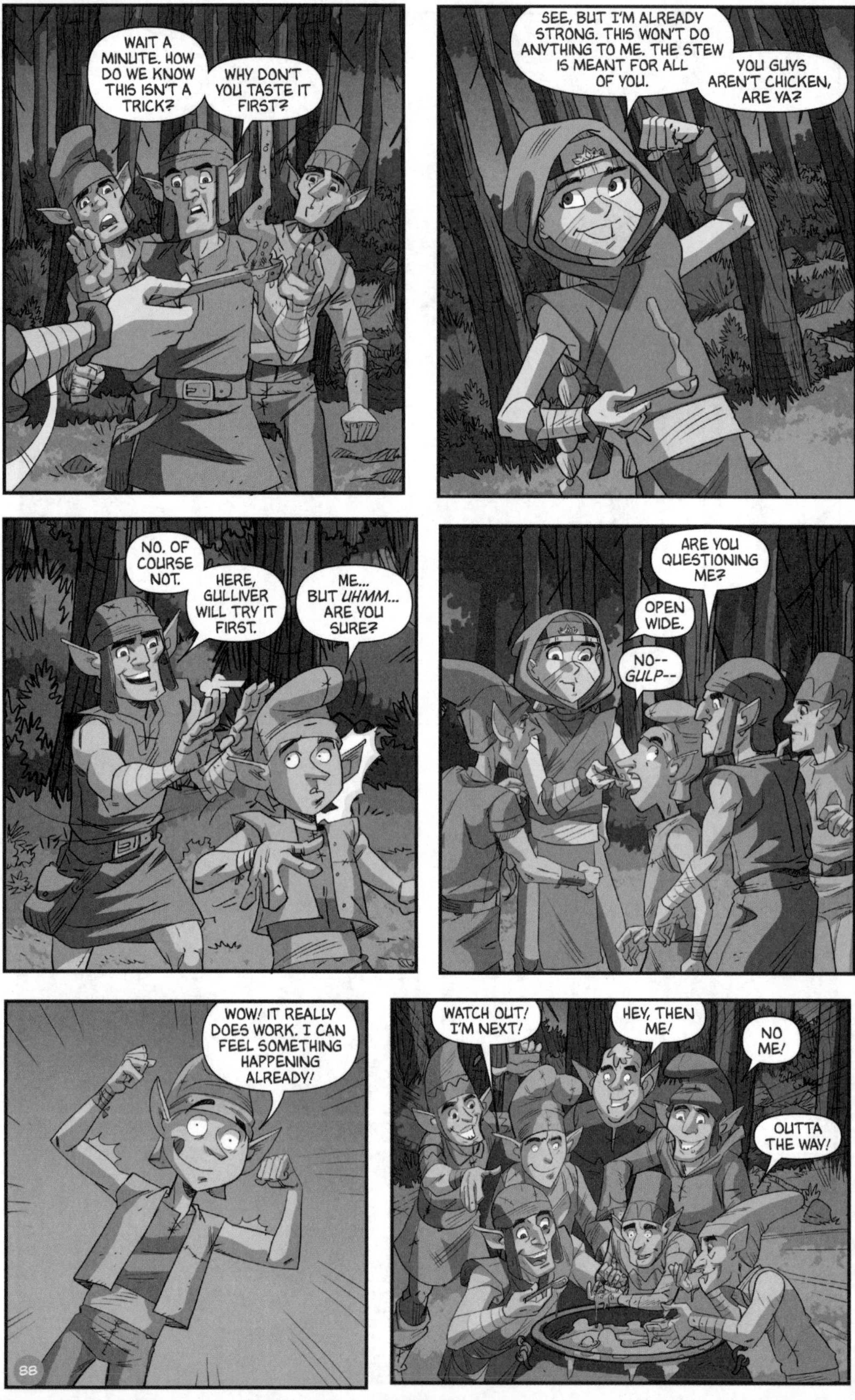
WAIT A MINUTE. HOW DO WE KNOW THIS ISN'T A TRICK?
WHY DON'T YOU TASTE IT FIRST?
SEE, BUT I'M ALREADY STRONG. THIS WON'T DO ANYTHING TO ME. THE STEW IS MEANT FOR ALL OF YOU.
YOU GUYS AREN'T CHICKEN, ARE YA?
NO. OF COURSE NOT.
HERE, GULLIVER WILL TRY IT FIRST.
ME... BUT *UHMM*... ARE YOU SURE?
ARE YOU QUESTIONING ME?
OPEN WIDE.
NO-- *GULP*--
WOW! IT REALLY DOES WORK. I CAN FEEL SOMETHING HAPPENING ALREADY!
WATCH OUT! I'M NEXT!
HEY, THEN ME!
NO ME!
OUTTA THE WAY!

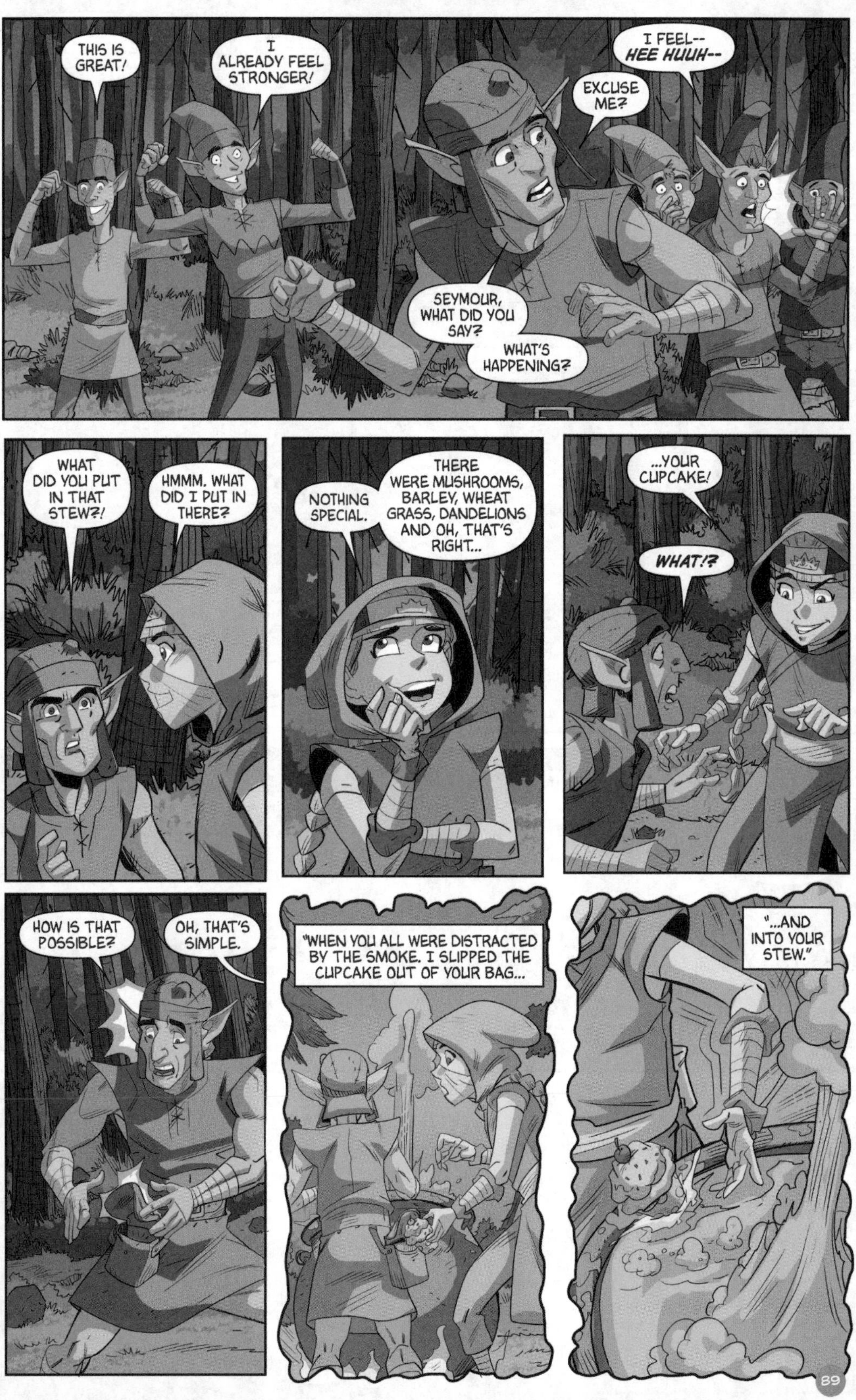
THIS IS GREAT!
I ALREADY FEEL STRONGER!
I FEEL-- HEE HUUH--
EXCUSE ME?
SEYMOUR, WHAT DID YOU SAY?
WHAT'S HAPPENING?
WHAT DID YOU PUT IN THAT STEW?!
HMMM. WHAT DID I PUT IN THERE?
NOTHING SPECIAL.
THERE WERE MUSHROOMS, BARLEY, WHEAT GRASS, DANDELIONS AND OH, THAT'S RIGHT...
...YOUR CUPCAKE!
WHAT!?
HOW IS THAT POSSIBLE?
OH, THAT'S SIMPLE.
"WHEN YOU ALL WERE DISTRACTED BY THE SMOKE. I SLIPPED THE CUPCAKE OUT OF YOUR BAG...
"...AND INTO YOUR STEW."

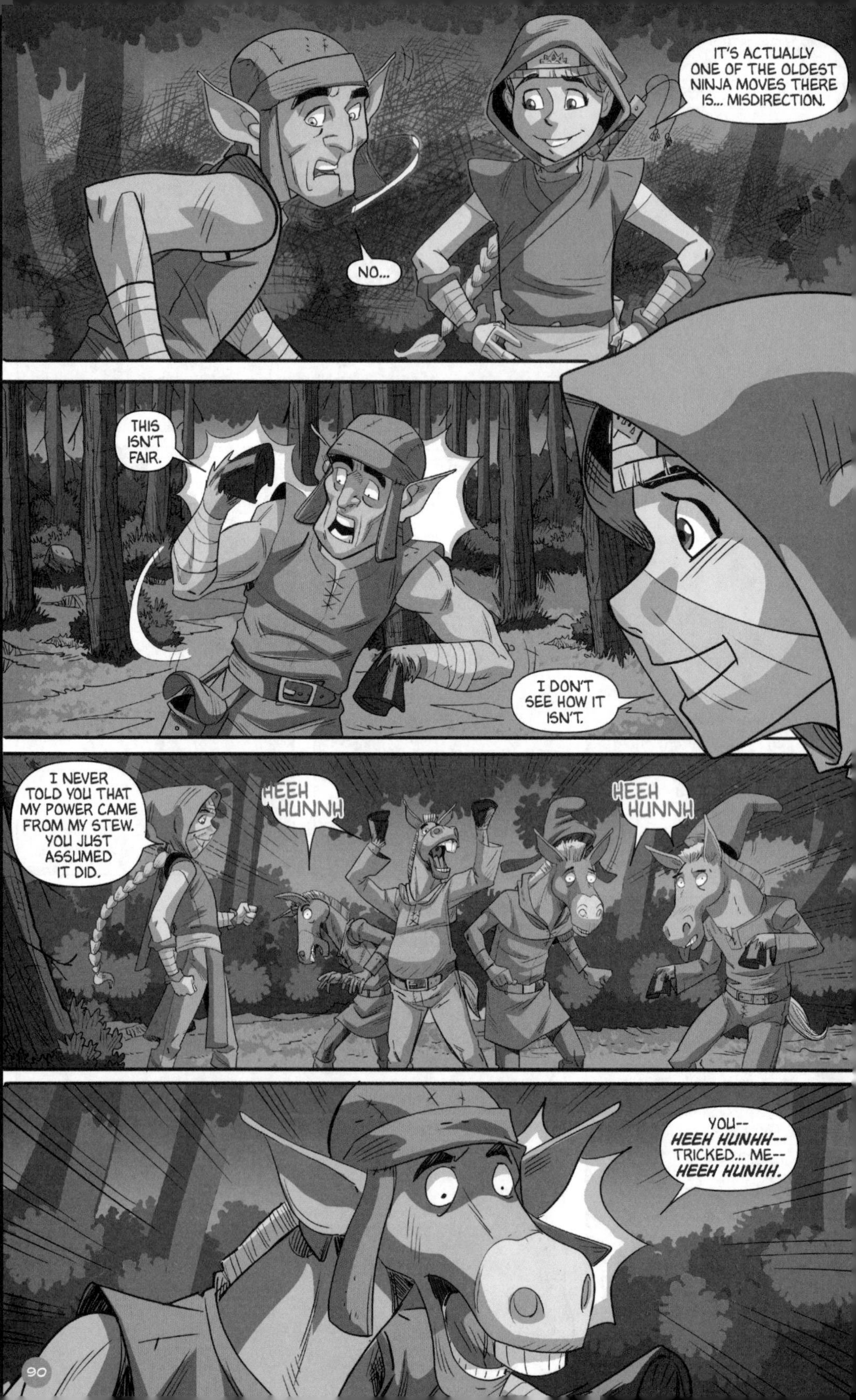
IT'S ACTUALLY ONE OF THE OLDEST NINJA MOVES THERE IS... MISDIRECTION.
NO...
THIS ISN'T FAIR.
I DON'T SEE HOW IT ISN'T.
I NEVER TOLD YOU THAT MY POWER CAME FROM MY STEW. YOU JUST ASSUMED IT DID.
HEEH HUNNH
HEEH HUNNH
YOU-- HEEH HUNHH-- TRICKED... ME-- HEEH HUNHH.

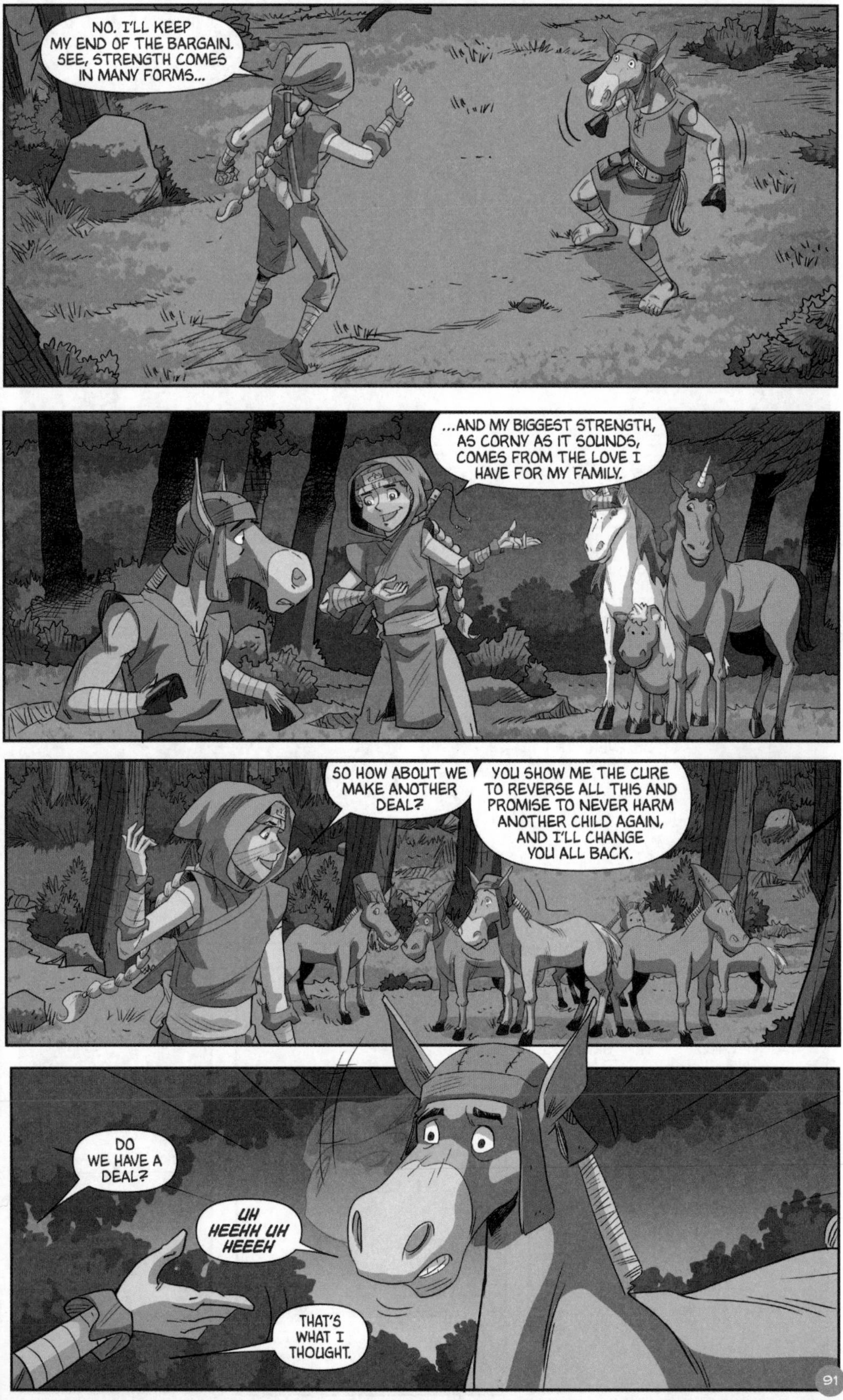

NO. I'LL KEEP MY END OF THE BARGAIN. SEE, STRENGTH COMES IN MANY FORMS...
...AND MY BIGGEST STRENGTH, AS CORNY AS IT SOUNDS, COMES FROM THE LOVE I HAVE FOR MY FAMILY.
SO HOW ABOUT WE MAKE ANOTHER DEAL?
YOU SHOW ME THE CURE TO REVERSE ALL THIS AND PROMISE TO NEVER HARM ANOTHER CHILD AGAIN, AND I'LL CHANGE YOU ALL BACK.
DO WE HAVE A DEAL?
UH HEEHH UH HEEEH
THAT'S WHAT I THOUGHT.

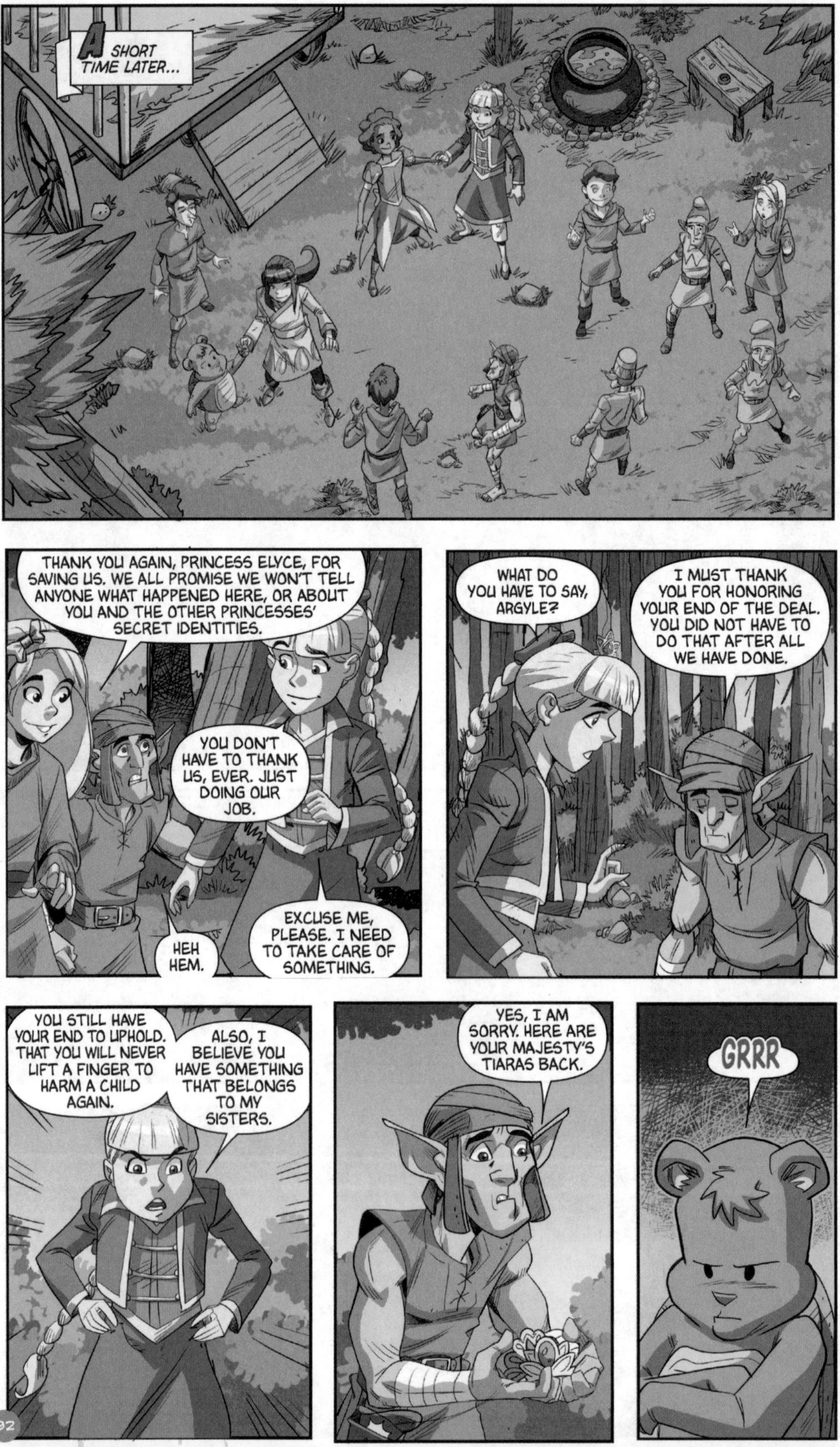
A SHORT TIME LATER...
THANK YOU AGAIN, PRINCESS ELYCE, FOR SAVING US. WE ALL PROMISE WE WON'T TELL ANYONE WHAT HAPPENED HERE, OR ABOUT YOU AND THE OTHER PRINCESSES' SECRET IDENTITIES.
YOU DON'T HAVE TO THANK US, EVER. JUST DOING OUR JOB.
HEH HEM.
EXCUSE ME, PLEASE. I NEED TO TAKE CARE OF SOMETHING.
WHAT DO YOU HAVE TO SAY, ARGYLE?
I MUST THANK YOU FOR HONORING YOUR END OF THE DEAL. YOU DID NOT HAVE TO DO THAT AFTER ALL WE HAVE DONE.
YOU STILL HAVE YOUR END TO UPHOLD. THAT YOU WILL NEVER LIFT A FINGER TO HARM A CHILD AGAIN.
ALSO, I BELIEVE YOU HAVE SOMETHING THAT BELONGS TO MY SISTERS.
YES, I AM SORRY. HERE ARE YOUR MAJESTY'S TIARAS BACK.
GRRR

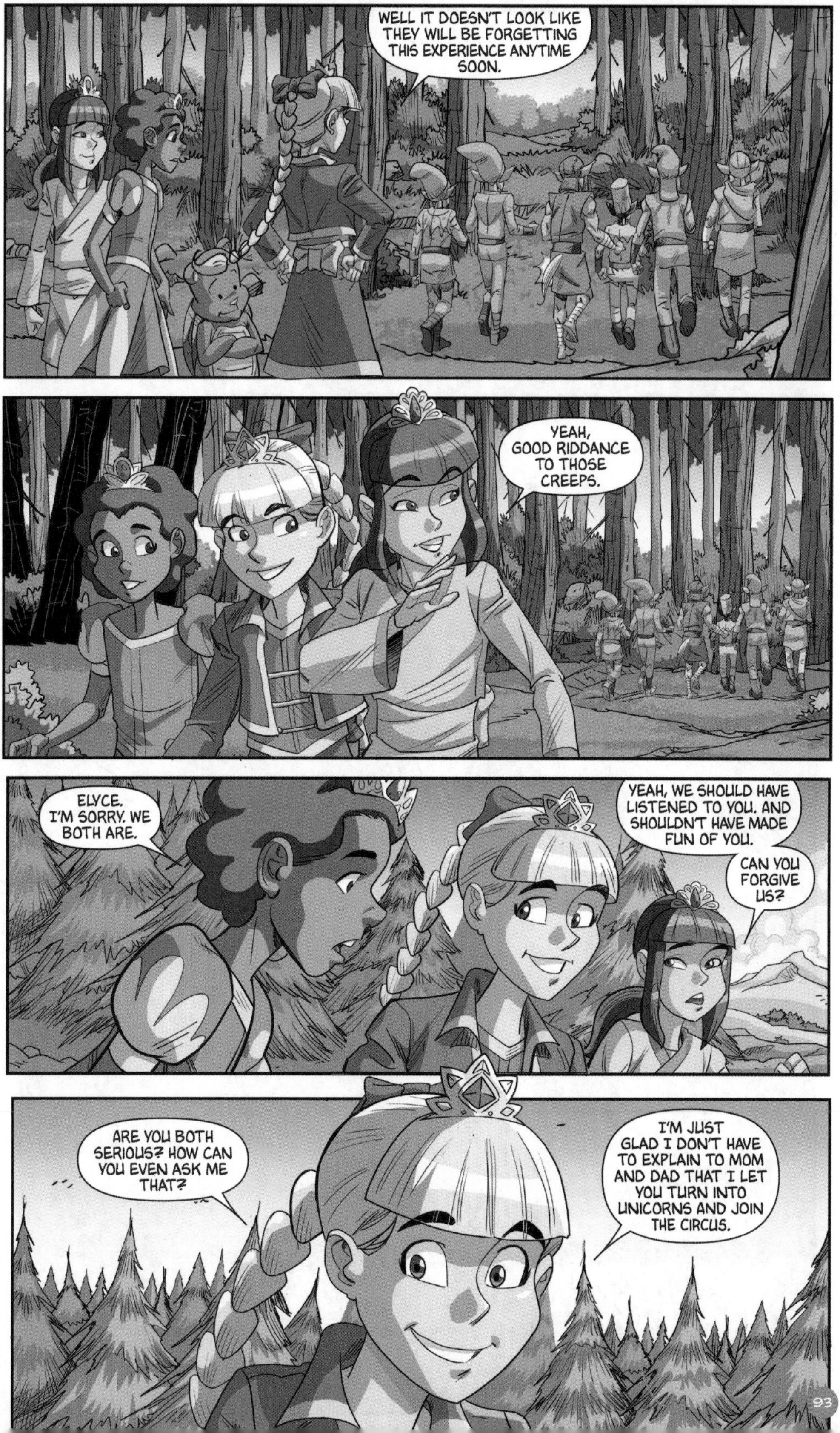
WELL IT DOESN'T LOOK LIKE THEY WILL BE FORGETTING THIS EXPERIENCE ANYTIME SOON.
YEAH, GOOD RIDDANCE TO THOSE CREEPS.
ELYCE. I'M SORRY. WE BOTH ARE.
YEAH, WE SHOULD HAVE LISTENED TO YOU. AND SHOULDN'T HAVE MADE FUN OF YOU.
CAN YOU FORGIVE US?
ARE YOU BOTH SERIOUS? HOW CAN YOU EVEN ASK ME THAT?
I'M JUST GLAD I DON'T HAVE TO EXPLAIN TO MOM AND DAD THAT I LET YOU TURN INTO UNICORNS AND JOIN THE CIRCUS.

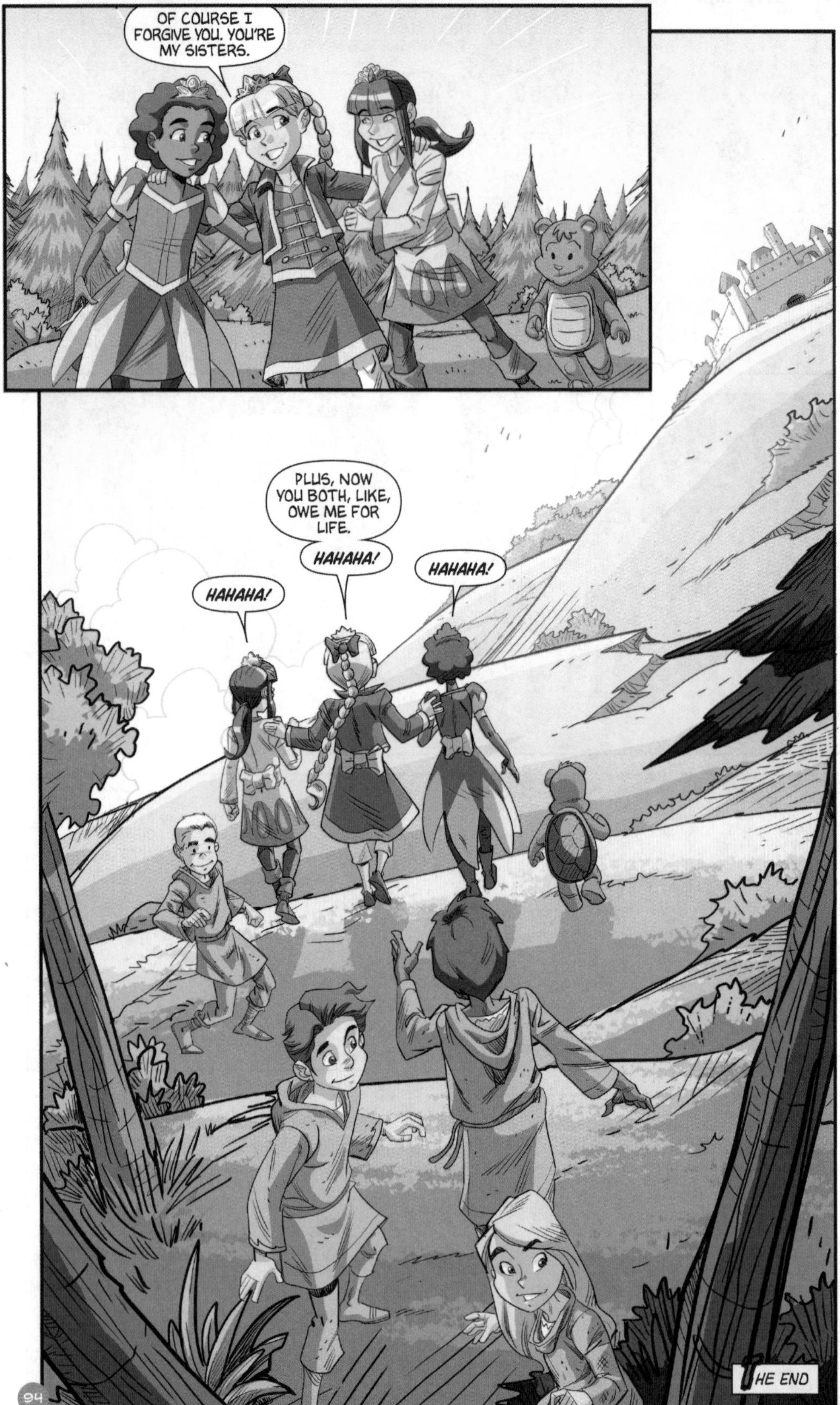

OF COURSE I FORGIVE YOU. YOU'RE MY SISTERS.
PLUS, NOW YOU BOTH, LIKE, OWE ME FOR LIFE.
HAHAHA!
HAHAHA!
HAHAHA!
THE END

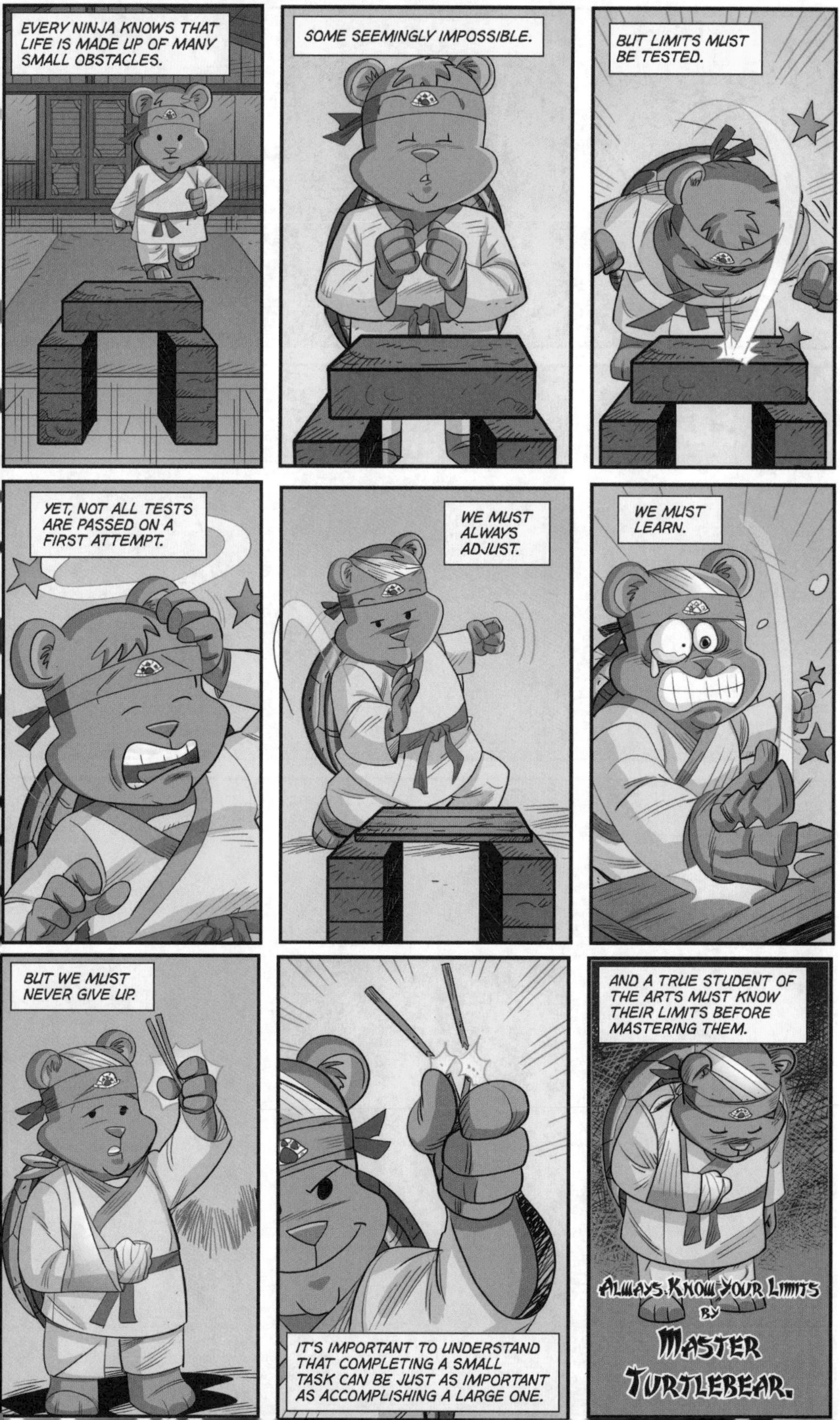
EVERY NINJA KNOWS THAT LIFE IS MADE UP OF MANY SMALL OBSTACLES.
SOME SEEMINGLY IMPOSSIBLE.
BUT LIMITS MUST BE TESTED.
YET, NOT ALL TESTS ARE PASSED ON A FIRST ATTEMPT.
WE MUST ALWAYS ADJUST.
WE MUST LEARN.
BUT WE MUST NEVER GIVE UP.
IT'S IMPORTANT TO UNDERSTAND THAT COMPLETING A SMALL TASK CAN BE JUST AS IMPORTANT AS ACCOMPLISHING A LARGE ONE.
AND A TRUE STUDENT OF THE ARTS MUST KNOW THEIR LIMITS BEFORE MASTERING THEM.
ALWAYS KNOW YOUR LIMITS
BY
MASTER TURTLEBEAR.

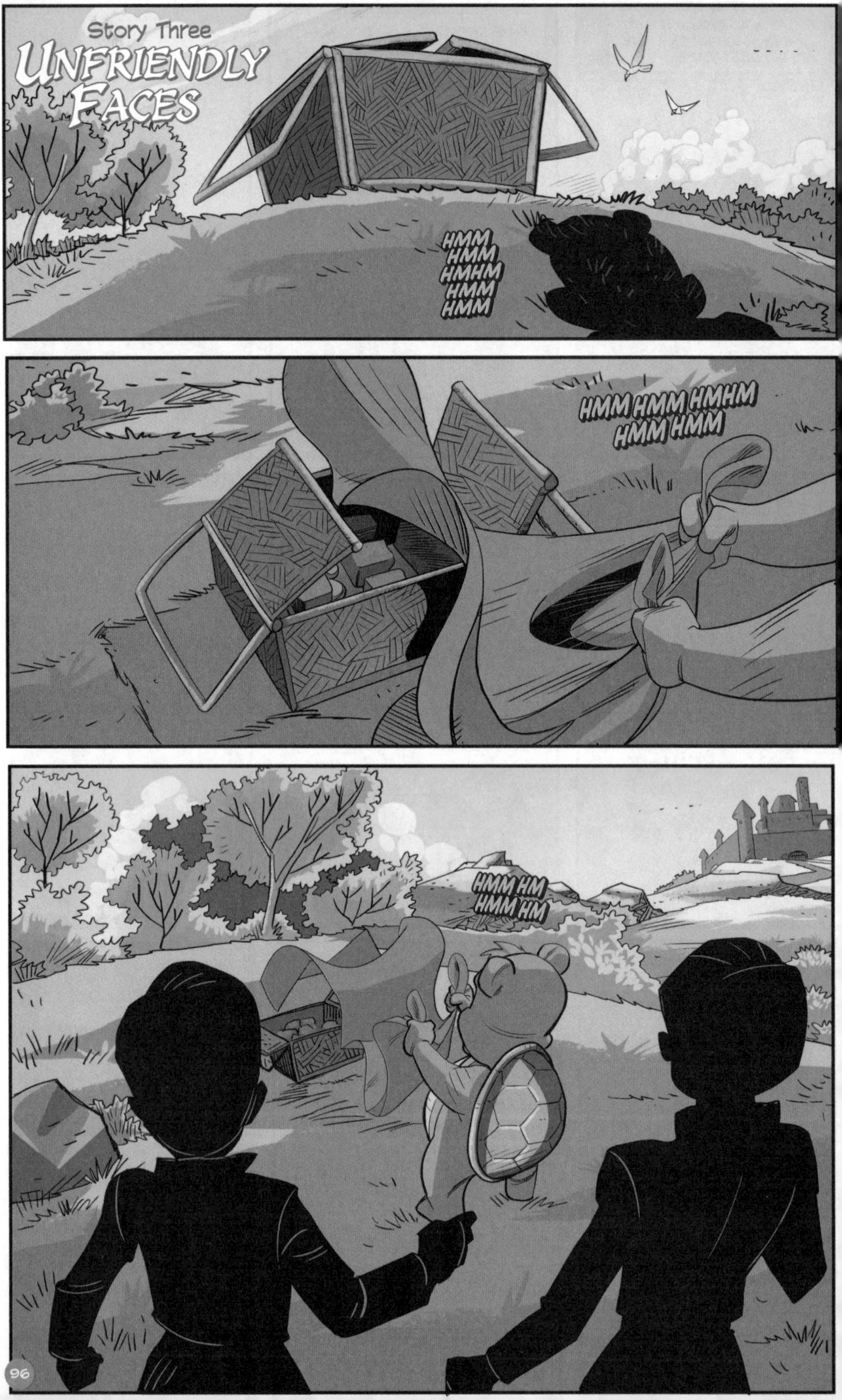
Story Three
UNFRIENDLY FACES
HMM HMM HMHM HMM HMM
HMM HMM HMHM HMM HMM
HMM HM HMM HM

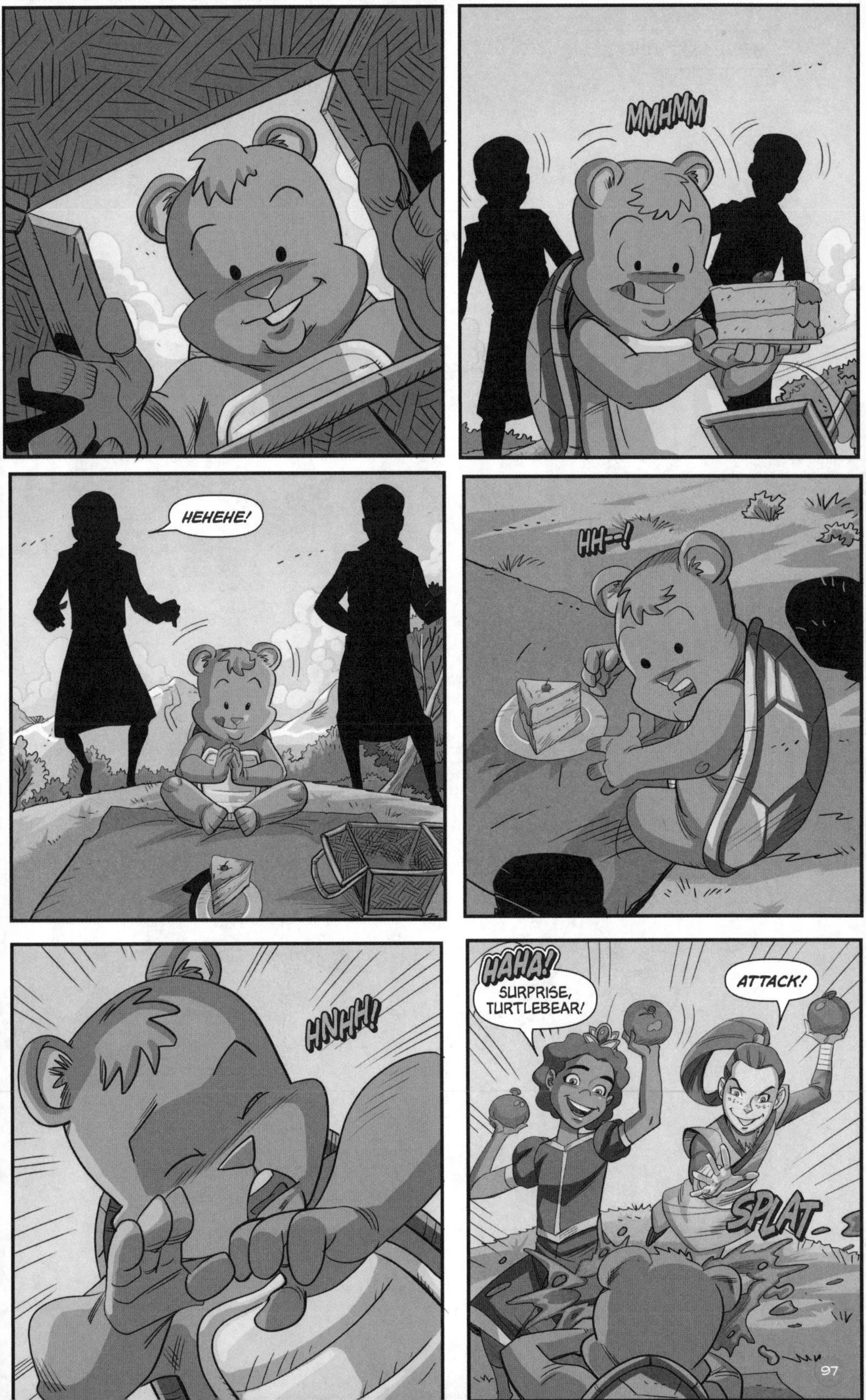
MMHMM
HEHEHE!
HH--!
HNHH!
HAHA!
SURPRISE, TURTLEBEAR!
ATTACK!
SPLAT

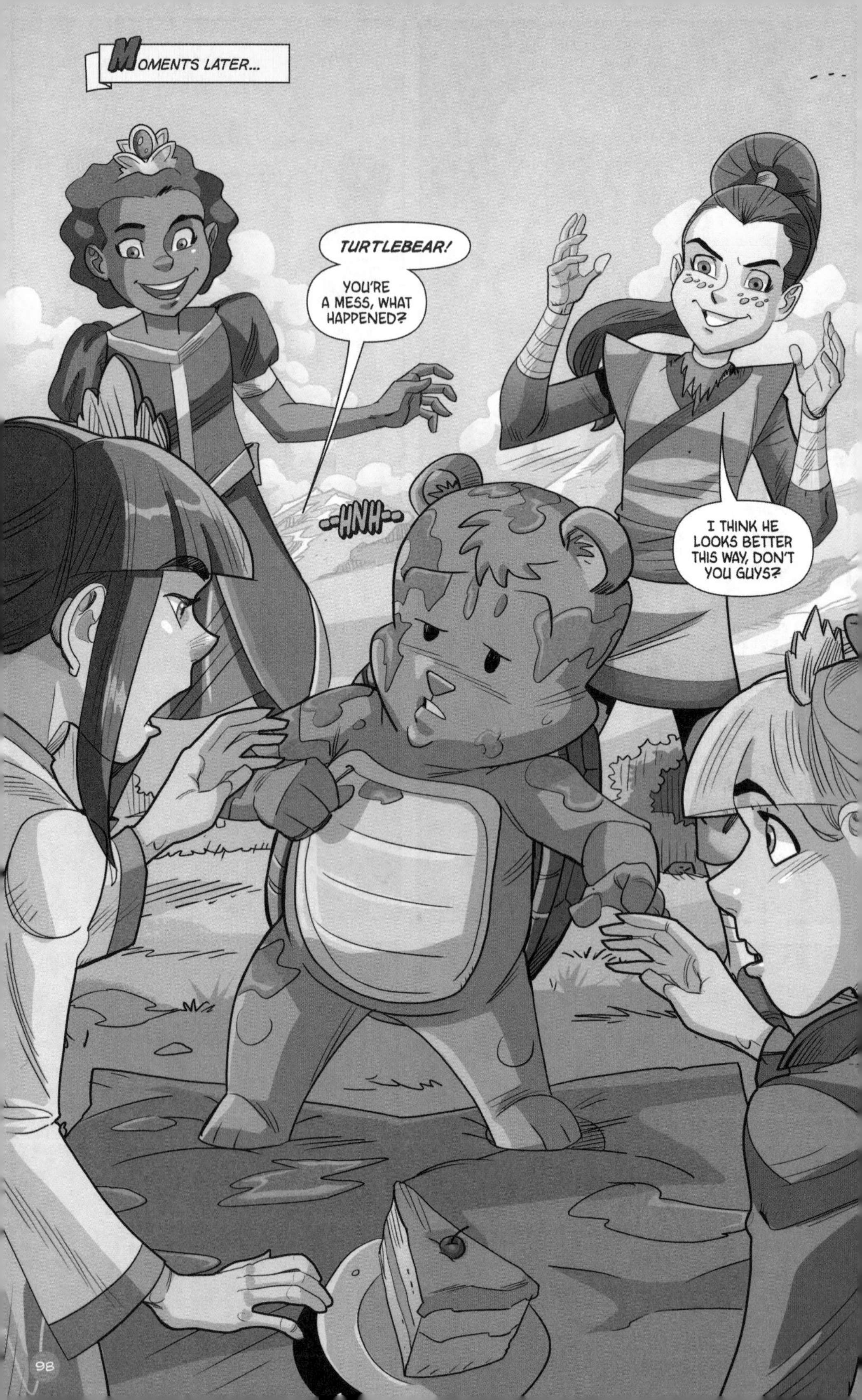
MOMENTS LATER...
TURTLEBEAR!
YOU'RE A MESS, WHAT HAPPENED?
-HNH-
I THINK HE LOOKS BETTER THIS WAY, DON'T YOU GUYS?

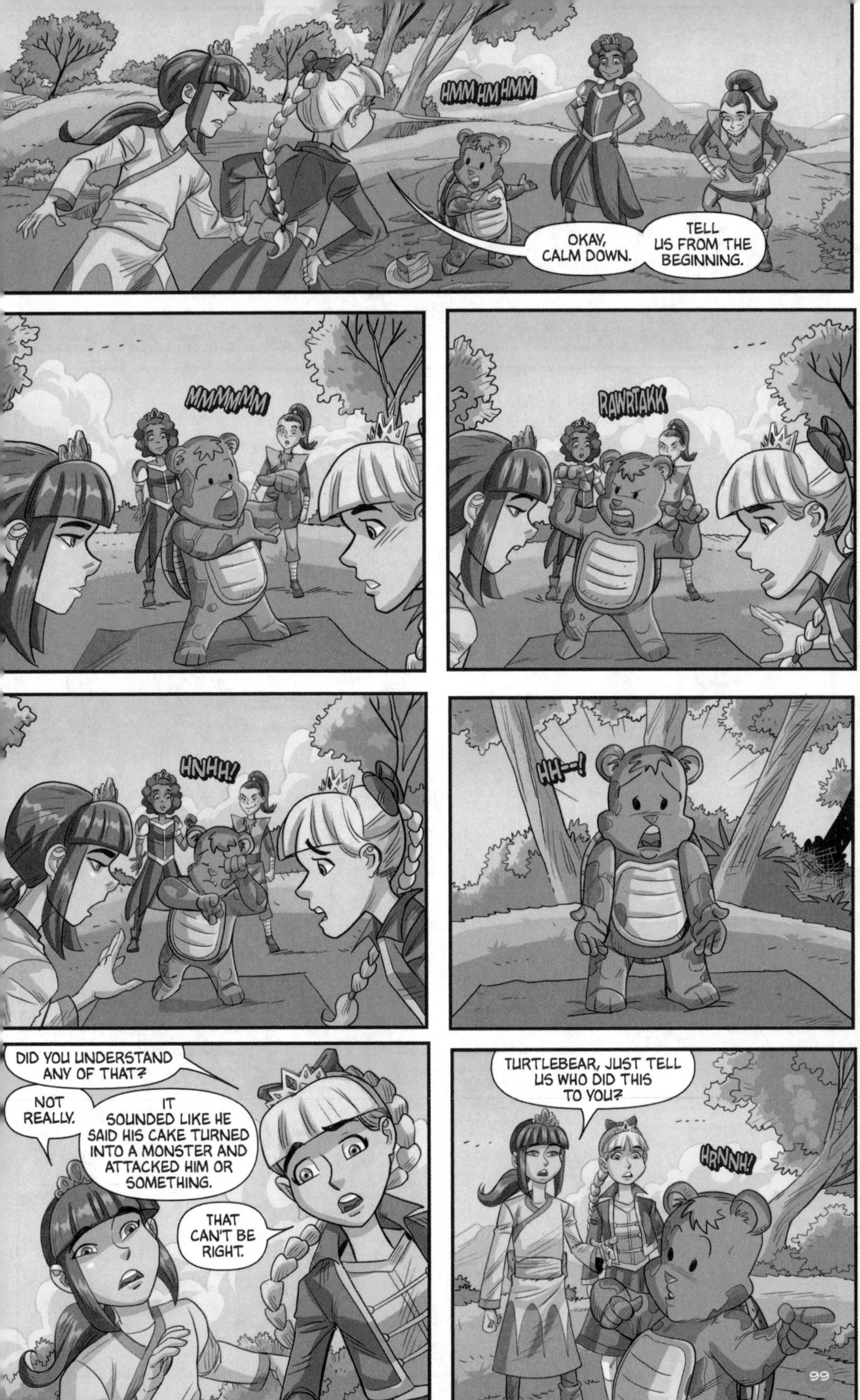

HMM HM HMM
OKAY, CALM DOWN.
TELL US FROM THE BEGINNING.
MMMMMM
RAWRTAKK
HNHH!
HH--!
DID YOU UNDERSTAND ANY OF THAT?
NOT REALLY.
IT SOUNDED LIKE HE SAID HIS CAKE TURNED INTO A MONSTER AND ATTACKED HIM OR SOMETHING.
THAT CAN'T BE RIGHT.
TURTLEBEAR, JUST TELL US WHO DID THIS TO YOU?
HRNNH!

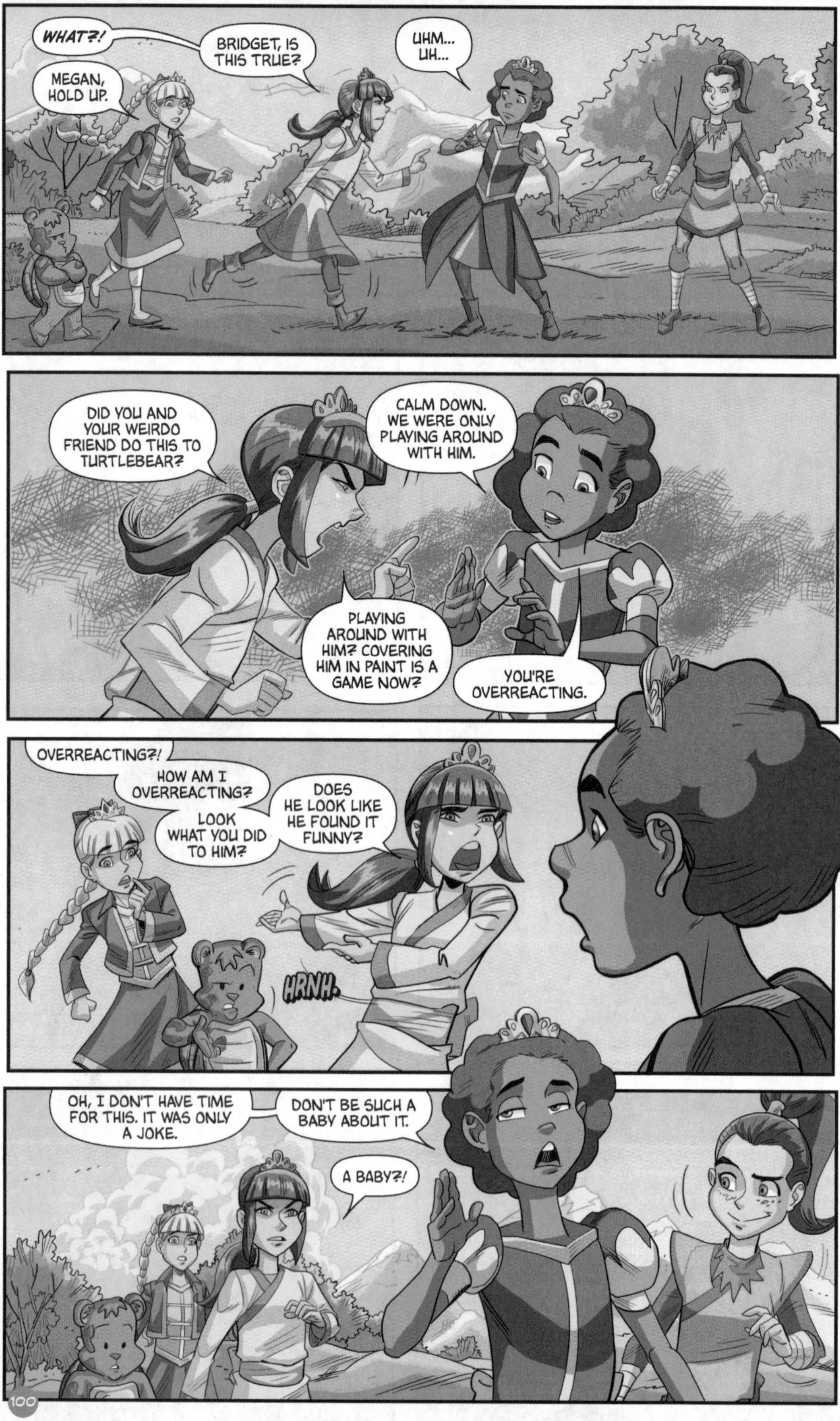
WHAT?!
MEGAN, HOLD UP.
BRIDGET, IS THIS TRUE?
UHM... UH...
DID YOU AND YOUR WEIRDO FRIEND DO THIS TO TURTLEBEAR?
CALM DOWN. WE WERE ONLY PLAYING AROUND WITH HIM.
PLAYING AROUND WITH HIM? COVERING HIM IN PAINT IS A GAME NOW?
YOU'RE OVERREACTING.
OVERREACTING?!
HOW AM I OVERREACTING?
LOOK WHAT YOU DID TO HIM?
DOES HE LOOK LIKE HE FOUND IT FUNNY?
HRNH!
OH, I DON'T HAVE TIME FOR THIS. IT WAS ONLY A JOKE.
DON'T BE SUCH A BABY ABOUT IT.
A BABY?!

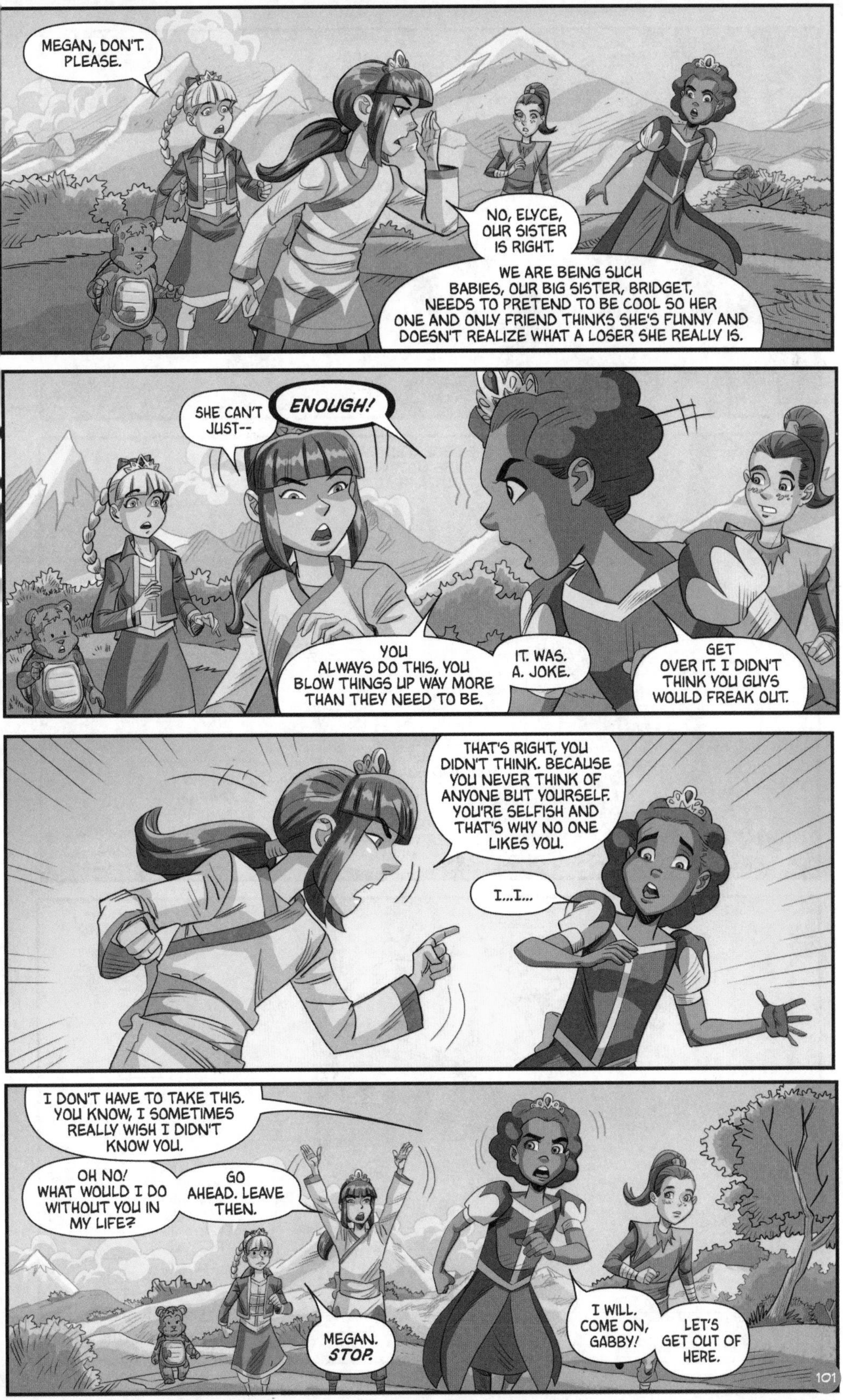
MEGAN, DON'T. PLEASE.
NO, ELYCE, OUR SISTER IS RIGHT.
WE ARE BEING SUCH BABIES, OUR BIG SISTER, BRIDGET, NEEDS TO PRETEND TO BE COOL SO HER ONE AND ONLY FRIEND THINKS SHE'S FUNNY AND DOESN'T REALIZE WHAT A LOSER SHE REALLY IS.
SHE CAN'T JUST--
ENOUGH!
YOU ALWAYS DO THIS, YOU BLOW THINGS UP WAY MORE THAN THEY NEED TO BE.
IT. WAS. A. JOKE.
GET OVER IT. I DIDN'T THINK YOU GUYS WOULD FREAK OUT.
THAT'S RIGHT, YOU DIDN'T THINK. BECAUSE YOU NEVER THINK OF ANYONE BUT YOURSELF. YOU'RE SELFISH AND THAT'S WHY NO ONE LIKES YOU.
I...I...
I DON'T HAVE TO TAKE THIS. YOU KNOW, I SOMETIMES REALLY WISH I DIDN'T KNOW YOU.
OH NO! WHAT WOULD I DO WITHOUT YOU IN MY LIFE?
GO AHEAD. LEAVE THEN.
MEGAN. STOP.
I WILL. COME ON, GABBY!
LET'S GET OUT OF HERE.

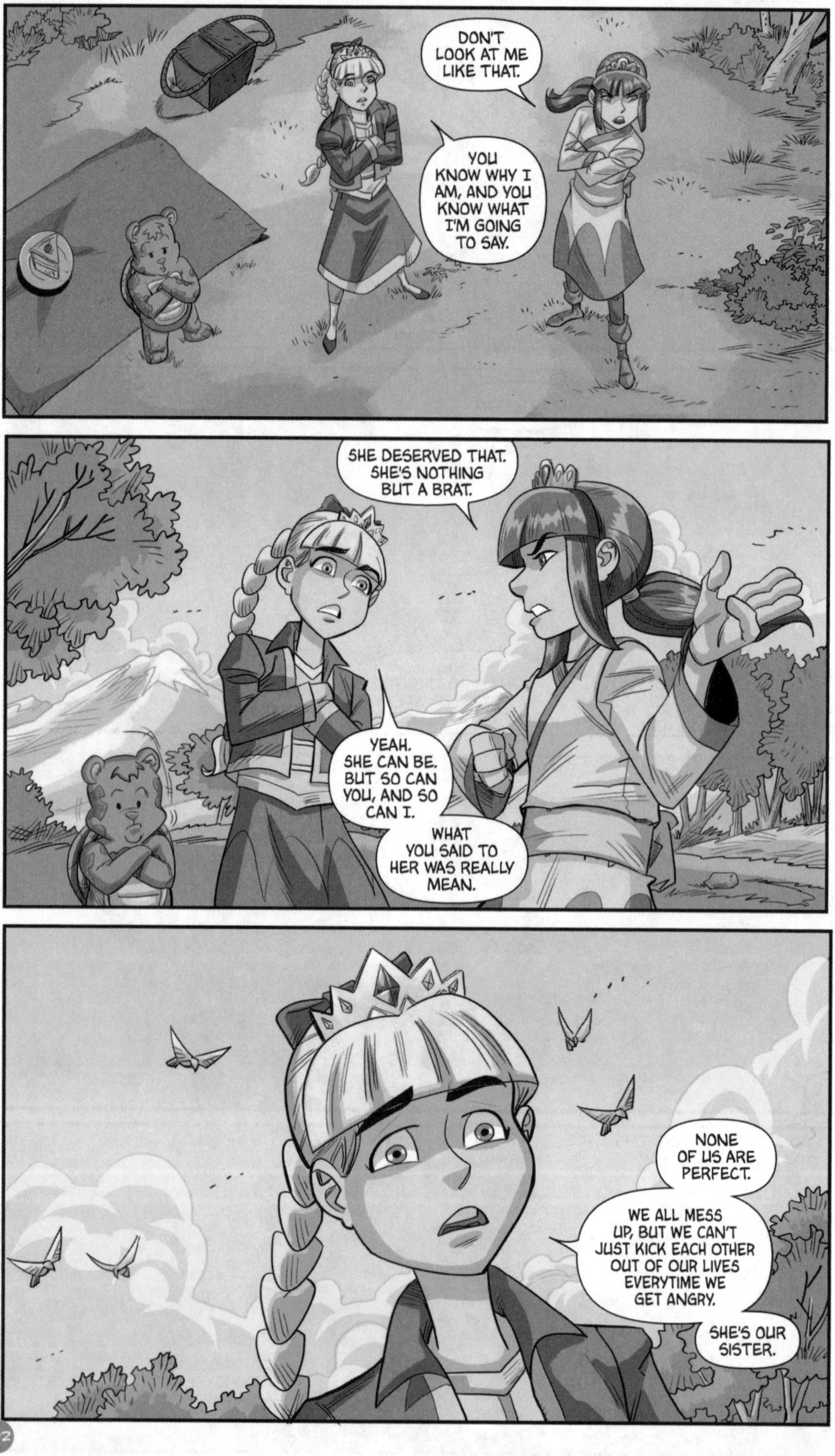
DON'T LOOK AT ME LIKE THAT.
YOU KNOW WHY I AM, AND YOU KNOW WHAT I'M GOING TO SAY.
SHE DESERVED THAT. SHE'S NOTHING BUT A BRAT.
YEAH. SHE CAN BE. BUT SO CAN YOU, AND SO CAN I.
WHAT YOU SAID TO HER WAS REALLY MEAN.
NONE OF US ARE PERFECT.
WE ALL MESS UP, BUT WE CAN'T JUST KICK EACH OTHER OUT OF OUR LIVES EVERYTIME WE GET ANGRY.
SHE'S OUR SISTER.

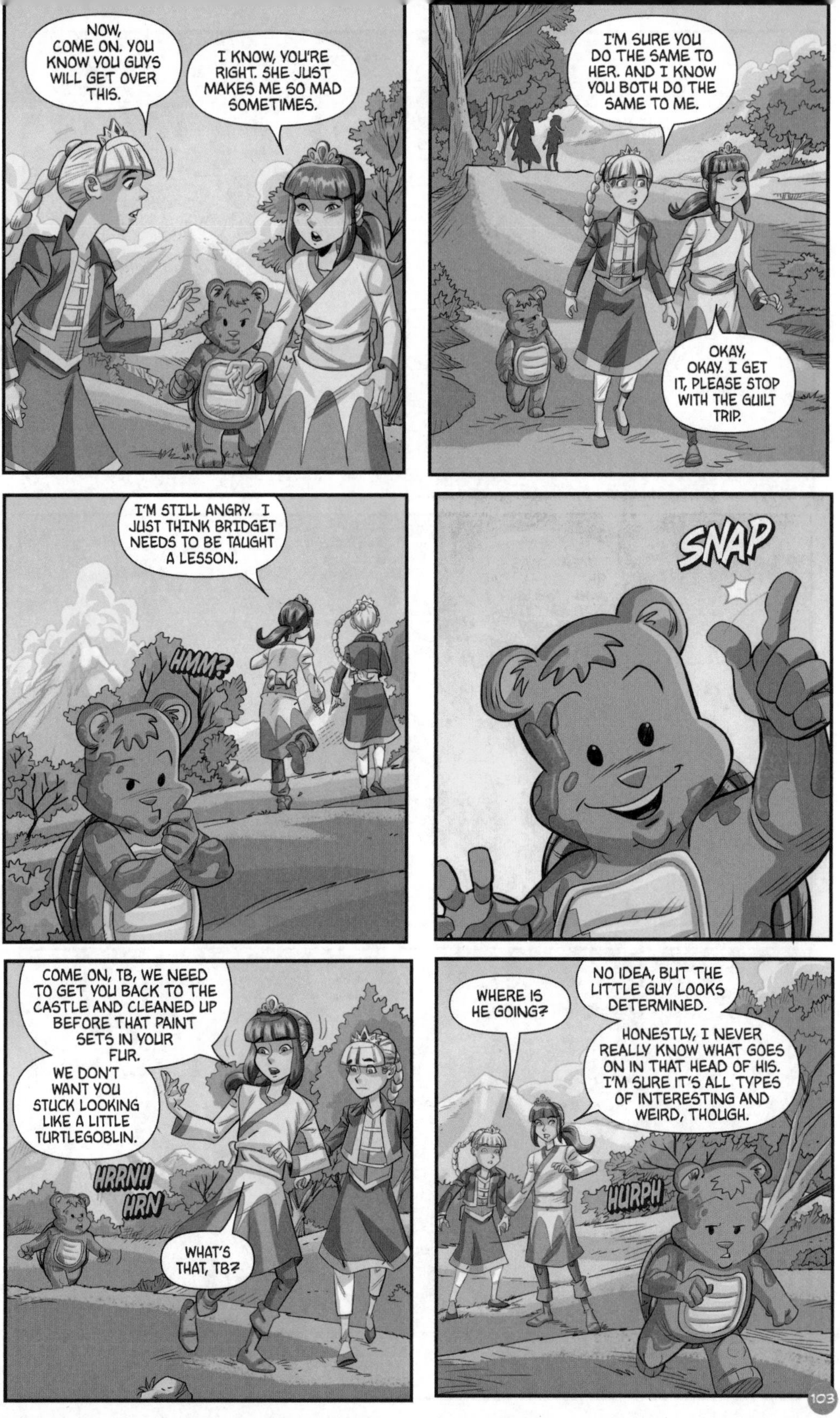
NOW, COME ON. YOU KNOW YOU GUYS WILL GET OVER THIS.
I KNOW, YOU'RE RIGHT. SHE JUST MAKES ME SO MAD SOMETIMES.
I'M SURE YOU DO THE SAME TO HER. AND I KNOW YOU BOTH DO THE SAME TO ME.
OKAY, OKAY. I GET IT, PLEASE STOP WITH THE GUILT TRIP.
I'M STILL ANGRY. I JUST THINK BRIDGET NEEDS TO BE TAUGHT A LESSON.
HMM?
SNAP
COME ON, TB, WE NEED TO GET YOU BACK TO THE CASTLE AND CLEANED UP BEFORE THAT PAINT SETS IN YOUR FUR.
WE DON'T WANT YOU STUCK LOOKING LIKE A LITTLE TURTLEGOBLIN.
HRRNH HRN
WHAT'S THAT, TB?
WHERE IS HE GOING?
NO IDEA, BUT THE LITTLE GUY LOOKS DETERMINED.
HONESTLY, I NEVER REALLY KNOW WHAT GOES ON IN THAT HEAD OF HIS. I'M SURE IT'S ALL TYPES OF INTERESTING AND WEIRD, THOUGH.
HURPH

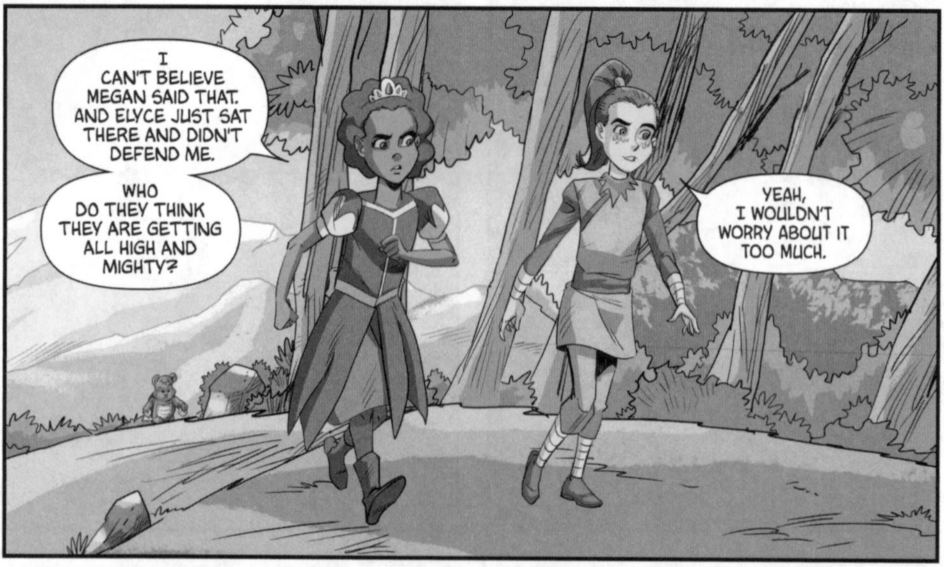
I CAN'T BELIEVE MEGAN SAID THAT. AND ELYCE JUST SAT THERE AND DIDN'T DEFEND ME.
WHO DO THEY THINK THEY ARE GETTING ALL HIGH AND MIGHTY?
YEAH, I WOULDN'T WORRY ABOUT IT TOO MUCH.

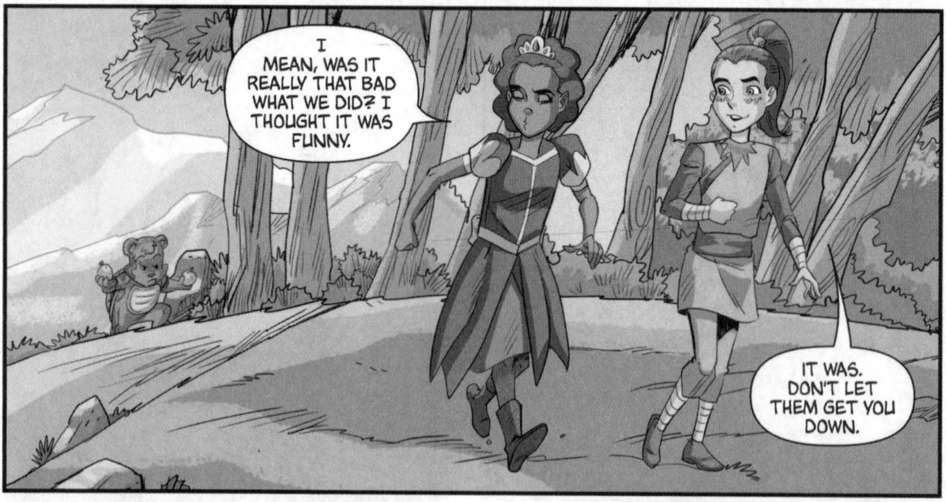
I MEAN, WAS IT REALLY THAT BAD WHAT WE DID? I THOUGHT IT WAS FUNNY.
IT WAS. DON'T LET THEM GET YOU DOWN.

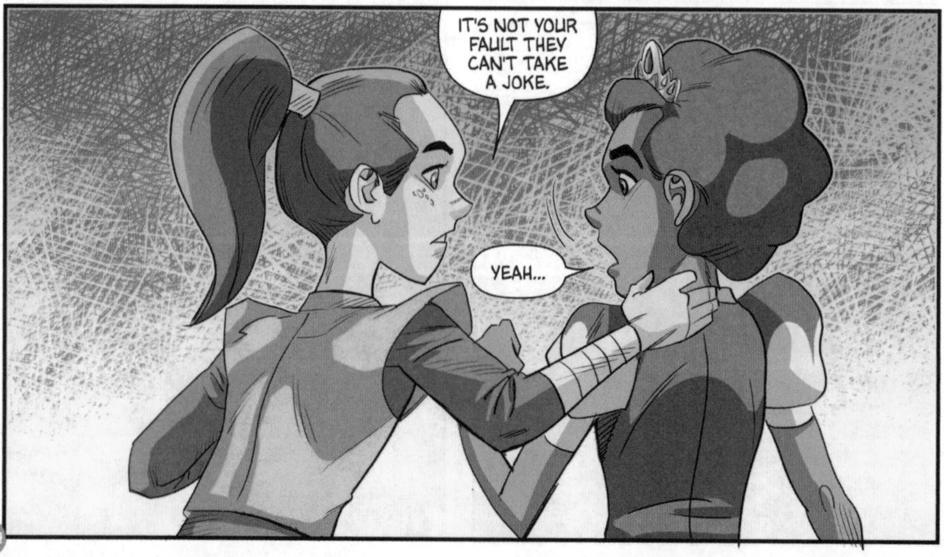
IT'S NOT YOUR FAULT THEY CAN'T TAKE A JOKE.
YEAH...

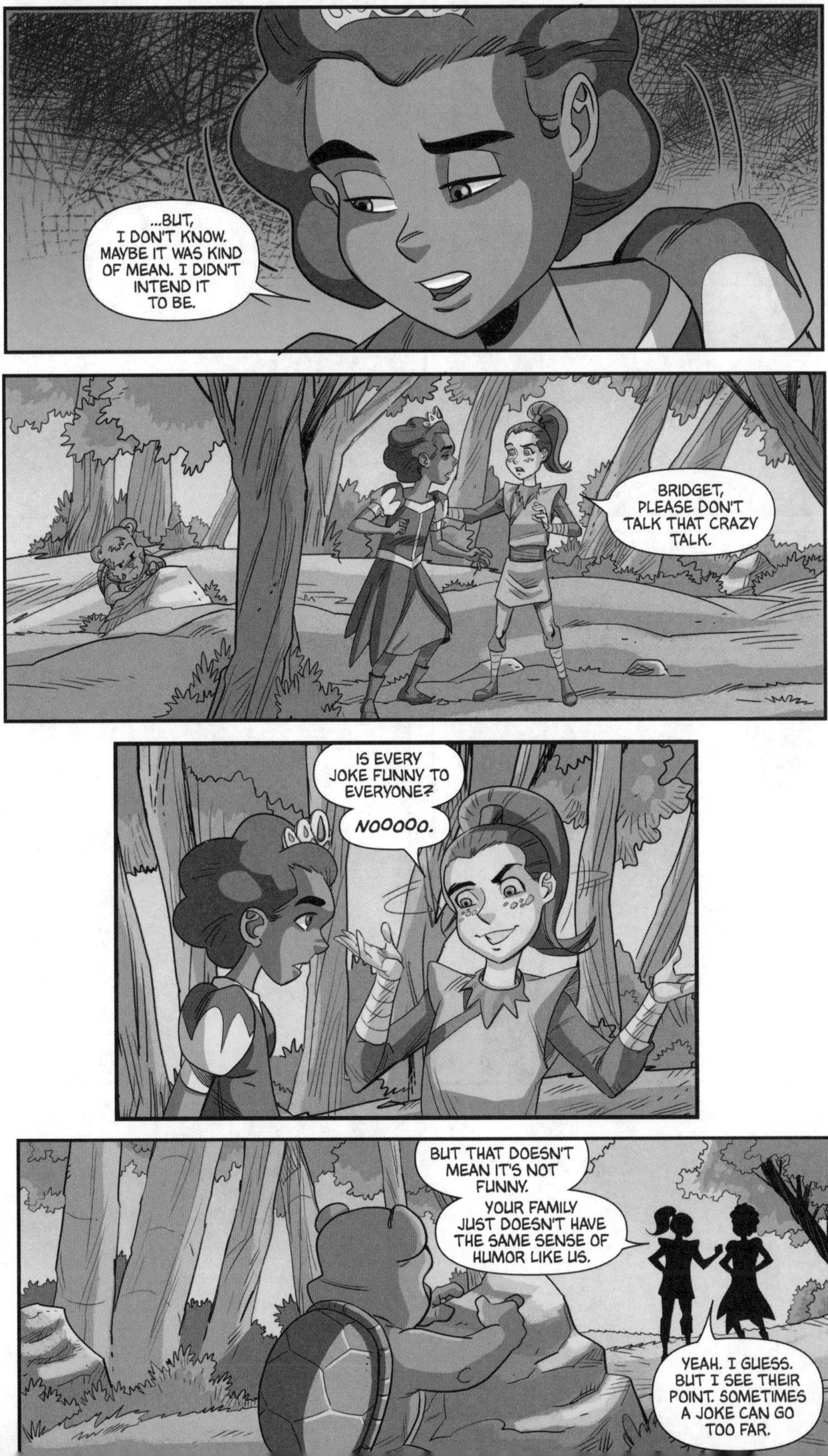
...BUT, I DON'T KNOW. MAYBE IT WAS KIND OF MEAN. I DIDN'T INTEND IT TO BE.
BRIDGET, PLEASE DON'T TALK THAT CRAZY TALK.
IS EVERY JOKE FUNNY TO EVERYONE?
NOOOOO.
BUT THAT DOESN'T MEAN IT'S NOT FUNNY.
YOUR FAMILY JUST DOESN'T HAVE THE SAME SENSE OF HUMOR LIKE US.
YEAH. I GUESS. BUT I SEE THEIR POINT. SOMETIMES A JOKE CAN GO TOO FAR.

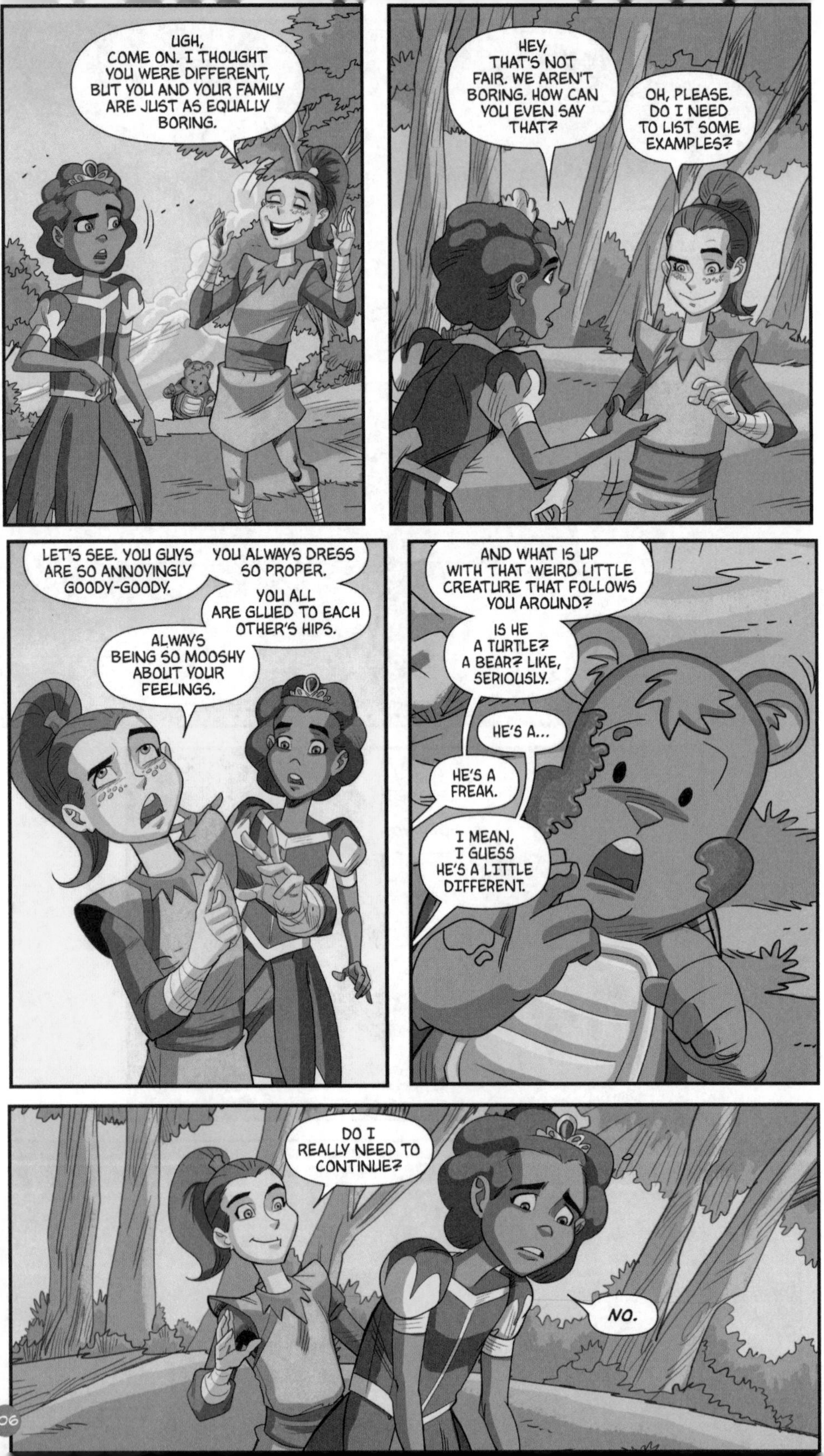
UGH, COME ON. I THOUGHT YOU WERE DIFFERENT, BUT YOU AND YOUR FAMILY ARE JUST AS EQUALLY BORING.
HEY, THAT'S NOT FAIR. WE AREN'T BORING. HOW CAN YOU EVEN SAY THAT?
OH, PLEASE. DO I NEED TO LIST SOME EXAMPLES?
LET'S SEE. YOU GUYS ARE SO ANNOYINGLY GOODY-GOODY.
YOU ALWAYS DRESS SO PROPER.
YOU ALL ARE GLUED TO EACH OTHER'S HIPS.
ALWAYS BEING SO MOOSHY ABOUT YOUR FEELINGS.
AND WHAT IS UP WITH THAT WEIRD LITTLE CREATURE THAT FOLLOWS YOU AROUND?
IS HE A TURTLE? A BEAR? LIKE, SERIOUSLY.
HE'S A...
HE'S A FREAK.
I MEAN, I GUESS HE'S A LITTLE DIFFERENT.
DO I REALLY NEED TO CONTINUE?
NO.

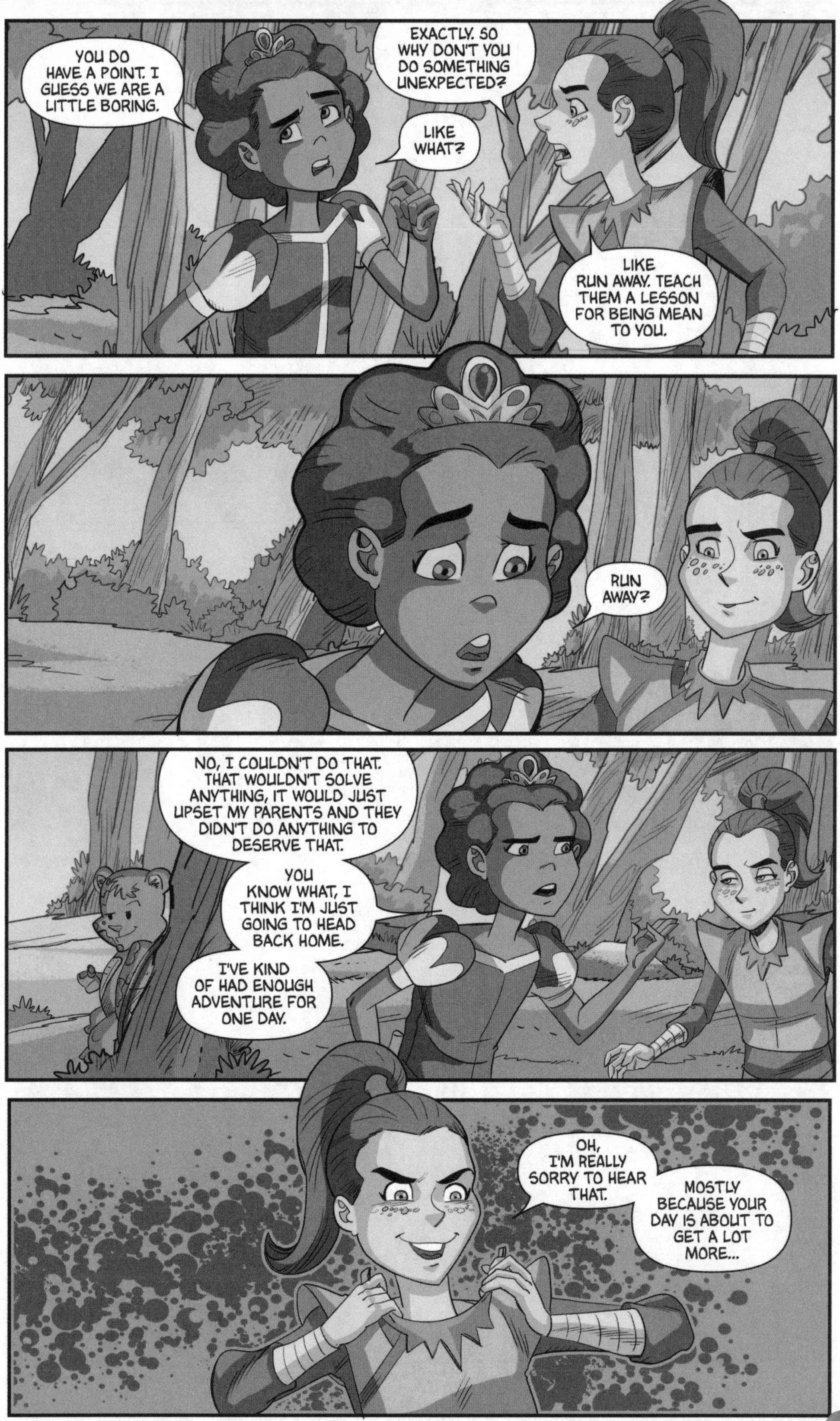
YOU DO HAVE A POINT. I GUESS WE ARE A LITTLE BORING.
EXACTLY. SO WHY DON'T YOU DO SOMETHING UNEXPECTED?
LIKE WHAT?
LIKE RUN AWAY. TEACH THEM A LESSON FOR BEING MEAN TO YOU.
RUN AWAY?
NO, I COULDN'T DO THAT. THAT WOULDN'T SOLVE ANYTHING, IT WOULD JUST UPSET MY PARENTS AND THEY DIDN'T DO ANYTHING TO DESERVE THAT.
YOU KNOW WHAT, I THINK I'M JUST GOING TO HEAD BACK HOME.
I'VE KIND OF HAD ENOUGH ADVENTURE FOR ONE DAY.
OH, I'M REALLY SORRY TO HEAR THAT.
MOSTLY BECAUSE YOUR DAY IS ABOUT TO GET A LOT MORE...

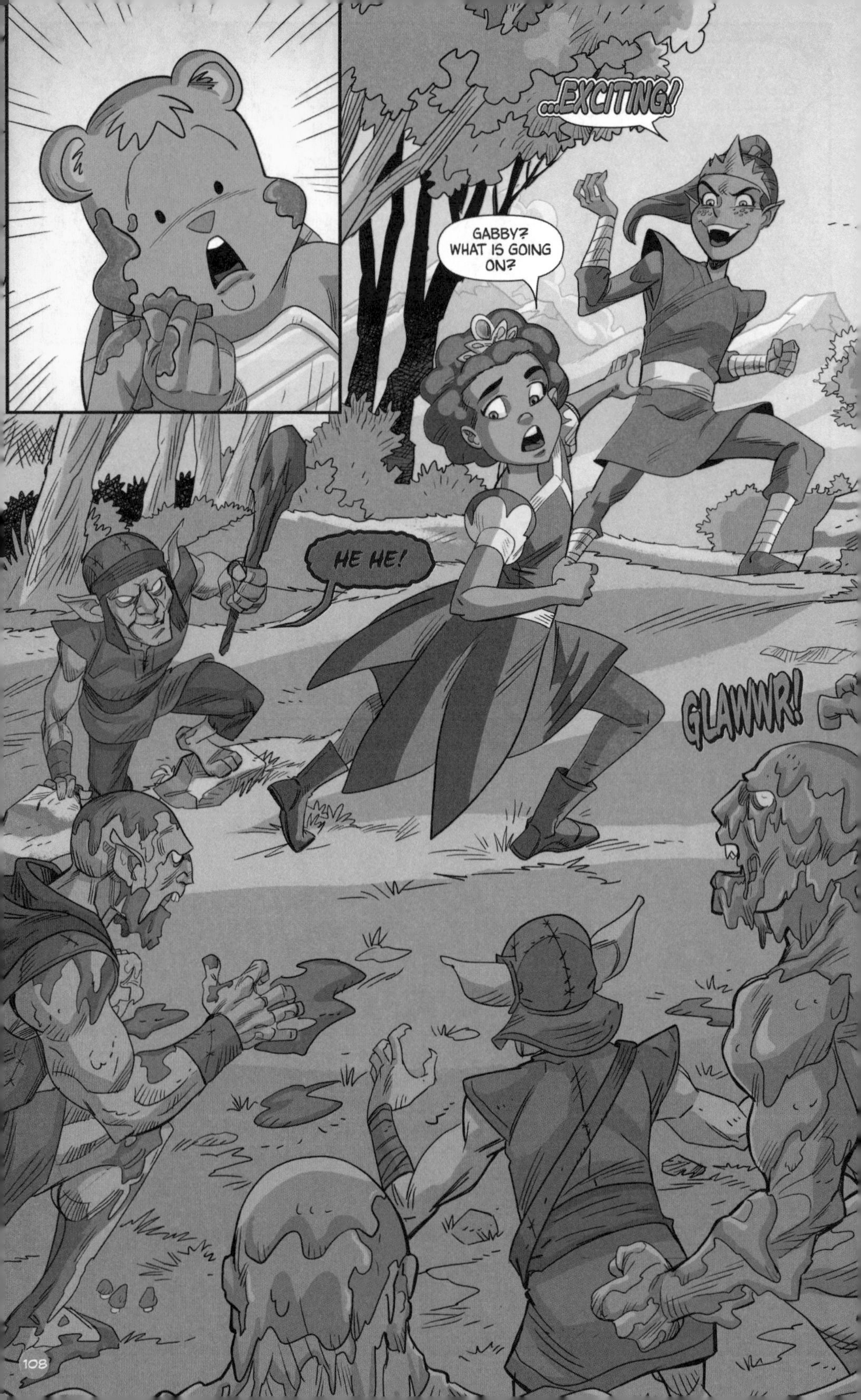
...EXCITING!
GABBY? WHAT IS GOING ON?
HE HE!
GLAWWR!

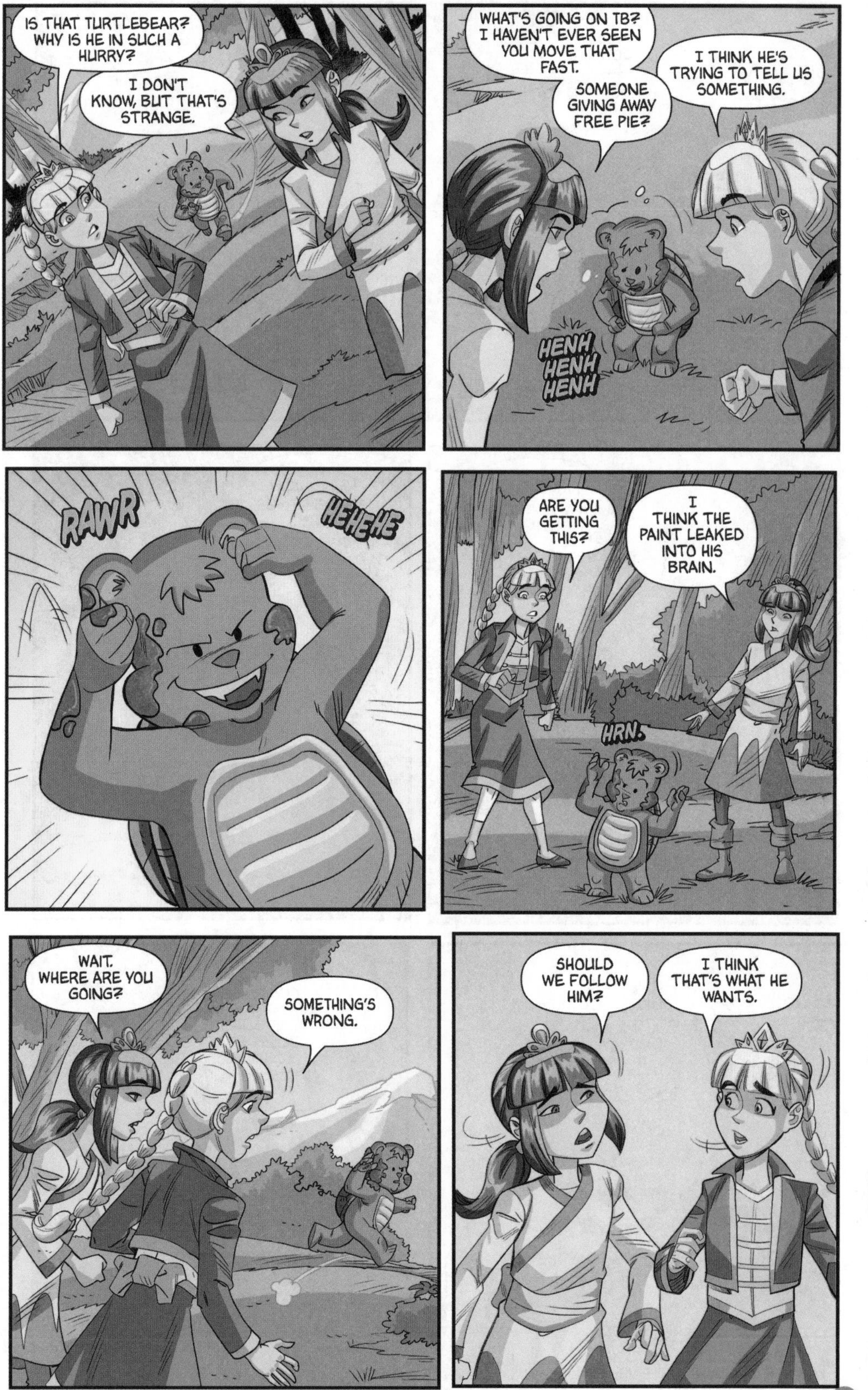
IS THAT TURTLEBEAR? WHY IS HE IN SUCH A HURRY?
I DON'T KNOW, BUT THAT'S STRANGE.
WHAT'S GOING ON TB? I HAVEN'T EVER SEEN YOU MOVE THAT FAST.
SOMEONE GIVING AWAY FREE PIE?
I THINK HE'S TRYING TO TELL US SOMETHING.
HENH HENH HENH
RAWR
HEHEHE
ARE YOU GETTING THIS?
I THINK THE PAINT LEAKED INTO HIS BRAIN.
HRN.
WAIT. WHERE ARE YOU GOING?
SOMETHING'S WRONG.
SHOULD WE FOLLOW HIM?
I THINK THAT'S WHAT HE WANTS.

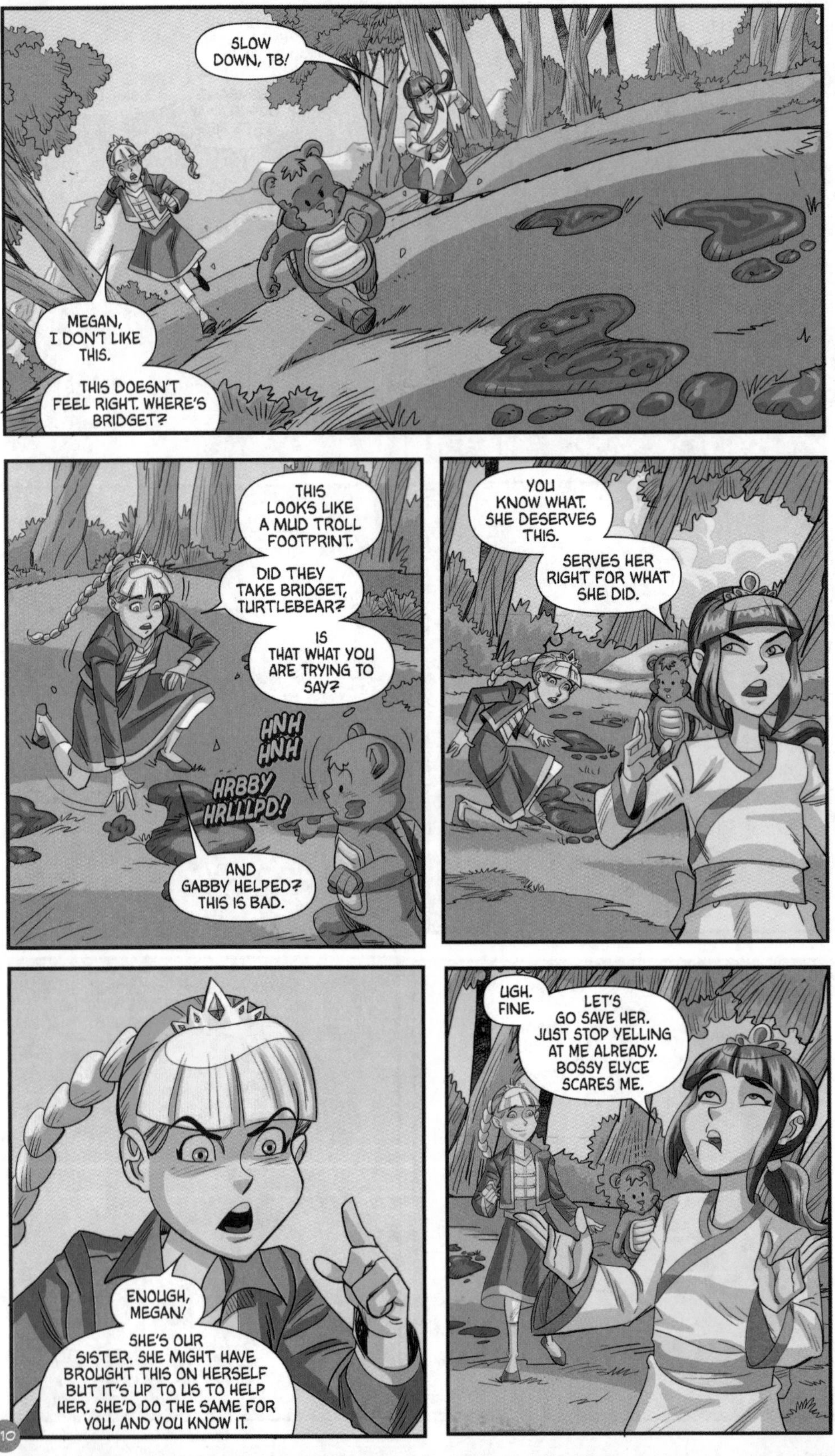
SLOW DOWN, TB!
MEGAN, I DON'T LIKE THIS.
THIS DOESN'T FEEL RIGHT. WHERE'S BRIDGET?
THIS LOOKS LIKE A MUD TROLL FOOTPRINT.
DID THEY TAKE BRIDGET, TURTLEBEAR?
IS THAT WHAT YOU ARE TRYING TO SAY?
HNH HNH
HRBBY HRLLLPD!
AND GABBY HELPED? THIS IS BAD.
YOU KNOW WHAT. SHE DESERVES THIS.
SERVES HER RIGHT FOR WHAT SHE DID.
ENOUGH, MEGAN!
SHE'S OUR SISTER. SHE MIGHT HAVE BROUGHT THIS ON HERSELF BUT IT'S UP TO US TO HELP HER. SHE'D DO THE SAME FOR YOU, AND YOU KNOW IT.
UGH. FINE.
LET'S GO SAVE HER. JUST STOP YELLING AT ME ALREADY. BOSSY ELYCE SCARES ME.

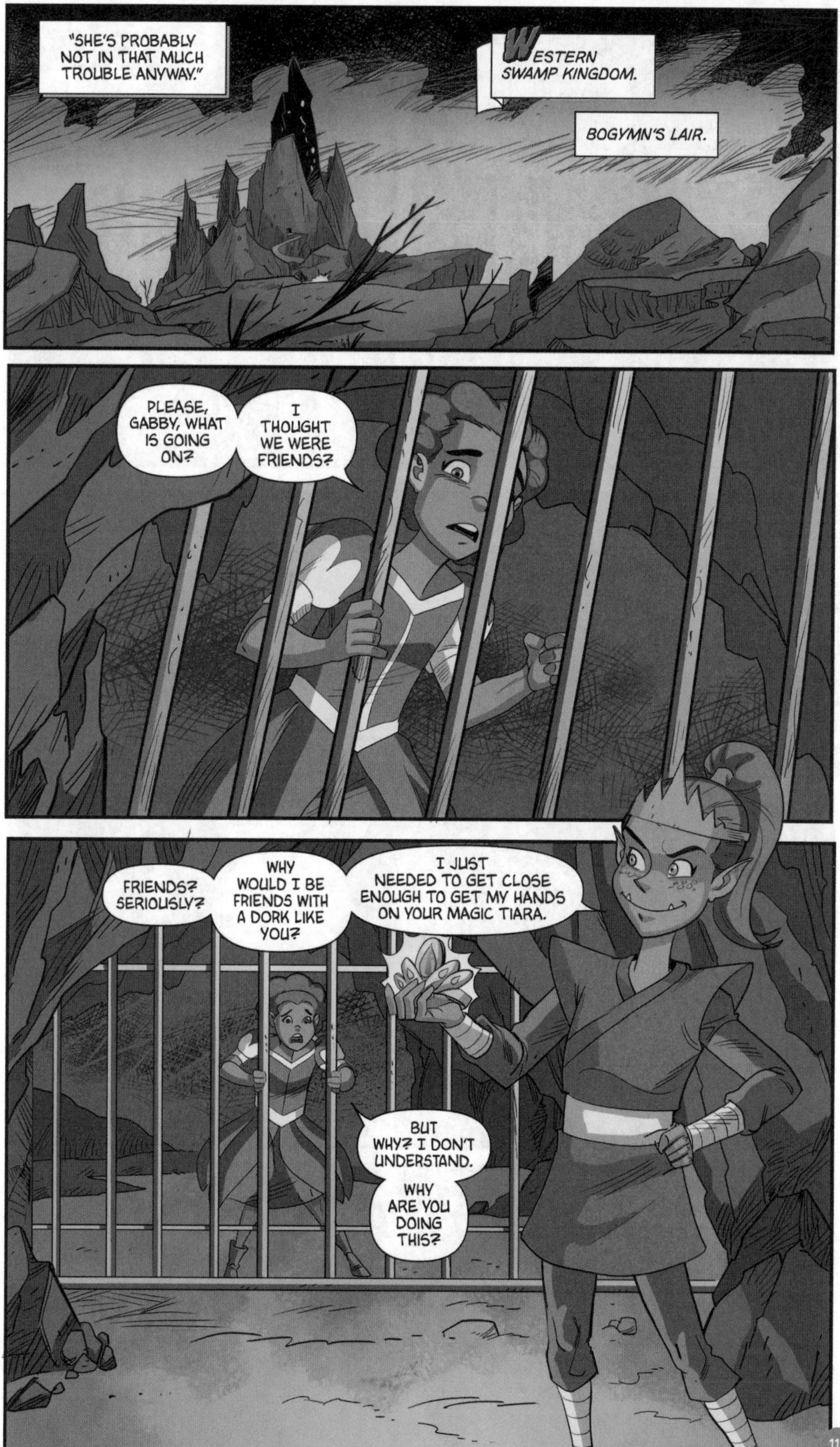
"SHE'S PROBABLY NOT IN THAT MUCH TROUBLE ANYWAY."
WESTERN SWAMP KINGDOM.
BOGYMN'S LAIR.
PLEASE, GABBY, WHAT IS GOING ON?
I THOUGHT WE WERE FRIENDS?
FRIENDS? SERIOUSLY?
WHY WOULD I BE FRIENDS WITH A DORK LIKE YOU?
I JUST NEEDED TO GET CLOSE ENOUGH TO GET MY HANDS ON YOUR MAGIC TIARA.
BUT WHY? I DON'T UNDERSTAND.
WHY ARE YOU DOING THIS?

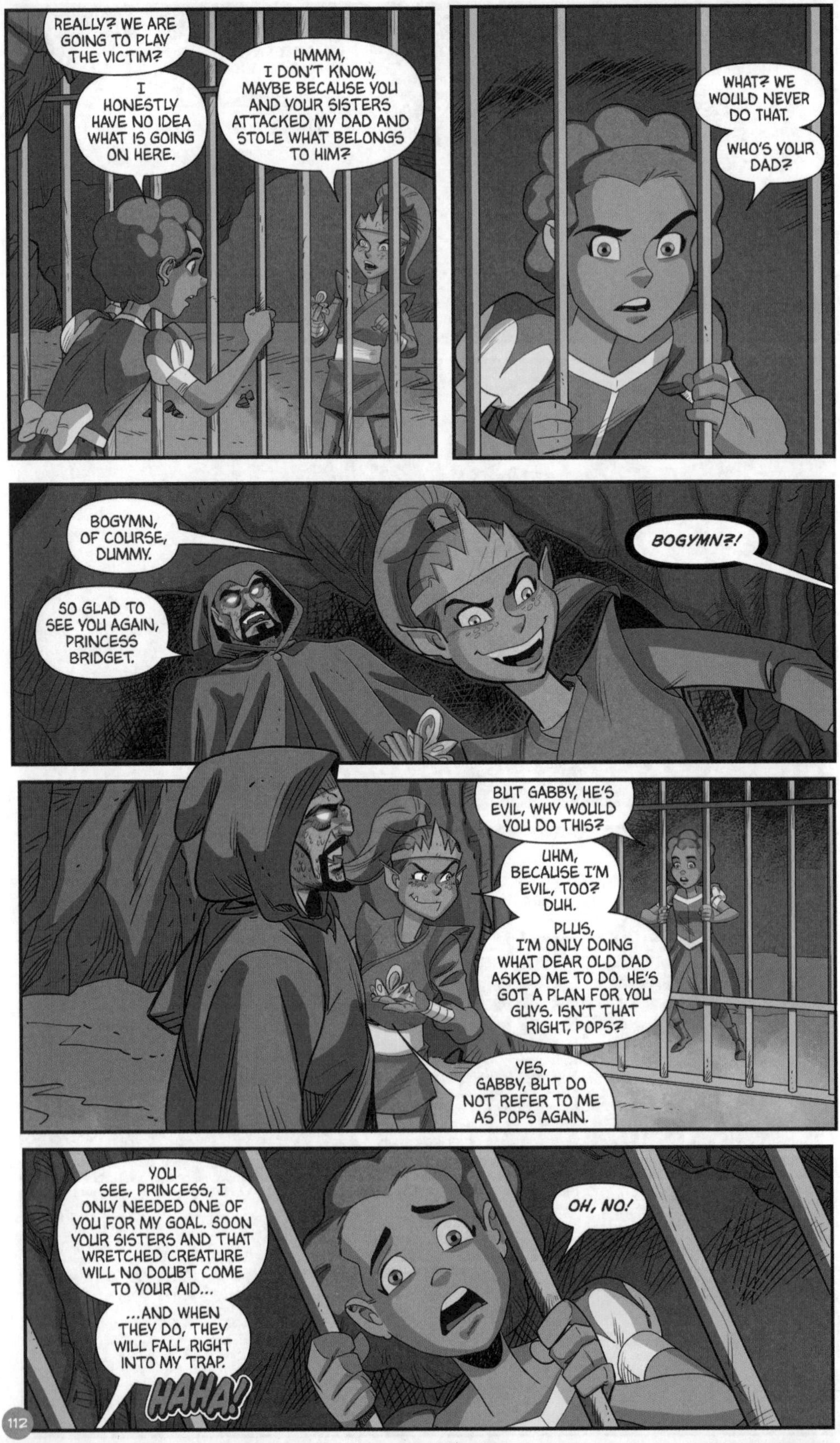
REALLY? WE ARE GOING TO PLAY THE VICTIM?
I HONESTLY HAVE NO IDEA WHAT IS GOING ON HERE.
HMMM, I DON'T KNOW, MAYBE BECAUSE YOU AND YOUR SISTERS ATTACKED MY DAD AND STOLE WHAT BELONGS TO HIM?
WHAT? WE WOULD NEVER DO THAT.
WHO'S YOUR DAD?
BOGYMN, OF COURSE, DUMMY.
SO GLAD TO SEE YOU AGAIN, PRINCESS BRIDGET.
BOGYMN?!
BUT GABBY, HE'S EVIL, WHY WOULD YOU DO THIS?
UHM, BECAUSE I'M EVIL, TOO? DUH.
PLUS, I'M ONLY DOING WHAT DEAR OLD DAD ASKED ME TO DO. HE'S GOT A PLAN FOR YOU GUYS. ISN'T THAT RIGHT, POPS?
YES, GABBY, BUT DO NOT REFER TO ME AS POPS AGAIN.
YOU SEE, PRINCESS, I ONLY NEEDED ONE OF YOU FOR MY GOAL. SOON YOUR SISTERS AND THAT WRETCHED CREATURE WILL NO DOUBT COME TO YOUR AID...
...AND WHEN THEY DO, THEY WILL FALL RIGHT INTO MY TRAP.
HAHA!
OH, NO!

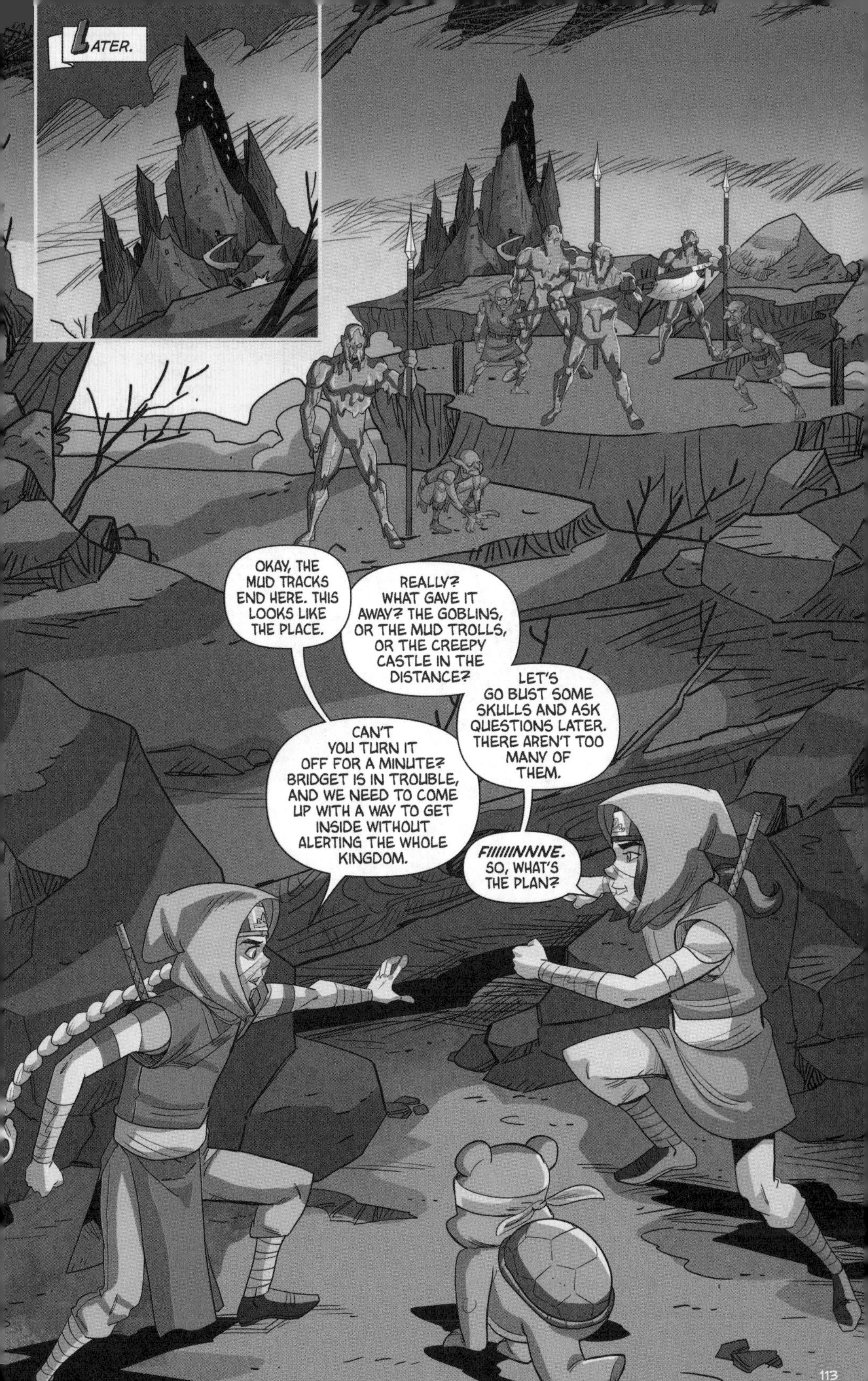
LATER.
OKAY, THE MUD TRACKS END HERE. THIS LOOKS LIKE THE PLACE.
REALLY? WHAT GAVE IT AWAY? THE GOBLINS, OR THE MUD TROLLS, OR THE CREEPY CASTLE IN THE DISTANCE?
LET'S GO BUST SOME SKULLS AND ASK QUESTIONS LATER. THERE AREN'T TOO MANY OF THEM.
CAN'T YOU TURN IT OFF FOR A MINUTE? BRIDGET IS IN TROUBLE, AND WE NEED TO COME UP WITH A WAY TO GET INSIDE WITHOUT ALERTING THE WHOLE KINGDOM.
FIIIIIINNNE. SO, WHAT'S THE PLAN?

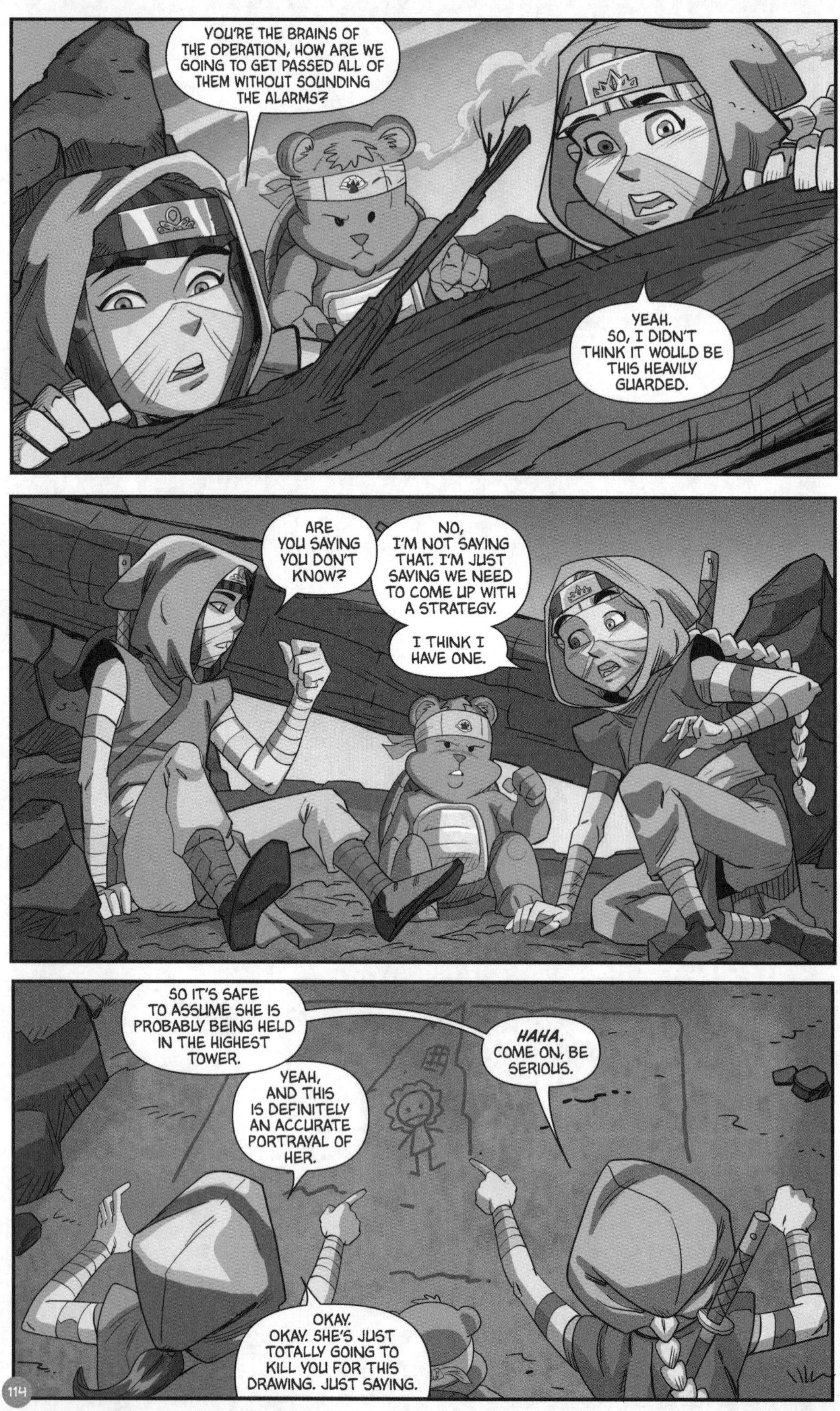
YOU'RE THE BRAINS OF THE OPERATION, HOW ARE WE GOING TO GET PASSED ALL OF THEM WITHOUT SOUNDING THE ALARMS?
YEAH. SO, I DIDN'T THINK IT WOULD BE THIS HEAVILY GUARDED.
ARE YOU SAYING YOU DON'T KNOW?
NO, I'M NOT SAYING THAT. I'M JUST SAYING WE NEED TO COME UP WITH A STRATEGY.
I THINK I HAVE ONE.
SO IT'S SAFE TO ASSUME SHE IS PROBABLY BEING HELD IN THE HIGHEST TOWER.
YEAH, AND THIS IS DEFINITELY AN ACCURATE PORTRAYAL OF HER.
HAHA. COME ON, BE SERIOUS.
OKAY. OKAY. SHE'S JUST TOTALLY GOING TO KILL YOU FOR THIS DRAWING. JUST SAYING.

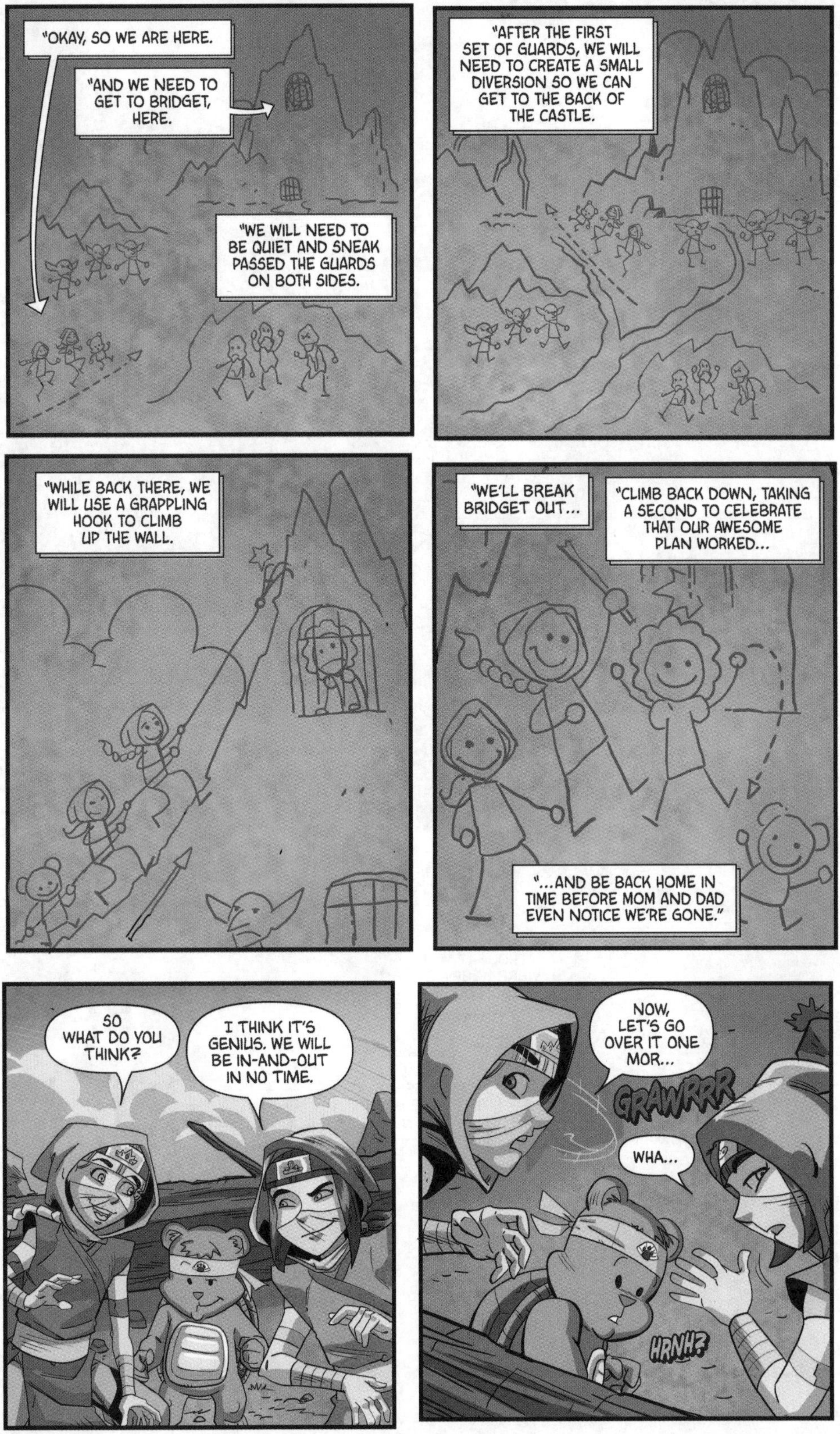
"OKAY, SO WE ARE HERE.
"AND WE NEED TO GET TO BRIDGET, HERE.
"WE WILL NEED TO BE QUIET AND SNEAK PASSED THE GUARDS ON BOTH SIDES.
"AFTER THE FIRST SET OF GUARDS, WE WILL NEED TO CREATE A SMALL DIVERSION SO WE CAN GET TO THE BACK OF THE CASTLE.
"WHILE BACK THERE, WE WILL USE A GRAPPLING HOOK TO CLIMB UP THE WALL.
"WE'LL BREAK BRIDGET OUT...
"CLIMB BACK DOWN, TAKING A SECOND TO CELEBRATE THAT OUR AWESOME PLAN WORKED...
"...AND BE BACK HOME IN TIME BEFORE MOM AND DAD EVEN NOTICE WE'RE GONE."
SO WHAT DO YOU THINK?
I THINK IT'S GENIUS. WE WILL BE IN-AND-OUT IN NO TIME.
NOW, LET'S GO OVER IT ONE MOR...
GRAWRRR
WHA...
HRNH?

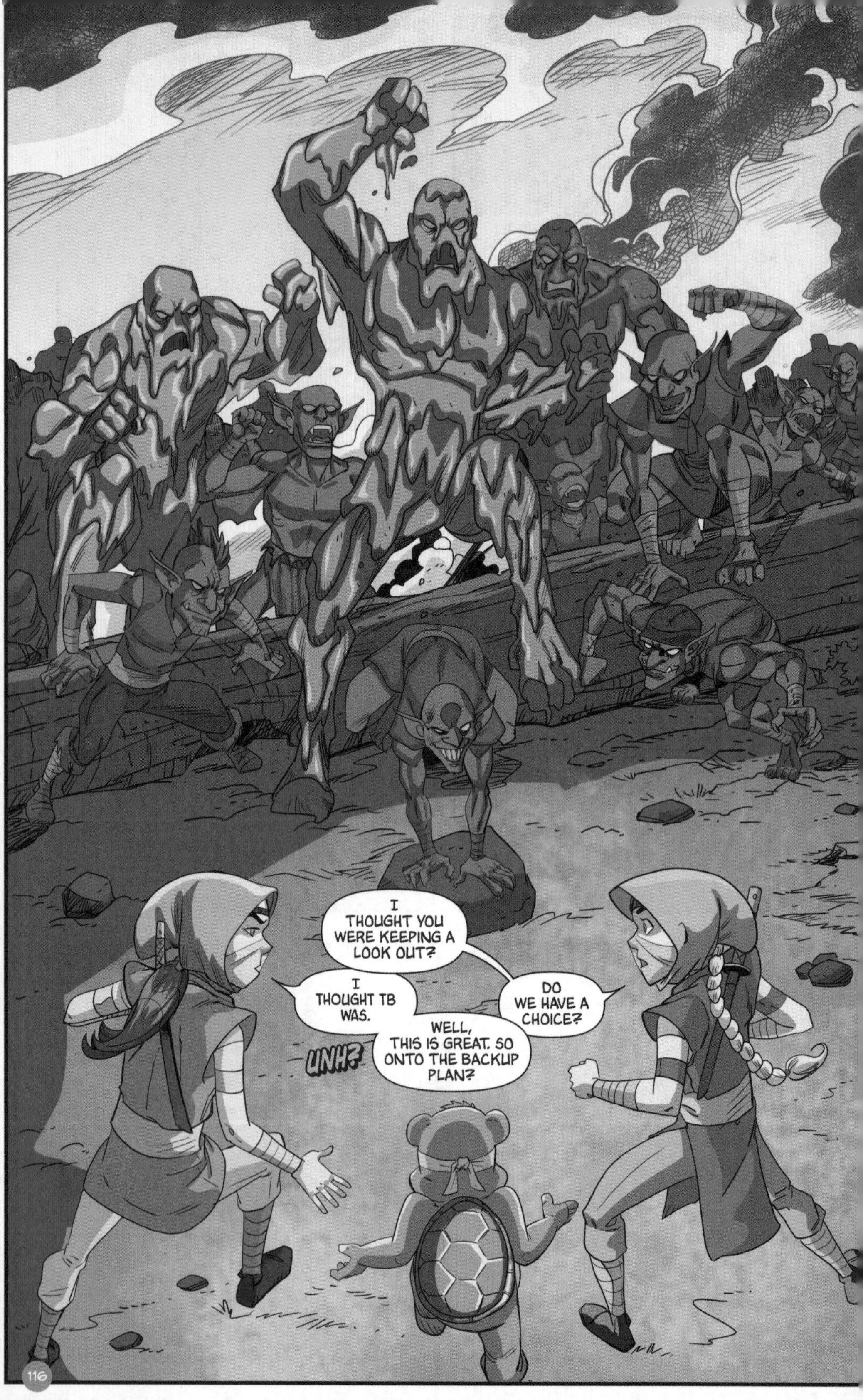
I THOUGHT YOU WERE KEEPING A LOOK OUT?
I THOUGHT TB WAS.
DO WE HAVE A CHOICE?
WELL, THIS IS GREAT. SO ONTO THE BACKUP PLAN?
UNH?

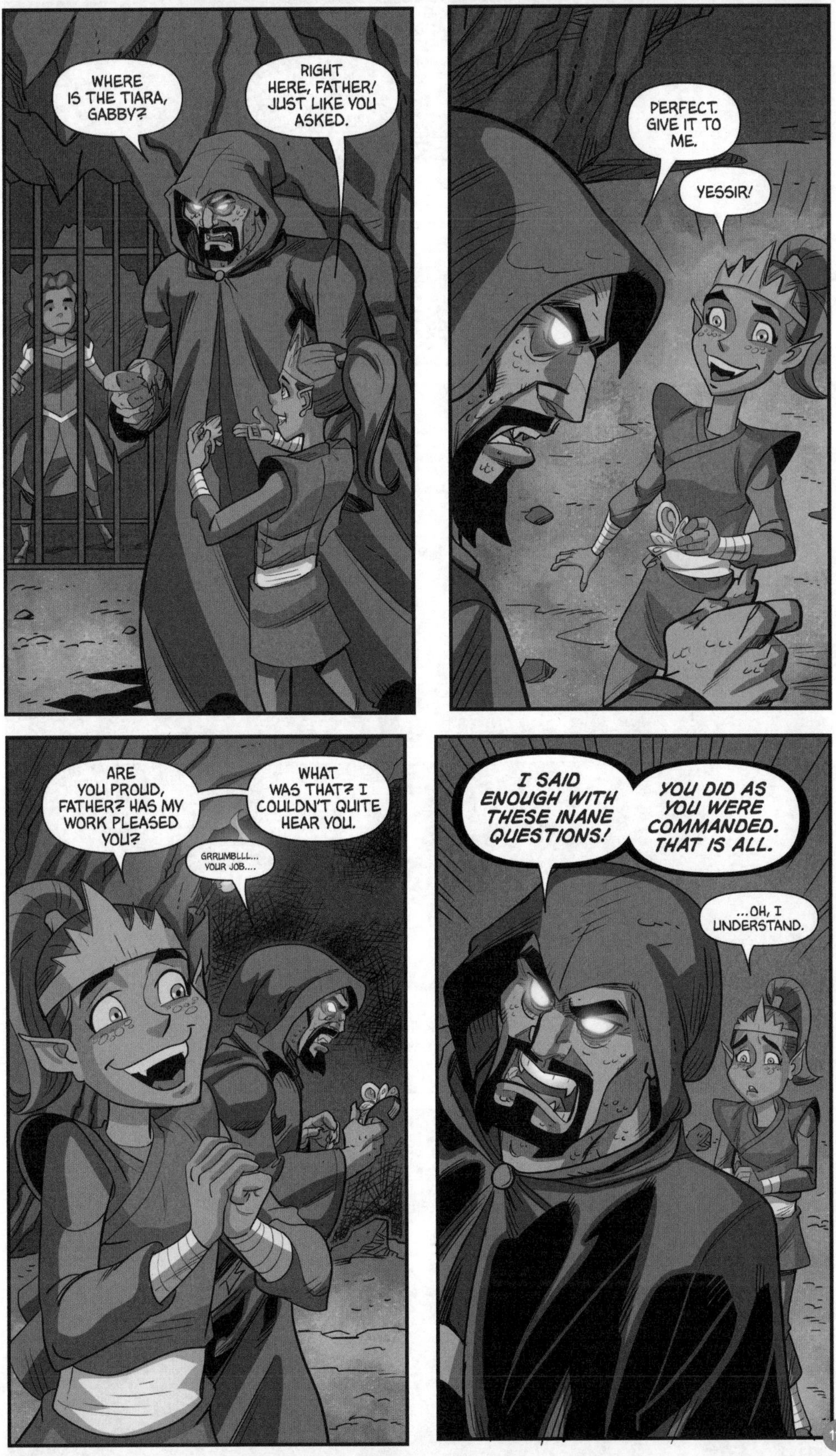
WHERE IS THE TIARA, GABBY?
RIGHT HERE, FATHER! JUST LIKE YOU ASKED.
PERFECT. GIVE IT TO ME.
YESSIR!
ARE YOU PROUD, FATHER? HAS MY WORK PLEASED YOU?
WHAT WAS THAT? I COULDN'T QUITE HEAR YOU.
GRRUMBLLL... YOUR JOB....
I SAID ENOUGH WITH THESE INANE QUESTIONS!
YOU DID AS YOU WERE COMMANDED. THAT IS ALL.
...OH, I UNDERSTAND.

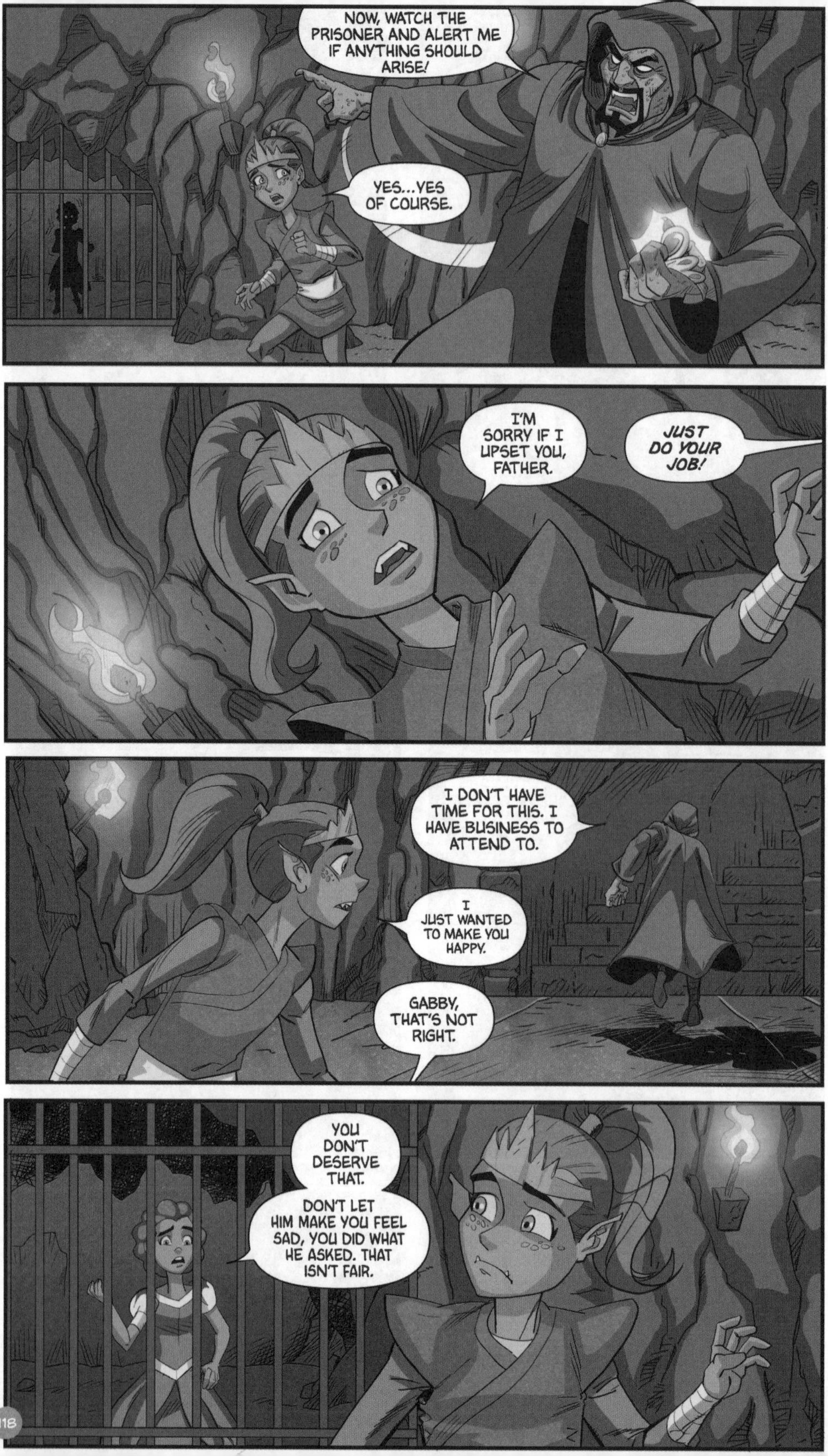
NOW, WATCH THE PRISONER AND ALERT ME IF ANYTHING SHOULD ARISE!
YES...YES OF COURSE.
I'M SORRY IF I UPSET YOU, FATHER.
JUST DO YOUR JOB!
I DON'T HAVE TIME FOR THIS. I HAVE BUSINESS TO ATTEND TO.
I JUST WANTED TO MAKE YOU HAPPY.
GABBY, THAT'S NOT RIGHT.
YOU DON'T DESERVE THAT.
DON'T LET HIM MAKE YOU FEEL SAD, YOU DID WHAT HE ASKED. THAT ISN'T FAIR.

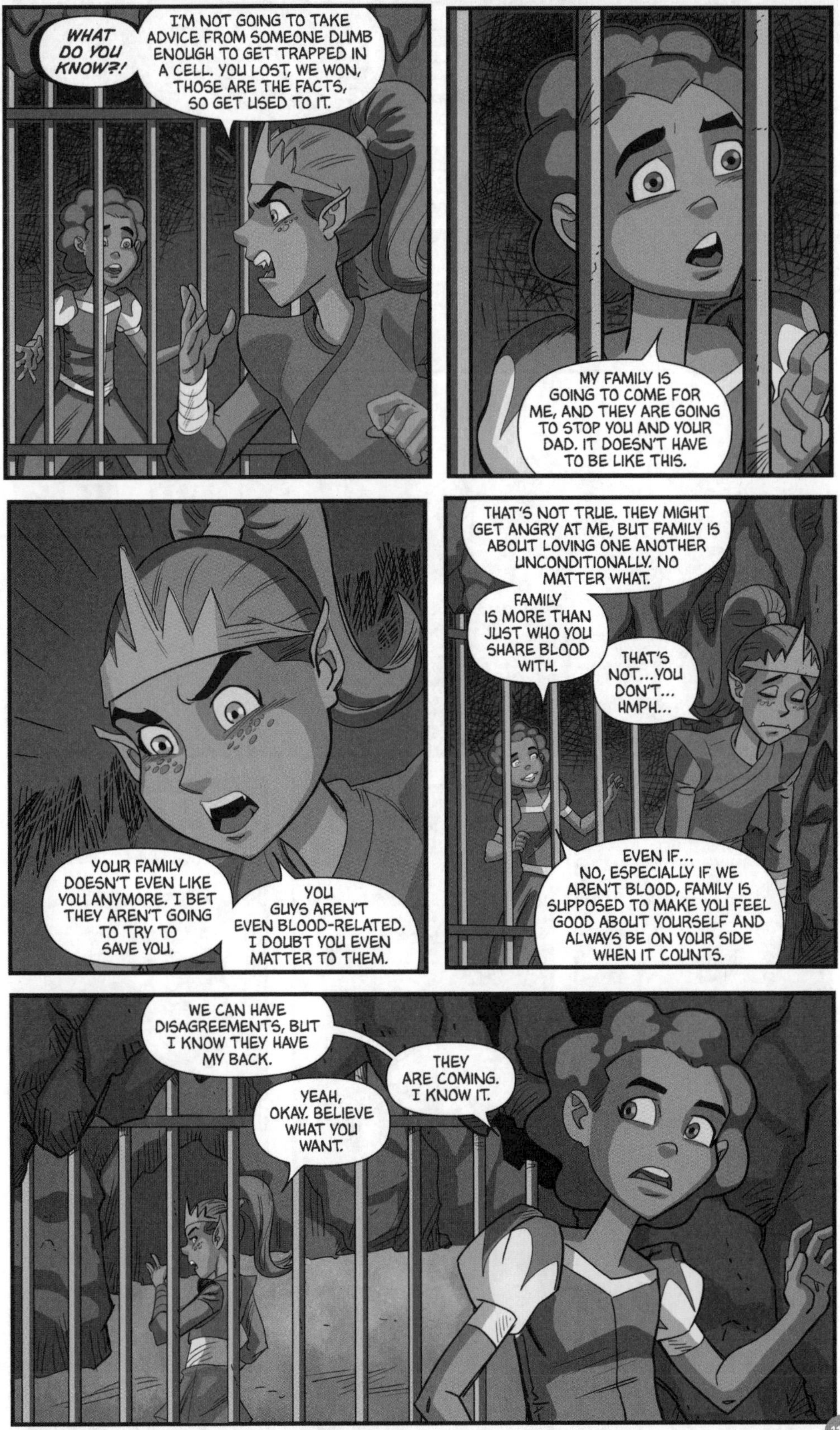
WHAT DO YOU KNOW?!
I'M NOT GOING TO TAKE ADVICE FROM SOMEONE DUMB ENOUGH TO GET TRAPPED IN A CELL. YOU LOST, WE WON, THOSE ARE THE FACTS, SO GET USED TO IT.
MY FAMILY IS GOING TO COME FOR ME, AND THEY ARE GOING TO STOP YOU AND YOUR DAD. IT DOESN'T HAVE TO BE LIKE THIS.
YOUR FAMILY DOESN'T EVEN LIKE YOU ANYMORE. I BET THEY AREN'T GOING TO TRY TO SAVE YOU.
YOU GUYS AREN'T EVEN BLOOD-RELATED. I DOUBT YOU EVEN MATTER TO THEM.
THAT'S NOT TRUE. THEY MIGHT GET ANGRY AT ME, BUT FAMILY IS ABOUT LOVING ONE ANOTHER UNCONDITIONALLY. NO MATTER WHAT.
FAMILY IS MORE THAN JUST WHO YOU SHARE BLOOD WITH.
THAT'S NOT...YOU DON'T... HMPH...
EVEN IF... NO, ESPECIALLY IF WE AREN'T BLOOD, FAMILY IS SUPPOSED TO MAKE YOU FEEL GOOD ABOUT YOURSELF AND ALWAYS BE ON YOUR SIDE WHEN IT COUNTS.
WE CAN HAVE DISAGREEMENTS, BUT I KNOW THEY HAVE MY BACK.
THEY ARE COMING. I KNOW IT.
YEAH, OKAY. BELIEVE WHAT YOU WANT.

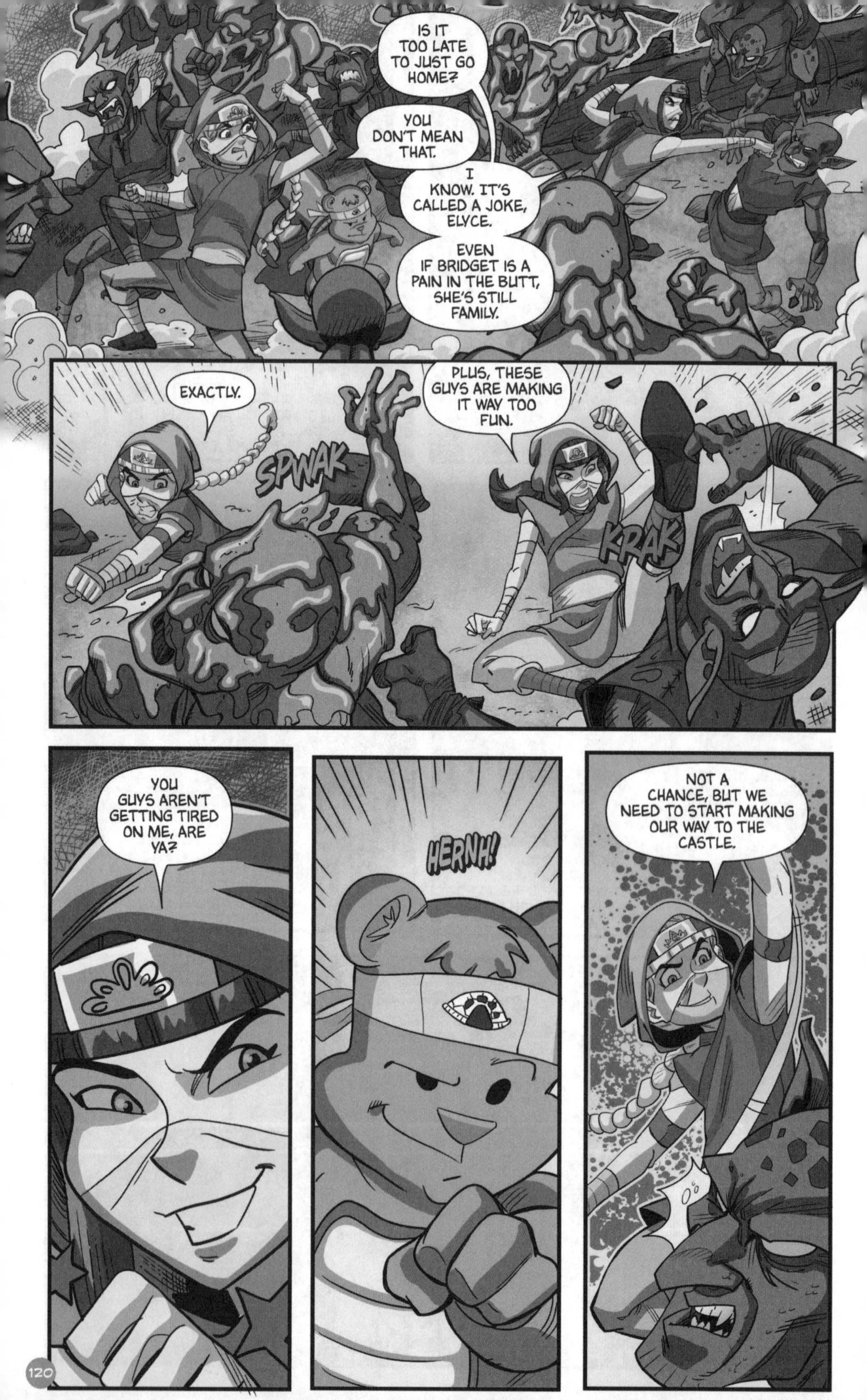
IS IT TOO LATE TO JUST GO HOME?
YOU DON'T MEAN THAT.
I KNOW. IT'S CALLED A JOKE, ELYCE.
EVEN IF BRIDGET IS A PAIN IN THE BUTT, SHE'S STILL FAMILY.
EXACTLY.
SPWAK
PLUS, THESE GUYS ARE MAKING IT WAY TOO FUN.
KRAK
YOU GUYS AREN'T GETTING TIRED ON ME, ARE YA?
HERNH!
NOT A CHANCE, BUT WE NEED TO START MAKING OUR WAY TO THE CASTLE.

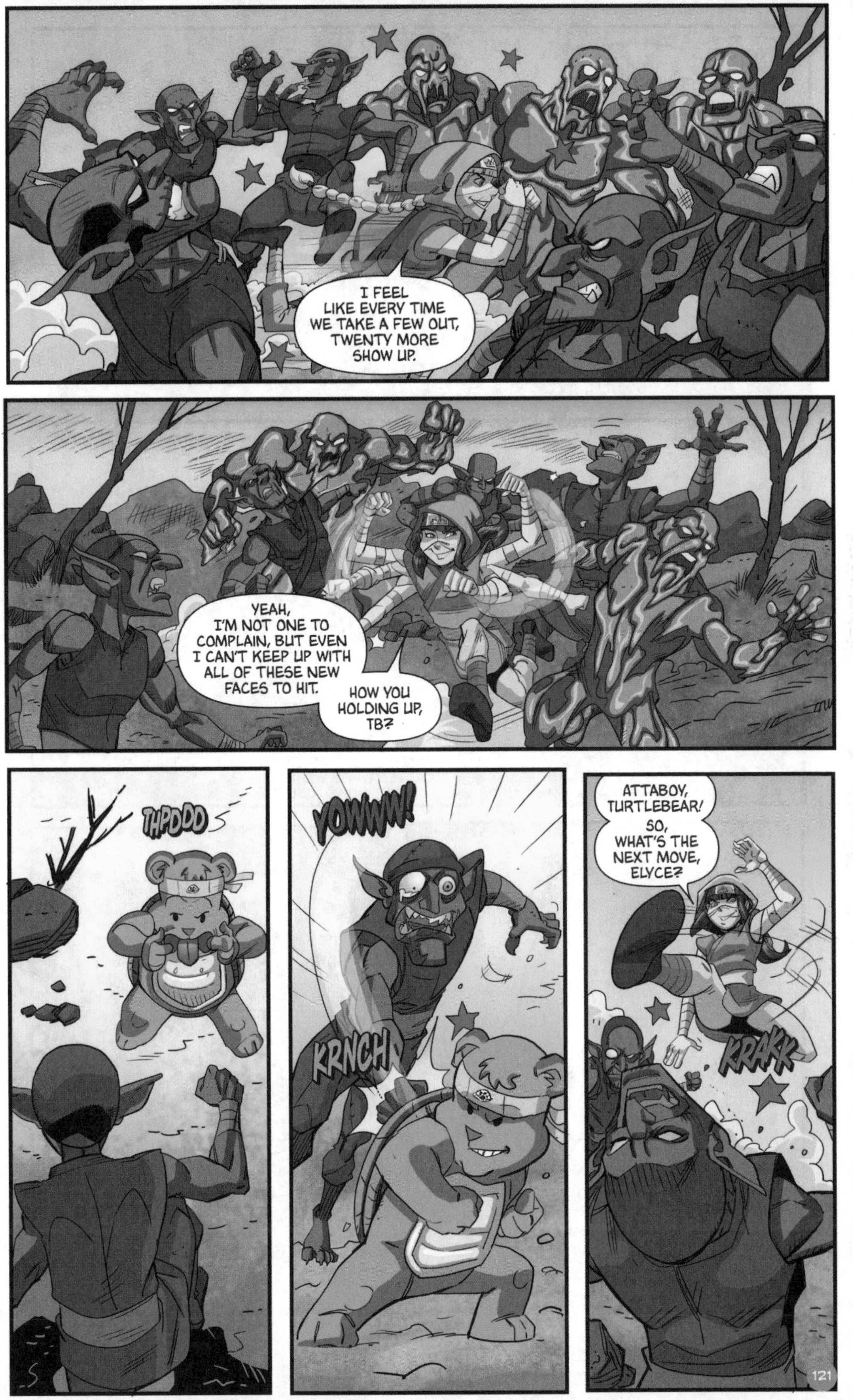
I FEEL LIKE EVERY TIME WE TAKE A FEW OUT, TWENTY MORE SHOW UP.
YEAH, I'M NOT ONE TO COMPLAIN, BUT EVEN I CAN'T KEEP UP WITH ALL OF THESE NEW FACES TO HIT.
HOW YOU HOLDING UP, TB?
THPDDD
YOWWW!
KRNCH
ATTABOY, TURTLEBEAR!
SO, WHAT'S THE NEXT MOVE, ELYCE?
KRAKK

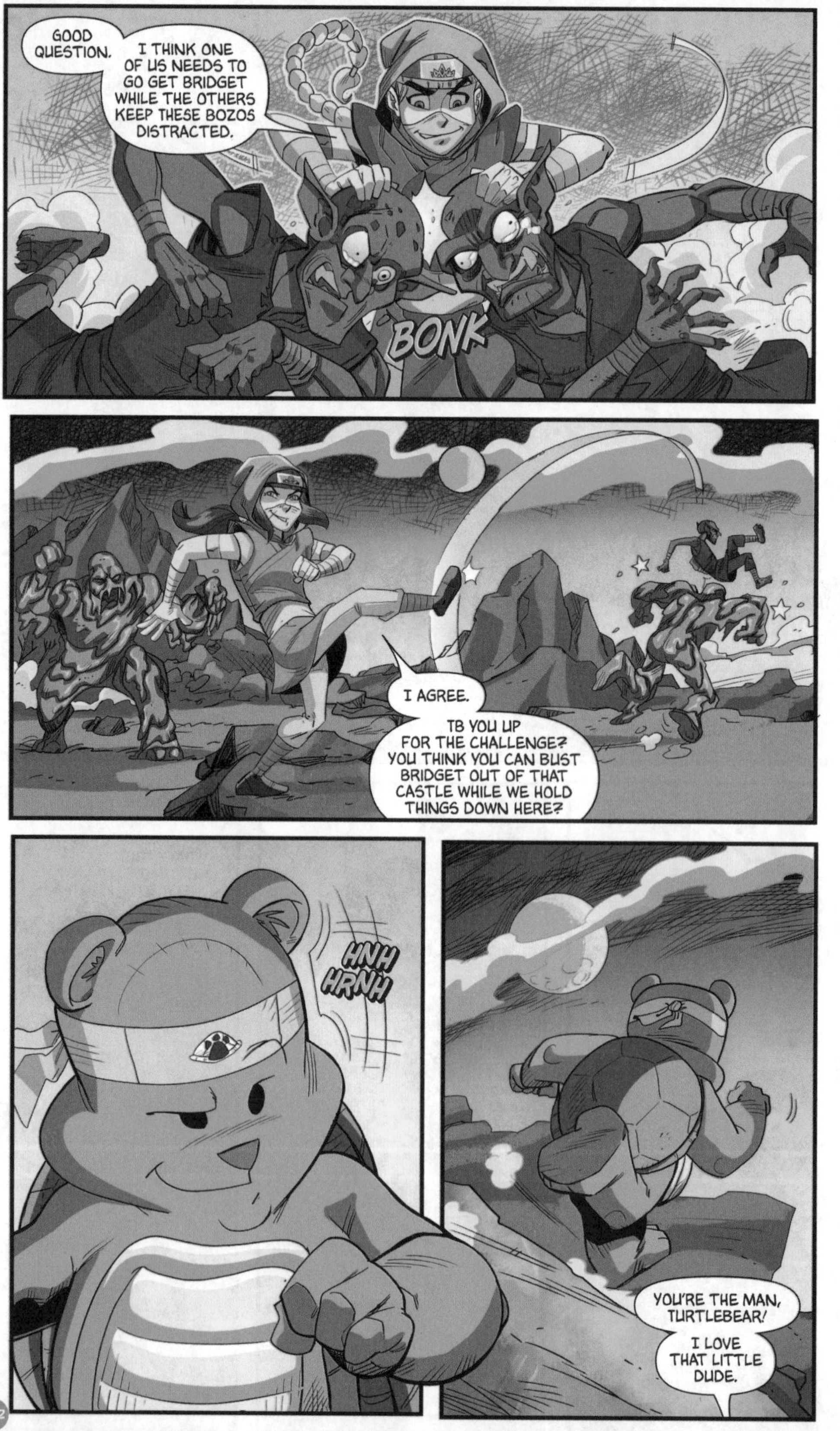
GOOD QUESTION.
I THINK ONE OF US NEEDS TO GO GET BRIDGET WHILE THE OTHERS KEEP THESE BOZOS DISTRACTED.
BONK
I AGREE.
TB YOU UP FOR THE CHALLENGE? YOU THINK YOU CAN BUST BRIDGET OUT OF THAT CASTLE WHILE WE HOLD THINGS DOWN HERE?
HNH HRNH
YOU'RE THE MAN, TURTLEBEAR!
I LOVE THAT LITTLE DUDE.

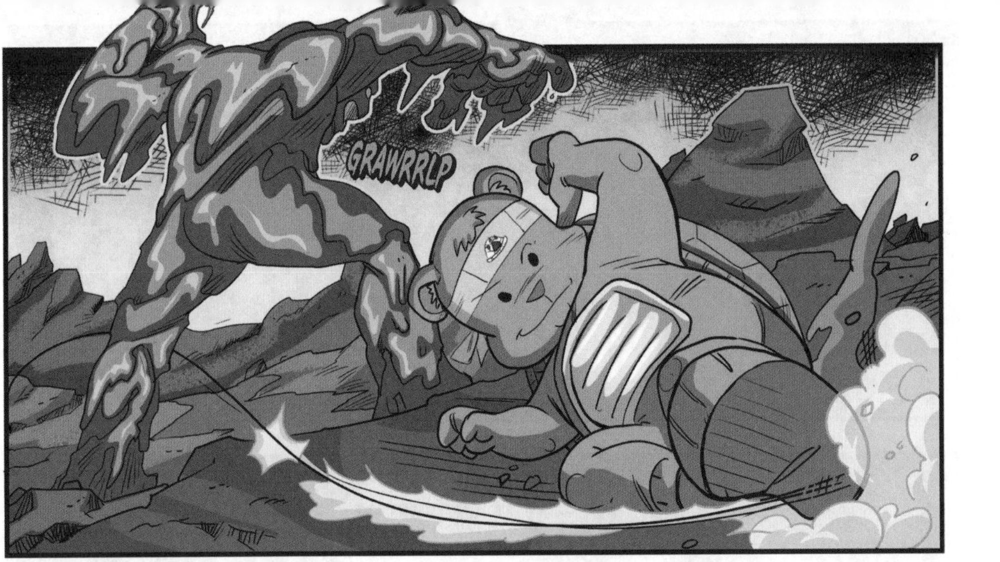
GRAWRRLP

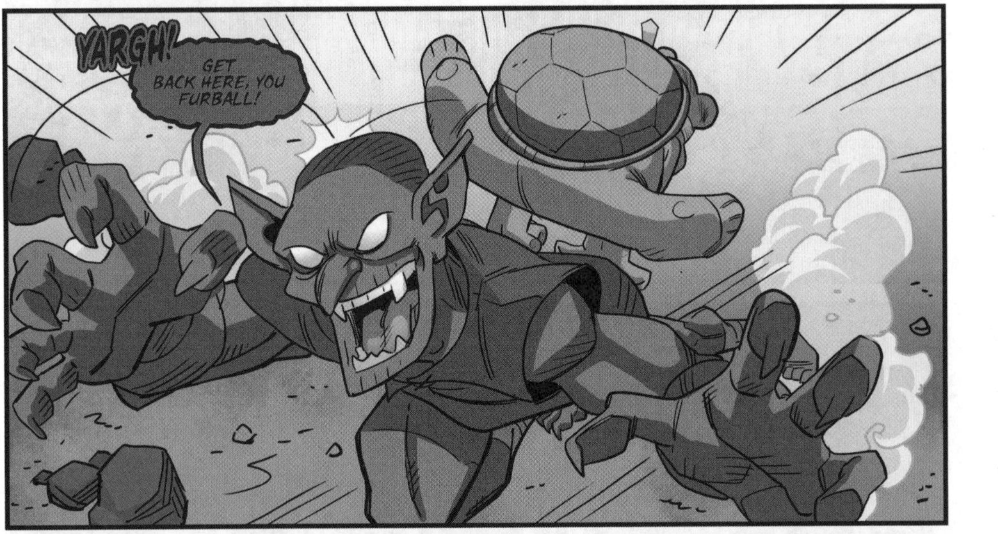
YARGH!
GET BACK HERE, YOU FURBALL!

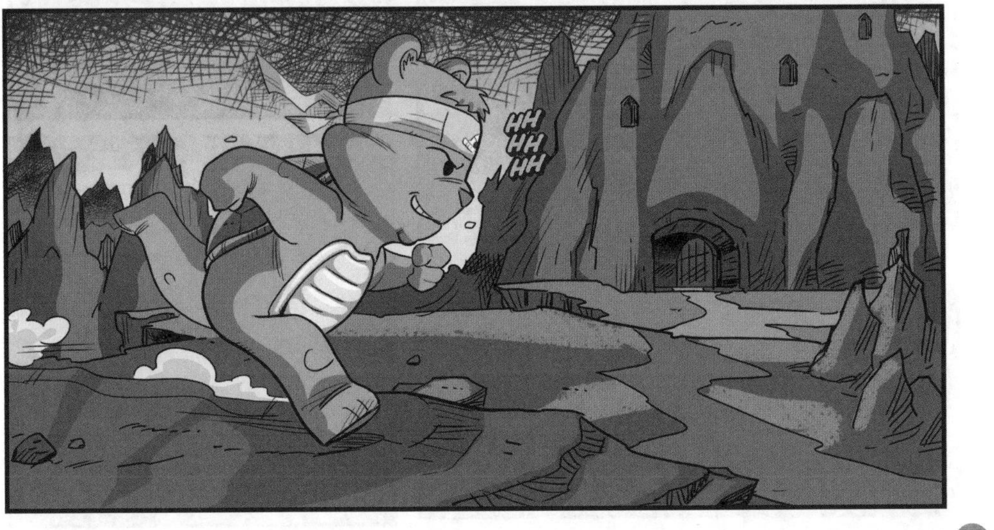
HH HH HH

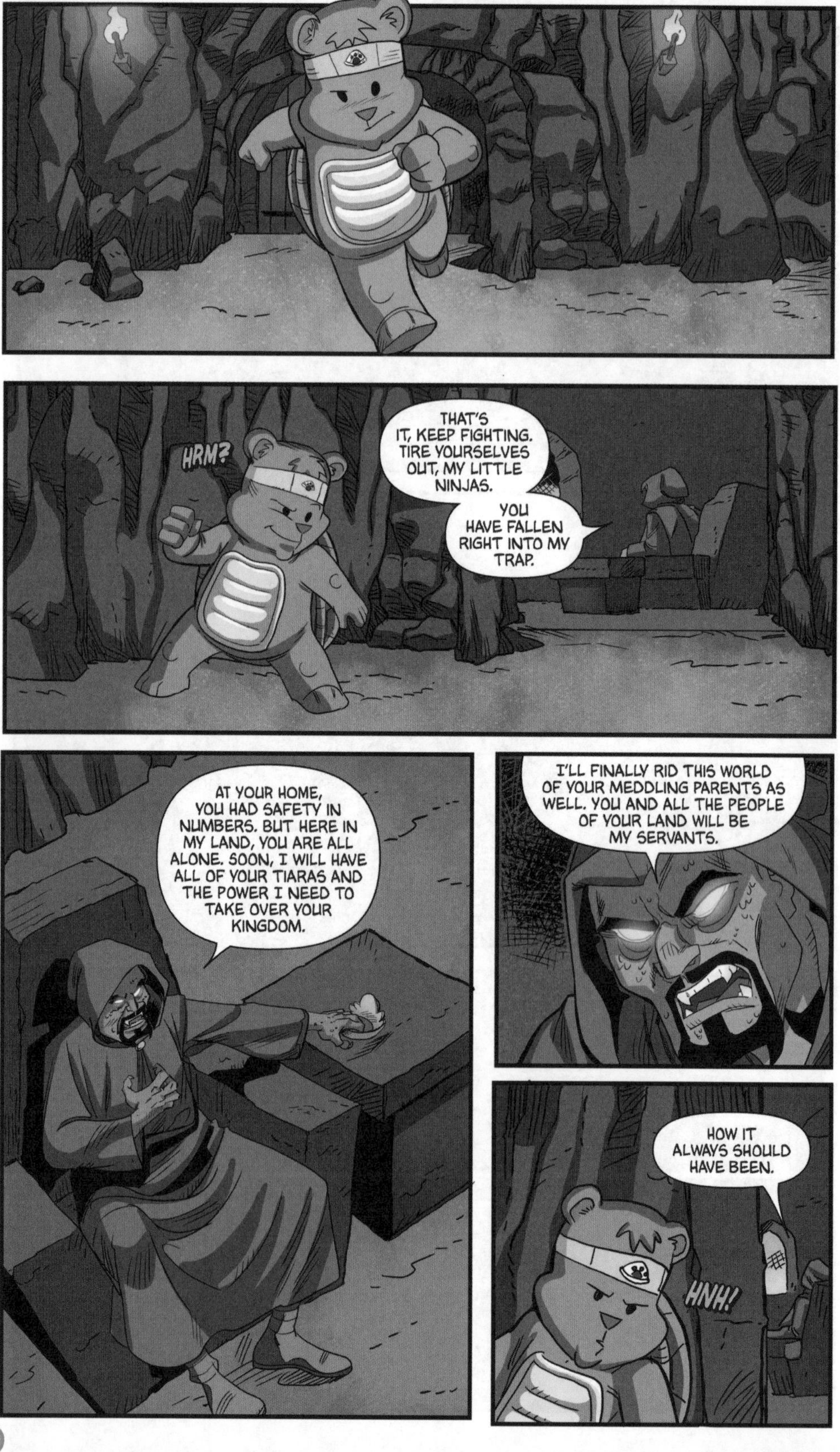
HRM?
THAT'S IT, KEEP FIGHTING. TIRE YOURSELVES OUT, MY LITTLE NINJAS.
YOU HAVE FALLEN RIGHT INTO MY TRAP.
AT YOUR HOME, YOU HAD SAFETY IN NUMBERS. BUT HERE IN MY LAND, YOU ARE ALL ALONE. SOON, I WILL HAVE ALL OF YOUR TIARAS AND THE POWER I NEED TO TAKE OVER YOUR KINGDOM.
I'LL FINALLY RID THIS WORLD OF YOUR MEDDLING PARENTS AS WELL. YOU AND ALL THE PEOPLE OF YOUR LAND WILL BE MY SERVANTS.
HOW IT ALWAYS SHOULD HAVE BEEN.
HNH!

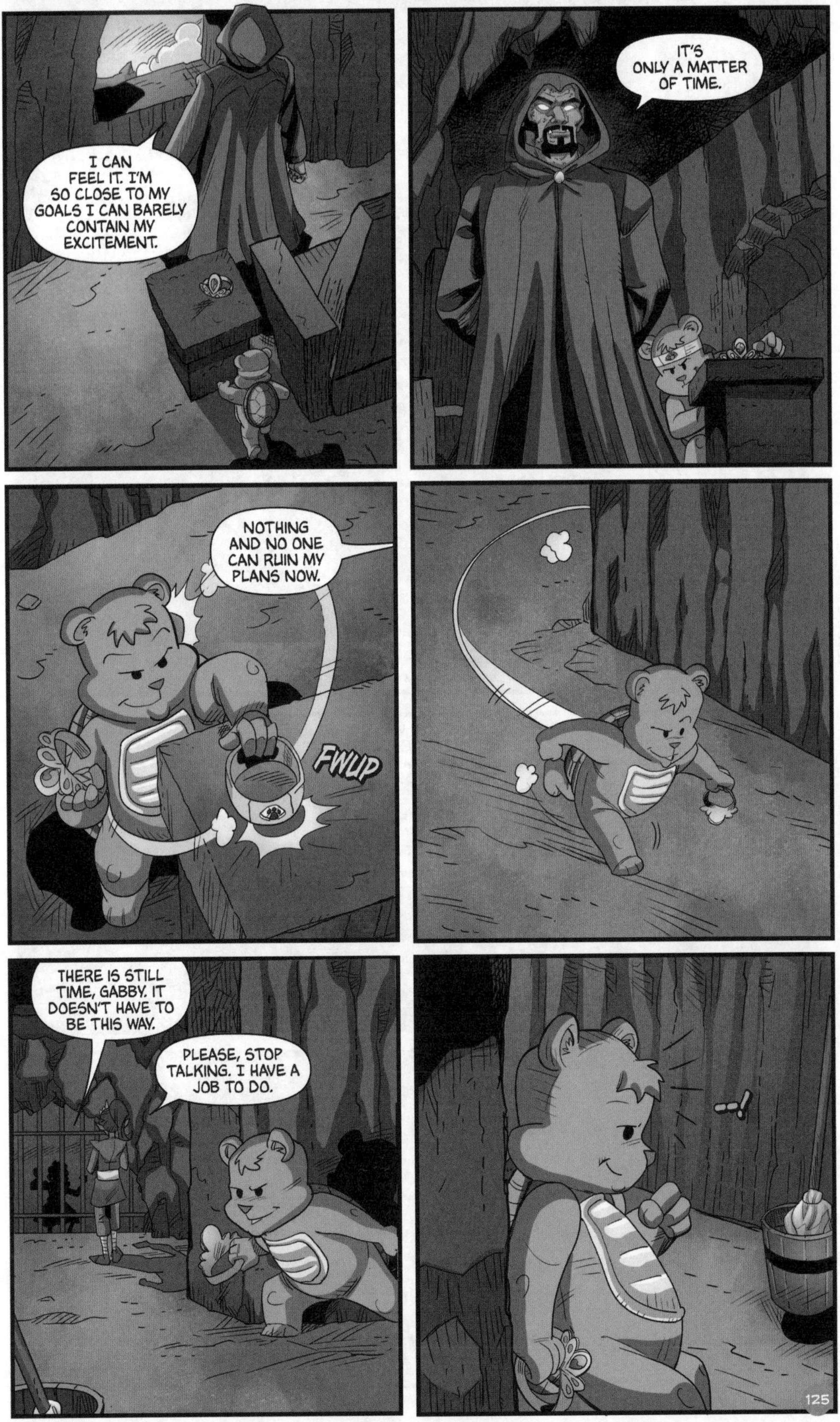
I CAN FEEL IT. I'M SO CLOSE TO MY GOALS I CAN BARELY CONTAIN MY EXCITEMENT.
IT'S ONLY A MATTER OF TIME.
NOTHING AND NO ONE CAN RUIN MY PLANS NOW.
FWUP
THERE IS STILL TIME, GABBY. IT DOESN'T HAVE TO BE THIS WAY.
PLEASE, STOP TALKING. I HAVE A JOB TO DO.

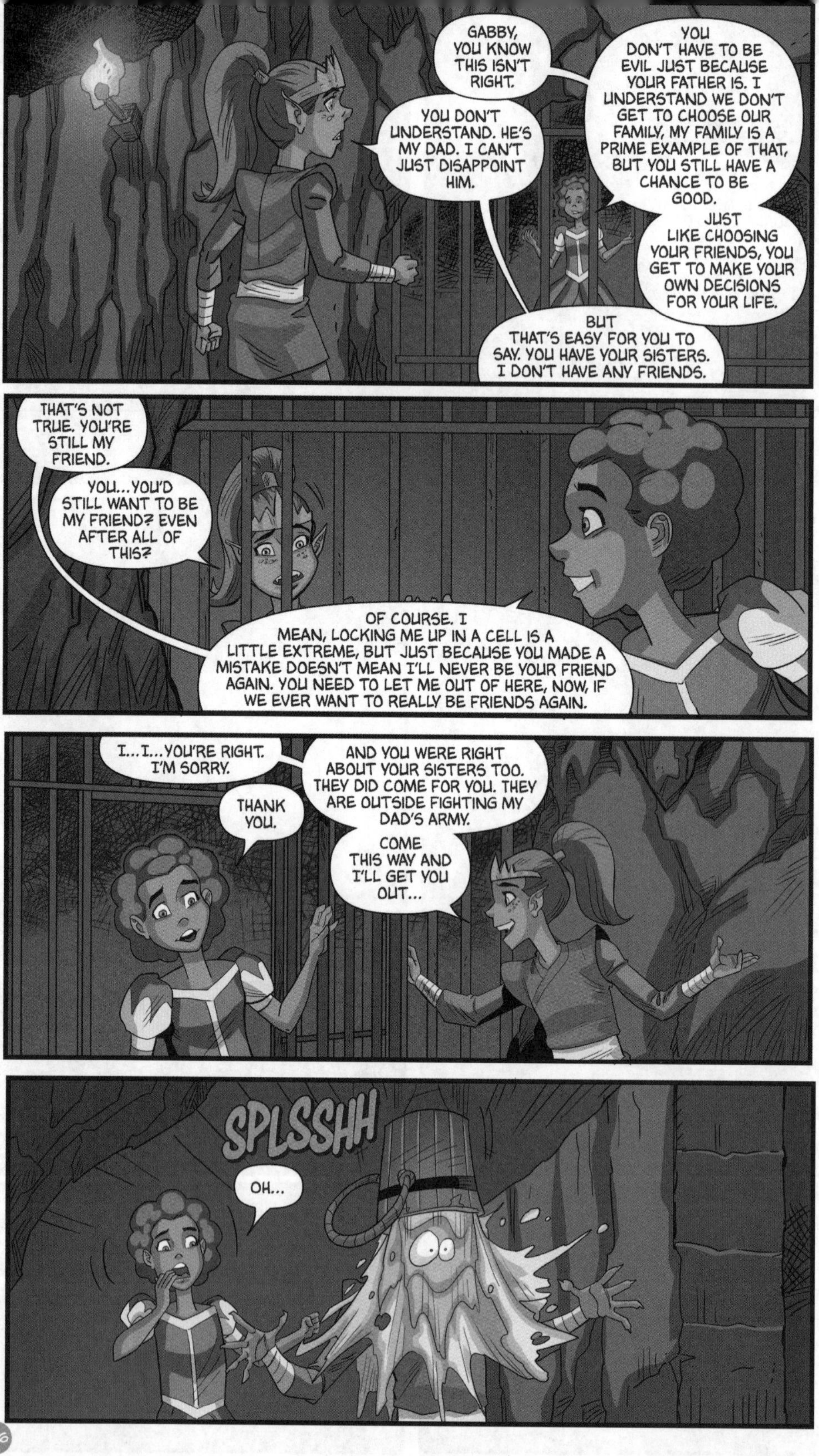
GABBY, YOU KNOW THIS ISN'T RIGHT.
YOU DON'T HAVE TO BE EVIL JUST BECAUSE YOUR FATHER IS. I UNDERSTAND WE DON'T GET TO CHOOSE OUR FAMILY, MY FAMILY IS A PRIME EXAMPLE OF THAT, BUT YOU STILL HAVE A CHANCE TO BE GOOD.
JUST LIKE CHOOSING YOUR FRIENDS, YOU GET TO MAKE YOUR OWN DECISIONS FOR YOUR LIFE.
YOU DON'T UNDERSTAND. HE'S MY DAD. I CAN'T JUST DISAPPOINT HIM.
BUT THAT'S EASY FOR YOU TO SAY. YOU HAVE YOUR SISTERS. I DON'T HAVE ANY FRIENDS.
THAT'S NOT TRUE. YOU'RE STILL MY FRIEND.
YOU...YOU'D STILL WANT TO BE MY FRIEND? EVEN AFTER ALL OF THIS?
OF COURSE. I MEAN, LOCKING ME UP IN A CELL IS A LITTLE EXTREME, BUT JUST BECAUSE YOU MADE A MISTAKE DOESN'T MEAN I'LL NEVER BE YOUR FRIEND AGAIN. YOU NEED TO LET ME OUT OF HERE, NOW, IF WE EVER WANT TO REALLY BE FRIENDS AGAIN.
I...I...YOU'RE RIGHT. I'M SORRY.
AND YOU WERE RIGHT ABOUT YOUR SISTERS TOO. THEY DID COME FOR YOU. THEY ARE OUTSIDE FIGHTING MY DAD'S ARMY.
THANK YOU.
COME THIS WAY AND I'LL GET YOU OUT...
SPLSSHH
OH...

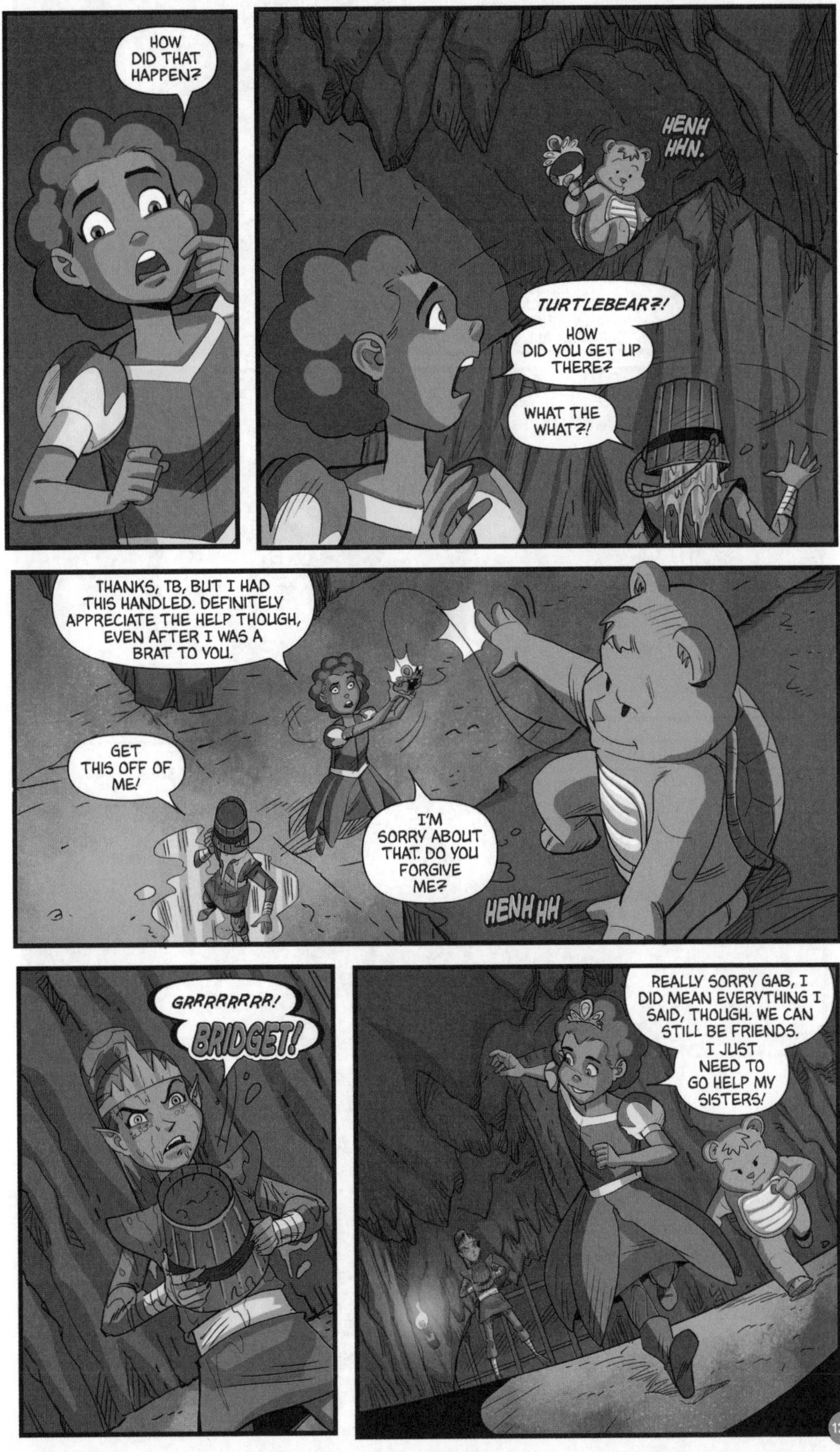
HOW DID THAT HAPPEN?
HENH HHN.
TURTLEBEAR?! HOW DID YOU GET UP THERE?
WHAT THE WHAT?!
THANKS, TB, BUT I HAD THIS HANDLED. DEFINITELY APPRECIATE THE HELP THOUGH, EVEN AFTER I WAS A BRAT TO YOU.
GET THIS OFF OF ME!
I'M SORRY ABOUT THAT. DO YOU FORGIVE ME?
HENH HH
GRRRRRRRR!
BRIDGET!
REALLY SORRY GAB, I DID MEAN EVERYTHING I SAID, THOUGH. WE CAN STILL BE FRIENDS.
I JUST NEED TO GO HELP MY SISTERS!

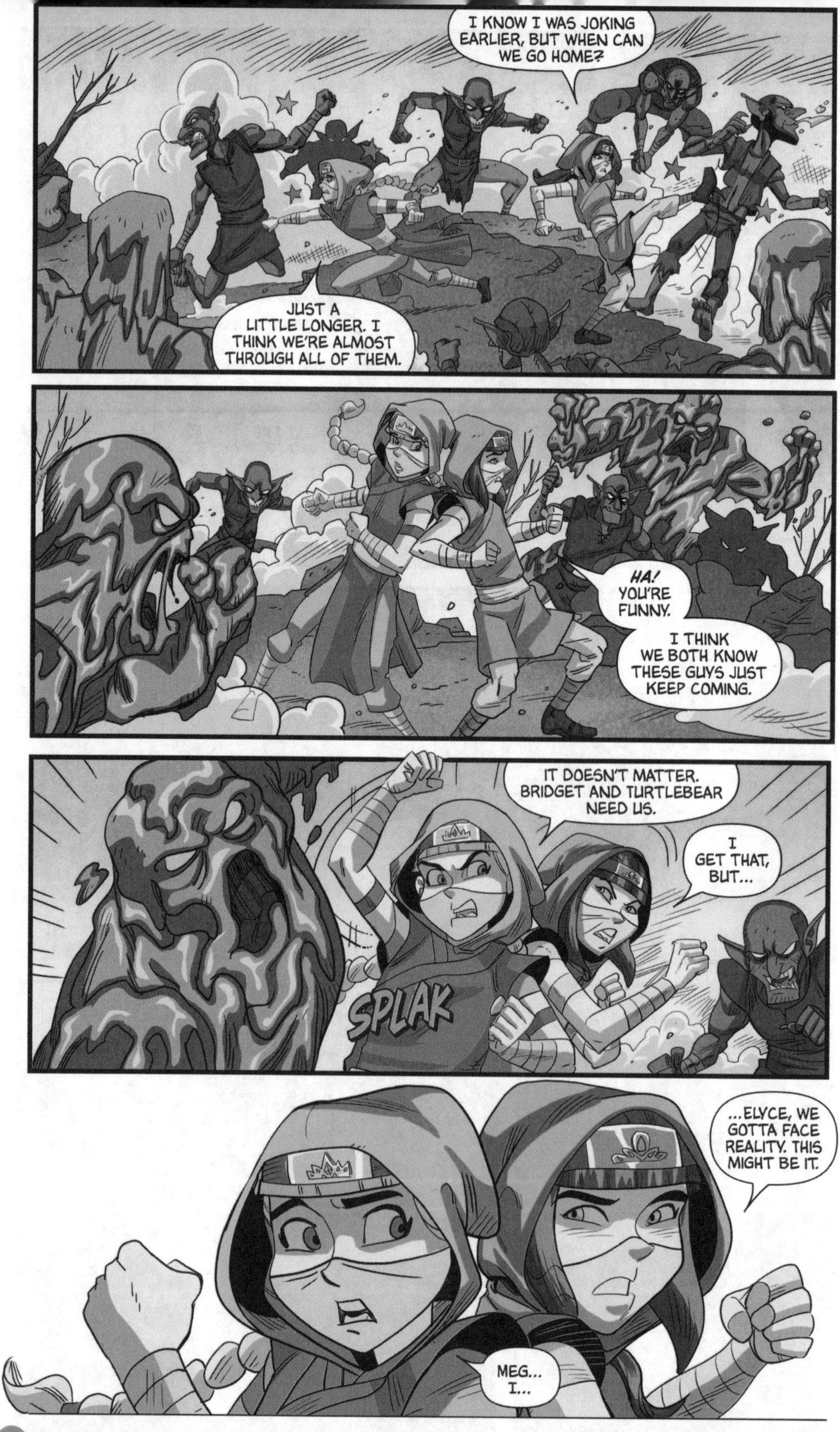
I KNOW I WAS JOKING EARLIER, BUT WHEN CAN WE GO HOME?
JUST A LITTLE LONGER. I THINK WE'RE ALMOST THROUGH ALL OF THEM.
HA! YOU'RE FUNNY.
I THINK WE BOTH KNOW THESE GUYS JUST KEEP COMING.
IT DOESN'T MATTER. BRIDGET AND TURTLEBEAR NEED US.
I GET THAT, BUT...
SPLAK
...ELYCE, WE GOTTA FACE REALITY. THIS MIGHT BE IT.
MEG... I...

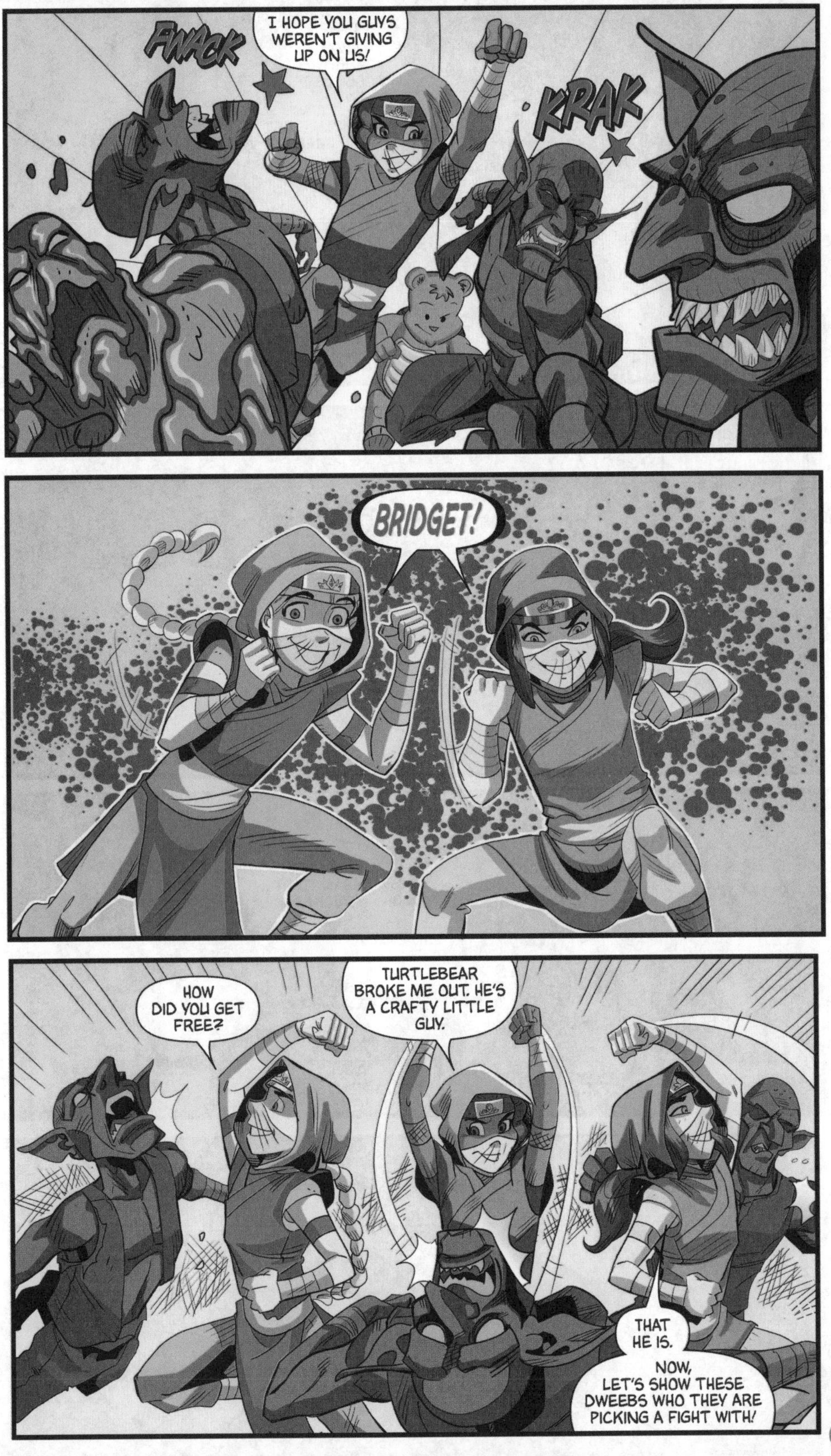
FWACK
I HOPE YOU GUYS WEREN'T GIVING UP ON US!
KRAK
BRIDGET!
HOW DID YOU GET FREE?
TURTLEBEAR BROKE ME OUT. HE'S A CRAFTY LITTLE GUY.
THAT HE IS.
NOW, LET'S SHOW THESE DWEEBS WHO THEY ARE PICKING A FIGHT WITH!

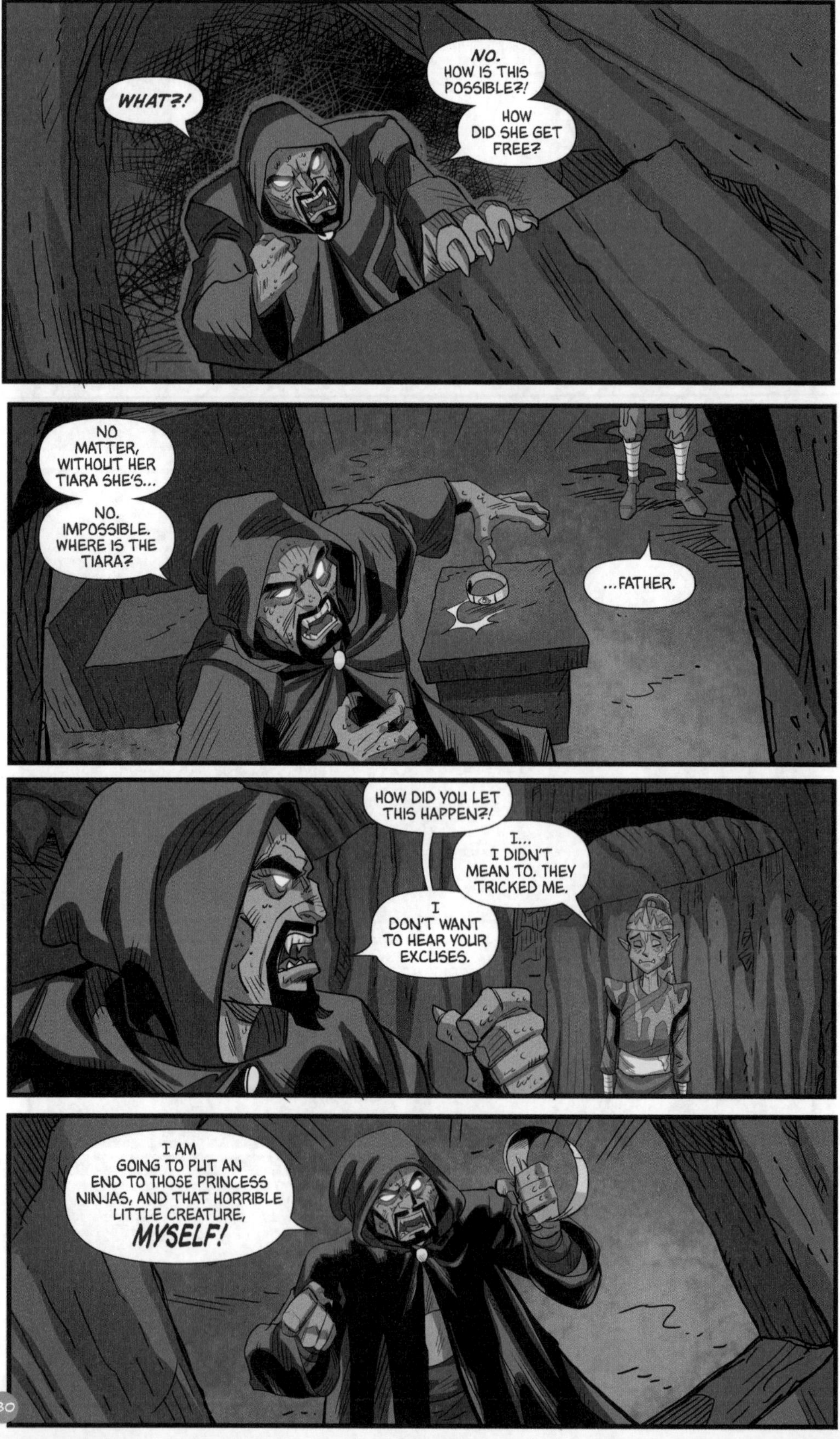
WHAT?!
NO. HOW IS THIS POSSIBLE?!
HOW DID SHE GET FREE?
NO MATTER, WITHOUT HER TIARA SHE'S...
NO. IMPOSSIBLE. WHERE IS THE TIARA?
...FATHER.
HOW DID YOU LET THIS HAPPEN?!
I... I DIDN'T MEAN TO. THEY TRICKED ME.
I DON'T WANT TO HEAR YOUR EXCUSES.
I AM GOING TO PUT AN END TO THOSE PRINCESS NINJAS, AND THAT HORRIBLE LITTLE CREATURE, MYSELF!

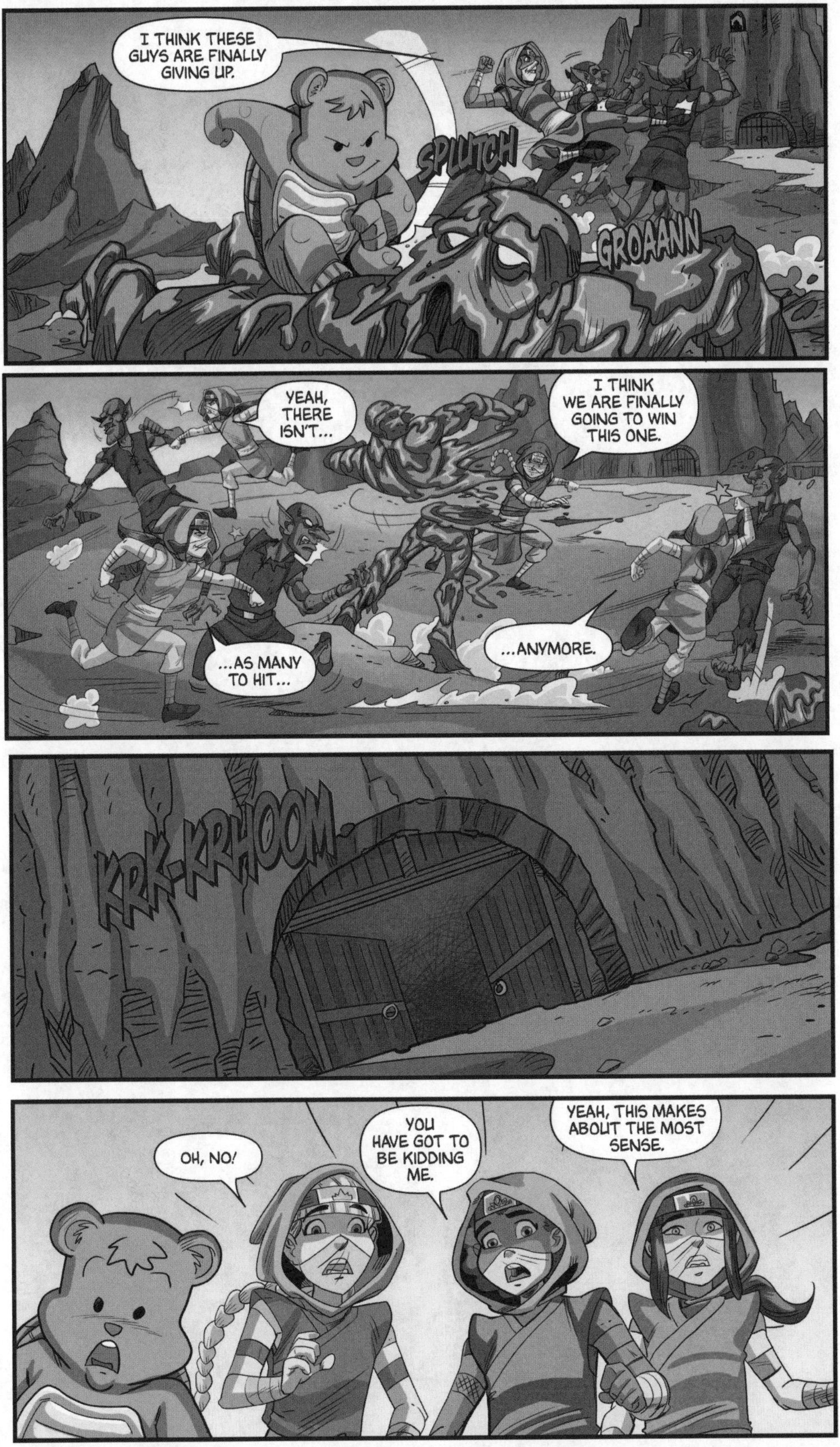
I THINK THESE GUYS ARE FINALLY GIVING UP.
SPLUTCH
GROAANN
YEAH, THERE ISN'T...
...AS MANY TO HIT...
...ANYMORE.
I THINK WE ARE FINALLY GOING TO WIN THIS ONE.
KRK-KRHOOM
OH, NO!
YOU HAVE GOT TO BE KIDDING ME.
YEAH, THIS MAKES ABOUT THE MOST SENSE.

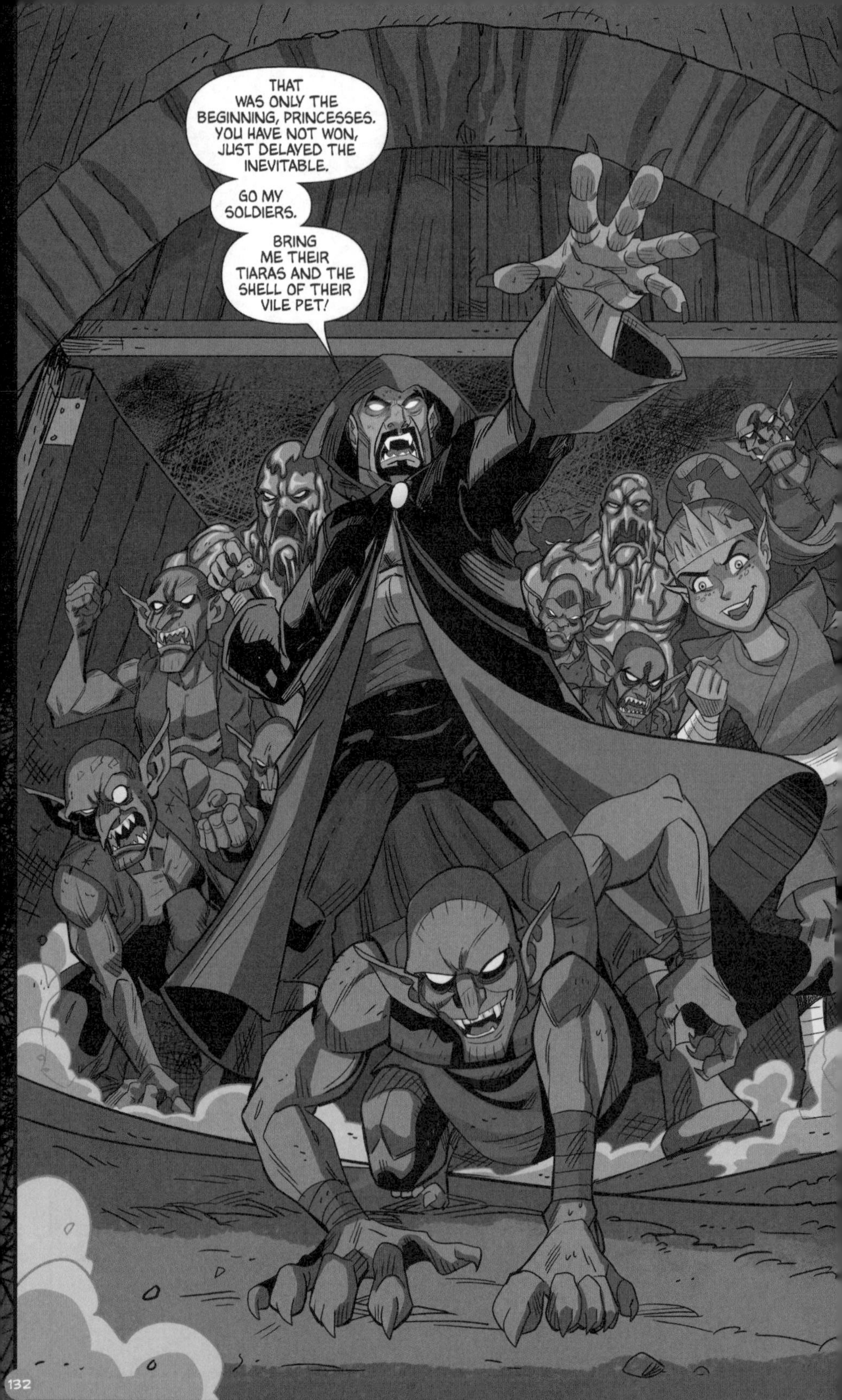
THAT WAS ONLY THE BEGINNING, PRINCESSES. YOU HAVE NOT WON, JUST DELAYED THE INEVITABLE.
GO MY SOLDIERS.
BRING ME THEIR TIARAS AND THE SHELL OF THEIR VILE PET!

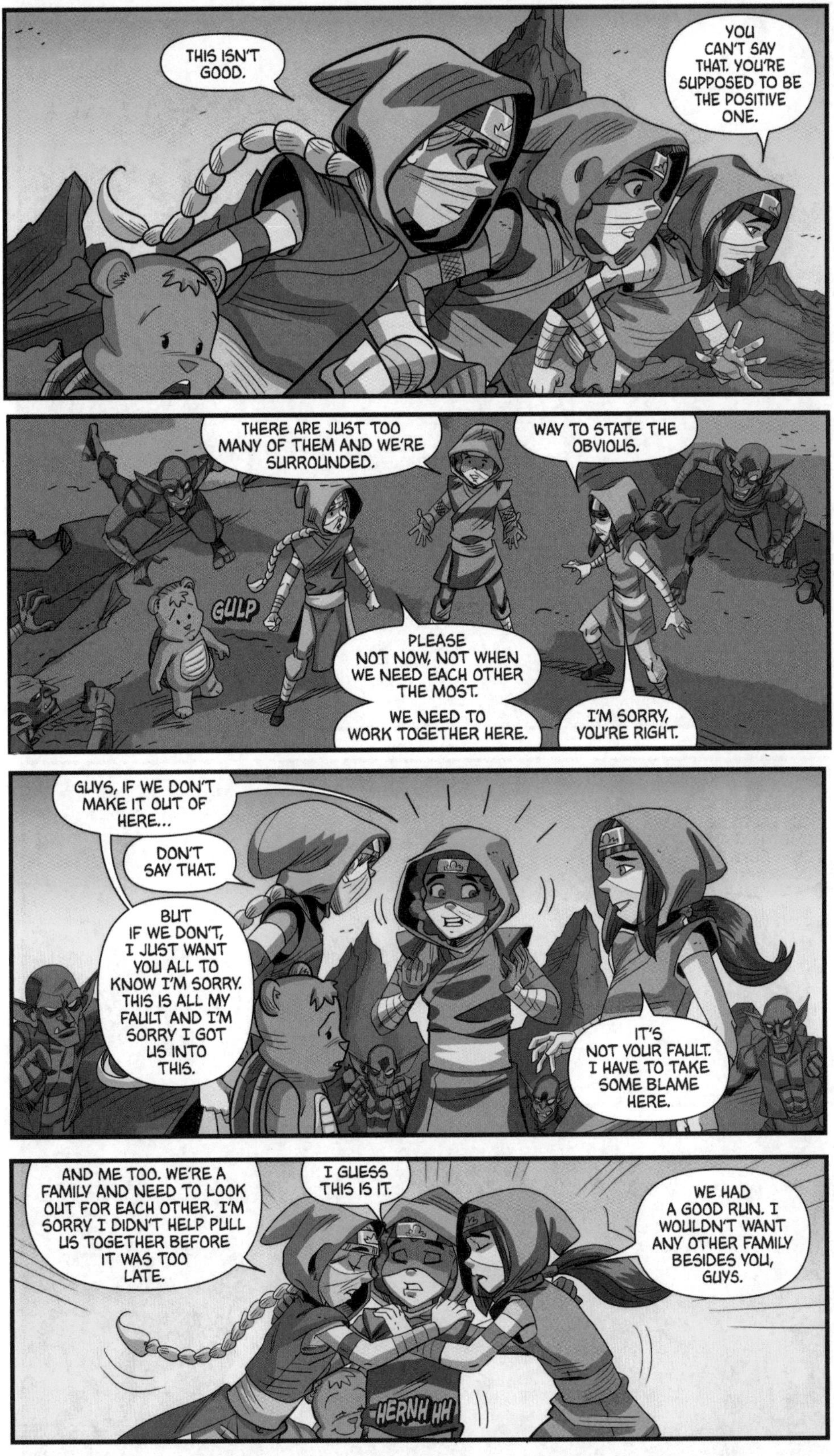
THIS ISN'T GOOD.
YOU CAN'T SAY THAT. YOU'RE SUPPOSED TO BE THE POSITIVE ONE.
THERE ARE JUST TOO MANY OF THEM AND WE'RE SURROUNDED.
WAY TO STATE THE OBVIOUS.
GULP
PLEASE NOT NOW, NOT WHEN WE NEED EACH OTHER THE MOST.
WE NEED TO WORK TOGETHER HERE.
I'M SORRY, YOU'RE RIGHT.
GUYS, IF WE DON'T MAKE IT OUT OF HERE...
DON'T SAY THAT.
BUT IF WE DON'T, I JUST WANT YOU ALL TO KNOW I'M SORRY. THIS IS ALL MY FAULT AND I'M SORRY I GOT US INTO THIS.
IT'S NOT YOUR FAULT. I HAVE TO TAKE SOME BLAME HERE.
AND ME TOO. WE'RE A FAMILY AND NEED TO LOOK OUT FOR EACH OTHER. I'M SORRY I DIDN'T HELP PULL US TOGETHER BEFORE IT WAS TOO LATE.
I GUESS THIS IS IT.
WE HAD A GOOD RUN. I WOULDN'T WANT ANY OTHER FAMILY BESIDES YOU, GUYS.
HERNH HH

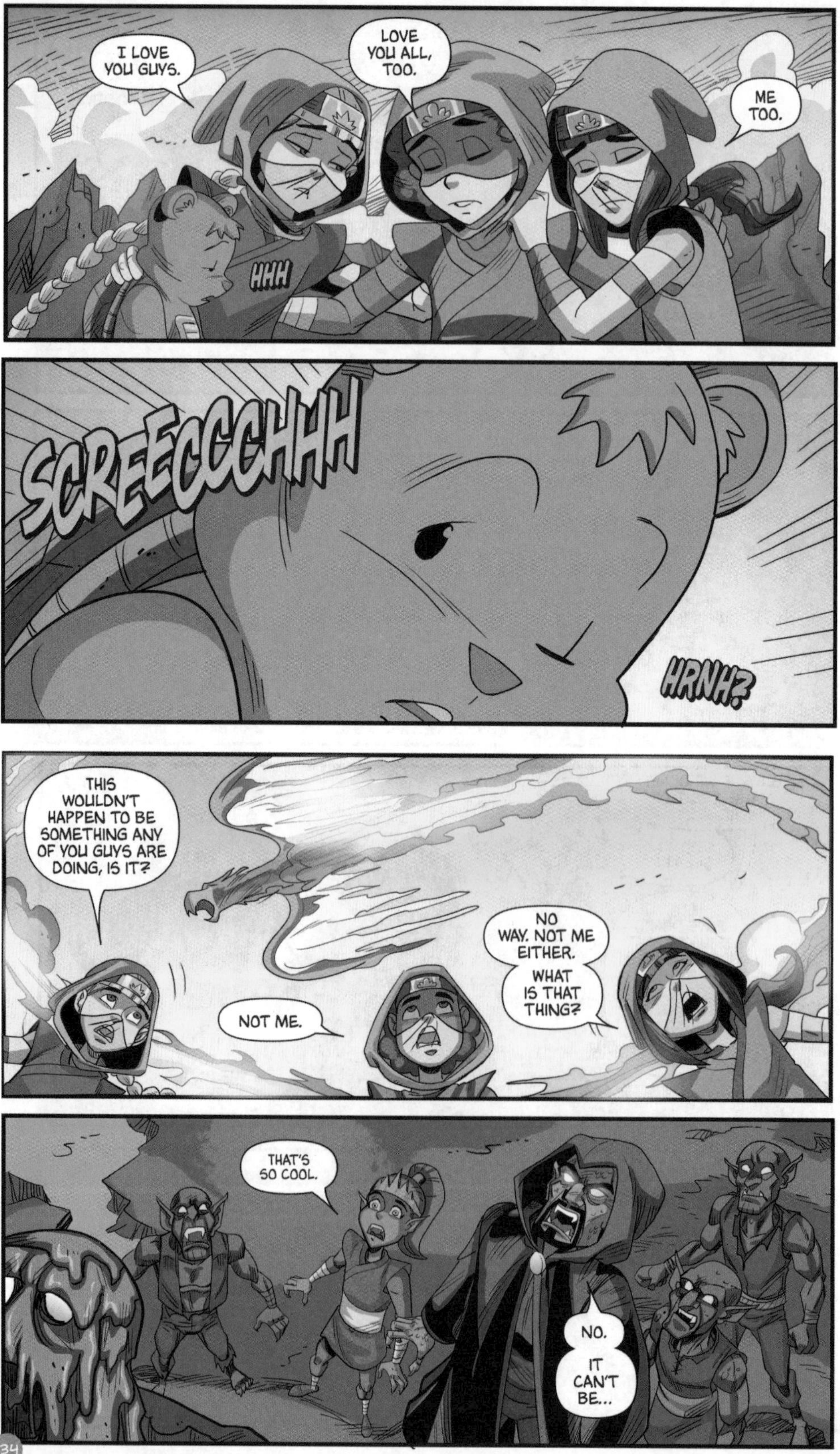
I LOVE YOU GUYS.
HHH
LOVE YOU ALL, TOO.
ME TOO.
SCREECCCHHH
HRNH?
THIS WOULDN'T HAPPEN TO BE SOMETHING ANY OF YOU GUYS ARE DOING, IS IT?
NOT ME.
NO WAY. NOT ME EITHER.
WHAT IS THAT THING?
THAT'S SO COOL.
NO.
IT CAN'T BE...

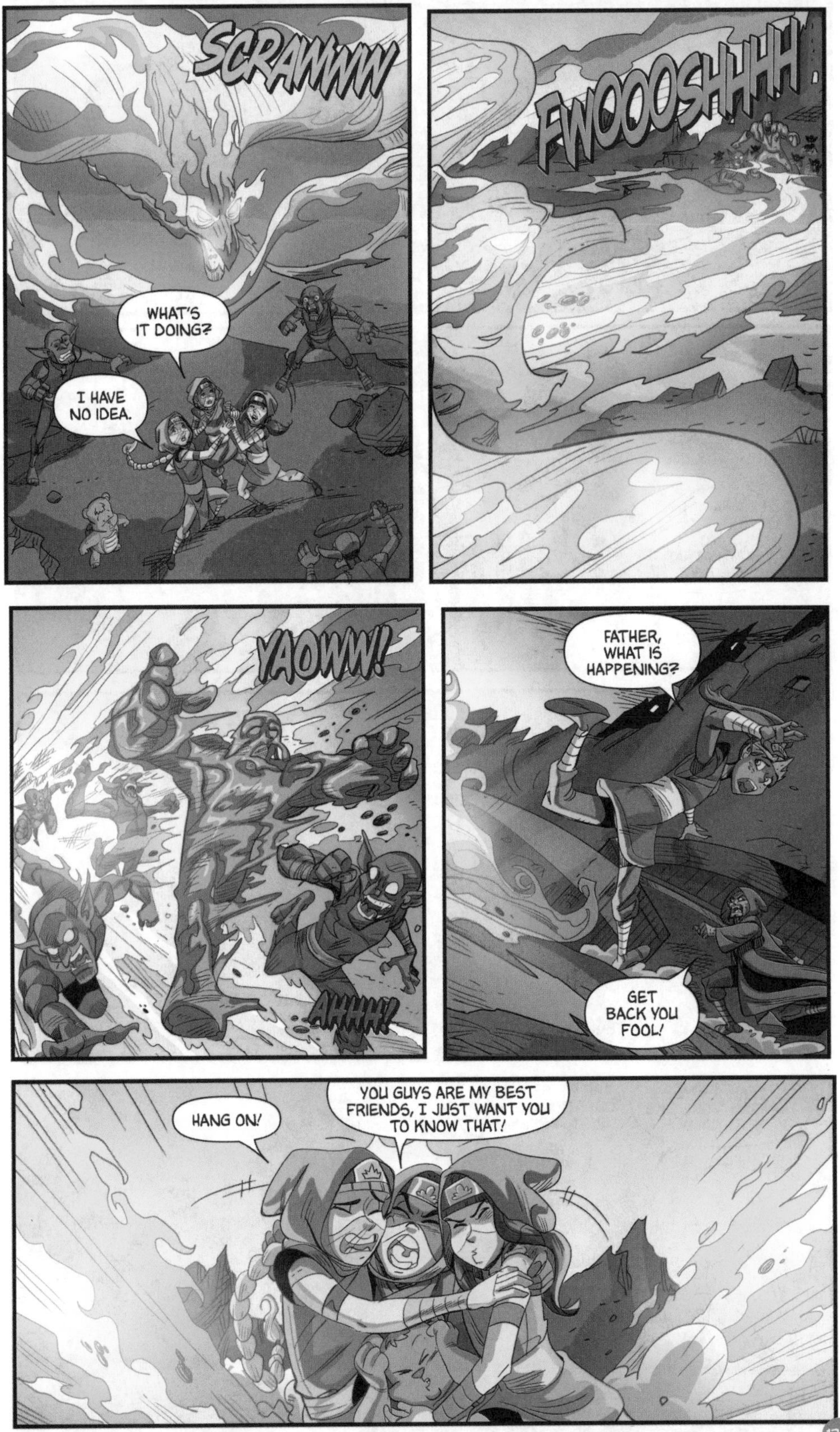
SCRAWWW
WHAT'S IT DOING?
I HAVE NO IDEA.
FWOOOSHHH
YAOWW!
AHHH!
FATHER, WHAT IS HAPPENING?
GET BACK YOU FOOL!
HANG ON!
YOU GUYS ARE MY BEST FRIENDS, I JUST WANT YOU TO KNOW THAT!

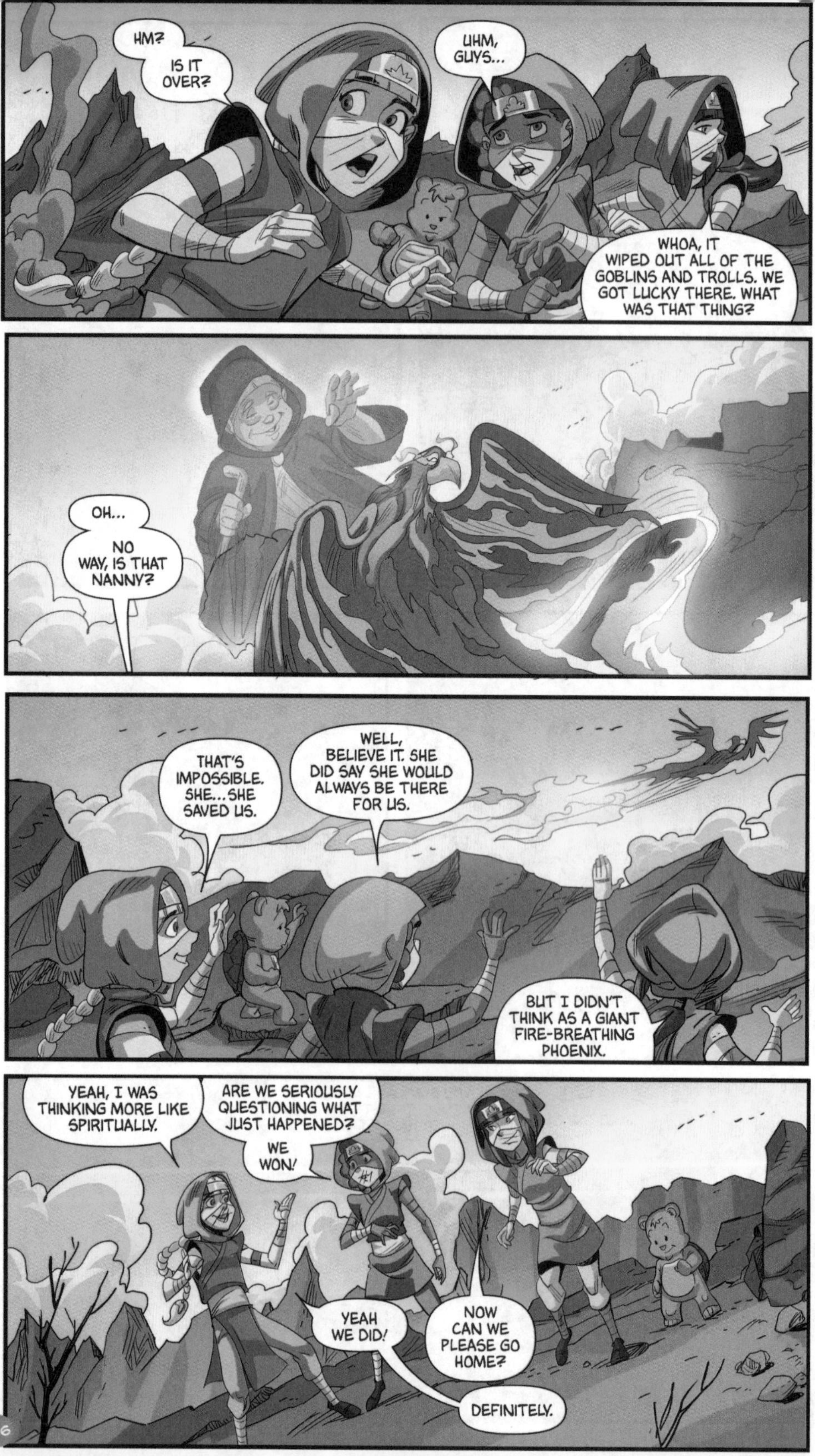
HM?
IS IT OVER?
UHM, GUYS...
WHOA, IT WIPED OUT ALL OF THE GOBLINS AND TROLLS. WE GOT LUCKY THERE. WHAT WAS THAT THING?
OH...
NO WAY, IS THAT NANNY?
THAT'S IMPOSSIBLE. SHE...SHE SAVED US.
WELL, BELIEVE IT. SHE DID SAY SHE WOULD ALWAYS BE THERE FOR US.
BUT I DIDN'T THINK AS A GIANT FIRE-BREATHING PHOENIX.
YEAH, I WAS THINKING MORE LIKE SPIRITUALLY.
ARE WE SERIOUSLY QUESTIONING WHAT JUST HAPPENED?
WE WON!
YEAH WE DID!
NOW CAN WE PLEASE GO HOME?
DEFINITELY.

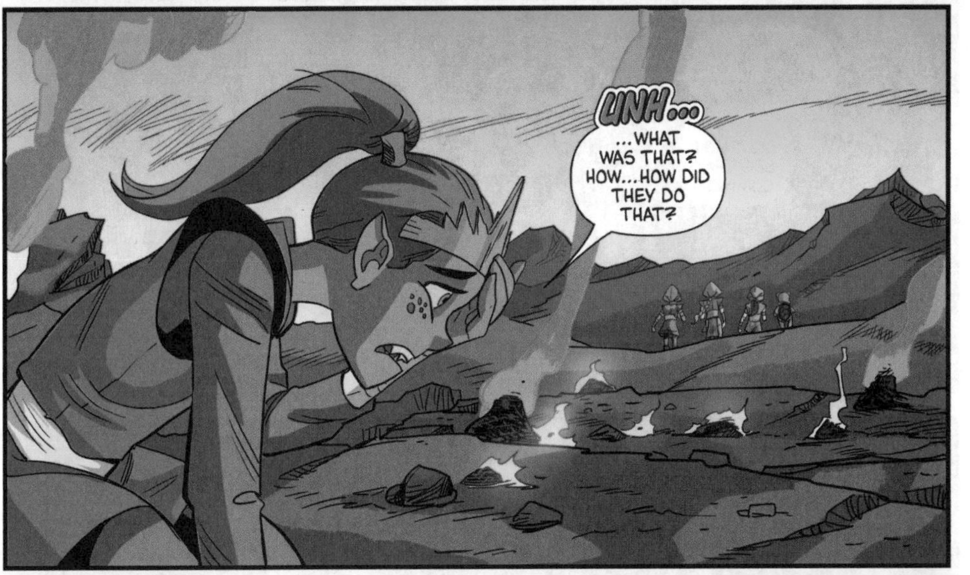
UNH...
...WHAT WAS THAT? HOW...HOW DID THEY DO THAT?

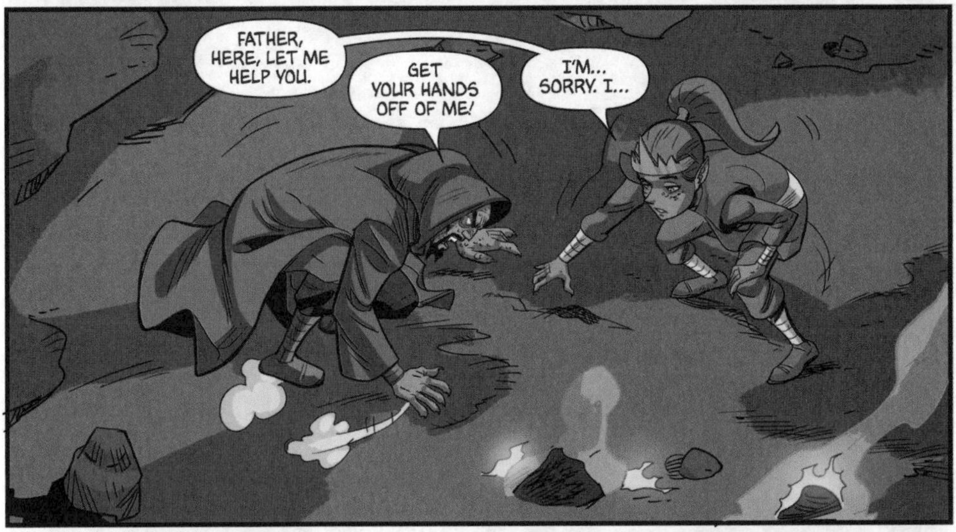
FATHER, HERE, LET ME HELP YOU.
GET YOUR HANDS OFF OF ME!
I'M... SORRY. I...

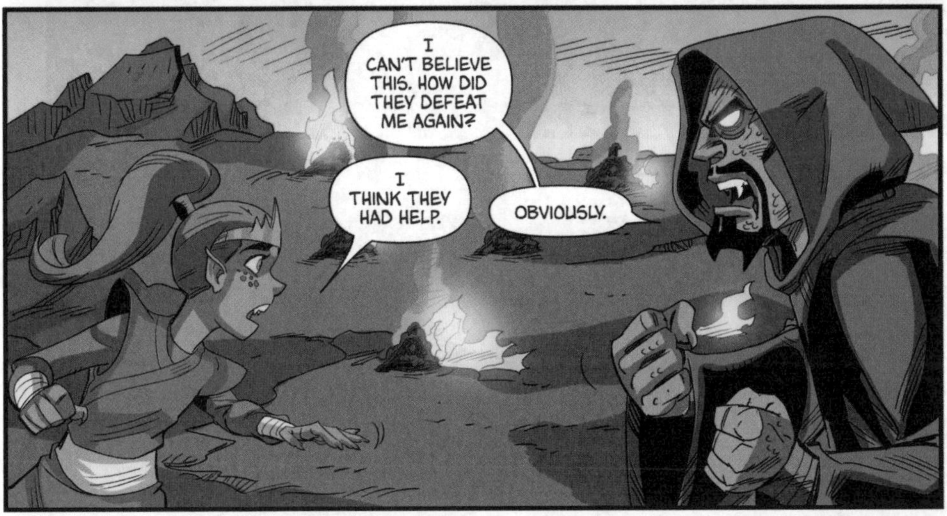
I CAN'T BELIEVE THIS. HOW DID THEY DEFEAT ME AGAIN?
I THINK THEY HAD HELP.
OBVIOUSLY.

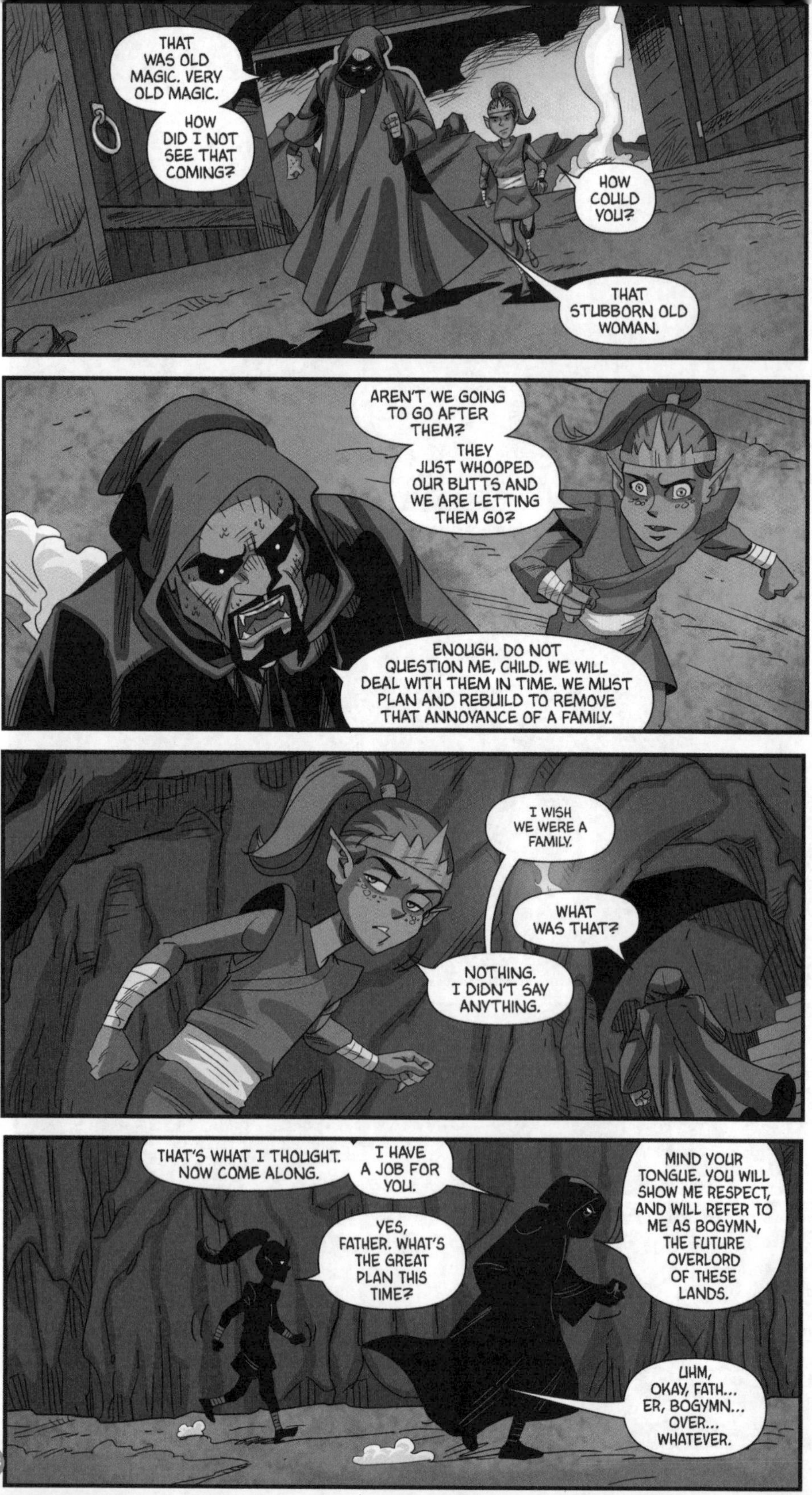
THAT WAS OLD MAGIC. VERY OLD MAGIC.
HOW DID I NOT SEE THAT COMING?
HOW COULD YOU?
THAT STUBBORN OLD WOMAN.
AREN'T WE GOING TO GO AFTER THEM?
THEY JUST WHOOPED OUR BUTTS AND WE ARE LETTING THEM GO?
ENOUGH. DO NOT QUESTION ME, CHILD. WE WILL DEAL WITH THEM IN TIME. WE MUST PLAN AND REBUILD TO REMOVE THAT ANNOYANCE OF A FAMILY.
I WISH WE WERE A FAMILY.
WHAT WAS THAT?
NOTHING. I DIDN'T SAY ANYTHING.
THAT'S WHAT I THOUGHT. NOW COME ALONG.
I HAVE A JOB FOR YOU.
YES, FATHER. WHAT'S THE GREAT PLAN THIS TIME?
MIND YOUR TONGUE. YOU WILL SHOW ME RESPECT, AND WILL REFER TO ME AS BOGYMN, THE FUTURE OVERLORD OF THESE LANDS.
UHM, OKAY, FATH... ER, BOGYMN... OVER... WHATEVER.

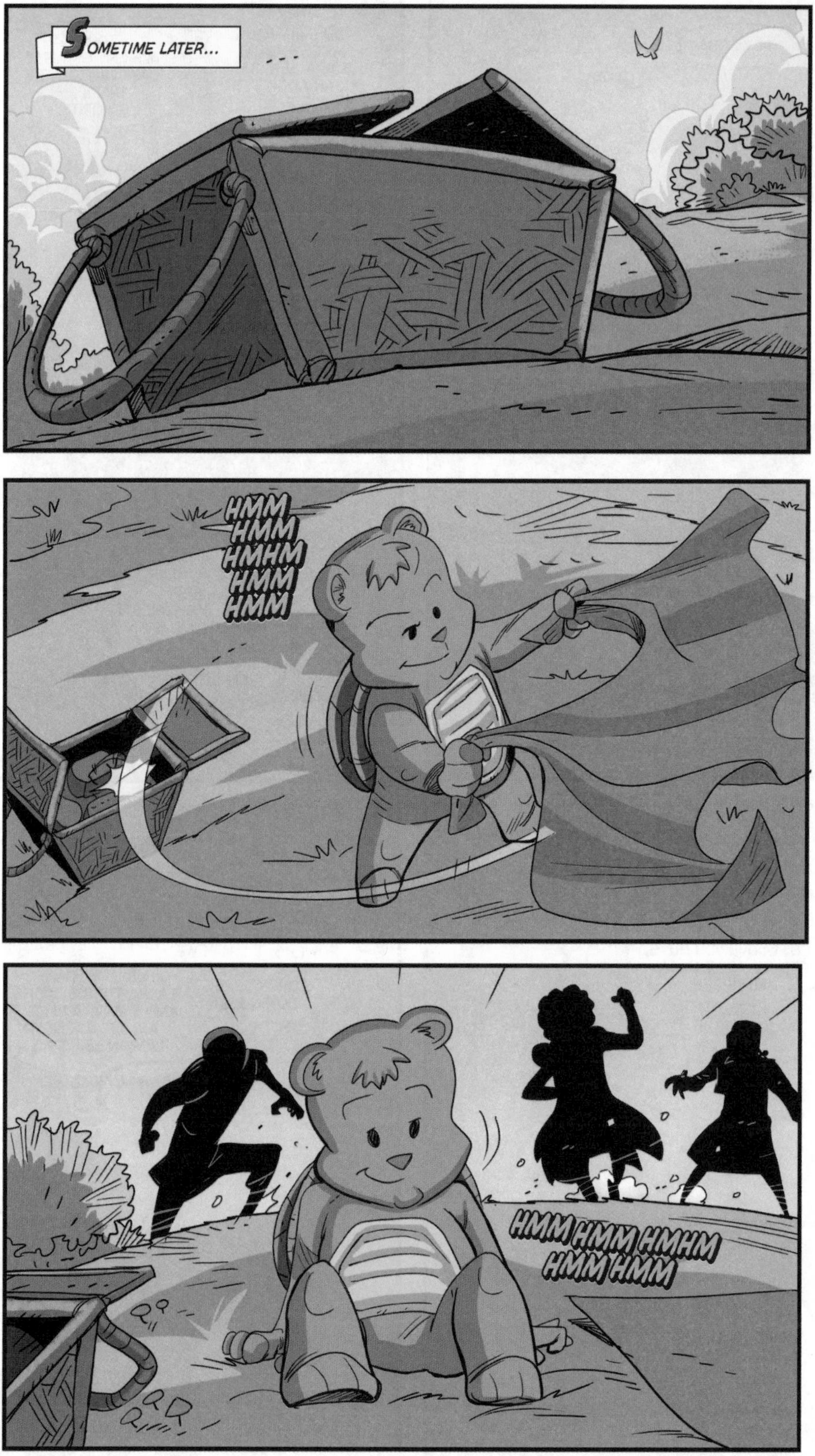
SOMETIME LATER...
HMM HMM HMHM HMM HMM
HMM HMM HMHM HMM HMM

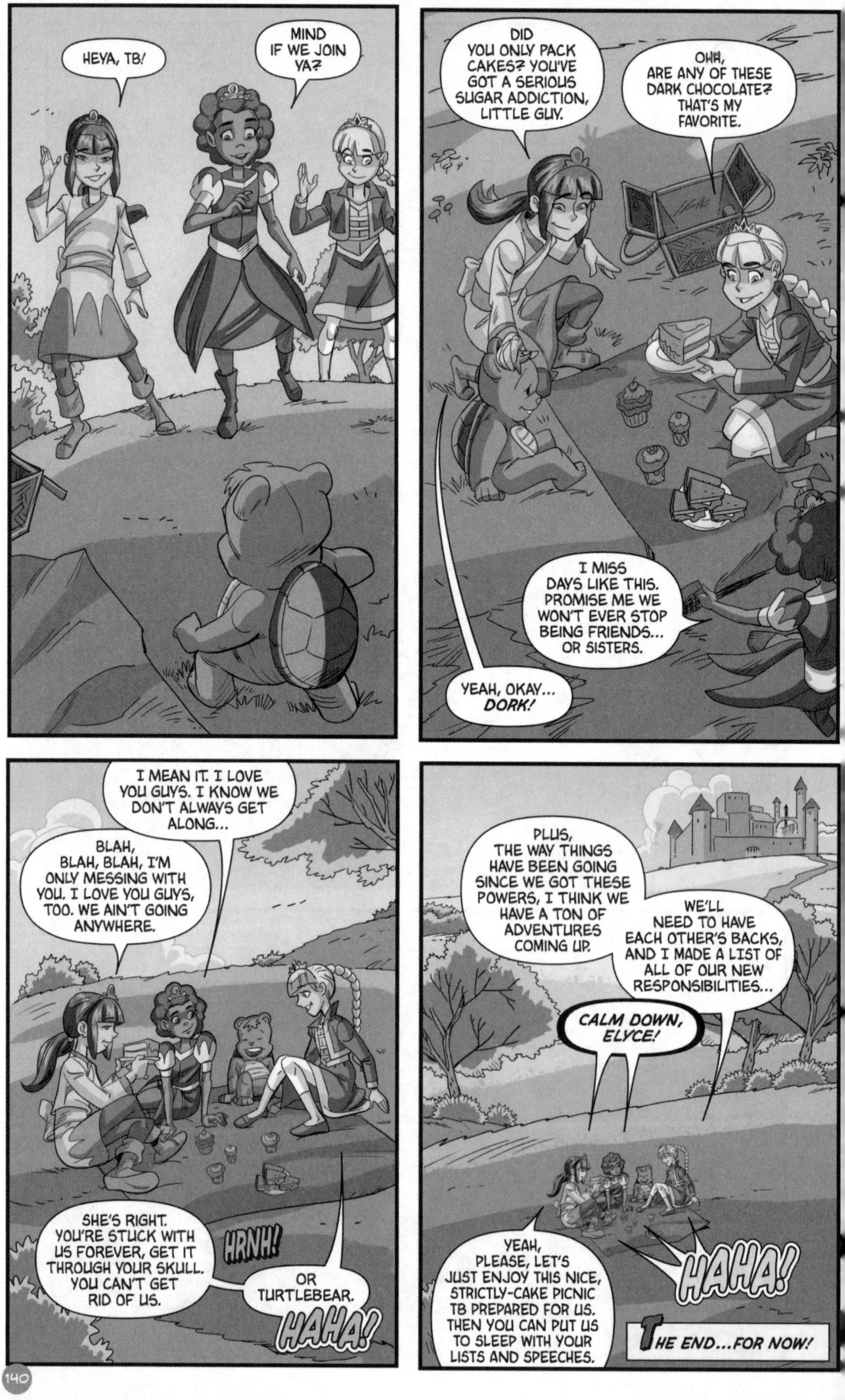
HEYA, TB!
MIND IF WE JOIN YA?
DID YOU ONLY PACK CAKES? YOU'VE GOT A SERIOUS SUGAR ADDICTION, LITTLE GUY.
OHH, ARE ANY OF THESE DARK CHOCOLATE? THAT'S MY FAVORITE.
I MISS DAYS LIKE THIS. PROMISE ME WE WON'T EVER STOP BEING FRIENDS... OR SISTERS.
YEAH, OKAY... DORK!
I MEAN IT. I LOVE YOU GUYS. I KNOW WE DON'T ALWAYS GET ALONG...
BLAH, BLAH, BLAH, I'M ONLY MESSING WITH YOU. I LOVE YOU GUYS, TOO. WE AIN'T GOING ANYWHERE.
SHE'S RIGHT. YOU'RE STUCK WITH US FOREVER, GET IT THROUGH YOUR SKULL. YOU CAN'T GET RID OF US.
HRNH!
OR TURTLEBEAR.
HAHA!
PLUS, THE WAY THINGS HAVE BEEN GOING SINCE WE GOT THESE POWERS, I THINK WE HAVE A TON OF ADVENTURES COMING UP.
WE'LL NEED TO HAVE EACH OTHER'S BACKS, AND I MADE A LIST OF ALL OF OUR NEW RESPONSIBILITIES...
CALM DOWN, ELYCE!
YEAH, PLEASE, LET'S JUST ENJOY THIS NICE, STRICTLY-CAKE PICNIC TB PREPARED FOR US. THEN YOU CAN PUT US TO SLEEP WITH YOUR LISTS AND SPEECHES.
HAHA!
THE END...FOR NOW!

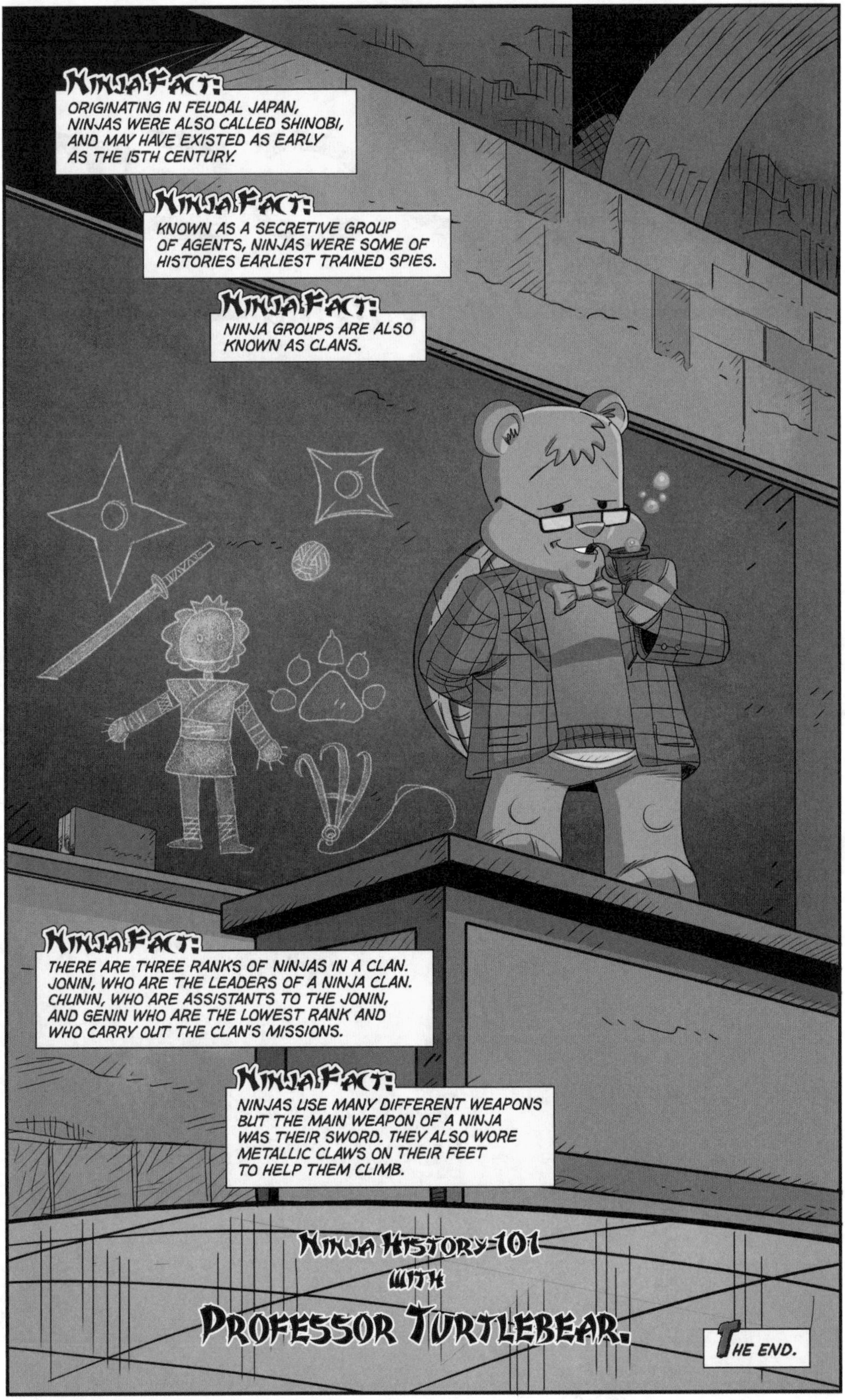
NINJA FACT:
ORIGINATING IN FEUDAL JAPAN, NINJAS WERE ALSO CALLED SHINOBI, AND MAY HAVE EXISTED AS EARLY AS THE 15TH CENTURY.
NINJA FACT:
KNOWN AS A SECRETIVE GROUP OF AGENTS, NINJAS WERE SOME OF HISTORIES EARLIEST TRAINED SPIES.
NINJA FACT:
NINJA GROUPS ARE ALSO KNOWN AS CLANS.
NINJA FACT:
THERE ARE THREE RANKS OF NINJAS IN A CLAN. JONIN, WHO ARE THE LEADERS OF A NINJA CLAN. CHUNIN, WHO ARE ASSISTANTS TO THE JONIN, AND GENIN WHO ARE THE LOWEST RANK AND WHO CARRY OUT THE CLAN'S MISSIONS.
NINJA FACT:
NINJAS USE MANY DIFFERENT WEAPONS BUT THE MAIN WEAPON OF A NINJA WAS THEIR SWORD. THEY ALSO WORE METALLIC CLAWS ON THEIR FEET TO HELP THEM CLIMB.
NINJA HISTORY-101
WITH
PROFESSOR TURTLEBEAR.
THE END.

BRIDGET

Air-Walking

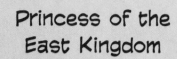

Princess of the East Kingdom

Likes the finer things in life

She believes it's important to always be well-dressed

Some... cough, cough, Megan... might say she can be a bit of a snob

MEGAN

Lightning Speed

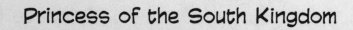

Princess of the South Kingdom

Outgoing, fun, and always ready for adventure or a good practical joke

Some... cough, cough, Bridget... might say she's a bit childish

Turtlebear is her best friend

ELYCE

Durability & Strength

Princess of the
North Kingdom

Bookworm and learning
enthusiast, with
know-it-all tendencies

Always willing to learn
and try new things

The peacekeeper of the
three sisters, and the glue
holding them together